ATTORNEY FOR THE DEFENSE

Beautiful and brainy Karen Perry-Mondari had it all. She was the rising star of a prestigious Florida law firm with a sterling record of winning lucrative cases. She was the wife of a handsome doctor who seemed to be the man of her dreams come to life. She lived in an exclusive gold coast community where she was welcomed by the best people.

Then she took the job of defending a man whom everyone knew was guilty of a crime that shocked the most hardened heart. And suddenly, it was not only this man who was on trial but everything Karen treasured. For what was revealed in the courtroom could bring her case—and her entire life—crashing down. . . .

DUE PROCESS

D0033347

SIGNET

 ONYX

RIVETING LEGAL THRILLERS

☐ **SUSPICION OF GUILT by Barbara Parker.** National Bestseller! What begins as a suspected forgery turns out to mask a brutal murder, and suddenly Miami attorney Gail Connor is caught in a web of violence and conspiracy. Her law firm—and her lover, criminal attorney Anthony Quintana want her to bow out, but she's in too deep to turn back, even as she puts herself at deadly risk. (177037—$5.99)

☐ **SUSPICION OF INNOCENCE by Barbara Parker.** This riveting, high-tension legal thriller written by a former prosecutor draws you into hot and dangerous Miami, where Gail Connor, a smart and successful young attorney, is suddenly caught in the closing jaws of the legal system—and is about to discover the other side of the law. (173406—$5.99)

☐ **THE SPIRIT THAT KILLS by Ronald Levitsky.** Native American Lakota leader Saul True Sky has been jailed for a savage murder. Now civil liberties lawyer Nate Rosen is flying in from Washington D.C. to take on a case of homicide and prejudice. But brutal shock-surprise and mounting peril are waiting for Rosen as he digs for buried secrets in a world where ghosts of the dead haunt the greed of the living. (405404—$4.99)

☐ **RUSH TO JUDGMENT by Irving Greenfield.** Captian Clark Gamrick must defend a sailor accused of murderously setting off an explosion that killed over thirty naval crewmen on the battleship *Utah.* Gamrick knows that before he can decide to defend a man with all the odds against him, he must come up with the real killer. For this is a death-penalty court-martial, where guilt is assumed and "justice" swift. (180887—$4.99)

Prices slightly higher in Canada

Buy them at your local bookstore or use this convenient coupon for ordering.

PENGUIN USA
P.O. Box 999 — Dept. #17199
Bergenfield, New Jersey 07621

Please send me the books I have checked above.
I am enclosing $_____ (please add $2.00 to cover postage and handling). Send check or money order (no cash or C.O.D.'s) or charge by Mastercard or VISA (with a $15.00 minimum). Prices and numbers are subject to change without notice.

Card #_____ Exp. Date _____
Signature_____
Name_____
Address_____
City _____ State _____ Zip Code _____

For faster service when ordering by credit card call **1-800-253-6476**

Allow a minimum of 4-6 weeks for delivery. This offer is subject to change without notice.

Catherine Arnold

DUE PROCESS

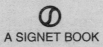

A SIGNET BOOK

SIGNET
Published by the Penguin Group
Penguin Books USA Inc., 375 Hudson Street,
New York, New York 10014, U.S.A.
Penguin Books Ltd, 27 Wrights Lane,
London W8 5TZ, England
Penguin Books Australia Ltd, Ringwood,
Victoria, Australia
Penguin Books Canada Ltd, 10 Alcorn Avenue,
Toronto, Ontario, Canada M4V 3B2
Penguin Books (N.Z.) Ltd, 182–190 Wairau Road,
Auckland 10, New Zealand

Penguin Books Ltd, Registered Offices:
Harmondsworth, Middlesex, England

First published by Signet, an imprint of Dutton Signet,
a division of Penguin Books USA Inc.

First Printing, December, 1996
10 9 8 7 6 5 4 3 2 1

Copyright © TEHA Productions, Inc., 1996
All rights reserved

 REGISTERED TRADEMARK—MARCA REGISTRADA

Printed in the United States of America

Without limiting the rights under copyright reserved above, no part of this publication
may be reproduced, stored in or introduced into a retrieval system, or transmitted, in
any form, or by any means (electronic, mechanical, photocopying, recording, or otherwise), without the prior written permission of both the copyright owner and the
above publisher of this book.

PUBLISHER'S NOTE
This is a work of fiction. Names, characters, places, and incidents either are the product of the author's imagination or are used fictitiously, and any resemblance to actual
persons, living or dead, events, or locales is entirely coincidental.

BOOKS ARE AVAILABLE AT QUANTITY DISCOUNTS WHEN USED TO PROMOTE PRODUCTS
OR SERVICES. FOR INFORMATION PLEASE WRITE TO PREMIUM MARKETING DIVISION,
PENGUIN BOOKS USA INC., 375 HUDSON STREET, NEW YORK, NEW YORK 10014.

If you purchased this book without a cover you should be aware that this book is
stolen property. It was reported as "unsold and destroyed" to the publisher and neither
the author nor the publisher has received any payment for this "stripped book."

ACKNOWLEDGMENTS

Though writing has its solitude, it's quite impossible for any author to work in a vacuum. In this effort, I was helped immeasurably by fellow lawyer Linda Hughes, encouraged and cheered on by husband, Harry, my agent, Jean Naggar, and my editor, Joe Pittman. I will be forever grateful.

This book is dedicated to my late mother and my hale and hearty father, both lawyers, who, as parents, nourished my soul and expanded my horizons, providing me with the kind of early encouragement, love, and support that all children need.

One

It had taken three tedious, frustrating years to bring this case before a judge and jury; three years of depositions, motions, hearings, and more hearings, all of them initiated by an arrogant, callous defendant intent on spending whatever it took to grind Karen Perry-Mondori's client into the dust of total despair.

With a platoon of lawyers fighting her every step of the way, Karen was expected to eventually advise her client to accept the settlement offered in the beginning, a light balm for the admittedly wrongful death of one Thomas Cole.

Cole was forty-two when he died. His death was attributed to his having been given the wrong medication by a frazzled, overworked pharmacist employed by Brister's Best Markets, one of the country's largest supermarket chains. His bereaved widow, Amanda, upon learning of the circumstances of her husband's death, had come to Karen in tears, asking for justice.

Justice.

A lawyer named Clarence Darrow had once declared that there *was* no justice—in or out of court.

At first blush, the case looked simple enough. Thomas Cole had undergone triple bypass surgery two months before he died. His doctor had prescribed blood thinners, but when Cole went to the pharmacy for a refill, he'd been given a treatment for gout. Unfortunately, the tablets were similar in size and color, and within a week, Cole was back in the hospital. His doctor asked Cole if he was taking his medication. Cole said he was. Had the doctor demanded to see the actual *prescription bottle,* Mr. Cole might still be alive. But the doctor did not do that. Instead, he doubled the dosage; Cole's blood was entirely too thick. And Cole died of a blood clot in the brain four days later.

An autopsy confirmed the lack of blood thinners in his system, and when the confused doctor, possibly worried about a malpractice suit, finally asked to see the medication his patient had been taking, he discovered the error and advised the bereaved widow.

When Karen filed suit on her client's behalf, the lawyers for Brister's made an immediate settlement offer of three hundred thousand dollars. Since Mr. Cole was earning $65,500 a year when he died, the offer was clearly insufficient, and after discussing the offer with her client, Karen rejected it. The lawyers for Brister's asked for a conference. Karen met with one of their senior legal eagles in a Tampa hotel room.

"This meeting is off the record," Stuart Livock began. He was an expensively dressed, attractive man, but haughty, a man who appeared to regard female lawyers as lesser beings. That was enough to get Karen's blood running for a start.

"Then we have nothing to talk about," she retorted.

"Oh, I think you better listen, Ms. Perry-Mondori. I'm giving you a break here."

"How's that?"

"We've been looking into the life and times of one Thomas Cole. He was a heavy drinker and a compulsive gambler. The drinking is what caused his heart problems in the first place. We have evidence that he was about to be fired from his computer programming job because of it. So, as for the loss of future income, there may not have been much future income."

"That's a matter for the jury to decide," Karen said.

"Be that as it may, Thomas Cole is black, and Tampa juries have a rich tradition to uphold; they aren't about to make his widow a millionaire, I guarantee you. As for the pharmacist's mistake, nobody's perfect. You'll never be able to prove recklessness in this case, and without that, you have no case for punitive damages. Bottom line? If you take this to court, you'll be lucky if your client gets half what we're offering."

Karen sighed. "You underestimate Tampa juries, Mr. Livock. Your being from Cincinnati, I can understand that. As for the case, you underestimate me. My preliminary investigation indicates that recklessness is very much a factor."

Some of the bravado left his soft face. "I see. Well, listen to me carefully, Counselor: if you proceed with this case, we'll drag it out for years. Mrs. Cole doesn't have the resources to see this through. Her husband's death benefits amounted to five thousand dollars. She used all of that to bury him. She has three kids, a job that pays seventeen thousand a year, and she and her family live in a small house in which Mrs. Cole has a five percent equity.

"In short, she's broke, lady. You're doing her a disservice if you don't recommend she accept this more than generous offer."

"I'll talk to her," Karen said.

"And?"

"I'll recommend she tell you to go to hell," Karen said.

Now, the case was finally being heard, and after five days of it, Karen had presented most of her case, all except for some witnesses held in reserve. The witnesses had told Karen they would testify on one condition: their jobs must not be placed in jeopardy. Karen thought she had a way to make that work, but it meant taking a risk.

A very calculated risk.

She'd anticipated that the defense would attempt to diminish the worth of Thomas Cole when it was time for them to present *its* case. And so they had. Now, they were engaged in an exercise designed to persuade the jury that Brister's was in no way responsible for what had happened to Thomas Cole. Karen sat beside her client, a client trembling in outrage, and listened to Brister's drug manager, Bruce Marshall, expertly guided by the corporation's lawyer, explain why Karen's client was entitled to a mere pittance upon the death of her husband.

Yes, Marshall was saying in answer to Livock's question, it was true that a pharmacist working for the defendant had made a mistake. Yes, he repeated, in answer to another softball question, it was true that the mistake might have contributed in some small way to the death of the man. But the corporation was not at fault. They had done *everything in their power* to ensure that such mistakes could never happen. The corporation had been diligent, aware, concerned, and vigorous in their training of pharmacists. If a mistake had been made, it was solely the fault of the pharmacist who had filled the prescription improperly, a pharmacist who had failed to follow well-established procedures.

The examination of Bruce Marshall droned on, Stuart Livock pounding away at a strategy designed to convince the jury that finding this fine, upstanding corporation at fault for a mistake made by one of their employees was anti-American, that, despite the precedents presented by the plaintiff's attorney, the pendulum had swung too far, to the detriment of everyone. The corporation was not as much as one percent responsible.

By the end of the day, Stuart Livock had done such a sterling job that the members of the jury were looking at Karen's client as if she were a leech, a money-grubbing whiner out to take this corporate saint for whatever she could get, aided and abetted by a bottom-feeding shark named Karen Perry-Mondori.

"Your witness," the judge said to Karen, at the conclusion of the direct examination.

Karen drew herself to full attention. "Your Honor, since the hour is late and I would prefer not to have my cross-examination of this witness interrupted, might I ask the court be in held recess until tomorrow morning?"

"Very well," the judge said. "Court is in recess until nine tomorrow morning. I caution the jury not to . . . "

Karen gripped her client's hand and looked into her eyes. "Don't be discouraged," she said. "Darrow was wrong."

"Who?"

"Never mind. I have to rush. I'll see you in the morning."

Karen left the courtroom and hurried to a small country-style restaurant twenty miles north of Tampa. When she entered the place, she found them waiting for her in a corner of the room, seven men and three woman, all nursing drinks, all waiting for her.

"You came," Karen said, as she took a seat beside them.

"Did you think we wouldn't?" one of them asked.

Karen Perry-Mondori stepped from the shower, toweled off, removed the little plastic cap from her head, let her soft brown hair fall to her shoulders, then leaned forward, staring intently at the fuzzy image in the mirror. She used a blow-dryer to clear the condensation, then looked at herself again. She detected very little puffiness around and under the large green eyes. A surprise, considering the lack of sleep. She straightened up, continuing to assess her thirty-seven-year-old body.

Not bad, really. Her face was still pretty, thank God. And thank you for the genes, Mother. You may be hell on wheels, but you have great genes. The high cheekbones, the long neck, the full lips were all gifts from her mother. Her father, whoever he might be, had probably given her the large eyes and the squarish chin. And the lack of height, damn it.

But not the drive. The drive came from her mother.

Her full breasts were still high, her waist still the same twenty-three inches, flaring out to hips that might have been wider—should have been wider. The scar on her abdomen, a constant reminder of a cesarean section that had almost come too late, was barely discernable. Thanks to regular workouts, her muscle tone was good, her skin still soft and supple. She turned and looked at her buttocks. Still no stretch marks, no real sign of aging. But soon. She knew that. The forces of gravity were unremitting.

Appearance counted in her profession, and at five feet, two inches, Karen Perry-Mondori was very aware of that. Being small was a detriment for any member of American society, but being small *and* a woman was an even bigger liability for a lawyer, especially a litigator. Some judges and many jurors resented female lawyers, especially in the South. Lawyering was man's work, pure and simple. Lawyers were leeches, snakes, and lizards. Women were supposed to be above all that.

Early in her career, when a judge would belittle her in court, Karen would fix him with a stare that could melt titanium. She would never comment, nor would she write letters of protest, for she understood the realities of the system. But she would stare. Stares did not appear on the record. The stare did not endear her to judges, but her courtroom demeanor did, for she rarely resorted to theatrics to make her points. She had a clear understanding of the law, a penchant for being on point, and an uncompromising regard for the truth as she perceived it. It had been years since a judge had deprecated her in a courtroom, though some, unable or unwilling to accept the new reality of the nineties, still called her "little lady."

Born and raised in Miami, she'd moved to Pinellas County at the age of eighteen. Miami had changed, and so had Karen's relationship with her mother—the wildly successful owner of a small chain of discount stores—and her half-brother, now a U.S. senator. Her estrangement from both, for different reasons, motivated her move to central Florida.

She worked her way through college and law school as a waitress, living in a small room she shared with a revolving trio of young women. But after passing her bar examination, her days of poverty were over.

Six months after joining the Clearwater law firm of Hewitt, Sinclair & Smith, Karen met Carl Mondori, a noted neurosurgeon, eight years her senior, whose specialty was back surgery. He wooed her like no other man ever had. He was a shining light in the rather dim cosmos that passed for social life in the Tampa Bay area, the most eligible of bachelors: handsome, witty, gregarious, urbane—and divorced.

For weeks, Karen fought to quell her interest in this man. It wasn't just the divorce that gave her pause. To be sure, she'd always had this romantic fantasy that the man she married would be unsullied by previous entanglements. The fact that there were no children from the previous marriage made it easier to accept Carl. But she knew—for he'd freely volunteered the information—that since his divorce, Carl had dated a great deal. Such candor, while appreciated, was terrifying. Could such a man remain faithful after marriage?

Carl swore he would, now that he'd found her. And chemistry being chemistry, Karen wanted desperately to believe him. Still, the decision to marry came a year after their first meeting.

Now, ten years married, Karen Perry-Mondori, mother, lawyer, and wife, was a rising star in the Florida legal community.

By the time she reached the kitchen, the room was empty. This being an operating day, Carl had risen at five and gone to the hospital. By seven, Michelle, the family's au pair, had fed daughter Andrea and taken her to a private school some twenty miles away. The daily commute was worth it, for the school was noted for its outstanding curriculum. Still, there were times when Karen felt guilty that she never had the time to take her daughter to school.

She gulped down some coffee and looked at her watch. She was due in court in just over an hour. This morning, she would finally get a crack at the unflappable Bruce Marshall. She could hardly wait.

Judge Randall Kane nodded to Karen. "Proceed, Counselor."

"Thank you, Your Honor."

Karen got up, patted Amanda Cole on the shoulder, stood at the lectern, placed a thick file in front of her, and leaned forward.

"Good morning, Mr. Marshall."

"Good morning."

"Yesterday, during direct examination, you testified that pharmacist Henry Travers was solely responsible for the mistake that resulted in the death of Thomas Cole, is that correct?"

"Yes."

"You also testified that you were aware that the computer program used by Brister's had a minor glitch, in that prescription data could be changed under certain circumstances, is that true?"

"I never called it a glitch."

"I'm sorry. What did you call it?"

"I called it a potential input programming error. But we . . . "

"Just yes or no answers, Mr. Marshall. I'm just reviewing some of your testimony to get it clear in my mind."

Marshall frowned.

"You testified that you sent a memo to all pharmacists explaining the potential input programming error, and warned them to be careful, is that correct?"

"Yes."

Karen looked at the judge. "Your Honor, I have a copy of that memo, which we offer as plaintiff's exhibit number twenty-three, and I'd like Mr. Marshall to read it to the Court and jury."

Livock was on his feet. "Objection, Your Honor."

Judge Kane peered over his glasses. "On what grounds?"

"The witness has already testified as to the content of the memo. If Ms. Perry-Mondori wanted to present the actual memo, she should have done so when she presented the plaintiff's case. There's no need . . . "

"Overruled."

Karen picked up the memo, gave a copy to Livock, presented it to the court clerk, then looked at the judge. "May I approach the witness, Your Honor?"

"Proceed."

Karen took the memo and handed it to Marshall. "Is this a true copy of the memo you sent to all pharmacists employed by Brister's?"

"It appears to be, yes."

"Well, is it or isn't it?"

Marshall hesitated. "Yes."

"Very well. Would you please read the contents of the memo to the Court and jury."

Marshall took a deep breath, then began to read. " 'To all pharmacists, from Bruce Marshall, OTC and Ethical Drug Manager. Date: March twenty-third. Reference: Using NDC Codes when inputting prescription data. Be advised that the new computer software recently installed is designed to be used with NDC codes only. When entering new prescription data, if you fail to use the NDC number, there is a potential input programming error. Pharmacists are instructed to be sure to use the NDC code when entering data and not the individual pharmacist codes as in the past. As well, when refilling prescriptions, pharmacists are instructed to refer to the original hard copy of the prescription.' It's signed by me."

Karen took back the memo and returned to the lectern.

"Mr. Marshall, since the Court and jury are not pharmacists, could you explain what this memo means?"

Again, Livock was on his feet. "Sidebar, Your Honor?"

Judge Kane gave him a look, then nodded. Karen followed Livock to the bench and listened as the lawyer presented his objection.

"Your Honor, the defense has already stipulated that the pharmacist made a mistake. We're prepared to pay for that mistake, and have offered the plaintiff a reasonable settlement. The only reason we're going through the agony of this trial is because of counsel's apparent greed. The settlement offered is, in light of the evidence already presented, more than adequate in this case. There's no need for us to drag this trial on and on with inconsequential questions that have no bearing on . . . "

Kane held up a hand. "No more, Mr. Livock," he whispered. "I will not allow you to slander opposing counsel. As you well know, counsel's questions relate to the question of reckless endangerment. She's entitled to pursue this issue. And if you use the word *greed* again, I'll hold you in contempt. Understand?"

Livock, red-faced with anger, nodded.

Judge Kane turned to Karen. "Step back, both of you. Proceed with the witness, Ms. Perry-Mondori." To the witness, the judge said, "Mr. Marshall, you may answer the question."

"Would you repeat it, please?"

Karen repeated the question.

"What it means is that all drugs, whether they are ethical or over-the-counter, bear a National Drug Code number. The memo instructed pharmacists to make sure they used this NDC number when they entered information into the computer."

"What happens if they don't enter the NDC number?"

"Nothing."

"Excuse me?"

"You asked me what happens, and I said nothing." He was being a smart-ass.

"Let me rephrase the question. At the time you wrote this memo, what could happen if the NDC number wasn't entered?"

"At that time, there could be a mistake."

"As happened in this case?"

"Exactly. But if the pharmacist had followed the instructions in my memo, this would not have happened."

"So, the pharmacist is solely responsible?"

"Yes."

Karen resisted the impulse to smile. "Mr. Marshall, why did you write that memo?"

"That should be obvious. Because we didn't want our pharmacists making mistakes."

"How did it come to your attention that by not using the NDC code, a mistake could be made?"

"I was advised by one of my pharmacists that the computer program allowed for certain drugs to be misidentified."

"What do you mean by 'misidentified'? Can you give me an example?"

"Well, take this case, for example. Mr. Cole came into one of our stores to get a refill for a medication he was taking. When the pharmacist looked up Mr. Cole's records, he saw that the prescription called for thirty tablets of Zubatin, ten milligrams each. That's what he dispensed. The mistake was made by the pharmacist who had entered the prescription in the first place. The prescription called for Zubatero, which is an entirely different drug. Instead of entering the NDC code, the previous pharmacist had entered a local code, which in this case was ZU10. In the store computer, the drug was entered as Zubatero, which was correct. But when the master computer in Cincinnati downloaded the weekly update, the data in the store computer was changed because the Cincinnati inventory control clerk used the code ZU10 as the local code for Zubatin."

"That sounds very confusing."

"That's because you're not a pharmacist."

"Are you?"

Marshall blushed. "Not officially."

"What does that mean, not officially?"

"I don't have a degree, if that's what you mean, but I've been managing pharmacists for fifteen years."

"I see. So you feel you're just as qualified as a pharmacist?"

Livock was on his feet. "Objection, Your Honor. Irrelevant and leading. Counsel is aware that the law in the State of Florida allows corporations to employ nonpharmacists as management."

"I withdraw the question," Karen said.

"Withdrawn. Proceed."

"So," Karen said, "the data in the store computer were overwritten?"

"Yes. But all the pharmacist had to do was look at the original prescription hard copy."

"Really. That's all?"

"Those were my instructions."

"I see. So, when you discovered that an error was possible, as a result of being told by one of your pharmacists, you sent out a memo. Did you do anything else?"

Marshall's eyelids flickered. "Yes."

"And what was that?"

"I discussed the matter with the company that sold us the software."

"And what was the result of that discussion?"

"Nothing."

"Nothing? Could you explain?"

"Objection!" Livock shouted.

"Overruled."

Karen gave Marshall the laser stare. "Isn't it a fact that the problem with the software originated when you, in your capacity as manager of both over-the-counter and ethical drugs, purchased the lowest priced of six available software programs, and used your own company's computer programmers to develop the balance of the program, against the express written advice of the software company's technical-support personnel?"

"That's not true."

"Isn't it a fact that you went to the software manufacturer and asked them to correct the problem, and when you were told the cost of fixing programming mistakes made by your company programmers, you again decided to use your own programmers to fix it?"

"Not at all. No."

"Isn't it a fact, Mr. Marshall, that your annual bonus would have been severely affected if you had taken the proper steps to correct this software problem?"

"That had nothing whatsoever to do with my decision!"

"And what decision was that?"

"To issue a memo."

"You thought that would cover it?"

"All they had to do was follow instructions."

"I see. After you issued your memo, were you contacted by pharmacists claiming that leaving the computer program the way it was would most assuredly result in scores of mistakes and that many of them could result in fatalities?"

"No! Nothing of the sort."

"Isn't it a fact that you hired an outside firm to correct the computer program two days after my client's lawsuit was filed, and that the fix cost was six hundred and eighty thousand dollars?"

"That's a distortion!"

"Isn't a fact that you were advised by many of your pharmacists that because temporary fill-in employees are often used in your stores, and that there was no time to train these people, it would be highly likely that mistakes would be made, some of them resulting in fatalities?"

"That's not true!"

"Are you aware of the penalties for perjury, Mr. Marshall?"

Before Marshall could answer, Livock was on his feet. Judge Kane overruled his objection immediately. "The witness may answer."

"I don't know what the penalties are, no."

"Well, you'll soon find out, Mr. Marshall. Does the name John Kelly mean anything to you?"

"Yes."

"Who is John Kelly?"

"He is one of my pharmacists."

"Did he write you a three-page memo in response to your memo?"

Marshall was beginning to pale. "No."

Livock was again on his feet. "Your Honor, this is unconscionable. Is Ms. Perry-Mondori prepared to present this person as a witness? If so, why did she wait until the defense began to present its case? This lays waste to discovery laws, Your Honor."

Kane looked at both attorneys. "I'll see counsel in chambers. The jury may retire to the jury room."

Karen and Livock followed the judge into his chambers. He removed his robe, hung it on a hanger, then took a seat in a high-backed leather chair. "What's going on, Karen?"

Karen took a deep breath. "Prior to this case coming to trial, I deposed ten pharmacists, Your Honor. All ten expressed the fear that they would lose their jobs if they came forward. They told me that after my client brought this action, the company corrected the programming glitch, and that the conditions that resulted in that particular error could never be repeated. They simply refused to give me any additional information.

"Since this is a civil matter, I don't have the power to subpoena these witnesses. Nevertheless, I wrote letters to all ten pharmacists asking them to come forward voluntarily. Last night, I was contacted by the ten pharmacists. They are now prepared to testify that they forwarded memos to Mr. Marshall begging him to fix the programming glitch. They were told that if they persisted in their memo-writing, they would be fired. After reading what's been going on in this trial, they no longer care. They want to testify."

Livock was almost purple with rage. "This is bullshit! You can't expect us to believe that ten pharmacists appeared on your doorstep last night all overcome with sanctimony. Give me a break!"

"That's exactly what happened, Mr. Livock," Karen insisted. "And all ten will so testify under oath. They are in this building and ready to do so. As for the laws of discovery, the witnesses are being presented to impeach your witness, and as you well know, witnesses brought forward for the purposes of impeachment are excluded from the witness list requirement because no one knows what testimony will eventually need to be impeached." She smiled. "Now we do."

Livock's eyes grew wide. "You set this up!"

"I did no such thing."

Judge Kane held up a hand to quiet both lawyers. To Karen, he said, "Are you saying to me that these ten pharmacists made contact with you last night based on a letter you wrote to them?"

"Yes, Your Honor."

"And they agreed to testify without some prior understanding between you?"

"Yes, Your Honor."

"Well, I'll eventually want to hear it from their lips. In the meantime, I would ask Mr. Livock what else he wants to say."

Livock hung his head.

"Mr. Livock?" the judge asked.

"I'd like to have a conference with opposing counsel, Your Honor."

"Very well," the judge said. "Let's get back out there. I'll recess court until two this afternoon."

"How much?" Livock asked, as he and Karen huddled in one of the small witness/lawyer conference rooms.

Karen shuffled some papers, then said, "First, Brister's will sign a document that guarantees that the ten pharmacists who came forward will not be subject to retribution in any way, shape, or form, as a result of their actions."

Livock just stared at her.

"Second, you will pay Mrs. Cole the lump sum settlement of ten million dollars."

Livock laughed. "Get serious!"

Karen shrugged. "Fine. This case is starting to get some press. By the time I'm through, it'll get a lot more. Brister's will receive a hundred million dollars' worth of bad publicity. The media have a habit of getting things wrong, as you well know. Everyone will assume that the problem still exists, that filling their prescriptions at Brister's could be fatal. That should knock a big hole in your precious profit margins."

"You're making a mistake, Counselor."

"How's that?"

"You're making this personal."

Karen smiled. "I seem to remember the word *greed* coming up in conversation with the judge. Damn right it's personal."

"Ten million dollars is crazy!"

"Fine. Let's tell the judge we can't come to an agreement."

Livock took a deep breath. "Be reasonable."

"Make me an offer I can take to my client."

Livock thought for a moment. "No public announcement of the settlement amount."

"Never!"

"Five million dollars, structured over twenty years."

Karen shook her head. "Not good enough. Make it a lump sum payment and I'll take it to my client."

"There's no way we're paying a lump sum settlement," Livock hissed.

"In that case, we have nothing more to talk about."

Karen turned and grabbed the door handle.

"Wait!"

At two o'clock in the afternoon, Karen stood stone-faced beside her client as Judge Kane addressed the jury. "Ladies and gentlemen of the jury," he intoned, "a settlement has been reached in this matter. You have conducted yourselves admirably throughout this arduous proceeding, giving all parties your full and devoted attention. I commend you for that, and while your services are no longer required, you are dismissed with the measureless thanks of the Court."

He looked at Karen. "The Court accepts the settlement agreement presented by the parties in all its elements. The order is so entered. I applaud both lawyers for working to bring this matter to a satisfactory conclusion."

He slammed his gavel. "This Court is adjourned."

Amanda Cole, tears streaming down her face, gave Karen a hug. "Thank you, you precious woman. May God reward you for what you've done."

"You're responsible for this, Amanda. Now, you can give yourself a rest and your kids a good education."

"Yes, oh yes!"

"Three and a half million dollars is a lot of money. I'd like you to speak to some people in my firm. They'll help you with some financial planning. No charge. And you're going to be pursued by every salesman in central Florida. Let me find you and the kids a place to stay until you have a chance to think this over."

"I would appreciate that very much."

"Good. Come with me."

As the two women left the courtroom arm in arm, Karen felt like shouting. But, as cameras clicked and flashguns fired, she simply smiled.

It felt so good to win.

Two

Karen took Amanda and her three children to a furnished apartment Karen had rented three days ago, in the event the trial turned out well. It was a precaution. The woman would be hounded by those trying to get their hands on big money, legally or illegally. Keeping Amanda and her children away from the sharks until such time as the woman could rearrange her life was, to Karen, almost as important as winning the case.

By the time Karen reached her office building, it was nearly four in the afternoon. She stepped off the elevator and took a moment to admire, for the hundredth time, the brass plaque mounted beside the thick glass double doors that led to the offices of Hewitt, Sinclair, Smith—and now—Perry-Mondori.

The brass plaque was a nice touch. It was one thing to have your name painted on a door; it was quite another to have it emblazoned on brass. It seemed Old World, more enduring, more meaningful.

Hewitt, Sinclair, Smith & Perry-Mondori was the biggest law firm in Clearwater, almost as big as some of the larger firms in St. Petersburg and Tampa, with forty-five associates, occupying the fourth and fifth floors of a building owned by the two original founders of the law firm, Brander Hewitt and Walter Sinclair.

She'd managed to survive those early years, but it

hadn't been easy. She could handle the crushing workload. She'd expected no less. But she was a woman, and in the South, men were still loath to consider women as equals in anything—even in Florida, a state considered more Yankeelike than Southern. It took extraordinary willpower to refrain from responding to the hundreds of blatantly misogynistic slurs issued in any given week, most of them unconscious offerings spoken without a thought to content. Old habits were hard to break.

For another, she was decidedly short, and short people, like fat people, were often the objects of overt derision.

And then there was Walter Sinclair, a partner who considered women purely as sexual challenges. In the pre–Anita Hill days, sexual harassment at Hewitt, Sinclair was the norm rather than the exception. Most of the women who refused to bed Walter in those early days were summarily dismissed, though the true reasons for the dismissals were always cloaked in rational embellishment.

Karen had tried to avoid Walter, but it was impossible. And when the inevitable confrontation finally took place, it took all of her wiles to turn him down and keep her job. But Sinclair was still a very big thorn in her side. As managing partner, he ran the office, and he was a terrible manager. Many good people had left the firm because of Walter.

Walter's prostate operation four years ago had brought his sexual escapades to a crashing halt and given him a perpetual sour disposition. He was now a lawyer-monk. God, in Her infinite wisdom, was just.

But Walter Sinclair was not.

It was Brander—the reason she'd joined the firm in the first place—who became Karen's mentor, imparting his experience and skill, taking an immediate liking to her, treating her almost like a daughter, showering her with opportunities, glowing with pride as she turned most of them into accomplishments, commiserating with her over the losses. Matters involving Walter Sinclair excepted, Brander was patient and wise, deceptively forceful, yet kind and almost all-knowing. She felt she owed much of her success to his tutoring.

As she pushed through the doors that separated the secretarial "pit" from the reception area, she was greeted with a loud cheer. Good news traveled almost as quickly as bad. At the back of the room stood the patriarch himself, Brander Hewitt, resplendent as always, his short arms crossed over his barrel chest, his dark eyes gleaming with pride behind thick, steel-rimmed glasses. As Karen approached, he held out both arms. "Well done, Karen. Well done, indeed."

She welcomed his embrace, his fatherly pat on the back, his genuine expression of affection.

"You are just as responsible," she said. "The firm allowed me to invest a lot of time on this case. That was your doing, Brander. No one else's."

Brander released her from his embrace and smiled. "But you won it, Karen. Congratulations, and may it continue."

"Thanks, Brander."

Karen smiled at some of the other well-wishers, then headed to her office. Liz, positioned just outside the office, jumped up, gave her a hug, and followed her in. "Way to go, Karen. I'm thrilled for you."

Karen slumped into her high-backed chair. "Thanks, Liz. After six days in court, it's great to be sitting in my office again. I miss anything here?"

Liz took a quick breath, then said, "Do you remember a man named Jack Palmer?"

Karen searched her memory for a face to go with the name. Nothing came immediately forward. "I'm afraid not."

"You prepared wills for Jack and Mrs. Palmer three years ago. According to the file, it was Law Day at the mall. You and three associates spent a few hours doing pro bono work on behalf of the Bar Association."

"Oh, yes. So, what's the problem?"

"Mr. Palmer has been calling for you all day. He's in county jail, charged with felony murder. I took it upon myself to have Colin go down and talk to him. No commitments. I hope you don't mind."

"No, that's fine. Felony murder?"

"Yes. And it's tawdry, Karen. He's charged with killing his lover's husband."

"That *is* tawdry."

"Did you read the *Times* this morning?"

"No."

"Well, if you get a chance, it's all over the front page."

Karen thought for a moment. "Is Palmer a quiet little guy, about forty?"

"Thirty-six," Liz said. She handed Karen the newspaper. Palmer's plain face was right there on page one. Suddenly, Karen felt as if someone had struck her in the chest. The blood drained from her face. "My God!"

"What is it?"

"It says here he killed Dan DeFauldo." She looked up, her face expressing shock. "I know the DeFauldos."

Liz's eyebrows rose. "Geez, I never thought . . ."

Karen devoured the newspaper report. The DeFauldos were neighbors, living a scant three blocks from Karen in an upscale Palm Harbor development known as Autumn Woods. Karen and Carl had played tennis with the DeFauldos a few times, even had dinner occasionally. They weren't friends by any account, but they were acquaintances.

To Karen, Dan DeFauldo seemed a vapid gladhander, as genuine as zirconia, and just as transparent. When he wasn't trying to con someone into getting involved with one of his complicated investment schemes, he was a brooder, sitting in a corner of a room, his hands wrapped tightly around a glass, his dark eyes burning with mysterious intensity, as if, like the earth itself, there burned within him some barely controlled nuclear reaction waiting to explode at the slightest provocation.

Caroline, on the other hand, appeared to be living in a fantasy world, perhaps due to her many appearances on local TV commercials and in little theater groups. The woman seemed the archetypical, beautiful airhead, slightly out of touch with reality, prattling on abut metaphysics and astrology charts, the lives and loves of movie and TV stars. Pleasant, but unfulfilling.

It wasn't often that violent crime touched Karen's circle of acquaintances; the occasional burglary, several divorces and DUIs, a few with drug problems. But murder? It was quite a shock. Karen leaned back in her chair and stared at the ceiling.

"Are you okay?" Liz asked.

"Just shocked."

Colin McBride, one of the firm's crop of eager associates, strode into the office. He was a tall, vigorous-looking man with uncontrollable wire for hair and the map of Ireland stamped firmly on his rugged face. At the age of fifteen, he'd immigrated to the U.S. with his impoverished parents, and despite his best efforts, had been unable to eliminate the lilting brogue. Colin had entered law school at age thirty-two, graduated in the top ten percent of his class, and was now the oldest of the "young" associates working at Hewitt, Sinclair. Enthusiastic and bright, he handled the quips about his age, appearance, and heritage with considerable poise, which endeared him to everyone. When Karen waved him in, he took a seat and wiped his brow with a white handkerchief.

"I hear you won the Cole case," he said. "It's all over the radio. That's marvelous."

"Thank you, Colin."

"Mind if I ask a question?"

"Go ahead."

"They said on the radio that the settlement was for five million, eight hundred and thirty-three thousand, three hundred and thirty-three dollars, and thirty-three cents. I'm a little new at this. How on earth do you arrive at a figure like that?"

Karen grinned. "I wanted my client to get three and a half million. Not a penny less. Take the settlement figure, deduct forty percent, and that's what she gets. Simple. Now, tell me about Jack Palmer."

Colin pulled a yellow legal pad from his attaché case. "Well, I talked to him, and I don't mind telling you he's a bloody mess. Almost incoherent, in fact. He broke down three times. It was hard to get a word out of him. He seems to be in a total fog."

"Did you check him out first?"

"I did. He's tapped out, as far as I can see. Everything he owns is joint with his wife. They have two kiddies. The chaps at the jailhouse say he called her three times, but she hasn't called us as yet, unless it happened while I was away."

Karen looked at Liz, who shook her head.

Colin pursed his lips for a moment, then said, "I realize she can't visit her husband until tonight, but I would have thought she'd want to talk to you. Maybe she's written the poor bugger off."

"Maybe," Karen said. "He has no personal assets at all?"

"None that I've been able to find. But . . ."

"But what?"

He took a deep breath. "I know it's not my place to say."

"Go ahead."

"Well, it would be nice if you talked to him before deciding not to take the case." He held up a hand to ward off the expected admonition. "I didn't commit to anything, mind you. I just told him I'd report back to you. He's so befuddled . . . it would take a terrific actor to fake it. And to fake such a story makes no sense to me."

Karen smiled at his obvious compassion. "You'd be surprised. Did he have his first appearance yet?"

"At eight this morning."

They looked at each other for a moment. Finally, Karen said, "All right. Tell me what he said."

Colin brightened. "He said he was with a woman last night, a lovely married woman he met while both were studying at some night college. He says they became quite close and, eventually, she invited him to her home for some hanky-panky. He says she was impossible to resist.

"They were hard at it, making love on the carpet in front of a roaring fireplace. Candles all over the place. Too bloody romantic, I'd say. In the middle of things, the husband walked into the room with a gun in his hand. Mr. Palmer says he was so shook up he almost fainted."

He looked at his notes again and said, "Mr. Palmer says that Mrs. DeFauldo somehow place a gun in Mr.

Palmer's hand and told him to use it. Her husband, she said, was about to kill them both. Mr. Palmer, after some hesitation, obliged."

Karen leaned forward. "He admitted he shot Dan De-Fauldo?"

"I'm afraid he did."

She groaned. "He admitted that to the police?"

"Yes."

Karen sighed. "Wonderful. What happened then?"

"Well, Mr. Palmer says he became quite ill. He ran off to the bathroom to be sick. When he came back, Mrs. DeFauldo was dressed and suggested he do the same, since the police were on their way. He got dressed. The police arrived, took him to one bedroom, while they took Mrs. DeFauldo to another. Mrs. De-Fauldo told the police a different story. After about a half hour of questions, Mr. Palmer was handcuffed and lodged in jail. Obviously, the police think Mr. Palmer is lying through his teeth."

Karen held out her hand. Colin handed her copies of the preliminary police report, a handwritten account of the events as reported to the police, plus a truncated catalog of obvious crime scene evidence.

Palmer's statement was almost identical to what he'd told Colin. Caroline DeFauldo's story, as Colin had said, was not in agreement. She had met Jack Palmer while attending a night course for adults. That much was true. She declared she thought he seemed like a nice man, though depressed about his work and his home life. She'd befriended him, and when he suggested they have dinner together in Tampa, she'd agreed because she felt sorry for him. At Jack's request, they'd taken separate cars and met at the restaurant. After dinner, they went their separate ways. That was supposed to be it. But five minutes after Carol

DeFauldo arrived home, Palmer showed up at her door. He put a gun to her head, forced her to disarm the security system, took her into the living room, and raped her.

When Mr. DeFauldo appeared on the scene, having arrived home early from his weekly poker game, Palmer shot him. Palmer's final words to Mrs. DeFauldo were that he would kill her—or have her killed—if she ever told the truth about what happened. She was to tell the police that they were lovers, that they had both mistaken the keys in Dan's hand for a gun. She was to claim that both lives were in immediate danger.

Only one gun was found at the scene. Ballistics and forensics reports were not yet available, but there was a preliminary report stating Palmer had tested positive for powder residue on his right hand. No powder burns were found on the victim, indicating the shots had come from at least six feet away. Mrs. DeFauldo had been checked at the rape crisis unit of Morton Plant Hospital. No report available at this time.

Karen threw the report on her desk. "Mr. Palmer has no money at all?"

"None."

"Then I guess the public defender's office will have to handle it."

Colin's face fell. "I think there's something amiss here, Karen."

She laughed. "Sorry, Colin, but that's the understatement of the year."

"He sounds very sincere. He really does."

She shook her head. "He might just be a very accomplished liar. I've met more than a few in my time. You have to let the evidence be your guide."

"I don't think so," he insisted. "At least not in this

case. I realize I don't have your experience, but . . . well, he seems to be in total shock. He just doesn't strike me as the kind of man who could do all this."

"He admits pulling the trigger," she said. "It takes a special kind of person to be able to pull the trigger of a gun aimed at another human being, no matter the circumstances."

"But if he really thought he was about to die . . . if you would just talk to him," Colin pleaded.

She was exhausted. She'd just completed a trial that had consumed much of her attention during the last three years. Besides, if Jack Palmer *was* telling the truth, he was still involved with another man's wife. Karen had precious little sympathy for men who cheated on their wives for whatever reason. As well, Caroline's story was plausible, at least on the surface.

But, as much as she hated to admit it, there was a niggling doubt in the back of Karen's mind. Something rang false. Though she didn't know Jack Palmer well, he didn't strike her as the rapist type. She remembered him as being meek. Rape was an act of violence, not sex. And then there was Caroline.

Karen didn't like Caroline much.

"Well?" Colin asked.

Karen looked into his beseeching eyes. "If you really want to make it in this business," she said, "you'll have to learn to be completely objective when it comes to clients. I know it sounds like a cliché, but you can't allow your personal feelings to dictate your actions."

His face fell. "You're right, of course."

"Does Mr. Palmer have a record?"

"No. I checked. Besides, I would have thought he'd call you if he'd ever been in trouble."

"I'm not really his lawyer. I simply did some wills for him and his wife."

"Still . . ."

Karen stood up and stared out the window. She tried to remember more of the encounter with Palmer and his wife, but the events of this morning took first place in her memory bank. After three long years, she'd finally triumphed, thanks to ten pharmacists willing to risk their careers for someone they didn't even know. She wished there were more people like that, willing to get involved, take a chance.

She was exhausted. The trial had consumed much of her energy. She wanted to take a few days off before catching up on a burgeoning caseload. Now that the news of the Cole win was a matter of public record, new potential clients would be knocking on the firm's door.

She was primarily a criminal attorney. Civil cases were usually handled by any of three of the firm's litigators. But Amanda Cole had touched Karen's heart. Now it was over, and she wanted a rest—needed a rest.

And then she thought of those ten pharmacists, willing to take a chance.

Take a chance . . .

She turned and faced Colin. "All right," she said. "No promises, but I'll talk to Jack Palmer."

Three

Ralph Vincenzo lifted his Hartmann suitcase from the Delta carousel at Tampa International Airport and strode quickly to the bank of elevators that would take him to the parking areas. He was an attractive forty, dark-haired, dark-eyed, his athletic build clothed in expensive Italian-designed clothes. He could well afford it. Even more now that the Ducerne deal was all but in the bag.

He got off the elevator at level five and entered the small, computer-operated tram that would take him to the long-term parking area. There, he unlocked his black Lexus, threw his suitcase and attaché case in the trunk, and started the engine. The cellular phone positioned just under the dash seemed to beckon. For a moment, he thought about using it to call the office, give Dan the good news, but he resisted. He wanted to see the expression on Dan's face, wanted to savor it, draw the pleasure out as long as possible.

The clock on the dash said four-fifteen. Lots of time left in the day. He could almost imagine the look on Danny Boy's face when Ralph gave him the good news. The very thought of it made Ralph laugh out loud.

He felt a slight buzz from the drinks he'd consumed on the trip. Ralph normally didn't start drinking until five in the afternoon, but the combination of a long trip—first the Concorde from Paris to New York, then the Delta flight from New York to Tampa—and exhilaration over closing the deal had caused him to make an exception this day. He reached into the glove compartment, found the small spray can, and spritzed his mouth. Dan didn't need to know he'd had a couple. The man was always bitching about Ralph's drinking.

Again he laughed. Dan had been especially concerned about this one, perhaps because the stakes were so high. But Ralph had pulled it off, just like he'd promised he would. All that remained was the actual transfer of funds.

Ralph had resisted the impulse to phone from Paris yesterday once the deal was signed, as he'd been expected to. He'd even refused to answer Dan's frantic calls. It was contemptible behavior, he knew, but there were times when Ralph could be positively diabolical, and for good reason.

Dan, an egoist of the first magnitude, was constantly lording it over him, always belittling him, reminding him that Dan was the most important member of this team. It wasn't true, of course. Each needed the other. Now, it was payback time, and Ralph fully intended to exploit the moment. As he wound his way through the parking lot to the exit, he slipped a Mozart CD into the player and lit up a Marlboro.

Ralph and Dan were full partners, though the company wasn't exactly structured that way. On paper, Vinde Investments was owned by Vincenzo, but the seed money had come from master salesman De-Fauldo. They'd known each other for ten years, ever since they'd worked together for Shearson in New York. A trust, born of necessity, had developed between them. Now they had what they'd always talked about, their own small investment firm specializing in limited partnerships that invested client money in risky offshore ventures.

Because of a tangle with the SEC during the go-go eighties, Dan was prohibited from owning stock in, or being associated with, any company dealing in investments. His name appeared nowhere on official corporate documents. Ralph was the one with his fingerprints on file, his name on the line, and his neck out a mile. But the partnership was working.

The average return on investment on the various limited partnerships so far this year had been phenomenal—over thirteen percent—due in part to the fact that people with money were scrambling to make that money work harder for them. With the traditional instruments like CDS and bonds paying lower yields, money was being transferred from the more secure havens to riskier, potentially higher-paying investments by people spoiled by the high-interest rates of the early eighties; people who also wanted to avoid paying taxes.

Impatience and imprudence combined to create opportunity for those with talent, and the Vinde Investments partners had talent in spades. Ralph was the one who picked the investments; Dan was the one who found the investors. Together, they funneled much of the money through a labyrinthine series of dummy companies set up simply to mask the true operation. It was a perfect business marriage.

Traffic on the causeway was heavy this Wednesday afternoon, and it took Ralph over an hour to get to his office building. As he got out of his car, he felt tired and wired at the same time. It was always like this after a big score, and this was the biggest yet.

Twenty-four investors, the maximum allowed, had

pooled their money—some two hundred thousand dollars each—in a limited partnership called Gaul LP1. Four million of the total amount would be invested directly in Ducerne Food Services of Paris, a new company with a two-year contract to supply ground beef to the second largest fast-food chain in France. The rest of the money would be paid to the managing partners, Ralph Vincenzo and Dan DeFauldo, over that same two-year period.

The investment was expected to return a minimum of fourteen percent (when one considered the tax-free nature of the deal) to the limited partners. But even if the numbers failed to reach those lofty heights, the managing partners would still receive their agreed-upon compensation: eight hundred thousand dollars for a few weeks' work. Not bad.

Their office was located on the second floor of a small building on Enterprise Boulevard. Ralph shunned the elevator and took the stairs two at a time, his attaché case in his hand. He took pride in the fact he was relatively unwinded when he reached the second floor.

When he entered the office, he was stunned by the appearance of Heather, their receptionist-secretary. She was the perfect woman for the job. She knew nothing of the real operation of the company, nor did she need to. She was a competent typist and had a charming personality and a very sexy telephone voice, but it was her large breasts that drew the attention of everyone. That's why Dan had hired her. Dan had a thing about large breasts.

Heather was dressed in her usual uniform, a business suit over a low-cut silk blouse that exposed a generous portion of creamy-white skin. But her normally perfect makeup was a mess. Her puffy red eyes and the long black streaks of mascara running down her cheeks gave her a ghoulish look. She was sitting rigidly at her desk, her hands clasped in front of her, hardly aware that Ralph had entered the room.

He stood in front of her desk. "Heather?"

She looked up and immediately burst into tears.

"What is it?" he asked, as he went around behind the desk and lifted her to her feet.

"Dan. Dan . . . was . . . murdered last night," she gasped.

four

How many times had she made this trip? Karen wondered. A hundred times? A thousand? Since the Pinellas County Jail and the criminal court building were in the same compound, litigators were often at one building or the other three or four times a day. Were it not for the ferocious traffic, she could do it blindfolded.

She drove to the jail compound, showed her Florida Bar card to the gate attendant, searched for a nonexistent parking spot, ended up parking on the grass, walked to the front door of the visitors' section, past the metal detector used only with nonlawyer visitors, she signed in, said hello to the busy desk sergeant behind the bulletproof glass via the little, beat-up speaker, then went through the sally port—electrically operated twin doors made of heavy brown-painted steel bars, only one of which could be opened at a time—down two hallways and into a small four-by-six room with the thick metal table bolted to the wall and floor. She took a seat on one of the two round metal stools bolted to the floor and waited.

For Karen, well known to the police officers in charge of the facility, the reception was always pleasant and cooperative. The people here respected most of the regular lawyers. They treated the prisoners in their charge with dignity as well—most of them at least.

There were some violent or especially antisocial prisoners who required special handling, but even they were treated with scrupulous attention to the rules, a basic requirement in these days of constantly hovering, cause-oriented apologists, considered by some as patrons of the criminal arts.

There were some lawyers, either unknown or having been found wanting in the past, who were required to submit to searches before seeing their clients.

Karen was not searched.

Jack Palmer, dressed in the dark blue prison outfit given major felony prisoners, was brought into the tiny room and told to sit on the one remaining stool. The door was closed. Lawyer and potential client were alone.

"Thanks for coming," he said softly.

"You're welcome," she said.

He looked pathetic, his red-rimmed eyes swollen from crying, his body slumped in defeat, his head hanging in abject surrender, the angry red scratches on his cheek begging attention. Karen remembered more about him now that she was sitting across from him. Her first fuzzy impression of him, gained three years ago, came into focus. He was plain-faced and bashful then. Now, he seemed thoroughly whipped. But the scratches on his face bespoke another kind of man, one with violent urges not heretofore expressed.

"Before we start talking about this case," Karen said, "and I know this sounds heartless, I'm required to discuss my fee. How much money do you have?"

He looked confused. Then, his faced flushed with embarrassment, he said, "Jesus. I never even thought about money. I have maybe three hundred dollars."

"What about your house?"

He shook his head. "It's just a condo. We have no

equity in it. It's worth less than I paid for it nine years ago."

Karen groaned inwardly. This was one part of the lawyer's life she hated. Preparing for trial, deposing witnesses, but especially being on stage employing every ounce of her intelligence—it all brought out the best in her. Discussing money seemed somehow squalid. It seemed to her that lawyers, especially litigators, should have assistants who discussed such things as money. Lawyers should be free to discuss the merits of a case, make their decisions based on some sense of justice. She was, at heart, a romantic. But not a hopeless one by any means.

"I know you have a wife," she said, smiling. "Two kids at last count. Any additions?"

"No."

"Okay, what about the rest of your family? Can they help? Or your wife's family?"

He shook his head. "My wife . . . I talked to her. She's pretty upset."

Karen could understand that. The woman's husband had been cheating on her. Now, he was charged with murder. His wife was probably trying hard to cope with her own world of hurt.

"And the rest?"

He shook his head. "I have no family. My mother died when I was six. My father died two years ago. He had cancer. The VA paid his medical expenses. Good thing, too, 'cause he was broke all the time. As for Ellen, her family has no money either."

"Do you have any friends?"

He thought for a moment, then said, "I have some friends, but not the kind who would ever lend me money." His eyes suddenly filled with fear. "Does that mean . . ."

"We'll see," she said. "You saw a judge this morning?"

"Yes." He looked even more panicky. "It didn't seem real. I was in this room with all the other prisoners, and the judge was on TV. I guess I was, too." Tears formed at the corners of his eyes. "I'm innocent, Mrs. Perry-Mondori. I swear to God!"

"Take it easy," she said, looking deep into his eyes, assessing. "What did the judge say to you?"

"He said I was charged with felony murder, which he explained is the same as first-degree murder." He seemed to choke on the words. "God! It's impossible."

"We'll get to that," she said. "What else?"

"He said I had seventy-two hours to get an attorney, or one would be appointed. I didn't want a stranger. I thought of you. You're the only attorney I know. I realize you're pretty famous now, but I didn't do this. I really didn't." His voice was beginning to sound like a child's. "I don't know how I can pay you, but doesn't the fact that I'm innocent count for anything?"

"If you're telling the truth," she said softly, "it counts for a great deal."

"How can I convince you?" he pleaded.

She hesitated for a moment, then said, "Are you willing to take a lie-detector test?"

"I'll do anything. Anything at all."

He looked lost and vulnerable, a man completely out of his element. There was no pretense, no posturing, no carefully calculated sentences. He was reaching out, grasping at what he perceived to be a lifeline. But for Karen, taking this case meant juggling her schedule, even shifting some paying clients to an associate. The clients wouldn't be pleased. Nor would the partners. A murder case usually involved at least a thousand hours at a fee of a hundred and eighty dollars an hour; that was a substantial investment. But that wasn't all. There were the out-of-pocket costs for experts, depositions, investigators, to name but a few. And, with appeals, the expenses could rise into the stratosphere. "Tell me about those scratches," she commanded.

Palmer's hand went involuntarily to his face. "I know how it looks."

"Never mind how it looks. How did you get them?"

"She scratched me while we were making love," he said sheepishly. "She scratched my chest, too."

"I see. You're saying it was part of lovemaking."

His gaze dropped to the table. "I thought it was, yes. I don't know much about lovemaking. I've never been involved with a woman like her before. In fact, until last night, Ellen was the only woman I'd ever made love to. I swear."

He looked into her eyes. She examined his face, looking for the little clues that nonpathological liars exhibit when they spin their tales. She saw none. But she wasn't ready to commit herself at this point. Though she might not take this case, she could at least take the time to impart some knowledge while she mulled things over.

"Let me fill you in on a few things," she said.

"Yes?"

"Bail is tough to get in a murder case. Besides, you couldn't make bail anyway, so you'll be here for a while. Do they have you in a cell by yourself?"

"Yes."

"That may change," she said. "It depends on how crowded things get. This is basically a short-term facility. But if it happens, don't get upset. Just keep your cool. Have you ever been in jail before?"

"Never."

"Well, it can be scary, but it's not the end of the

world. Tell whoever represents you that you want them to send a letter to the commander requesting that no one talk to you about this case. A copy of that letter will be posted right outside your cell. If *anyone* tries to discuss this case with you, show them the letter. Say nothing to anyone except your lawyer, got it?"

He looked crushed. She was preparing to tell him she wouldn't represent him. And why should she? He had no money. Money made the world move, not innocence.

"I understand," he said.

"This is one of the better jails in the country," she continued. "They'll treat you all right so long as you're polite and don't cause problems. Did they give you breakfast before your court appearance?"

"Yes, but I couldn't eat it. I've been throwing up a lot. This is more than I can handle."

"You have to settle down, Jack," she said, still assessing. "All meals are served at your cell, as you've already discovered. You'll get an hour a day of exercise and no hassles, just as long as you keep out of trouble. If you need a doctor, just ask. You'll get one. If you feel extremely nervous or anxious, they can give you a sedative. Don't be afraid to ask. This is not a torture chamber.

"If you need to talk to your lawyer, call. You're allowed as many collect phone calls as you like, and your lawyer is allowed to see you whenever he or she wants. But don't call your lawyer at three in the morning unless you have a very good reason."

"I won't."

He seemed genuinely terrified. Was it an act? Act or not, the prudent thing would be to leave now. But his eyes, those beseeching eyes, held her fast. It was more than just the eyes. It was the way he held his body, the way his mouth worked when he talked, the way his hands seemed to have a life of their own. Hands that trembled. Old man's hands. He projected an image of despair and hopelessness, a man, with little self-esteem to begin with, having lost what small fragments remained.

"Everything you tell me is confidential. Are you aware of that?"

"Yes."

"Good. I don't make judgments, I defend people. But if you're guilty and you lie to me, you'll only be fooling yourself. You'll suffer, not me. So don't waste my time with false denials. Understood?"

"Yes."

Karen opened her case and removed a legal-size yellow pad. "Tell me what happened," she said. "From the beginning."

He told her how he'd met Caroline while both were attending adult education classes. He was an auto parts salesman but wanted to be a writer. Caroline was a glamorous model and actress who also wanted to write. They had something in common. To his astonishment, she was very friendly to him. He'd seen her on TV many times, doing commercials for various local concerns. Being able to talk to a celebrity of sorts was thrill enough, but having this gorgeous creature treat him as if he were somebody was mind-bending.

"The third week," he continued, "she gave me this short story to read. It was a very sexy story." He shook his head. "I thought she was trying to tell me something. The next week we were talking after class, sitting in her car. We started necking."

He closed his eyes, remembering, perhaps savoring. "She was really getting to me. Then she said she wanted us to get together. You know?"

"She was suggesting sex?"

"Yes."

"It was her idea?"

"Absolutely. I swear."

Karen made a note. "You said you were necking. How serious was the necking?"

He blushed. "We both kept our clothes on. It was just kissing and touchy-feely stuff. She was really hot. At least, I thought she was. She acted like she was hot."

"This short story she gave you. Do you still have it?"

"No. When she gave it to me she said she needed it back. She said something about trusting me. So I gave it back when I gave her the first couple of chapters of my novel to read."

"When she suggested you have sex, what did she say?"

"She said her husband would be out of town on the tenth, giving us the perfect opportunity. She had it all arranged. We'd take our own cars and meet in Tampa for dinner, then I was to come to her place. I was to park the car about a block away and come on foot. I couldn't believe it. I couldn't sleep for almost a week. I've never cheated on Ellen before, but I couldn't resist Caroline. She was all I could think about."

He sighed, then said, "So that's what we did. After we had dinner in Tampa, I showed up at her place and she let me in. She was dressed real sexy. The fireplace was going and there were candles all over the place. She gave me a glass of liqueur and we sat down in front of the fire. Within minutes, we had our clothes off and were making love. That's when she scratched me. I never even felt it. I was feeling kinda sick . . . I guess from all the excitement . . . but I didn't care."

"What happened then?"

He thought for a moment. "A light went on in the

kitchen. At that point, it really hit me. I thought I was going to throw up. I saw this guy coming toward us with a gun in his hand. All of a sudden, Caroline gave me this gun and said I better shoot or he'd kill us both."

"Back up a minute. What time did you arrive at the house?"

"I don't know, really."

"Approximately."

"Ahhh, I guess it was a little before eleven."

"Okay. You and Mrs. DeFauldo were on the floor making love. How long had you been making love before the light in the kitchen went on?"

He let out a deep sigh. "I can't really say. Five minutes, more or less. I wasn't really paying attention. She was really into it. She let out this really loud yell. It scared me. I thought the neighbors might hear her. And then I heard this other noise, like a door closing. And then he turned on the kitchen light."

"Who did?"

"Mr. DeFauldo."

"You saw him do it?"

"No. I just saw the light go on."

"Go on."

"Well, I heard him call her name. Like I said, there were candles all over the place, but the light was still pretty dim in the living room. I couldn't see him, really . . . just this shape, like a silhouette. But his voice was loud. I didn't know who it was, and then Caroline said it was her husband."

"How exactly did she express herself?"

"She said, 'God, it's my husband, Dan.' Something like that."

"And he called her name?"

"Yes."

"Go on."

He pinched his face in concentration. "She was holding her blouse to her chest, trying to cover herself. I was frozen. I couldn't move. Then I saw him walking toward us with the gun in his hand. I figured I was dead right there.

"Then . . . there was a metal bucket by the fireplace, filled with those logs you buy in the supermarket, you know? Caroline . . . Mrs. DeFauldo . . . reached inside and pulled this thing out. I didn't know it was a gun until it was in my hand. She told me that Dan was crazy, that he was going to kill us both. She looked scared out of her mind."

His hands started to shake violently. He placed them flat on the table to stop the shaking.

"How far away was he when you first noticed the gun?"

"About twenty feet."

"How was he dressed?"

"Dressed?"

"Yes. What was he wearing? Tie? Jacket?"

"No. I think he was wearing a short-sleeved shirt and slacks. You know, business slacks."

"And when did you see the gun in his hand? Before or after you could see his face?"

"Oh, before. Way before."

"What did the gun he was carrying look like?"

"It was big. I'd guess a nine-millimeter or .45 semi-automatic. Nickel-plated. The light from the candles reflected off it."

Karen made a note, then said, "What do you mean you didn't know Caroline had handed you a gun?"

"Well, I was staring at the gun in her husband's hand. Then I felt this thing in my hand. I looked down, and there it was. The gun, I mean. Caroline was holding a rag of some sort. Maybe a dish towel. Some cloth with stripes on it. I figure she'd wrapped the gun in it before."

"She handed the gun to you wrapped?"

He shook his head. "No. She unwrapped it and dropped it in my hand. She kept telling me that Dan was going to kill us."

"You saw her unwrap it?"

"No. I told you. I was staring at Mr. DeFauldo. I felt this weight in my hand."

"And you saw her take it from the bucket?"

"I saw her take something wrapped in a cloth out of the bucket."

"But you said you were staring at Mr. DeFauldo."

"I *was*. But out of the corner of my eye, I saw Caroline move. I thought she was trying to duck, but she was reaching for something in the bucket. Then she straightened up and dropped the gun in my hand."

Karen felt a strange chill run down her spine. Warning bells. "What kind of gun was it, the one she gave you?"

"A semiautomatic. I don't know the caliber."

"You're familiar with guns?"

"A little."

"Do you own one?"

"No. I hate guns."

"Then how is it that you're familiar with them?"

He seemed embarrassed. "I'm writing a novel," he said, blushing. "I have to read a lot for research. There's a part in my novel where the hero has to use a gun, so I thought I better read about guns. I've fired a rifle, but I've never fired a handgun in my life."

Karen nodded. "Okay. Back to your story. Caroline dropped the gun in your hand. What happened then?"

He stared past Karen, thinking, his mind whirling.

Karen prodded him. "Go on. The gun is in your hand. Then what happened?"

His concentration returned. "I saw him walking toward us. He never said anything. He pointed the gun at us. When he was about ten feet away, I could see him clearly. There was a weird look on his face. I was sure he was about to pull the trigger. Caroline was screaming at me to shoot. I finally did."

"How many times?"

"I don't remember exactly. I think the first one missed, because he kept coming. The second one hit him in the stomach. I saw the blood. But he didn't fall. He just stood there, still aiming the gun at us. I closed my eyes and fired again two or three times, and he kinda slumped to the floor."

"How big is the living room?"

"Big. Maybe thirty, forty feet long."

"Are you aware that Caroline DeFauldo says you raped her, that you killed her husband in cold blood? That you threatened to kill her if she told the truth?"

He started breathing hard. "I know she says that. But it's not true!"

Karen leaned forward. "The police think it is. And the evidence supports Mrs. DeFauldo's story. No other gun was found, just the one you used. There are scratches on your face and body. You see how it looks?"

"Yes."

"Why would Caroline lie?"

"I don't know."

He buried his head in his hands and moaned. If he was a liar, he was a very good one. As he fought to get himself under control, Karen evaluated his story. It was too appallingly outrageous to be a total lie. Like any human being under intense pressure, his memory might have played tricks on him, making him believe certain events had taken place when, in fact, they had not.

"I know it's tough," Karen said, "but if what you're telling me is true, something is very wrong."

"You don't believe me," he mumbled.

"I didn't say that."

He leaned back in his chair and said, "I don't know what I'm supposed to say. I'm telling you the truth. It's the only thing I can do."

She gave him another hard look. "Let's move on. Dan DeFauldo is lying on the floor. What happened next?"

It took him a moment to answer. "I crawled over to him. He was lying on his back. It was easy to tell he was dead. There was blood all over him. It was sickening. I knew I was going to puke. I ran to the bathroom and was sick. Real sick. After about ten heaves, I lay on the floor. I was shaking and covered in cold sweat. I thought I was going to pass out. I managed to put a towel in the sink and get it wet. Then I put it over my face. God! The room was spinning."

"Where was the gun? The one you used?"

"I dropped it on the floor after he fell."

"And then?"

"I came back into the living room. Caroline was already dressed. She'd put a blanket over the body. My clothes were still on the floor She told me to get dressed, that the police were on their way over."

"How was she dressed?"

"The same way as before. She had on that white blouse and a long black skirt."

"Were the candles still burning?"

He thought for a moment, then said, "I don't remember."

"What did you do while you waited for the police?"

"There *was* no wait. They were there as soon as I was dressed."

"Did they knock on the door?"

"No. They just walked in. The door was open. She must have opened it. They were all over the place. They took me into a bedroom and closed the door. They asked me what happened. I told them everything. Then, a black guy in plainclothes came in and asked me if I wanted a lawyer. I said no. He told me I didn't have to talk to them and made me sign something. I signed it. Then he told me what Caroline was saying, that I had forced her to have sex. I went nuts. I started screaming at him. Then I threw a punch at him."

"You what?"

"I threw a punch at him. I know it was stupid, but I was out of my mind. I'd just killed a man, and they were telling me things I couldn't believe. I thought it was a crazy nightmare. It made no sense to me. I was sure they were lying. When I finally realized they weren't, I told them I didn't want to talk to them anymore. They told me I was under arrest, and they brought me here. I didn't know your home phone, so I waited until this morning to call you."

Again, he buried his head in his hands and started to weep.

Karen stood up, leaned against the wall, and listened to him whimper for a while. His obvious weakness troubled her. Weak men made for bad witnesses. But that same weakness, if genuine, precluded the possibility of him having committed rape and murder.

She'd had clients like Jack before. While the shock of what they had done was still powerful, they were capable of lying like champions, acting on survival instincts, playing roles with extraordinary aplomb. But as they were dragged deeper into the maw of a voracious criminal justice system, the shock subsided and the clients had trouble remembering the lies. Confronted with reality, they confessed to their lawyer, and the stage was set for a plea bargain.

Jack fit the profile. If he was lying, it wouldn't be long before he'd crumble. On the other hand, if he was telling the truth, he'd need a hell of a lawyer.

"I'll represent you, Jack."

His face jerked up, filled with hope. "You will?"

"Yes."

"But I have no money."

"I know. I'll take the three hundred dollars as a retainer. We'll have to see what we can do about the rest later. For now, let's not worry about the money. But understand this: If you're lying to me, I'll find out. I'll drop you so fast your head will spin. If you murdered the man, tell me now. I'll still defend you."

"Everything I've told you is true," he said. "Everything."

"I hope so, for your sake."

five

Ralph Vincenzo told his distraught receptionist to take the rest of the day off. It would have been a nice thing to do, except for the fact that she'd already worked almost an hour past normal quitting time waiting for Ralph to show.

He then placed a message on the answering machine to the effect that the office would be closed until Tuesday. It was only proper, after all. He used a marking pen to prepare a sign displaying the same message, stuck it to the front window, locked the door, closed the blinds, and retreated to his office. He read the newspaper accounts of the crime, all the while shaking his head in bewilderment. Incredible! Poor Caroline! As terrible an ordeal as she'd suffered, it still would have been better had the madman raping her finished his business and left the house before Dan arrived home. At least Caroline was still alive. As for Dan, it seemed a case of being in the wrong place at the wrong time.

Ralph mourned the loss of his partner in the only way he knew how. He sat at his desk and drank, ignoring the dozen or so messages that Heather had left on his desk. He and Dan had been business partners a long time, and while Ralph didn't always appreciate Dan's mood swings, his braggadocio, or his often obstreperous rantings about politics, Ralph marveled at the man's extraordinary sales ability.

Dan was unique. In the four years they'd been together as partners, they'd put together over forty limited partnership deals, and all but three had been successful. While Ralph employed no false modesty in assessing his own worth to the firm—he was, after all, the one who picked the investments—he knew that without the inflow of capital the entire enterprise would fail. Money made it all work, and it was Dan who consistently brought in the capital.

Halfway through the journey that he hoped would eventually dim the pain, Ralph began to wonder how in the world he would find someone to replace Dan. He needed someone in a hurry. He knew several men working for other investment companies, men with much experience and good track records. While no one could ever replace Dan, there were some who might come close. Ralph would have to start interviewing almost immediately, and with absolute discretion. What he and Dan had been doing the past four years was well over the often blurry lines established by various government agencies; it was flat-out illegal. But as long as everyone involved made money and paid taxes on the open transactions, they'd be all right.

Ralph made out a list of names, then determined he'd better approach these prospects in person. It would take some time. He had to get started.

But not today, not right now. Today, he had to conclude the Ducerne deal. Normally, he would have taken care of that important business immediately, but the stunning news of Dan's death had unhinged him more than even he realized.

Now, his emotions dulled by alcohol, he turned on the computer and began the rather laborious series of entries that would electronically transfer the four million dollars being held in a special reserve account to the bank in Paris. Once the Paris bankers acknowledged receipt of the money, the signed contract with Ducerne would automatically be in effect. And while he mourned the loss of his partner, Ducerne was expecting the money. Business was business.

When he entered the code known only to Dan and himself, the screen normally filled with data. But this time, there was nothing but the blinking cursor and the message "Directory does not exist . . . create?"

He thought at first he'd entered the wrong codes. But when he carefully retraced his steps, the result was the same. Perhaps there was something wrong with the computer.

He brought another directory to the screen. This one seemed to be fine.

Okay, nothing wrong with the computer.

He rebooted the computer and did a directory search. The directory was gone.

Wrong drive? No.

Beginning to sweat now, he rebooted the computer and started over again. The results were the same. The GaulLP1 directory, the entire record, had been erased.

An accident? Impossible!

He leaped out of his chair and rolled back the small teak book cabinet that decorated part of one wall. Then he spun the combination lock on the safe and opened the heavy door. Inside was a box filled with backup floppy disks. He rummaged through them looking for the one marked "GaulLP1."

It wasn't there.

His stomach was starting to ache. His temples were pounding. Large drops of perspiration appeared on his forehead and upper lip.

Oh, God!

He grabbed the telephone. It took fewer than thirty seconds to get an account executive on the telephone. It was nighttime in Switzerland, but the efficient Swiss worked twenty-four hours a day, not wanting to miss any opportunity to make a buck.

"Mr. Haggar here."

"This is Ralph Vincenzo," he said to the man with the clipped English accent. "I'm inquiring as to the balance in account number UZ334–333."

"Of course. Your code, sir?"

"Yes. Timberline–B."

"Would you spell that, please?"

"Yes. T-I-M-B-E-R-L-I-N-E. Then a dash. Then B as in Bob. Got it?"

"Yes. One moment, please."

Waiting was agony. Ralph's hands were so sweat-covered, the receiver slipped out of his hand. He grabbed it and held it tightly.

"Mr. Vincenzo?"

"Yes."

"Yes, I have that information. I simply need the second code to verify that you are Mr. Vincenzo."

"Jesus! 3777488."

"Thank you, sir. That account is inoperable, sir."

Ralph's heart stopped beating for an instant. "What do you mean, inoperable?"

"The account has been closed."

"Closed? Are you nuts?"

There was a pause, then, "As you know, under the agreement signed by both you and Mr. DeFauldo, precautions were taken in the event . . ."

"Yes! I know all that."

"Well . . . under the terms of that agreement, the account requires but a single signatory, either you or Mr. DeFauldo. The account was closed by Mr. DeFauldo."

"Closed? Where did the money go?"

"Into a new account opened by Mr. DeFauldo. A private account. Under the terms of the agreement . . ."

"What the hell are you saying?"

"I'm trying to explain, sir. The contents of the account in question were transferred to another account at the request of Mr. DeFauldo. Date was November nine."

The pounding in Ralph's head intensified fourfold. He was standing now, screaming into the telephone. "Cut the crap. What's happened to the money?"

There was another pause, then, "It would appear to me, sir, and I wish there was a more delicate way to phrase this, that you need to have a chat with Mr. DeFauldo, or perhaps your attorney. I shouldn't be telling you this, but . . . on November nine, Mr. DeFauldo made sixteen transactions. All of the transactions resulted in money being taken from various accounts and transferred to this new account. I can tell you that the new account now holds a zero balance."

"What!"

"The money in the new account has been transferred to another bank. It's completely out of our hands, Mr. Vincenzo. I suggest you talk to Mr. DeFauldo as soon as possible."

Ralph's eyes were beginning to spin within their sockets. "I can't!" he screamed. "He's dead!"

"Oh, my. That's most unfortunate," the man said.

"But I need to get that money back!"

"That's quite impossible, sir. We followed instructions agreed to by both you and Mr. DeFauldo. It would depend on the agreement Mr. DeFauldo signed with the new bank as to a disposition of the account upon his death. As I said before, it's completely out of our hands."

Ralph tried to think. "What's the name of that other bank?"

"I wish I could help you, sir, but . . ."

"You mean to tell me that my partner can steal over six million dollars and you're not going to lift a finger to help me get it back? Didn't you hear me? The son of a bitch is dead!"

"I'm truly sympathetic, Mr. Vincenzo. But the rules established are for the protection of all clients. I'm sure you understand. I'm unable to be of further assistance to you. Good day."

Ralph screamed something into the mouthpiece, but he was wasting his breath. The line was dead.

By seven-thirty that evening, Ralph was quite drunk. He'd been sitting stiffly at his desk for the past half hour, drinking and rereading newspaper accounts of Dan DeFauldo's death and trying to comprehend what the hell was really happening.

Some of it seemed clear enough. Dan, his trusted partner Dan, had stolen all of the money in the Ducerne account—plus a lot more. In fact, he'd gutted all of the accounts. Ralph was ruined. Of that, there was no question.

The constant ringing of the telephone, calls he refused to answer, were obviously those of frantic investors who had heard the news of Dan's death, investors wondering if their precious money was still safe. What was he supposed to tell them? What *could* he tell them? How many people would believe he was stupid enough to have created a situation where one partner could crush the other?

Fact was, no one *would* believe him. Once it was discovered that the money was missing, the investors, at least the ones involved in the legitimate deals, would assume Ralph was in on it, too. The others, the tax evaders, would be less forthcoming. But two hundred thousand dollars was a hell of a lot of money, no matter how rich a man was. The big shooters might have their own ways of settling a score.

It all spelled trouble.

Jesus. Once the straight arrows started screaming to the feds, the ball would start rolling downhill. The feds would investigate. Then, the creeps from the IRS would swoop down like angry wasps. The local police would join the federal investigation, and Ralph would be smothered under a swarming hive of cops and lawyers. Even if, by some miracle, they failed to stick him in prison, they'd hound him to death.

He took inventory of his personal assets. He had sixteen thousand dollars in his personal account, about fifty thousand dollars in bonds in a safe-deposit box, and that was it. He'd invested everything else in the company. He lived alone in a rented condo and drove a leased car. The money would last him less than a year, and then what? He'd never be able to work in the securities business again, not after this fiasco.

Ralph buried his head in his hands. He'd never felt so miserable in his life.

He stood up and started pacing, weaving from side to side. There was a part of this he couldn't understand at all. Dan's taking the money? Okay. That was always a possibility. Ralph had trusted Dan, not because he thought Dan was honest, but because he was sure the guy didn't have the guts to steal. Not Dan. Dan was a blowhard salesman—crooked, sure, but only when he was sure he could get away with it.

Ralph had been wrong about that.

Why had Dan picked November 9 to pull the plug? Because there was more money available than ever before, that's why. Okay. That made sense.

But why wait around? Why hadn't Dan taken Caroline and left the country before Ralph got back from Paris? That was the big question. What the hell was he doing calmly playing poker with his buddies after he'd stolen the money? How could that be? And why had he called Ralph in Paris? What was that all about?

He cursed himself for not having taken the calls.

Another question. Was Caroline in on this, or was Dan going to leave her flat? He shook his head. That was impossible. The two were inseparable.

Then again, why had Dan waited?

He flopped back down on the chair and rubbed his throbbing temples as he ran the sequence of events through his memory bank one more time. And still the little question kept coming back like a bad penny, haunting him.

Why wait?

The question loomed larger and larger in his mind. Waiting made no sense, unless—

Jesus!

Ralph leaped to his feet. For a moment, the room started to spin. He held on to the desk for support until the room slowed down. Jesus! He staggered to the door.

Caroline. Bitch. She had to be the one! Yes! It was the only thing that made sense. Caroline had done this. She'd taken the money, then set up Dan. Hired this poor schlub to kill Dan, then turned on the poor sucker and left him hanging. Sure! That was it. That *had* to be it. Maybe Caroline and Dan *weren't* inseparable at all! Caroline was an actress, wasn't she? Maybe this lovey-dovey stuff was all an act.

There was only one way to find out. Caroline was still here. He had to see her. Had to make her talk. She'd talk, by God. Ralph would make her talk. He'd take the .38 sitting in his glove compartment and stick it up her pretty nose until she did talk.

Yes!

He lurched out of the office and into the Lexus. It took a while to get the key into the ignition, but he finally managed.

Have to drive slow, he thought. Can't get a ticket right now. Have to talk to Caroline. One way or another, Caroline knows where the money is.

The money.

He eased the big car into the heavy flow of traffic. God! Even at this hour, the highway was a mess. Who the hell were all these people? Why weren't they at home? Goddam Nineteen, three lanes in each direction, speed limit fifty-five, cluttered with blind old men and women in their eighties and nineties, still driving on a highway that was too dangerous even for young kids. Accesses every hundred feet. Crazy. A hodgepodge of stores on both sides of the highway. In and out. People making turns from the wrong lanes. Crashes every hour. Always a mess.

He heard a horn honk. Shit! He was weaving. He gripped the wheel tighter and tried to steer straight. He had to talk to Caroline. It was a big goddam hoax. Jesus. She'd ripped them both off. Now she was setting Ralph up to take a fall.

Fuck that. Nobody was going to stick it to Ralph Vincenzo.

Another horn blast. Insistent. Bastard! He opened the window, stuck out his hand, and flipped his middle finger.

Stop for the red light at Tampa Road. Then Nebraska,

left at Alderman. Minutes away from Caroline now. Minutes away from answers. He felt his heart pounding. Caroline would shit her pants when he stuck that gun in her face.

The sound of the siren made him jump. Jesus. Flashing lights. Sheriff. Gotta look straight. Pull over. Be nice.

He pulled into one of the many strip malls that faced the highway and stopped. The police car was right behind him. He looked in his rearview mirror and saw the cop getting out of the car, ambling slowly toward him. He pressed the button that lowered the window and stuck out his head.

"What seems to be the problem, Officer?"

The cop was beside him now, peering at him from behind dark sunglasses. "Would you step out of the car, sir?"

Ralph smiled. "Normally, I'd have no problem with that, but you see, I'm really in a hurry. I have to talk to Caroline."

"Step out of the car, sir."

Louder this time. More demanding. Ralph opened the door and stepped outside. He leaned against the car.

"Have you been drinking, sir?"

Ralph waved a hand in front of his face. "Maybe a little, but I have a good reason. My partner just stole all the money. I have to talk to Caroline, don't you see? She'll know where the money is. She has to."

"Would you turn around and face the car, sir?"

"What for?"

"Just do it."

Ralph turned around and fell down. He felt his arms being pulled behind him, heard the metallic sound of handcuffs being placed on his wrists. Heard the deep voice say, "You're under arrest, sir. Now, I want you to stand up and get into my cruiser. I'll call someone to take care of your car. I don't want you getting excited. Just be cool, okay?"

Ralph shook his head in frustration. "You don't understand," he said plaintively. "Caroline took all the money."

Six

Karen used a pay phone in the jail to contact the detective in charge of the case, a veteran cop named Charles Simms. She'd worked on cases he'd handled before. Like most of the detectives in the Pinellas County Sheriff's Department, Charlie was a pro in the finest sense of the word. He regarded defense attorneys as part of the system, not part of the problem, a fine distinction due in part to the fact that the county's highly respected sheriff was not only a former cop but a former defense attorney.

Palm Harbor, being an unincorporated section of the county despite its seventy thousand residents, had no police force of its own. Instead, it relied on the services of the county's law enforcement agency.

"Is the crime scene still secure?" she asked, after an exchange of pleasantries.

"It was a busy night," he said. "The techs didn't get there until five in the morning. They wrapped it up about an hour ago, but I don't think the house has been officially cleared yet. Hold on."

She waited while he checked. When he came back on the line, he said, "It's secure until six tonight."

"I'd like to come down and look the house over," Karen said. "Will you okay it, or do I need to get a court order?"

There was a pause, then, "If you can do it right now, I'll meet you there."

"Thanks, Charlie."

She stopped off at the courthouse, just a short walk from the jail, gave the clerk of the Court official notice that she was Jack's attorney, and left a copy of a handwritten note given the jail commander requesting that her client not be questioned outside her presence. Then she found the name of the assistant state attorney and judge assigned to the case, groaned inwardly, and rushed back to Palm Harbor.

Yellow ribbons still marked off the front lawn of the DeFauldo house. A uniformed officer stood guard at the front door. Across the street, the usual crowd of curious neighbors had gathered, some of whom Karen knew. They stared at her in recognition. She didn't wave. This was business. And Susan Brooks, a reporter for Channel Seven News, was rushing toward her, a microphone in hand, a cameraman in tow.

"Karen! Wait up!" she called.

Karen waited. Susan, an attractive twenty-eight-year-old determined to make it in the tough world of television news, stopped in front of her, caught her breath, and said, "Can we talk?"

"Off the record, for now," Karen answered.

"No way. We're taping. Come on, Karen. I'm just doing my job. Our producer just called and says you filed notice you're representing Jack Palmer. Can I ask you why you're representing the man accused of raping Mrs. DeFauldo and murdering her husband? Isn't it true that you and the victims are practically neighbors?"

Susan, as usual, was being very cunning. Karen didn't allow the heavily loaded question to goad her. Calmly, she said, "Right now, I'm here to talk to the police and examine the crime scene. After I've done that, I'll give you a statement."

Before Susan could answer, Karen turned away and walked quickly toward the front door, introduced herself to the cop, and asked for Charlie. The cop opened the front door. Karen walked across the tiled entryway and spotted Charlie slumped in a chair, his eyes closed, his open mouth offering soft snores.

A former linebacker in college, Charlie was big. His chocolate-colored skin covered 240 pounds of muscle and bone. He looked deceptively peaceful in sleep. He was a man who hated using his gun, preferring to employ his quickness and strength to subdue the bad guys, especially when the bad guys were barely past puberty. But in these turbulent times of weapon-loving, violence-oriented, drug-crazed lunatics, it wasn't always possible. Kids and guns were rapidly becoming synonymous.

"Charlie?"

He opened his eyes and grinned. "Hi, Karen. Sorry. It's been a long night. How've you been?"

"Good. You?"

Charlie shook his head to clear the cobwebs. "About as well as can be expected." He looked around the room. "At least this one involves grown-ups. I'd call that good luck, at least for me. You want to look around?"

"I do," she said.

They were alone in the big house. A six-inch-wide splotch of blood and several smaller ones stained the lush off-white carpet about fifteen feet from the hearth. They were outlined in black chalk. The same black chalk was used to draw seven small circles, which Karen realized were the locations of spent cartridges. They were in no particular pattern, running from the fireplace to the body. Another larger circle marked where a gun had been found.

Parts of the remains of two fireplace logs clung to the grate, the ashes underneath. There were no candles in sight. Across the room, black marking pens had been used to outline two bullet holes in the wall. Yellow strings went from the bullet holes to a spot two feet below the fireplace mantel, indicating the path of five of the slugs. More strings went from the floor to the ceiling, the paths of two more slugs. That made seven in all.

Karen checked her notes. The murder weapon was a Walther PPK. That meant a full clip and one in the pipe.

She went to the kitchen, then retraced the steps Dan had made when he entered the house, stopping at the outline marked on the carpet. She walked over to the fireplace and looked inside a brass bucket. Nothing but logs.

"What are you looking for?" Charlie asked.

"Just looking. When do you figure you'll have a report ready?"

"Forty-eight hours," he said. "But you'll have to talk to the ASA." The ASA assigned to this case was Assistant State Attorney Brad Keats.

"I know that," Karen said.

Charlie shoved his big hands into his pockets. "What on earth you doin' defending this scuzzball?"

"Community service," she said, smiling. "How do you figure it went down?"

"You read the preliminary report?"

"I did."

"Then you know."

Karen shook her head. "Just like that?"

"Just like that."

"What makes you so sure?"

"You see your client's face?"

"I did."

"She scratched him pretty good. That's one thing. He admits he shot the guy. That's half the battle right there. He says the guy had a gun, but we never saw but one, just the one Palmer used, and we looked real hard, Karen. But what it boils down to, aside from the evidence, is this: when we talked to Mrs. DeFauldo, she was very convincing. He just wasn't."

"She have any bruises?" Karen asked.

"Not where I could see them, but we'll leave that to the doctors."

Karen pulled the preliminary report from her attaché case and read it over again. A call had gone in to 911 at 11:13 P.M. Another call at 11:14. The first call was from a neighbor concerning gunshots being heard coming from this address. The second call was from Caroline.

The first police unit arrived at 11:20. Three additional units arrived at 11:21, along with the paramedics. Simms got to the scene at 11:40. According to Jack Palmer, he was in the bathroom being sick. That meant Caroline was on her own for at least three or four minutes.

"How convincing was she?"

"Very. She was real shook up, pale and shaking. Palmer had warned her he'd kill her if she talked. At first, she was reticent, but finally opened up. When we confronted Palmer with her statement, he got *real* upset." He laughed. "When you look at him and her together, it all fits. The guy thought he could bluff his way through. Strictly an amateur."

Karen ran a hand through her hair. "If he's lying, doesn't his story sound a little stupid to you?"

"Come on, Karen. How many smart killers do you know?"

He had a point. Most killers had IQs well below average, especially the domestic variety—the husbands and wives who settled arguments with guns or knives. The less developed the cerebral cortex, the more potential for killing.

"Mind if I look in the other rooms?"

He struggled out of the chair. "I'll go with you. But let's make it quick, okay?"

He followed her as she wandered through the rooms, looking at anything and everything, making copious notes. When she reached the bathroom closest to the living room, she inspected it carefully. It was the guest bathroom, a room designed for guests to change clothes. One door led to the living room, another to the pool area. Karen checked the outside door. It was locked from the inside. She looked at the toilet. There were no signs it had been dusted for prints.

"Did you check the toilet for prints?" she asked.

Charlie nodded. "Crime unit tries not to mess up the entire house unless they have to. Used a laser."

"Did they find any?"

"You'll have to ask them."

She left the bathroom and looked at the elaborate security system's main station near the front entrance. A small green light signaled that the system was off. She was familiar with the system, having had a similar unit installed in her own home. There were several circuits incorporated into the design. Should a burglar appear at the front door with a gun, the owner of the house was to warn the burglar that the alarm would sound unless disarmed. In fact, turning the system off sent a signal to the security firm, who in turn notified the police that a robbery with violence was occurring. Only a special code number would deactivate the system. It was usually a waste. Most experienced burglars knew security systems forward and backward. And the druggies didn't care. As soon as police arrived, the druggies usually started shooting at anything and everything. The system was most effective in an empty house.

"Did she disarm this system?" Karen asked.

"She had to. He was hip. He told her if she entered the warning code, he'd kill her."

As Karen continued her examination, Charlie asked, "What exactly are you looking for?"

"I just left Palmer," she said. "Unlike you, I found him pretty convincing."

"You kiddin' me? I thought you were slicker than that."

She knew he wasn't being disparaging. Like most cops, once someone was arrested, that was that. Case closed. Cops didn't like to think of themselves as capable of making mistakes. Mistakes could get you killed. Confidence was a prime requisite if one was to be a successful cop. Confidence, sometimes mistaken as cockiness, spilled over into everything. While Karen had her doubts about Palmer, those doubts would not be shared with Charlie. That would be unethical.

"Charlie," she said, "you know as well as I do that most of the people I defend are guilty as charged. But there's something about this guy that's different. Just between us, I really do believe the guy, and that's not just lawyer talk."

He looked hurt. "You can't be serious."

"I'm very serious," she said. "Caroline DeFauldo is an actress. Did you know that?"

He was wary now that Karen had declared herself so definitively. There was a big difference between a lawyer's simply defending a client, working to get the shortest possible sentence, and a lawyer who sincerely thought the client was being railroaded. For the latter, the best defense was offense, and that involved making the police look bad, a bunch of incompetents jumping to false conclusions. It was one reason Crime Scene Units had been established all over the country.

"Yeah," he said. "I've seen her on TV selling Fords. Almost makes me want to go out and buy one. I gotta tell ya, she looks even better in person."

Karen cocked her head. "Maybe she just played her greatest role."

"You're dreaming," he said.

They were back in the living room. "Was the fire-place going when you got here?"

"Uh-huh."

"What about candles? Any candles burning?"

"I don't think so. I wasn't first on the scene. Deputy named Cox got here first. Waited for backup, then came inside with a couple other uniforms."

She looked more carefully at the carpet. "The victim was lying on his back?"

"Uh-huh. You'll get the pictures along with the rest of the stuff."

"Was there a blanket around?"

"Yeah. Cox had pulled it off him by the time I got here."

"Did Cox mention anything about candles?"

"Can't say he did."

Karen made another note. "She claimed rape, right?"

"Right."

Karen sensed the change in Charlie's attitude. But he was still answering questions, still being cooperative, still being the pro. "Did she change her clothes before they took her to the hospital?"

"You know better," he said. "Rape cases, we want them just as we found them."

"You talked to her first?"

"I did. I got her story, then sent her down to the hospital. Then I talked to your client."

"And you were sure he was lying."

Charlie smiled. "Karen, I've been at this awhile. When I told him what she said, he went nuts. He was ready to kill me."

Jack had said as much. But she didn't want Charlie to know that. "How so?"

"He went wild. He started throwing punches at me."

Karen thought about that for a moment. Jack's actions could be interpreted two ways: he could be perceived as a violent man unable to control his emotions or as a man so shocked at hearing Caroline's story that he simply lost it. Obviously, the police interpretation was the former.

"Does that seem rational to you?" she asked. "He's in a room with three or four cops and he wants to fight?"

Charlie grinned. "I never said he was rational. It happens all the time. You know how that goes. Violent people react violently to every damn thing. It's all they know."

Karen nodded. "Are you aware this guy has never been arrested for anything?"

"I'm aware of that. There's always a first time. Besides, Mrs. DeFauldo is also as clean as a whistle." The grin disappeared. "Tell me something, Karen. You got two people telling two different stories. Hers checks out. His doesn't. What the hell am I supposed to do?"

She took a moment to answer. "In the case of felony murder, I'd give the investigation a tad more time."

"That's not my decision."

"It is if you're not satisfied."

"But I am satisfied."

"Then I'd say you're too easily satisfied, Charlie."

Charlie made a face. The tired cop decided to put a stop to this. There was a limit to his patience. "Karen, I'm bushed. I'm not the guy you gotta convince. You want to argue this, talk to the ASA. I just do my thing and make a report. The ASA makes the decisions."

"Okay," she said, "I'm through here. I'm just going to look outside for a bit. Thanks for letting me take a look, Charlie. I really appreciate it."

"No big deal," he said. "I'm outta here."

"Where is Caroline now?" Karen asked, as they reached the front door.

"I understand she's staying with a friend for a few days, least until they put new carpet in this place and fix up the wall."

They stepped outside. Charlie closed the door behind him, spoke to the uniformed officer, then waved good-bye to Karen. Karen slowly walked the perimeter of the house. In the gathering darkness, it was getting hard to see, but there was enough light for her purposes. She noted a large, screened-in swimming pool, which dominated the back of the house. Like most of the pool screens in the area, it was partially covered with brown pine needles. While the tall pines added a certain majesty to the development, they were dirty trees, always shedding needles in a rain or wind. Pool enclosures had to be cleaned weekly, no easy task. And when the squirrels took to the trees to feast noisily on tasty pine nuts, the unwanted part of the cones, the scales and cores, rained down like so much confetti.

Beyond the pool was a retention pond for water runoff. Farther away, the backs of houses on the street running parallel to this one.

These were big lots, and the houses on either side of the DeFauldo house were at least forty feet away. Karen made a note, then walked toward the street. Susan was waiting. There was no escape. The questions would have to be answered.

She steeled herself.

Seven

Brander Hewitt, his thinning white hair carefully coiffed, his soft face set in an expression of majestic solemnity, his gold cuff links gleaming in the harsh light of the late-afternoon sunlight streaming in the window, leaned back in his high-backed brown leather chair and shook his head.

As senior partner and cofounder of the firm, he occupied one of the four corner offices on the top floor of a five-story stainless steel and glass building on Highway Nineteen, just north of trendy Countryside Mall. His was, by far, the most sumptuous of the four corner offices, facing west and north, with over six hundred square feet of space. Two walls were plate glass. Another boasted original art by a now-dead New York artist, a series of vividly colored scribbles and blotches that, for reasons not understood by Karen, commanded high prices. The fourth wall was decorated with three dozen certificates, sheepskins, and awards given the firm for its philanthropic efforts. The venerable head of Hewitt, Sinclair believed that law firms should be part of the community, and he often put his money where his mouth was. At this moment, however, he wasn't thinking of philanthropy. Just the opposite.

"I'm disappointed," he said. "The news of your stunning victory of yesterday has barely had a chance to make the rounds. I expect the phone will be ringing off the hook today, that in the coming weeks, this office will be overflowing with excellent opportunities to represent clients willing to pay staggering amounts of money to have you represent their interests."

He slapped his hand on the desk. "But instead, you've committed to represent a man without assets in a case that reeks of negative images, one sure to draw the attention of the tabloids like vultures to fresh roadkill. I just don't understand it, Karen. Aside from the revenue you're throwing away, such a decision sullies your image. I wish you'd talked it over with me before making such a commitment."

It wasn't often that Brander took her to task. For one thing, it was rare for her to do something that would raise his dander. For another, it was left to Walter to ream out the attorneys when a situation called for it, even the partners. But when it came to Karen, Walter usually steered clear of her, for she frankly baffled him. Every time he'd start to talk to her, she'd level a gaze that seemed to go right through him. It was as if she knew his innermost secrets. Secrets that elicited nothing but scorn.

Karen would take it from Brander. Such was her respect for the man, an icon of sorts, the kind of man who'd drawn her to the profession in the first place.

Brander waved a well-manicured hand in the air. "There are also any number of lawyers willing and able to represent the man for the sixty dollars an hour the state allows. Let *them* be the missionaries, not you. You bill out at a hundred and eighty dollars. Your client can't afford you. Neither can this firm afford you to indulge yourself."

Karen's eyes narrowed. "As a partner in this firm, I'm entitled to choose my clients. My contributions to this firm's financial well-being are second to none. If you want to criticize, now is not the time. It's uncalled for, and I won't accept it."

She stood up and placed her hands on his desk as she leaned forward, glaring at him. "I never thought of you as a man to whom money was everything. What's changed?"

He lowered his head and peered at her over his glasses. "Nothing," he said. "It's just . . ."

"Just what?"

"Have you read this morning's *Times*?"

"Yes. It doesn't make any difference. I've already made the decision to represent Jack Palmer. I expect the full support of this firm. I've earned it, dammit. You've never acted like this before. What's really eating you, Brander?"

He took a deep breath, then said, "I would have thought that you, being a woman, would understand."

"Understand what?"

He exploded in anger. "Jack Palmer entered that poor woman's house, held her at gunpoint while he raped her, then murdered her husband. Such violence! Why would you defend such a man?"

Karen sat back down, awestruck. "That isn't like you, either," she said softly.

"Why not? The facts support *her* story, not his."

Karen shook her head. "I can't believe you're saying this. The man was arrested less than forty-eight hours ago. You don't have all the facts. Neither do I."

"You don't see it, do you?"

"See what?"

"By defending Jack Palmer, you're saying Caroline has to be lying."

Karen's eyebrows arched. "Caroline? You know her?"

He blushed. "I've met her. Some charity function a few years ago. I found her to be quite engaging."

"Engaging? Really! So that's why you're so upset!"

"Nonsense. I'm upset because you failed to consult with the partners before accepting this man as a client. This is a business. I don't have to tell you the staggering costs involved in defending someone charged with murder. You've been involved in enough capital cases to know. All I'm saying is that you should have discussed this matter with the partners before agreeing to take this on. There's nothing personal here. Besides, it's quite clear the man is guilty."

That was an unusual declaration from a man like Brander. "Ninety-eight percent of the criminals I defend are as guilty as hell. What's the difference here?"

"They pay," Brander said bluntly.

"So it *is* the money."

He slammed a hand on the desk. "Stop saying that."

"Why? It's the truth. You just said so."

His smooth cheeks flushed with exasperation, he looked away, playing with his watch fob for a moment. "Yes, you have the right to pick your own clients, but when the case impacts the profits of this firm, you have a moral obligation to allow us some input before you make your decision. And I have every right in the world to be critical of your decision to bypass us."

He was talking in circles. It was the money. It *wasn't* the money. She'd failed to consult. But he knew she had the right to choose her clients. It was personal. It *wasn't* personal. Whatever the real reason, he was upset. It was prudent to give it time.

"Perhaps you're right," Karen said softly. "I should have discussed it with you."

"Then why didn't you?"

She said nothing.

He was still angry. "I would submit," he said, "that you, flushed with your recent dramatic success, developed a swelled head in record time, and decided you needn't be a team player any longer. To hell with the firm, to hell with your existing clients, to hell with any considerations other than the stroking of your own ego. I find that distressing."

She was deeply hurt, and it showed. "Is that how you perceive me? I'm an egotist?"

His cheeks flamed. He'd gone too far, and he knew it. "Perhaps I have overreacted."

"God, I hope so."

For a moment, neither said anything. Finally, Karen, in her softest voice, said, "I'm committed, Brander. Do I have your support or not?"

Their eyes met with powerful intensity, Karen standing, her body rigid, her hands balled into fists, her lips nearly bloodless. Brander was still in his chair, now drawn close to the desk, his hands clasped one on top of the other to keep them from flying in the air. He, too, was hurt. She could see it in his eyes.

"It's your decision," he said finally.

"Thanks," she said. She strode quickly out of the office.

Lawyer Jonathan Walsingham looked up from the brief he was reading and smiled at his secretary, standing in the doorway of his office. "What's up?"

"I have Caroline DeFauldo on the telephone. She's very upset. She's asking for an immediate appointment."

"With me?"

"She asked for you personally."

"DeFauldo? The wife of the man who was murdered?"

"The same."

"Did she say what she wanted?"

"Only that she wants to see you as soon as possible."

"How's my calendar today?"

"You're booked solid."

"Who can we shift?"

"Perhaps Mr. Calder? He's in no rush."

"Do it. Slot Mrs. DeFauldo."

The secretary smiled knowingly. "I'll take care of it."

Two hours later, Caroline DeFauldo, dressed in a simple black dress, was ushered into Jonathan's office. Jonathan came out from behind his desk, showed Caroline to a chair, then asked if she'd like some coffee or tea.

"No, thank you."

Jonathan took a seat across from this stunning woman, marveling at her composure. He'd seen her many times on television, doing commercials for various local concerns. She was much more attractive in person, even in these trying circumstances.

"I appreciate very much your seeing me on such short notice."

"No problem. I offer my deepest sympathies on your tragic loss. How can I help you, Mrs. DeFauldo?"

"Please call me Caroline."

"As you wish."

She took a deep breath. "You obviously know who I am. How much do you know of the circumstances surrounding the death of my husband?"

"Just what I've read in the newspapers and seen on television. From what I understand, your ordeal was absolutely terrifying. I'm amazed that you can even function."

She gave him a bitter smile. "I'm not sure I am functioning. My doctor has me on so many pills I can hardly stand up. It doesn't seem to help the pain much. I just can't . . ." She removed a white handkerchief from her handbag and dabbed at her eyes.

"Can I get you some water?"

She shook her head. "Give me a moment. I can't seem to stop crying. I'm all right for a while, and then I start to see it happening all over again. It's like I'm watching a movie scene, over and over and over . . ."

Jonathan shifted uncomfortably in his chair. "What caused you to call this office?"

"I talked to some friends. They said you were the best. And I want the best. No. I *need* the best."

Jonathan looked surprised. "You are in need of legal representation?"

"Oh, yes. Very much. I'm a victim twice over, Mr. Walsingham. I don't much like being a victim. And I'm not about to stand aside and be made a victim all over again."

"I don't understand," Jonathan said.

Caroline took a deep breath. "I'm sorry. I told you I'm having trouble functioning. It's just . . ." She started to weep.

Jonathan stood up and placed an arm around her shoulder, trying to comfort her. When she finally regained control of her emotions, he returned to his chair and looked into her eyes. Marvelous eyes. Her makeup was streaked from the crying, but the eyes were still magnetic.

"This is very difficult," she said.

"Of course. Take your time. There's no rush."

"It's also very, very embarrassing. It would be embarrassing at any time, but coming so close after the death of my husband, it seems much worse. But I have no choice."

He had no idea what the hell she was talking about. Whatever medication her doctor had prescribed, that and the horrific shock, caused her to ramble. But Jonathan was in no hurry. He enjoyed being in the company of beautiful women, no matter the circumstances. He was sure she was coherent enough to eventually get to the point.

"You see," she said finally, "it has to do with the man who raped me and killed my husband.

Jonathan leaned forward. "What about him?"

"Do you know a lawyer named Karen Perry-Mondori?"

"Of course. I know Karen quite well."

"Are you aware she's representing the bastard who killed Dan?"

"I read that, yes."

"Well, that's why I'm here. Karen hates me. She's trying to get me. That's why she's defending Jack Palmer. To get at me."

Jonathan's jaw dropped. "But why? What reason would Karen Perry-Mondori have to hate you?"

She started to week again. "That's . . . that's what's so embarrassing."

Karen was still puzzling over the scale of Brander's reaction when she arrived home, exhausted, feet throbbing, head aching, her neck muscles protesting from the tension of the day. She's had to shuffle some clients, prioritize her "must-do" list, and spend much of the day on the phone, placating those who were being shunted aside in favor of a dead-bang loser with no money. Several clients were unhappy. Karen had to be her diplomatic and persuasive best the entire day, and she was worn out. All she wanted was to sink into a soft chair, put her feet up, and sip a rare, very dry martini.

She parked her silver Beemer beside Carl's black Infiniti in the three-car garage, went through the door leading to the kitchen, kissed her daughter, Andrea, on the cheek, and sniffed the food being prepared by Michelle.

Michelle was good at most things, but her culinary skills were abysmal. For the first month the family had dined on pedestrian, starchy fare with little imagination. Mere fuel. Karen had given Michelle several cookbooks and encouraged her to pay heed. The woman had promised to do so. The food had gradually improved, but Michelle still had trouble understanding a calorie chart.

"What is this?" Karen asked, hovering over the stove.

"Boeuf et poivron chez nous," Michelle said proudly. "Beef and peppers, a specialty of the house. Low in calories, like you asked for."

"A specialty of whose house?"

"This house," Michelle said. "From now on."

It smelled delicious.

Michelle was a treasure, always cheerful, great with Andrea, who, at the age of six, was a handful. Michelle took Andrea to school every day, picked her up, and, when at home, kept her busy with crayons and paper, and especially books. Thanks to Michelle's readings, Andrea had developed a wonderful interest in reading. Michelle was a whirling dervish with vacuum and duster. She even did windows.

"Look, Mommy," Andrea cried, holding up a drawing for approval. "It's a picture of Daddy."

It was indeed.

"That's very good," Karen said, giving her daughter a big hug. "How was school today?"

"All right, I guess."

"You guess?"

"Well . . . I still don't like Mrs. Collier. She's real mean."

"How so?"

"She took Missy to the principal's office just for talking during class."

"Well, maybe Mrs. Collier is trying to show all of you that when she says there's to be no talking in class, she means it. School is not just for play, my love; it's for learning. And learning is serious business. Though you might not realize it today, Mrs. Collier has your best interests at heart. You should try to see things from her side."

Andrea made a face. "Oh, Mommy. You always say that."

"That's because she's usually right," Karen said. She looked in the living room. Carl was standing, waiting for Karen, the expression on his face even more wrathful than Brander's. His hands were in his pockets, his chin stuck out the way it did whenever he was upset. Karen kissed Andrea on the forehead and entered the living room.

Carl was forty-five, still ruggedly handsome, his European looks a match for any of the models that graced the male perfume ads. He stood just under six feet, tall for an Italian, all muscles and tight skin, with smoldering dark eyes and slicked-back dark hair, thick eyebrows, and full lips. She'd been inordinately attracted to him the first time she saw him, at a fund-raising party for Helen Ellis Memorial Hospital in Tarpon. The party had been held at the Innisbrook Hilton Resort, and the memory of that night was still as vivid as the sun.

He'd come with two other doctors and their wives. He was unaccompanied by a woman because his date had taken ill earlier in the day. Karen had just broken up with Wayne, the football player, and had reluctantly attended the party with Brander and his wife. After dinner, the dancing started, and Carl appeared magically at her side, asking for a dance. She'd looked up into his eyes and felt her heart stop.

Never before had she felt such a strong and instant attraction to a man. In the past, her love affairs had evolved slowly, for Karen was supercautious in these days of short attention spans and sexually transmitted death. There'd been just two men in her life, and it had been months before either of the relationships had been allowed to progress beyond what used to be a finite barrier breached only by marriage.

Her rather old-fashioned attitude had driven away those interested only in sex. And that was fine. Both lovers had become friends first, someone she could trust while she explored the possibilities. But there was a limit to trust. She had yet to have sex with a man not wearing a condom.

"So, what do you do?" Carl asked as he held her in his arms, gliding her across the floor with an experienced dancer's expertise.

"I'm an attorney."

She could tell he was immediately disappointed.

"You don't like lawyers?" she asked.

"I'm being sued."

"Why?"

"Malpractice."

"You're a doctor?"

"Yes."

"And lawyers are the enemy?"

"Some are. They encourage frivolous actions."

"I'm glad you said some."

"It's true, is it not?"

"With some, yes."

"How refreshing. But not with you."

"I try to be ethical."

"As do I."

"That's nice. There are some doctors I'd place in the same dungeon with the bad lawyers."

"I'm glad you said some."

She smiled. "It's true, is it not?"

"You're teasing me," he said.

"Would you like to talk about something else?"

"Yes. You're an incredibly lovely woman. Your left hand is at the back of my neck. I can't see if you're wearing a ring. Are you?"

"What would you say if I told you I was married?"

"I'd say it's been lovely dancing with you."

"That's it?"

His face darkened. "Yes."

"Why so serious?"

"I was married once. My wife betrayed me. I take adultery very seriously."

"Oh. Well, I'm not married."

"I'm very happy to hear it. I would like to take you to dinner Saturday night. Are you free?"

A bolt of electricity zapped through her body. "I'm free."

"I'll pick you up at seven if that's okay."

"Seven would be fine."

"I'll need your address."

He took her to a small Italian restaurant on Nineteen—a delightful place called Mulberry Street, where the food was terrific, the atmosphere convivial, and the waiters as efficient as fighter pilots. They sang along with the strolling guitarist, drank Ruffino, ate veal, and talked about everything. And when they made love later that night, it was Carl who suggested the condom.

He was patient and giving, his surgeon's hands soft and knowing, his technique utterly astonishing. He took her over the edge, made her lose control, summoned the most powerful string of orgasms she'd ever experienced. She was left drenched in perspiration and slightly woozy. And he held her close and stroked her hair while he nuzzled her cheek and her ear.

They said nothing for fifteen minutes.

And she knew.

Their courtship lasted over a year. It was spectacularly romantic. Both were extremely busy people, but with unwavering precision, each carved precious time from their schedules to be together, to blend the intellect with the interest, to explore, compare, question, and make love.

In some ways, Carl was predictable. In others, he was a free spirit. Once, he invited her to his modest apartment for a Chinese dinner. She thought he meant takeout. She was wrong. He answered the door wearing nothing but a clear plastic raincoat and a spatula in his hand.

"I'm using the wok," he explained mischievously. "I don't want to get grease on my clothes."

"Or your skin."

"That would really be bad," he said.

They ate the Chinese food in the nude. He was a hell of a cook.

Crazy stuff. But wonderful. Fabulous. Memorable. She'd managed to repress her initial fears and accept his candor about his former promiscuity as simply refreshing honesty. Even now, after ten years of marriage—mostly smooth flying with occasional heavy storms—he still had that effect on her. But not at the moment. At the moment, a tempest lay straight ahead.

"Something wrong?" Karen asked tentatively, starting to fix the martini.

"I had to hear about it from the nurses," he said.

"Hear about what?"

"You know what! The DeFauldo killing . . . and your involvement."

Karen dropped an olive into her glass, stirred the drink with her finger, then stuck her finger in her mouth. "Did they mention the Cole case, by any chance?"

"That's yesterday's news. Today, the talk is about you defending some creep instead of letting the public defender's office handle it. On the way home, I had to listen to the talk show guys wondering why. What *I'm* wondering is why you never even mentioned this to me last night. Not a goddam word!"

She sighed. "I didn't mention it because we were celebrating, if you remember. I meant to tell you, but by the time we finished celebrating, you were asleep. Besides, I didn't really want to put a damper on yesterday. Days like yesterday are all too infrequent. It's nice to bask in the glow of having done something you perceive as worthwhile. Defending criminals isn't very rewarding in the soul department. Is that so hard to understand?"

"You still should have told me. I have to find out from my nurses? That stinks. It makes me look like an idiot."

"I'm sorry. You're right. I should have told you."

He wasn't ready to let it go. "I can't believe you'd represent that Palmer asshole. The DeFauldos are friends and neighbors. How could you?"

She stared at him, astounded. "Friends? Good grief,

Carl, I'd hardly call them friends. We went to dinner with them a couple of times, and neither of us could stand them."

"That's not the point. People *think* we're friends. It makes us look bad."

"I can't help that," Karen said. "I took the case for several reasons. Though I don't know him well, I don't think Jack Palmer is capable of cold-blooded murder. In the second place, the preliminary evidence is too pat."

She stood in front of him and smiled. "Are you going to kiss me hello, or is this going to be a big issue?"

He stared at her, his eyes filled with incredulity. "You're saying Caroline made it all up?"

Unkissed, Karen kicked off her shoes and sat in one of the heavily upholstered chairs fronting a long glass coffee table. "I'm not saying Caroline made it all up. My *client* claims she's making it up."

"And you believe your client? Is that what you're saying?"

It wasn't the whole truth, for there were serious doubts in Karen's mind about Jack Palmer's guilt or innocence. But she resented being questioned like some student nurse. "It may be a fine distinction, but yes, I think he's telling the truth."

Carl threw his hands in the air in utter exasperation. "That's crazy!"

"Crazy? Just because we've know the DeFauldos doesn't mean we owe them unquestioning fealty for the rest of our lives. Daniel DeFauldo was shot to death. Jack Palmer shot the man all right, but the circumstances as to *why* he shot him are at issue. If my client is telling the truth, Caroline had to have arranged this whole thing for reasons not yet determined. I'm sorry, but these things do happen, even in the best of families."

Carl's right hand cut through the air, slamming into the palm of his left. "They live three blocks away. We've dined with them several times. Maybe they aren't close friends, but Dan DeFauldo was my patient just two years ago. By taking this Palmer guy as a client, you make it appear you're going against Caroline. That makes us look very bad."

"I'm not against Caroline," she said. "I'm defending a man who is charged with murder, a man who says he was set up. Until I've had the chance to thoroughly investigate, I have to assume he's telling me the truth. If it turns out he lied to me, I'll deal with it. I don't like being lied to. You know that."

Carl threw his head back in frustration. "Palmer's a nothing. You defend him, and everyone in the neighborhood will drop us like a hot rock. Don't you understand?"

Karen took a sip of her drink, then put it back on the coffee table. "Carl," she said, "I'm truly sorry if this embarrasses you. I can't help it. I'm a lawyer. It's what I do. If our *real* friends drop us because of this, I'll be very surprised, but I'm not going to let others dictate what I do with my life—not even you. I don't interfere with your medical practice, and you've never before interfered with my legal practice."

She took another sip of the drink, swallowed, then sighed. "It's been a very long day. Can we just relax, have dinner, maybe watch some TV? I'm completely shot. I really don't want to argue with you."

He sighed, shook his head, then sat down. "Your decision is final?"

"It was made yesterday."

"It's a big mistake, Karen." His voice sounded ominous. "Perhaps the biggest in your life."

Michelle announced that dinner was ready. Not a moment too soon.

The *boeuf et poivron chez nous* was delicious, even given the tension that cloaked the room. Karen made a mental note to check the calorie count in the cookbook. It tasted too good to be low-cal. With Carl in a funk, Karen conversed with Andrea. A perceptive child, she sensed the strain, but displaying a sophistication that often amazed her mother, Andrea acted as if nothing was amiss.

There was a knock at the door. "I'll get it," Karen said, getting up from the table, eager to break the mood. She saw next-door neighbor Rosemary Perkins through the narrow window adjacent to the door, then pulled the door open.

"Come on in, Rosemary. Have some coffee."

"I can't," Rosemary said. "The plane leaves at six in the morning, and I'm not even close to being packed."

Karen had forgotten completely. "Oh, right," she exclaimed, "you're off to Hawaii, you lucky dogs."

Rosemary grinned, then did her version of the hula. "Ten glorious days. I just wanted to make sure you still had the keys to the house and cars. You know, just in case."

"Oh, sure. I'll check."

Karen went to the kitchen and looked in the key organizer by the pantry. When she returned to the front door, she said, "Everything's there. House key, car keys. Do you want me to water plants or anything?"

"No. I didn't want to trouble you. Marty said she'd come by and do it."

"Marty?"

"You know. Our twice-a-week soap-opera-addicted

housekeeper. I think the only reason she works so cheaply is because we have a wide-screen TV."

Karen smiled. "You're sure you won't come in for a moment and have some coffee?"

"I'm sure. Gotta run. I'll be up all night packing."

"Well, have a ball."

Rosemary grinned, "I intend to."

When Karen returned to the dinner table, she sat there dreamy-eyed for a moment.

"Who was that?" Carl asked.

"Rosemary. They're off to Hawaii in the morning. That's something I'd like us to do one of these days."

"It's too commercial," Carl said.

"I'm sure Waikiki is, but there must be some spots that are still unspoiled."

His dark eyes grew cold. "Hawaii holds unpleasant memories for me, Karen."

"Why?" she asked without thinking. And then, from the look on his face, she realized she'd struck a nerve. He'd told her about it once, how his first wife had cheated on him while they were vacationing in Hawaii.

"Hawaii," he said bitterly. "That was the first time. I wasted another six years thinking it was the only time."

"What are you talking about?" Andrea asked.

"We're talking about Hawaii," Karen said. "Your father doesn't care for Hawaii."

Andrea looked at her father. "You lived there for six years?"

"Not exactly," he said. "I was saying I had a bad experience there. It took me six years to get over it."

"What bad experience?"

"Nothing we can talk about at the dinner table."

"Why not?"

"Because there are some things that shouldn't be discussed during dinner."

"Is that why you haven't said anything?"

Carl took a sip of his wine, put the glass down, and said, "Tell me about Mrs. Collier. Is she really as bad as you say?"

After dinner, Karen walked aimlessly through the house while Carl retreated to his home office. She tried to calm the fires that burned within her. It wasn't the first time Karen and Carl had argued. Carl was, after all, a surgeon, a member of that elite group of doctors who, with their skill and experience, saved human lives on a regular basis. That kind of power fueled an already prodigious ego, for surgeons without egos were as rare as snowstorms in Tampa.

Carl, the hot blood of his Roman ancestors coursing through his veins, was not one to back away from an argument, nor was he prone to sudden fits of contrition. It was always left to Karen, not without ego herself, to cool the fires, to make the move toward reconciliation. It was a role she accepted with grace, for she felt the rewards far outweighed the penalties—there were two sides to Carl's passion.

Andrea was reading. "How'd you like to go for a bike ride?" Karen suggested.

"Super!"

The sun had almost set, but there was enough light for a short ride. They were a block away from the house when Andrea asked, "Why is Daddy angry with you?"

Why indeed? Karen brought her bike to a halt and stood beside it. "What makes you say that?"

"I heard you fighting. Daddy was yelling at you and you were yelling back."

"We weren't fighting. People disagree sometimes. It doesn't mean they don't love each other."

"I know that."

"Good."

"But what were you fighting about?"

Karen tried to explain. "A man has been charged with a very bad crime. I'm his lawyer. We've talked about this before, Andrea."

"I know. Even a bad man has a right to a lawyer."

"Exactly. But in this case, there's someone else involved. Someone your father and I both know. By defending this man, it makes it look like I'm turning against this person your father and I know. Your father thinks that's wrong."

"What do you think?"

Karen took a moment to answer. "I'm not really sure. Can you give me some time to think about it?"

Andrea shrugged. "Sure. But I hope you don't stay mad at each other very long. I really hate it when you're made at each other."

"We're not mad at each other. We're just not in agreement. There's a difference."

Well," she said, with a child's lack of pretense, "it sure looks like you're mad at each other."

Karen was in bed reading when Carl finally finished his work, entered the bedroom, undressed, then showered. He said nothing to her as he slipped into the king-size bed without so much as a glance. Karen reached out and touched the silky coolness of his skin.

"How long is this going to last?" she said softly.

Nothing.

"Carl, I don't like to end the day like this. Let's talk it out."

He rolled over on his back and stared at the ceiling.

"I won't ask you to understand why I've taken this

case. All I ask is that you show me the same respect I show you. Is that too much to ask?"

Finally, he looked at her. "Of course not," he said. "That isn't the issue. It's just . . . well, it would be nice if you consulted with me when a case comes along that involves people we both know. You're so wrapped up in the mechanics of your profession, you can't see the forest for the trees."

"I don't know what you mean," she said.

"Sure you do. There are a hundred scruffy lawyers who would take this case for the publicity alone. Your client would be well served by any of them. By defending this man, you force our friends to take sides, and they will. I don't mind fighting battles of principle when I believe in the principle, but I resent being forced to defend a position taken by you with which I disagree. When people say to me, 'Oh, I see your wife is defending the creep who raped Caroline and murdered her husband,' what the hell am I supposed to say? Had you chosen to include me in your thinking, you might not have taken the case."

Karen pulled her hand away. "You expect me to consult with you before taking on a client?"

"When it involves people we know? Yes. When it affects our social life? Yes. Only then, and only because it affects *both* of us. I'm not just being selfish here."

She sat up. Softly, she said, "Carl, if you'll remember, we agreed I would never take a medical malpractice case because of the problems it could create for you."

"I do remember, and I appreciate your consideration."

"Thank you," she said. "I can't run to you every time I have to make a decision."

"I'm not asking you to. This isn't about *me*. This is

about *us*. Most of our friends know the DeFauldos. Did you know Caroline has moved in with the Clarks?"

"No, I didn't."

"Well, she has. I stopped off at the club on the way home. Harold Clark was there, alone, looking like shit. He said he had to get out of the house. He says it's a zoo at his place. He and Lila had to make the identification of Dan's body today. It shook Harold up pretty good. He says Caroline's devastated, not even functioning. Harold came right out and asked me what the hell you were trying to prove. He was pissed, Karen. They're all pissed.

"I walked by Ben Gould's table, and he barely spoke to me. And it's just begun. I fail to see why someone else can't defend this guy."

She put her face inches from his. "Do you really think our friends will shun us because I'm doing my damn job?"

"Yes," he said. "They don't really give a shit about right and wrong. Their concern is that you, by representing this man, are attacking one of our own. That makes you a traitor to your class. If that sounds elitist, too bad. The class system is alive and well in this country.

"There are those who feed the system, and there are those who feed *on* the system. You align yourself with one side or the other. In this case, you've chosen the wrong side. Now, we'll both have to pay for it."

He rolled over and placed a pillow on top of his head. The discussion was over.

Karen switched on the bedside TV. It was almost eleven. Susan Brooks had the lead story. She was standing in the halogen-lit darkness, in front of an office building in downtown St. Petersburg, looking quite pretty in her power-red dress, her eyes gleaming with excitement.

"The death of Dan DeFauldo has shocked the quiet community of Autumn Woods," she began, "a community known more for its lovely, well-landscaped homes than for violence. But I have an exclusive story that adds an entirely new dimension to this case."

Karen sat bolt-upright in bed. She felt Carl moving beside her.

Susan turned to her right. "I'm joined here in Saint Petersburg by attorney Jonathan Walsingham, who now represents Caroline DeFauldo, the widow of Dan DeFauldo and a victim in her own right. Mrs. De-Fauldo claims she was raped by the man accused of killing her husband. And that's not all she claims."

As the camera slowly zoomed back, Susan looked up at the lawyer. "Mr. Walsingham, why have you entered this case?"

Karen could feel the adrenaline coursing through her veins. Something was very wrong. Jonathan Walsingham, forty-eight, was a senior partner with one of St. Petersburg's largest law firms, a handsome man of quiet dignity, a towering reputation, and a penchant for beautiful women. Karen had first met him during a deposition taken four years ago, a grueling exercise involving a charming con man who was also a pathological liar. At the conclusion of the depo, Jonathan had smoothly sidled up to Karen and asked her to dinner, ostensibly to discuss the case. She'd refused. Jonathan had followed that with phone calls and letters requesting a case conference. When he finally got the message that his efforts would be in vain, he sent her a dozen roses with an unsigned card that read, "At least I tried."

Now he was standing in the street at eleven o'clock at night, looking professional, the words coming out of his mouth having the effect of nuclear bombs.

"I've just returned to my office after a long talk with Mrs. DeFauldo," he said. "I was retained by Mrs. De-Fauldo after she learned that Ms. Karen Perry-Mondori is representing the man accused of killing Dan De-Fauldo. Ms. Perry-Mondori is one of our most respected criminal attorneys, but Mrs. DeFauldo, quite rightly, I fear, is concerned that the motives here are other than to make sure that the accused receives a fair trial."

"I don't understand," Susan said innocently.

Walsingham looked grim. "I'll be filing a motion on behalf of Mrs. DeFauldo in court tomorrow morning, requesting that Ms. Perry-Mondori be removed from this case. It embarrasses me almost as much as it does Mrs. DeFauldo to have to say this, but the truth of the matter is . . . Mrs. DeFauldo had a short-lived affair with Ms. Perry-Mondori's husband some two years ago."

Karen's heart stopped beating.

"I'm afraid," Walsingham continued, "that Ms. Perry-Mondori's motive for taking this case is more a matter of vengeance. Clearly, Ms. Perry-Mondori is more interested in destroying Mrs. DeFauldo than defending her client."

He shook his head sadly. "We just can't have that in the legal profession."

Eight

She was curled up at one end of the large sofa in the den, alone in the semidarkness, her legs brought up beneath her, a drink in her hand, the tears on her cheeks gleaming in the reflected light of the bright streetlight that stood about thirty yards from the window. She saw him pad softly into the room and take a seat in a chair facing the sofa. For a moment, he simply stared at her, his face expressing more anger than remorse.

"Don't look at me like that," she said. "I'd appreciate it if you'd just leave me alone."

He didn't move. Nor did he speak. He just stared his angry stare. She couldn't bear to look at him, so she moved to the far wall where the bar was and sat on a stool, the drink in her hand, her back to him. He followed her, taking the stool next to her, his silk pajamas seeming to glow in the gloom. Her body felt like a coiled spring.

"Look at me," he commanded.

She couldn't do it. She could smell his smell, hear his breathing, and that was more than she could bear. She was afraid to look at him. It would rip out her heart.

She heard him sigh, then say, "You think you're hurt?"

She didn't answer.

"How interesting," he said. "Weren't we just talking about selfishness, about how you often have this way of considering your own needs before those of others? This is a perfect example of what I was talking about."

Almost involuntarily, her hand lashed out, crashing across his face with such force that he jerked back. She wanted to scream, but a tenuous connection with reality warned her that Michelle, who slept in a downstairs bedroom, would hear. It was bad enough already.

Carl touched a hand to his nose, then reached for a box of tissues. He was bleeding. Karen couldn't not look at him now, her expression an impossible mixture of anger and compassion. "I'm sorry," she said. "I didn't mean to do that. Does it hurt?"

He stood there, dabbing at his nose, shaking his head. "Let me tell you about pain," he said softly. "Pain is not a bloody nose. Pain is not even assuming that your husband has had an affair. That's nothing. Pain, the real McCoy, is lying in bed watching television and listening to someone utter a complete lie, then have your wife *immediately* accept that lie as truth without so much as a question or even a glance. She simply leaves your bed, comes downstairs, fixes a drink, and sits in the darkness feeling sorry for herself."

He took a deep breath, then said, "Now, *that's* pain."

"Are you saying you never had an affair with Caroline?"

He sneered. "It's nice of you to ask. Finally. The answer is I never had an affair with Caroline. Ever."

"I don't believe you," she said.

"That's obvious."

She stared at the ceiling. "You were so upset when I

took this case. Is that what you were afraid of, that I'd find out about this?"

"No. I told you my concerns. They are legitimate, reasonable concerns. At least they were. I would imagine they mean little now. Since Caroline's lawyer is claiming you're out to get her, it must be true. A lawyer would never lie. Which means you'll be off the case. Our friends, our newly screwed-up marriage notwithstanding, will embrace us with new fervor, hoping that one of us will spill some of the juicy details so that they can all take sides and become involved spectators."

"I never knew about the affair," she said. "They can't remove me from the case for cause. It just isn't true."

Suddenly, he laughed. "How rational you are! You can glibly accept one proposition and ignore the other. You can accept the lie that you took the case to wreak vengeance on Caroline, but you ignore the lie that there was an affair in the first place. That is truly amazing!"

They stared at each other. She'd never seen him so angry, yet controlled. She could almost feel the fury within him, and for the first time since her life had suddenly turned to dreck, she doubted herself. "Why would Caroline say you'd had an affair if you hadn't? It makes her look like a slut."

He didn't answer right away. Instead, he poured himself some brandy. After sipping some of the amber liquid, he put the bulb-shaped glass on the bar and, in a voice thick with ridicule, said, "You have to ask? Karen Perry-Mondori, the celebrated attorney-slash-sleuth has to ask? When the answer was right there in front of you?"

"I'm not in the mood for any of your bullshit, Carl."

He drank some more of the brandy, then said, "Nor are you in the mood for intelligent conversation. You're always spouting off about the rights of those you defend, yet here you are accusing me of having an affair. Not for a second do you disbelieve what you heard that lawyer say. You've accepted it whole, without question. And that makes you a hypocrite, Karen. A fake. I deserve better."

His words stung her deeply. He was right, of course. Her own anger was now being assailed by the logic of his words, and that hurt her even more.

"So," she said, "explain it to me, since I'm so stupid."

"You're not stupid," he said, "but there are times when you act stupidly. Like now. If I remember correctly, you told me that you took this case because you believed your client was innocent. True?"

She didn't answer.

"Ergo," Carl said, "if your client *is* innocent, Caroline DeFauldo is guilty of something. Of what, we're not quite sure at this time. But if what I heard on the news is true, your Jack Palmer is unable to afford a lawyer of your caliber. True?"

Karen said nothing.

"You've been on your soapbox for some time now, proselytizing, trying to get your fellow lawyers to understand that public defenders don't get paid enough to do a proper job in complex criminal cases. Knowing you, it's probably one of the reasons you took this case. You think you can show the world that justice is available to those with means, while those without means receive short shrift. You're a crusader, Karen. Too bad you don't practice what you preach.

"But I digress. The reason Caroline has come up

with this destructive lie is to get you off the case. With you defending the guy, using all your intellect and financial resources, you might just find something that Caroline doesn't want you to find. Getting you off the case ensures that your client will be represented by someone you regard as not up to the job. Which means your client will be convicted and Caroline is off the hook. Not much mystery there.

"And she has succeeded. Whether or not her lawyer prevails in court, you're certainly off this case. You're filled with such self-pity, I doubt you can hold your head up high enough to even be seen in court. The seeds of doubt have already been cast. A jury will be judging *you,* not your client."

She could feel her heart banging against her rib cage. There was such logic to what he was saying! Could it be? Or was he being glib, using his considerable powers of persuasion to deflect reality?

"The mystery to me," he continued, "is why you would so readily accept that I would have an affair with Caroline. Which makes me wonder. Just how strong is this marriage?"

He drained the remains of his brandy, placed the glass on the bar, and headed back upstairs.

Later, Karen found him in the guest bedroom. She sat on the edge of the bed, trying to think of something to say. He rolled over and glared at her. "Would you like me to take a lie-detector test, Counselor?"

"Would you?"

Without hesitation, he said, "No. I've done nothing wrong. If you can't trust me, you can't trust me. I just wish I'd known your true feelings ten years ago. It would have saved both of us a lot of heartache."

He turned his back to her. "Think what you want,

Karen, but leave me alone. I have to operate in the morning. I need some sleep."

Karen stared at his back for a moment, then slowly walked back to the master bedroom, her mind a painful boiling cauldron of inner conflict.

Nine

The small lawyer-prisoner conference room was occupied by Ralph Vincenzo and Victor Ganza, a young firebrand attorney.

Victor was short and very muscular, with a cockiness about him that was off-putting to most people. His long black hair was tied back in a thick braid, and a long gold earring hung from his right earlobe. He wore a black silk shirt, a matching black silk suit, and a wildly colored silk tie. With his puffy cheekbones and mashed-in nose, he looked more like an ex-boxer than a lawyer. His badly scarred face was simply a legacy from an early life in one of the rougher areas of Queens, New York.

As a short kid, Victor had learned the hard way that there was no way to hide from bullies. His father taught him how to fight in the streets. By the time he was sixteen, Victor could beat the best of them. Orphaned at the same age, he was taken under the wing of a retired uncle, who persuaded him that life in the streets was a dead end. Being a professional, the uncle said, was like being a god.

Victor eventually decided being a lawyer would be cool. The uncle helped him learn how to study, and Victor, after struggling through the first two years of college, finally put his life in order. The rest was astonishingly easy.

Choosing Florida for its weather, he developed a thriving practice, mostly criminal cases, for he understood the criminal mind. But he did take on a few commercial accounts, just to keep his hand in, all of them companies run by people who appreciated a lawyer who thought taxes were a cancer.

As the attorney for Dan and Ralph's business for the past four years, he was privy to everything, had in fact helped set up the offshore banking deal that now hung like a dark cloud over Ralph's future. At the time, Victor had suggested that two Swiss accounts be kept—one in each name—both of them trust accounts payable to the surviving partner upon the death of the other. It was the most logical choice. But with the Swiss banking authorities becoming more and more cooperative with the American IRS than in previous years, there was always a risk that secrecy might not be maintained.

Neither partner was willing to accept such a deal. They would rather be forced, they said, to trust each other. Against Victor's advice, they opened an account that required just such a trust. Both had access to the account, much like a husband-wife joint checking account. Victor had always figured it was only a matter of time before one partner screwed the other into the ground. Now, with Dan dead, it looked, at first blush, as if the boys had done it right after all, but he was about to learn he'd been right all along.

Ralph, his head pounding, his eyes red, his stomach heaving, was finally realizing how incredibly stupid he'd been. As he related the story of his arrest to Victor, he kept hitting himself in the chest, literally beating himself up, until Victor grabbed his arms and made him stop. "You're acting crazy," he said.

Ralph took a deep breath, then said, "When can you get me out of here?"

"Not until morning," Victor said. "You have to make a first appearance. They'll set bail, and we'll pay it. You'll be on your way by nine o'clock. This is your second offense, my friend. You got trouble."

"Oh, I got trouble all right," Ralph said.

"What do you mean?"

Ralph leaned forward. In a raspy, low voice, he said, "You think I got drunk because of what happened to Dan?"

"I assumed that was the reason, yes."

"Not so," he said sadly. "I got loaded because that miserable cocksucker took all the money."

"Dan did what?"

Ralph threw his hands in the air. "He took it all! Everything. Not just the Ducerne money, but everything else as well."

Victor let out a low whistle. "When did this happen?"

"The day before he got himself killed. I got back from Paris and heard about Dan gettin' killed. I almost dropped. When I went to make the money transfer, the computer file was wiped clean. I called Zurich. They told me Dan had gutted the accounts. And that's all they'd tell me."

Victor blinked, fought to suppress an I-told-you-so smile on the missing money, then asked, "You still drunk?"

Ralph gave him a look, then said, "Listen to me, asshole. The money's gone. All of it. It was transferred to an account supposedly set up by Dan on Tuesday. Then, the whole thing was transferred to another bank altogether. The Zurich bank won't tell me who or where.

All they'll say is that it's gone. All of it. Every last fucking dime. Six million dollars, Victor. Gone."

He shook a fist at Victor. "Now, you tell me something. Dan takes all the money, right? Then he hangs around just long enough to get his brains blown out. Does that make any sense to you?"

Victor said nothing. He was still digesting the news of the theft of the money.

"Or," Ralph went on, "would it make more sense if Caroline found the codes and took the dough, then had Dan bumped off. How does that sound?"

Victor thought for a moment, then said, "It doesn't sound like something Dan would let happen. He ran that woman pretty good. And I don't think Caroline has the smarts to pull this off." He shook his head. "It's all gone—you're sure?"

Ralph rolled his eyes skyward. "What, you think I was so drunk I couldn't make a phone call? Yes, it's gone."

Victor had been right after all. There was some satisfaction in knowing that he hadn't lost his touch when it came to assessing human character. In this case, it wouldn't have happened had they listened to him. He felt little sympathy for the suffering client before him.

"The timing *is* a tad weird," he said, getting back to the question. "I'll give you that much."

Ralph was still thinking out loud. "Hell, maybe Dan gave Caroline the codes. Maybe he wanted her to have the money if something happened to him. Who knows? But she can't wait. She wants the money now. So she takes it, then arranges for Dan to take a hit. She hires this dumb jerk to do it, says she'll back up his stupid story, then hangs him out to dry. Doesn't that make more sense to you?"

Victor was still a page behind. "Are you telling me you're tapped out?"

Ralph frowned. "You worried about getting paid?"

"No. I'm worried about you surviving. What the hell are you going to live on?"

Ralph waved a hand. "I've still got a few bucks in my personal account, but the company accounts are wiped out. Forget about that. Think about what I said about Caroline."

"Forget about Caroline," Victor said. "I read the paper. There's no way Caroline set this up. I told you, she hasn't got the smarts. It's gotta be an incredible coincidence, that's all. But one thing's for sure, there's gonna be some serious investigations."

"I already figured that out," Ralph said.

Victor looked worried. "That's not good, Ralph. Not good at all."

"So what the hell am I supposed to do?"

"I'm not sure," Victor said.

"You're a great fucking help."

"Quiet," Victor said, serious now. "I gotta think this thing out."

"Well, while you're thinking, I want you to have a talk with Caroline."

"For what?"

"For what? Is that what you said? You nuts? Ask her about the money. She's gotta know something. Shake her tree a little. Tell her you know she had Dan knocked off. See what that does. But find out where that money is. If we don't find that money, you and me both are in deep shit, Victor."

Victor's eyes narrowed. "Not me, pal."

Ralph pointed a finger at him. "Yeah, you. You set this up. I'm not going down this road alone."

Now Victor was getting a headache. "Listen," he

said harshly. "I'm not stupid enough to leave a paper trail, my alcoholic friend. You mention my name, and you'll be sucking wind. There's nothing to tie me to anything illegal done by you or your pal. I set up the legitimate corporations in this country, that's all. If you and your partner chose to take the money from those and use it for something else, that was your doing, not mine. I'm not on the board of directors, pal. I got no connection with your illegal shit. I did you a *favor,* asshole. So don't be making threats, Ralph. Not unless you want to get yourself another lawyer."

Ralph looked into Victor's dark eyes and nodded. "Okay. Sorry. I'm just a little pissed, you know? But you see the problem, Victor? We can't just sit back and let Caroline get away with this, can we?"

Victor gave him a look, then said, "If you're right, that's one thing. But I think you're way off on this."

"Maybe. But you tell me how come somebody cleans us out on a Tuesday, and on the next day Danny gets killed. Something doesn't fit, Victor. You see what I'm saying?"

"I see it," Victor said. "I'll think about it."

"We gotta stop her before she takes off," Ralph said. "And she's gonna take off for sure."

Victor thought for a moment, then said, "Why hasn't she done that already? Why would she stay here?"

Ralph had an answer. "It would look bad, don't you see? If she waits until this clown she hired gets convicted, she's in the clear. Then, she can do what she wants."

Victor wasn't convinced. "You keep saying Caroline did this. I don't see it. The cops are satisfied. You have nothing to go on. Nothing!"

"Maybe not, but you tell me, pal. How come Dan

waits around after he takes the money? Answer that for me. You talk about crazy. *That's* crazy!"

Victor rubbed his aching forehead. Ralph had a point. "Like I said, I'll give this some thought. I should have some suggestions for you in the morning."

"Case Number PC—37774—GD. Ralph Vincenzo."

At the sound of his name, Ralph got up from his seat and moved to a position in front of a TV camera. Two TV monitors, their screens filled with the image of a judge, flanked the camera.

It wasn't like the old days. In the old days, someone charged with a crime actually showed up in court during a first appearance, which under Florida law had to take place within twenty-four hours of the arrest. Now, for reasons of expedience, those charged with crimes were herded into a large room in the jail, their images transmitted to the nearby court via closed-circuit television.

Victor stood beside him and spoke into the microphone. "Victor Ganza representing Mr. Vincenzo, Your Honor."

The judge looked at his papers. "Mr. Vincenzo, you are charged with driving while intoxicated and refusing to take a breath test. Arraignment is set for November twenty-third. Bail is set at ten thousand dollars. Your driving license is hereby revoked until trial. You'll surrender it to the clerk. Since you have an experienced lawyer present, I'll let him explain the rest to you. Can he make bail, Mr. Ganza?"

"He can, Your Honor."

"Fine. See the clerk."

"Thank you, Your Honor," Victor said.

As the clerk called the next case, Ralph tugged on Victor's arm.

"Don't we plead not guilty?" Ralph asked.

"Not here. That comes later. I'll make arrangements for your bond. You'll be out in half an hour. I'll meet you in the parking lot."

"Where's my car?"

"In the pound. You can't drive. Your license has been suspended. I'll get somebody to pick it up."

"The way I see it," Victor said later, as he drove his Lincoln Town Car toward a nearby restaurant for breakfast, "you got no choice."

"What are you talking about?" Ralph said.

"Just listen for a minute."

Ralph sighed and looked out the window. He felt tired. Jail was not conducive to sleep, especially the drunk tank with its moaners and screamers and pukers. His clothes were filthy and smelled of urine and vomit. Not his. Someone else's. Jesus.

"You can't run," Victor said, "so that's out. They'd find you sure as hell. Fact is, you didn't take the money, and you can prove that. The transactions were done while you were out of the country, and you can prove that as well. The Swiss will probably tell it like it happened, especially since the account was moved from their bank. So, even though you were screwing the IRS and breaking a few other laws, the maximum penalty is only ten years if you're convicted of every damn thing. And the odds are that you won't be. But if you go to the feds and spill the beans, let it all come out, I think a jury is going to feel sorry for you. They're not supposed to, but they're only human. And going to the feds now makes you look good."

Ralph stared at him in shock. "Are you nuts?"

"Not at all. Think about it, Ralph. Other than the tax angle, you set up a very legitimate deal with Ducerne.

All along, your deals have been straight. We can bring ten guys into court who will swear they made good money with you. You never planned to screw anybody except the government. Hell, *everybody* screws the government."

"I don't *want* to go to court," Ralph yelled.

"I know that, but it can't be helped. Now that the money's gone, court is where you'll end up sooner or later. Better it should happen on your terms. The way I got this figured, you might not spend a day in jail."

"Got what figured?"

Victor pulled the car into a parking lot near the St. Petersburg–Clearwater airport and shut off the engine. He turned and faced his client. "What you said earlier about Caroline. You might be right, you know? Maybe there's more to this murder thing than meets the eye."

Ralph lit a cigarette, inhaled deeply, then said, "You can't smoke in jail. Did you know that?"

"Yes, I did."

"If I go to jail for a year, that means I can't smoke for a year. That would kill me, Victor."

"No, it wouldn't. It would be good for you."

Ralph laughed. "I know a guy who spent time in jail. He said it was funny. You could get booze, drugs, whatever. But no cigarettes. They could smell the cigarettes."

He turned and looked into Victor's eyes. "So, you think I'm right about Caroline?"

"You just might be."

"So, go talk to her."

"I can't do that, Ralph. Wouldn't do much good anyway. If she's smart enough to pull this off, she's smart enough not to talk."

Ralph took another drag, then said, "So what's your bright idea?"

Victor opened the window to let the smoke out. "I'm suggesting we do several things. First, we hold a press conference and tell the world that you and your clients got screwed by Dan DeFauldo. Then we go to the cops and tell them what happened. We get everything on the record. You'll get arrested for tax and securities violations, but the bail won't be bad. You'll be out right away. While you're waiting for your trial, the feds will be trying to figure out where the money went. We let the feds chase the money. They'll eventually come to the same conclusion you did, that Caroline knew something about this. They'll be all over her ass.

"Then there's Jack Palmer's lawyer. I know her. Very sharp. She's gonna think the same thing. She'll be climbing all over Caroline as well. Between the cops and the lawyers, somebody ought to be able to shake her loose. Maybe they'll find out what Dan did with the money. Hey, with the feds involved, they can pull some strings with the Swiss bank.

"Now, and this is the good part, if Caroline did have him killed, she hasn't had time to spend the money. The money's gotta be somewhere. The feds find it, get it back, you pay a fine, and you're on your way. The fine will be less than your end of the money. The clients get their dough back, and you get a slap on the wrist. Sound good?"

"No way," Ralph said. "I'd lose my license. I'd never be able to work securities again."

Victor shook his head. "You just don't get it, pal. That's already a given. No matter what you do, you're out of the securities business. But if you play this my way, there's a chance you may get the money back. Would you rather be out of business and broke or out of business and rich?"

Ralph just stared at him.

"You got no choice, Ralph. None at all."

Ralph turned away. "I don't wanna hear no more of this crap. I'm not about to give myself up to the feds."

"You have a better idea?"

Ralph nodded. "You don't want to know, Victor."

Ten

She hated to leave her office, for it was her sanctuary, a place to hide from the embarrassing glances, the outright openmouthed stares, even some cruel smirks. As with any group, there were some at Hewitt, Sinclair who took pleasure in witnessing the discomfort of others. And while Karen was generally well liked, those who envied her success felt vindicated by the fresh knowledge that Little Miss Perfect was incapable of keeping her husband in line. The bravest among them let her know it by their expressions, while those who empathized with her were more inclined to ignore her. There but for the grace of God . . .

Hers was the smallest of the corner offices, less ostentatious and a lot more feminine. When she'd been made a partner, she'd been advised against having a feminine-looking office.

"Clients, by they male or female, expect an attorney to be strong," Brander had told her. "An office decorated in a feminine fashion presents an image of softness, and that's not good for a lawyer."

"Things will have to change," she'd told him, one of the rare occasions in which she'd disagreed with her tutor. "If I think the client needs to be jacked up, we'll hold our meetings in one of the small conference rooms. But I have to work in this office, and I'll be spending more waking hours in it than in my own home. If it's all the same to you, I'll decorate it to suit myself."

Her assertiveness was one of the reasons Brander had decided to push for her partnership. That, and the possibility she'd move on if she wasn't made a partner. This was one associate he didn't want to lose. He'd acquiesced gracefully by saying, "It's your office, Karen. You may do with it what you wish."

And so she had. Her office had the least interesting vista of the four corner units, facing east and overlooking a crowded housing development. In the distance, she could see both Lake Tarpon and Old Tampa Bay, but the immediate view was uninspiring, so she'd paid particular attention to the window. The pattern of the drapes matched the coverings on the sofa and two chairs, all of it done in soft pastels. The walls were painted rather than covered, and featured traditional works of art that Karen had brought from home. Her desk was thick glass, as was the coffee table, and a small table in the corner bore a crystal vase filled with fresh-cut flowers that were changed every second day.

It was a cozy and comfortable office, a suitably peaceful environment, almost a respite for a woman who spent much of her time in the profoundly charged atmosphere of the courtroom. The office was especially welcome this morning after a night spent wide awake, a night filled with torment, doubt, and fear.

But she had to leave.

The Friday morning staff conference, held in the southern-facing conference room, was attended by the usual dozen people, all of them making a conspicuously conscious effort to ignore the obvious, pretending they'd never heard last night's newscast. They proffered broad smiles and glad hands, but their eyes

betrayed them. For her part, Karen accepted the charade, and while her stomach was churning, her exterior
seemed calm enough—at least as calm as a Xanax
tablet could make her.

Brander was there, of course, and Darren Smith, the
owlish-looking former IRS agent who now fought the
agency with a vengeance, handling client tax problems
with his computerlike mind. Like reformed smokers
who treat their former comrades-in-certain-death with
consummate disdain, Smith leaked hatred of the IRS
from every pore. Having once been on the inside, he
knew from firsthand experience the depths to which
IRS agents would sink to win a case. Perhaps fueled by
remorse, he defended his clients with a passion that resulted in a win record second only to that of the
Houston-based Michael Minns.

And Walter Sinclair. The managing partner, once the
happy-go-lucky type, was also a changed man. His new
life of forced sexual chastity had left him hungering for
something that could never be again. His sullen, hollow-
eyed comportment was enough to depress anyone.

Karen sipped coffee from a foam cup and scanned the
faces of the others, all associates on the fast track, the
worker bees of this particular hive, lawyers who might
be made partners if they continued with the firm. Some
wouldn't wait around, choosing instead to fly away to
bigger or smaller firms, usually for more money.

As managing partner, Walter was the one who set the
salary and bonus levels. To say he was tight-fisted was
like saying Attila the Hun was insensitive. It was an accepted fact that lawyers who came to Hewitt, Sinclair
usually did so because they considered the firm a training ground—a kind of lawyer's boot camp—with exposure to major cases almost certain. Once they had the
experience they were after, many moved on. There was

no shortage of those willing to take their place, and that suited Walter just fine.

The issue had been raised at more than one meeting of the partners. Karen had spoken in favor of salaries being more competitive, and more associates being made partners. The firm's ratio of partners to associates was near the lowest in the entire country. At one stormy meeting, Karen had presented a detailed essay proving, at least on paper, that high turnover rates were inefficient. The cost of training new people more than offset Walter's imaginary savings. She'd backed up her claim with several recent supportive studies.

Walter, as usual, took Karen's position as a personal attack, reacting like a petulant, spoiled child. The matter was dropped. But after the meeting, Darren Smith stepped into Karen's office and volunteered to develop comprehensive internal data to prove her point. Another battle loomed on the horizon.

"We'll come to order," Walter snapped, taking his position at one narrow end of the table. "I realize you're all chomping at the bit to make it a long weekend," he intoned, "but there's much to discuss, so let's get with it. First, let me officially congratulate Karen for her excellent work on the Cole case."

There was a round of applause. Walter held up a newspaper. "I see we received some positive press in the local paper. Nice picture, Karen."

He was overcompensating, but Karen appreciated it. Her appreciation was short-lived, however. Walter was, after all, Walter.

"I also note that in the same edition, there is a report of the death of one Mr. Dan DeFauldo. I understand that Karen is representing Jack Palmer, the man accused of killing Mr. DeFauldo. Let me, therefore, inquire of Karen as to her plans for the Palmer case. Is this going to be pled out in a hurry?"

All eyes focused on Karen. Walter was pretending nothing had happened during the past ten hours. And everyone knew it. Karen decided to play it straight.

"I've talked to Mr. Palmer," she said softly, "and I don't think a plea is on his mind. I'm arranging a polygraph examination. In the meantime, I'm proceeding as if we'll be taking this all the way. I want Colin to assist me."

Walter's face took on the appearance of a gathering thundercloud. "I am given to understand you have agreed to take this case pro bono. Is that correct?"

Karen glared at him. "Not officially. I have accepted three hundred dollars as a retainer."

They stared at her in awe.

"Is this some kind of joke?" Walter asked.

"Not at all," Karen said, stoned-faced. "While it's true Jack Palmer has no funds, I expect this case, by its very nature, to be a high-profile one. As such, it will attract the media. You know what happens when the media starts hyping a murder case. Groups with a wide range of causes are attracted to the light along with the less-minded interests. It's possible a defense fund will be set up. Perhaps you, Walter, would accept the responsibility of managing such a fund. As well, you might consider approaching our client with a view to having him sign over his rights to possible commercial considerations such as books or movies."

It was nonsense, of course. This was not the kind of case that attracted causes. A child sexually ravished by sick parents, a young girl left paralyzed after a vicious attack, old folks beaten and bashed by marauding youths—those were the kind of cases that made people get up from their seats in front of the TV and reach for their checkbooks. A man accused of raping another man's wife and then murdering her husband—not in a million years. She had to express her anger.

"At worst," Karen continued, "as a pro bono case, we will satisfy the state requirements for the next three years. In addition to Colin, I expect I'll need the help of other associates as we move along. And should we actually win this case, the resultant publicity won't hurt. All in all, this case will be good for us, Walter."

Brander had heard enough. He could see Karen was about to boil over. He tapped his pencil on the table, cleared his throat, and said, "I've already told Karen she has our complete support. Considering the fact that, thanks to her diligent efforts, a seven-figure amount was deposited to our account yesterday, I'd suggest we get off the subject of money. There are more important considerations."

Walter looked at Brander as if the man had lost his mind. He shook his head slowly, then looked at Karen. "What about your current caseload? What about potential new clients? How are you going to—"

"I'll take care of it, Walter," Karen said sharply, cutting him off. "Can we move on to something else? If you have concerns, see me after the meeting. Perhaps I can successfully allay your fears."

He glared at her for a moment, then shrugged. "Halder versus Halder. Mr. James?"

Walter did not deign to visit Karen after the meeting, but Brander did. He entered her office, closed the door behind him, and said, "I think we should talk this over."

As he stood in front of her desk, Karen fought the strong desire to dissolve into tears. She pointed to a chair. Brander sat. He looked at the pile of pink message slips sitting on her desk.

"Reporters?"

"Mostly. Jonathan's little exercise has enticed the snakes from their pits."

He made a face. "Have you considered what this means?"

"Excuse me?"

His face was flushed. "Perhaps you should reconsider your decision to represent Mr. Palmer."

Karen took a deep breath. "I wasn't completely honest with you yesterday."

"How so?"

"I'm not at all convinced Jack Palmer is telling the truth."

Brander was dumbfounded. "Then why did you accept his case?"

She took a moment to answer. "When I talked to him, he seemed sincere. I decided to take him on until such time as I could better determine what really happened. I told him I'd drop him if I discovered he'd lied to me. And I will. But I'm not going to let Caroline push me out. What she's done is hateful. I can't let her get away with it."

Brander seemed disappointed. "You'll play right into her hands. You'll make this personal."

"I can't help that. If she and Carl did have an affair, I'll have to find a way to deal with that. But the alleged affair had nothing to do with my reasons for representing Jack Palmer. Walking away now would be tantamount to admitting she was right. I won't let that happen."

Brander said nothing. Karen sat nervously. Waiting.

"I was up most of the night," he said finally. "I was thinking about your case, wondering why Caroline would go to such lengths. There appears to be but one viable conclusion, and that is that she wants you not to represent Mr. Palmer. And when I evaluate her motivation, I sense that she fears you. If the events leading to the death of her husband are as she claims, why should she fear you? Why should she fear the truth?"

"Carl said almost the same thing to me last night."

Brander's eyebrows rose. "Really. Perhaps I was wrong about Caroline DeFauldo. Perhaps she lied about the death of her husband. Perhaps she also lied about having an affair with your husband."

"Perhaps. But I don't think Caroline is clever enough to fabricate all of this."

"Is it possible you underestimate her?"

"Of course."

"Well, after last night, it wouldn't be unfair to suggest that your present attitude is tainted. You'd be inhuman if you were capable of total subjectivity."

"I can't argue with that assessment."

"Which brings me to this: I think I should be the one to argue against Jonathan's motion."

"I can do it."

"I know you can. I'm only suggesting you shouldn't. Judge Brown is not the kind of man to pass up an opportunity to humiliate you or any other female attorney. This is what he lives for. He'll stretch this out until you break. In saying that, I'm not suggesting you are weak, but I do submit that you are emotionally involved, and no matter how strong you are, you will be unable to withstand Judge Brown's callousness for hours on end. I, on the other hand, have an edge. In addition, I can argue the law forcefully and impartially."

Karen leaned back in her chair and nodded. "You're right, of course. And thank you, Brander."

"You're entirely welcome." He smiled his fatherly smile. "I've come to know you over the years, Karen.

You're quite right. You can't walk away from this now, not after this perverted and disgusting challenge. In point of fact, Jonathan knows very well that Carl's alleged infidelity is irrelevant to this case. The issue is your motivation, and you've given no one cause to suspect that your motivation is anything but proper. Mr. Palmer contacted you. We can prove that."

He leaned forward. "Have you asked Carl if he'll appear at the hearing, assuming there'll be one?"

Karen shook her head.

Brander stood up. "I realize how difficult this is, but it would be wise if you asked him. I'm sure Jonathan will press for an immediate hearing. I'd be in favor of one myself. I'd like Carl to testify."

She said nothing.

"I'll see the judge this morning. Are you in agreement that the hearing should be right away?"

"I am," she said.

He headed for the door and opened it. Then he turned and looked at Karen and said, "And while it's none of my business, unless the evidence presented is irrefutable, I would give your husband the benefit of the doubt."

He closed the door behind him. She was alone in her sanctum, alone with her pain and confusion, her fear and anxiety. She felt a muscle twitching in her left arm, felt the emptiness in the pit of her stomach, felt the waves of uncertainty wash over her intellect. Silently, she cursed the name of Jack Palmer.

Her respite was brief. When Colin knocked on the door, she told him to come in and waved him to a chair. "You wanted to see me?" he asked.

"Yes. What have you got going at the moment?"

"Oh, nothing much. A few contracts, a real estate closing, just minor stuff."

"Can it wait a few days?"

"Sure," he said, "all except the closing. That's on Tuesday. Won't take more than an hour."

"Good. I want you to help me on the Palmer case. You'll be sitting in the second chair should this get to court. I want you in from the beginning."

He lit up like a Christmas tree. "Thanks, Karen."

"You may think twice about thanking me when I tell you we've drawn Judge Brown."

Colin's face fell. "Oh, no."

"I'm afraid so. The luck of the draw, as they say."

"He's hopeless. And he hates you."

"Hate is much too soft a word," she said. "Start writing."

Colin grabbed a yellow pad.

"First," Karen told him, "I want you to interview all the people who live within earshot of the DeFauldo house. Pay particular attention to what they heard, what they saw, and when. You'll find most will be reluctant to discuss it, but use your Irish charm. Be precise with your questions. Then, get over to the Tarpon Springs campus and find a list of everyone who attended that word processing class. I want them all interviewed. Without putting words in anyone's mouth, I want them to comment on what they saw happening between Jack Palmer and Caroline DeFauldo during the five sessions. Was there affection shown? If so, when, what, and where? I also want you to talk to the campus security people. Jack says he and Caroline necked one night. Maybe someone saw them. We need witnesses, Colin."

"When do you want me to start?"

"Immediately. Oh, and add the Tampa restaurant to the list. Find the waiter who served them. See if he overheard any of the conversation. You'll have to move fast and hard. There's a lot of ground to cover."

"You want me to work the weekend?"

She smiled at him. "I wouldn't ask that of an associate. Of course, if you were to volunteer . . ."

"I get the picture."

"Fine. Be thorough. Don't rush. And be good."

"I'll do my best," he said.

"Okay. Now, page two, as what's his name likes to say."

Colin's jaw dropped.

"I want a complete profile on the DeFauldos," she said. "I want to know everything there is to know about them both, business as well as personal. And I mean everything. Keep that in mind as you work your way through page one. Talk to Ralph Vincenzo. He won't be in jail long.

"Finally, and perhaps this should be higher on the list, I want you to talk to people Dan DeFauldo played poker with the night he was killed. The word I have is that he usually played until the wee hours of the morning. Find out why he left early that night."

"I'll do my best," Colin said.

"Good. You'd better get started."

He headed for the door, then stopped. "Karen, I don't know how to say this, but . . ."

She sighed. "Go ahead."

"Well, I was thinking about it all night. You know, Jonathan Walsingham might just be trying to upset you. Have you thought of that?"

She nodded.

"Well, I just wanted you to know, I hope that's what it is. I really do. And I'm truly sorry this has happened. You don't deserve this kind of garbage."

She gave him a weak smile. "Thanks, Colin."

Liz poked her head in the door. "I have Mr. Palmer on the phone," she said. "Do you want to talk to him?"

Karen picked up the telephone.

The condo complex consisted of 226 units, arranged in clusters of twenty or so condos per stark white, vinyl-sided, tired-looking building, twenty of them in all, looking more like public than private housing. They ranged in size from 890 to 1,230 square feet, the smaller units selling for a paltry fifty-three-thousand dollars.

Jack Palmer lived in Building G, the one closest to the highway. The Palmer unit was on the second floor, where the ceaseless growl of truck engines and relentless whine of tires resonated from the busy nearby highway, the cacophony washing over Karen like dirty rain as she pressed the doorbell to unit 210.

A six-year-old with blond curly hair and startling blue, anxious eyes, opened the door and stared at her. "Who are you?" asked the tentative, suspicious, little-girl voice.

"Hi," Karen said, stooping down to be at eye level with this child already wounded by cataclysmic events outside her control. As always, it was the children who suffered the most. "My name is Karen," she said cheerfully, "and I'm here to see your mommy. Is she here?"

"I'm here," a gruff voice called out.

Ellen Palmer came to the screen door and pushed it open. She was a tall, thin, plain-faced woman, her pale complexion accentuating the deep pouches under her cold, dark eyes. "Come in."

The interior of the condo looked like a war zone: cramped, messy, furnished in early Kmart. A big TV took center stage, around which were assembled a variety of mismatched chairs, a sofa, a chipped walnut coffee table brimming with TV fan magazines, sports magazines, and supermarket tabloids, and a tilting bookcase filled to overflowing with paperback books. The walls were bare, except for a small section of framed photos of the children, taken at various stages in their young lives. The most recent one of the boy featured oddly tormented eyes that matched those of the man now sitting in jail.

The kitchen, surprisingly large, boasted a sink filled with dirty dishes and a small table cluttered with the remains of three TV dinners. The whole place smelled of mildew, dried sweat, and dust. Karen removed some plastic toys from a worn chair and sat.

"Go in the bedroom with your brother," Ellen ordered the child.

The girl with the blue eyes did as she was told, closing the door quietly behind her. Ellen slumped down on the sofa and threw an arm over the back, eyeing Karen as one would examine excrement. "So," she said, her voice thick with contempt, "you're Jack's lawyer. Looks like you and I have the same problem with cheating husbands."

Karen blushed. "I'm here to talk about Jack."

The woman sneered, then said, "I didn't tell the kids who you are. Let's leave it that way, okay?"

"Fine," Karen said. "How are you making out?"

Ellen snorted. "How do you think? I'm not very good at selling real estate, and now that Jack's in jail, we're sure to lose this place. God knows where we'll end up."

There was little warmth in this woman. There were deep grooves around her tightly clenched mouth that seemed to be a manifestation of her personality. What life there was in her eyes was fired by undisguised hostility. Jack had said the couple had few friends. It wasn't hard to understand why.

"As I told you on the telephone," Karen said, "I believe Jack is innocent of the charges."

Ellen shrugged. She was wearing a green sweater that did nothing to offset her pallid complexion. Nor did the gray slacks do anything to enhance her appearance. She was a woman without a modicum of taste.

"It doesn't really matter much," Ellen said.

Karen's eyes widened in surprise. "It doesn't matter that your husband may be innocent?"

Ellen shrugged again. "Not really. He was in that woman's house, and there's no denying that. He was there cheating on me, and you can't say that isn't so."

"I'm not saying it isn't so. I'm saying he isn't guilty of murder."

The woman was unmoved. "You're his lawyer, so you've got to say what's best for him, but I don't really care. Jack ended this marriage when he started messing with her, and now he's in jail. As far as I'm concerned, he's abandoned me and his children for a roll in the hay with some rich bitch. Even if you're smart enough to get him off, he'll never get his old job back. He may never get *any* kind of a job. That means no support money. I'm left with full responsibility for bringing up the kids. Just me, making less than thirteen thousand a year. What the hell am I supposed to do?"

Karen looked at her for a moment, then said, "I don't have an answer to that question."

"I didn't think you would."

Karen took another tack. "I'm sure you're hurt and upset, Mrs. Palmer, and while Jack is not blameless for getting involved with Mrs. DeFauldo . . . it's possible he was seduced by a very clever woman with an agenda."

Ellen waved a hand in the air, dismissing the thought. "A man can't be seduced unless he wants to be. That goes for your husband, too."

"Let's keep my husband out of this conversation, all right?"

"Suit yourself."

Karen took out a small notebook. Enough small talk. She wasn't here to comfort this bitter woman. If she dallied much longer, she'd be engaging in a dialogue with no purpose. "What kind of man was Jack before all this happened?"

Ellen sighed. "Nothing special."

"Was he abusive to you or the children? Either physically or verbally?"

That brought a cruel smile to the woman's lips. "Jack? He was never like that. Jack was a wimp. I bugged him for years to talk to his boss about a raise. He wouldn't do it. He was afraid they'd fire him."

"Maybe he was right," Karen said defensively. "Corporations are cutting back all over the country."

"Maybe so," Ellen said, "but Jack's sales were higher than two other salesmen, and he got paid less. If he had any guts, we'd be a lot better off."

She was unrelentingly negative. Karen could feel her own resentment building. "Did Jack own a gun?" she asked.

"No way. Not with kids in the house."

Karen fought to put a smile on her lips. "You're very wise. Does that mean that he once expressed a desire to have a gun in the house?"

"No. But if he had, I wouldn't have allowed it."

"So," Karen said evenly, "you never saw him with a gun at any time?"

"No. Jack wasn't into guns."

"He wasn't a hunter?"

"Hell, no. Jack couldn't hurt a fly. He used to get up-set when he saw dead animals on the road. Like I told you, he's a wimp."

Karen fought back a retort. "Was he a good husband, aside from the recent . . ."

"He was all right," she said, matter-of-factly. "Bor-ing, but all right. He never got drunk or tried to slap us around. He was on the road most of the time. When he got home, he'd just sit and read books. Or he'd mess with that novel of his." She laughed. "I could write bet-ter than him. God, what a waste. We couldn't afford to go out much. Jack doted on the kids, but he didn't like to talk to me much."

"Why was that?"

"Ask him."

Karen looked around the room. Something made no sense. "You say you're earning about thirteen thousand a year. Jack claims he was making thirty. Is that about right?"

Ellen frowned. "So?"

"Well, that's a better than average family income. Do you mind if I ask where that money goes?"

Ellen glared at Karen for a moment, then said, "It's not all that great. It's expensive having a family these days. Both Jack and I have to pay our own expenses. We both need cars. Then there's the health insurance. Add it all up, and there isn't much left. What with the fund for the kids, we're lucky to eat. Now, I guess we can forget about eating."

"The fund for the kids?"

She took a moment to answer. "Jack never went to college. He wanted to make sure the kids did, so he started a fund when they were born. A hundred dollars in each account every month."

Karen made a note, then asked, "Was this the first time Jack ever cheated on you?"

Ellen laughed. "Who knows? Like I said, he was on the road most of the time. I never thought so before, but now . . . I'd guess he was screwing other women all the time."

"But none that you know about?"

"Why don't you ask him?"

"But if he did, he never discussed it with you. Some men, when they have affairs, seem to have a need to confess. Jack never mentioned an affair, did he?"

"No. But that doesn't mean much. I never knew he was seeing this one either. All that proves is that he can keep his mouth shut, which is most of the time anyway."

Karen put her notebook away and leaned back in the chair. "Mrs. Palmer," she said softly, "I realize you're hurting. It's never pleasant in these situations. But the fact is, your husband is in jail charged with a murder I don't think he committed. Putting that aside for the moment, he is presumed innocent until proven guilty."

"Sure. That's why he's in jail."

"No. He's in jail because the law requires that he appear to answer to the charges. In any event, he's still the father of your children, and, as such, he has certain rights."

The woman sneered at her. "He asked you to come here, didn't he?"

"He did, but I would have come anyway. If I'm to win this case, I'll need your help."

Suddenly, Ellen stood up, her eyes flashing with anger. "Let me tell you something, Miss Hot Shot Lawyer. As far as I'm concerned, he can rot in that prison. I want nothing more to do with Jack Palmer."

Now Karen was on her feet. "He deserves better than

this," she said. "I'll grant you he was unfaithful, but the penalty for adultery is not a lifetime in prison. If you want to divorce him, that's up to you. If you want to wash your hands of him, that's your privilege. But it seems to me that, while your marriage may not have been made in heaven, Jack was a decent provider and a reasonably good husband and father. The jury should hear that, and the words should come from your lips. It's nothing less than the truth."

Ellen's eyes glowed hot with righteous indignation. "He gets nothing from me. Nothing! Just like what he'll be giving us from now on."

Karen took a moment to get her own anger under control. Finally, she said, "Be that as it may, Jack is entitled to speak to his children. He's not asking that they be brought to the jail. He doesn't want to expose them to that. But he does want to talk to them on the telephone. If you refuse to allow that, I'll have to get a court order."

"So get one."

Karen took a deep breath. "Look," she said, "the law is quite clear on the issue. All you'll be doing is making it more difficult for yourself, your children, and Jack. I can understand your pain, but this is not the way to punish your husband. You're punishing your children, too."

Ellen Palmer's face was like stone. "He's not talking to the kids. Court order or no court order."

"That isn't the way things work," Karen said softly. "If there's a hearing, and if Jack prevails, and if you refuse to obey a court order, you'll be held in contempt. That means jail for you, too. Is that what you want?"

There was no answer. Karen looked at her watch.

"Jack is going to call again in about an hour. For everyone's sake, let him talk to the kids, okay?"

The woman remained silent. Karen walked slowly to the door, then outside. It slammed behind her.

Karen smiled inwardly. The visit with Ellen Palmer had not been a total waste. In her own perverse way, this bitterly resentful woman would make a terrific witness—whether she liked it or not.

Karen got behind the wheel of her car. Almost immediately, Ellen Palmer was all but forgotten. The critical question of Carl's fidelity, a question that had dogged Karen throughout the day, began to dominate her thoughts. As she sat behind the wheel of her car, thinking about Carl, envisioning him with Caroline, her head began to pound. She rested her head on the steering wheel and let the tears come.

Eleven

Karen listened to the six o'clock news on the car radio. They played up the intriguing story of the woman defending the man accused of murdering the man married to the woman who had had an affair with the woman who—they were having great fun with it. Lots of fun. And when they finally got around to reporting the actual news, it was to say that Judge Joe Brown had granted an immediate hearing—immediate meaning Monday morning—on the question of whether Karen would be allowed to defend accused rapist and killer Jack Palmer.

She parked her car in the garage beside Carl's and went inside the house. From the dining-room window, she could see Carl cavorting in the backyard pool with Andrea. With her heart pounding so hard she could actually hear it, she dropped her attaché case off in her home office, leafed through the day's motley collection of letters, junk mail, and magazines, then headed to the pool area. She could stall no longer. It was time to face Carl.

She stepped out to the screened-in pool area, every nerve in her body tingling with tension. Carl was throwing Andrea high into the air, letting her make a terrific splash as she tumbled back into the water, arms and legs akimbo, screaming with pleasure. Karen felt a tug at her heart, watching them together. Among other things, Carl was a spectacular father. And this was a spectacular evening, one she would normally enjoy to the fullest.

November was the perfect time of year in central Florida, with clear, warm, sun-filled days, and crisp, starry nights. Gone was the thick, suffocating humidity of the summer, the violent thunderstorms, the threat of hurricanes. November and April were the months that made the summer almost tolerable. In November, the air conditioner was turned off, the windows were opened, and the house itself seemed to take deep, satisfying breaths. But although the weather was cool and dry, Karen felt as if she had been thrown inside a blast furnace.

"Hi," Carl said, waving, a smile on his face. "There's some wine in the cooler. Pour me one, too, will you?"

She was stunned. Yesterday seemed like ancient history, wiped clean from the slate.

"Sure," Karen said.

"Hi, Mommy!" Andrea cried.

"Hi, sweetheart," she called back.

With shaking hands, Karen took the wine from the cooler and half filled two chilled tulip-shaped glasses. Carl placed Andrea atop a floating plastic alligator and pulled himself from the pool. Dripping wet, he sank into a chair beside Karen.

"We have a problem," he said softly. The smile was gone momentarily, replaced by a look of implacable pain. "When I got home today, Andrea greeted me with a question. She wanted to know if you and I were getting divorced. She was terrified."

Karen's hand flew to her mouth. "Oh, my God!"

"I've settled her down some, but you'll have to talk with her. Better yet, we'll do it together. The kids at school teased her all day. They told her since I'd had an affair with somebody, you would certainly divorce me. They told her that's how things worked, and she'd better decide now who she wanted to live with. You know how cruel kids can be."

His words had immediate effect. Karen choked back a sob. At that moment, she despised herself, so caught up in self-pity that she'd completely ignored the obvious. *Of course* the kids at school would have known about the news report. *Of course* they would have teased Andrea relentlessly. And Karen should have anticipated it.

She jumped to her feet. "It has to be now. Right now. I'll change into my suit."

Carl said nothing. Karen dashed back into the house, where Michelle was preparing dinner. "How was Andrea when you picked her up?" Karen asked.

Michelle avoided Karen's stare. "She was crying. She was upset."

"What did you tell her?"

"I told her it was a lie. What else could I say? She was very upset until she talked with Dr. Mondori."

Karen wanted to kiss her. "Thanks, Michelle. You did the right thing."

Karen changed into a swimsuit in less than two minutes. She ran back downstairs and out to the pool area. Carl and Andrea were splashing water at each other. She dived in and joined them. She clutched her daughter to her chest and hugged her tightly, fighting back tears. She reached out to Carl and pulled him close.

"You listen to Mommy and Daddy," she said sternly. "We love each other very much. We both love you more than life itself. What you heard at school today is a lie. You know that people sometimes lie, don't you?"

Andrea answered, "Yes," in an uncertain voice. "But why did they say you were getting a divorce?"

"We've talked about what Mommy does for a living before," Karen said. "You know that there are times when I have to deal with people who aren't very nice."

"Uh-huh."

"Well, this is one of those times. A very nasty person said something on TV that was a lie. I don't know why she said it, but she did. People who don't know Mommy and Daddy believe those things just because they've been said. That doesn't make it true. Mommy and Daddy are not getting divorced, understand?"

Andrea, her face a portrait of innocence, asked, "Then why were you fighting last night?"

Karen was speechless. Carl took up the cause. "People have arguments," he said. "Mommy and Daddy have argued before, right?"

"Yes."

"And we didn't get divorced, did we?"

"No."

"You see? When Mommy and Daddy argue, it doesn't mean they don't love each other. When we punish you for doing something wrong, we still love you. You understand that, don't you?"

"I guess so."

"You guess so?"

Andrea made a face. "I don't want you to get divorced."

"We're not getting divorced," Karen insisted.

"Promise?"

"Promise."

Andrea gave them both a big hug.

Karen ate very little during dinner. She was concentrating hard on acting nonchalant, but her stomach was churning. And after dinner, she devoted every second to Andrea, reading to her, reassuring her, laughing and smiling and hugging and kissing. And when Andrea finally went to bed, Karen felt drained.

Andrea, bright and sensitive, inquisitive and somewhat impulsive, the product of two busy people, alone with hired help most of the time, perceptive enough to play one parent against the other if allowed, and obviously insecure enough to be driven close to panic by the vicious taunts of classmates.

The insecurity troubled Karen deeply. As parents, Karen and Carl strived to provide as natural an environment as possible, but they knew there was a tendency to spoil her. They had to guard against that, for it was easy to give the child everything she asked for. They were successful professionals, with prodigious reservoirs of love and affection. But, as with most dedicated people, there were priorities. The job could be a bully, sucking up all one's attention.

In their parenting, there was an inclination to overcompensate for what was often denied the child—their presence. Karen wondered if that was the root cause of the child's frightening insecurity. Or was this simply a normal reaction to the taunting of her schoolmates?

It was so hard to know.

Karen joined Carl on the backyard deck. He was holding a snifter of brandy and staring at the stars.

"We have to talk," she said.

"Did Andrea get to sleep all right?"

"Yes, thank God."

"Good. I'll be glad to put this day behind me."

"Me, too."

"We have to talk about the hearing," she said.

He looked crestfallen. "Ahhh. The case again. Interesting. I thought you wanted to talk about us. But I guess the case is more important."

Karen blushed. "It's not that at all."

"No? Then explain something to me." His angry eyes appraised her. "Caroline DeFauldo says Jack Palmer murdered her husband. You have a talk with Mr. Palmer and decide Caroline's lying. Then Caroline DeFauldo says I had sex with her. You have a talk with me and decide *I'm* the one who's lying. How does that work, exactly? What's Jack Palmer's secret?"

"The two situations are not related."

"Oh, but they are. You'll believe the words of a stranger, but not those of your husband. I'd like a goddam explanation."

There was no escape. She had to tell him.

"When I first met you," she said, "I fell in love with you immediately. And even after you told me you loved me, too, I was afraid."

"Afraid of what?"

"You don't realize the image you project. You're handsome and bright and witty. You're sexy as hell, Carl. Before we married, you told me that, after your divorce, you screwed every woman you could get your hands on. You were insatiable, and everyone knew it. You had quite a reputation."

"You just said I told you all about that."

"I know. But throughout our marriage, I've been waiting for the other shoe to drop. I've been terrified that I could never really satisfy you, that you'd eventually look elsewhere. And even if you weren't looking, I know how surgeons are revered by the nurses at hospitals. There are surgeon groupies, just like rock star groupies, women who will do anything to get their hooks into a man they see as a god. If you were the ugliest man on earth, you'd still be pursued. And you happen to be gorgeous, which makes you all the more magnetic to these women. Don't try and tell me you haven't seen it happen with some of your colleagues."

He shook his head. "Jesus Christ! Now I know where Andrea gets her insecurity. It comes from you! You sell yourself short, Karen. Sure, I went nuts after the divorce. And why not? I was a good-looking guy, making lots of money, pretty good in bed, and my wife had to get it on with a bunch of nothings. What the hell do you think that did to my ego? I felt like you feel now, the difference being, I had a *reason*.

"Yes, I screwed around. I needed validation. I needed to feel wanted. And then I met you. And it all stopped. And yes, there are nurses who chase doctors. I won't deny that, but when I tell them I'm not playing that game and they'd better lay off or look for work elsewhere, they do."

"I want to believe that."

"You'd better believe it," he said harshly. "I don't deserve this. If it's impossible for you to accept I've been faithful to you all these years, I suggest we see a counselor damn quick. This cannot continue. I'm being punished for something I didn't do. It needs to be resolved now. I won't stand for this any longer. You understand?"

She dropped her head. "I understand."

"I'll set it up next week."

"Fine."

"Now, as far as your precious case goes, there's no need for you to be concerned. Brander called me at the hospital this afternoon. He told me the hearing has been scheduled for Monday morning. He asked me to clear my schedule. He wants me to testify. I said I'd be damn happy to do it. I'll be saying it under oath, Karen. Maybe that will help."

Karen's stomach rumbled. Her throat started to constrict. "I . . ."

"Never mind. Brander said to tell you he doesn't want you anywhere near that courtroom on Monday. He was adamant. He wants Caroline to be the center of attention."

She brought a hand to her eyes. "This is all so . . ."

"Yes, it is. Brander came to the hospital to see me after we talked on the phone. He asked all sorts of questions and wanted records. Now that he has a copy of Caroline's lawyer's motion, he knows what to look for. He's pulling out all the stops for you. You should be grateful."

She didn't speak. She couldn't.

He grabbed her arm. "Look at me."

She did.

"I've told you I didn't appreciate your taking sides on this thing. It makes us look bad. Well, the Hamptons' twentieth anniversary bash is tomorrow night and I want us to be there. I refuse to crawl into a cave and hide. I won't do it."

The party had completely slipped her mind, and it showed.

"You forgot, right?"

She nodded. She was still too emotional to speak.

"Want to chicken out?"

Again, she nodded.

"I figured that," he said. "No dice. We'll have to confront these people sooner or later. Best we get it over with. Especially now, with Andrea so worried, we have to keep up appearances, as they say. We have to pretend everything is just fine. I don't want any argument on this."

Karen simply sighed.

* * *

They spent much of Saturday at Busch Gardens. It was Andrea's first time, and she was in absolute heaven. They avoided the more strenuous rides, choosing to spend their time looking at the incredible variety of animals. It was a lovely day, cool and bright, the smell of hops hanging thick in the air.

Andrea's eyes widened as she saw real alligators for the first time, and zebras, and giraffes, and an eighteen-foot boa constrictor. She had the courage to wait in line for a chance to touch the huge snake's skin, which was dry, not slimy as she had expected.

They arrived home exhausted. Andrea seemed happy. Karen was so tight she thought she'd snap.

The Hamptons lived eight houses away. Carl and Karen walked. As they neared the Hampton house, they saw cars lining both sides of the street. It was just ten minutes past the announced eight o'clock start of the celebration. Obviously, no one wanted to be late for *this* party. Karen, always observant, recognized most of the cars and started laughing.

"What's so funny?" Carl asked.

She pointed to a red Cadillac. "Henry and Grace Caulfield. They live three houses away. How lazy can you get?"

"It's an ad," he said. "Not everyone was invited to this bash. Henry wants the neighbors to know he's on the 'A' list."

She stopped walking. "This is really tough, Carl."

He shrugged. "Think of Andrea."

"I *am* thinking of Andrea, and I'm beginning to wonder if this is such a good idea."

"They didn't cancel the invitation."

"I know, but . . ."

"Look," he said, "if it gets uncomfortable, we'll leave. What the hell, maybe you can make a short speech about the criminal justice system."

"This has nothing to do with the criminal justice system."

"Then make it sound like it. A diversionary tactic, as you like to say. Think of them as a hard-nosed jury. And if that doesn't work, screw them. I don't really care anymore. I just want to get this goddam party over with."

Like most of the houses in Autumn Woods, the Hampton house was huge, with a living room large enough to accommodate thirty guests comfortably. The party-goers were all huddled in the center of the room. A man in a tux sat at the seven-foot black Steinway that dominated one corner of the room, playing soft jazz, accompanied by a drummer and a bass guitar player. Two uniformed maids skirted the outer perimeter of the circle, bearing trays of finger food and drinks. Well-dressed people with drinks in their hands stood nose to nose, laughing and talking—until Carl and Karen entered the room. The extraordinary silence caused the pianist to look around, wondering what had happened.

"Carl, Karen," Mary Hampton gushed, her cheeks aflame with embarrassment, rushing up to them and hugging them both. It was a signal of sorts, and the low rumble of conversation began anew. The jazz man looked at the other members of his trio, shrugged, and slipped into his version of a pop tune.

Karen handed Mary a gift-wrapped package. "Congratulations," she said.

Fred Hampton was now standing right behind his wife. "Glad you could make it," he said.

"Wouldn't miss it," Carl told him. "Twenty years. It's just wonderful."

Fred hugged his wife. "You bet it is. Come on in, have a drink."

They knew nearly everyone. They nodded to some, shook hands with others, hugged the ones they knew best. All smiles, all warmth, and all a facade. They knew they were the center of attention, for wherever they turned, all eyes focused on them, the facial expressions running the gamut from abject disgust to admiration.

But it was twenty minutes before someone mentioned the case. As might be expected, it was the loquacious Carrie Lander who broke the artificial barrier. She sidled up to Karen, her large plastic breasts almost spilling out of her red dress, her gold chains smothered beneath her many chins, her voice a conspiratorial whisper. "I never liked Caroline much," she said. "Always thought she put on airs, you know? She calls herself an actress. Big deal. She does a few commercials and acts in little theaters that seat a dozen people. Some actress. Well, we all know about actresses, don't we."

"I'd rather not talk about it," Karen said softly.

A circle was quickly beginning to form. "I'm just saying," Carrie went on, "that there's something fishy about this whole thing, if you ask me."

Louis Haller stood behind Carrie. "You only say that," Louis said, "because you've never seen Caroline act. I have. She's appeared with several touring groups before audiences of two thousand or more. Got good reviews, too. There's nothing fishy about this at all. If Caroline DeFauldo says she was raped, I believe her."

Louis smiled sheepishly at Karen. "I know how the law works, Karen. A man has a right to be defended by an attorney. Just because you're defending the guy who killed Dan doesn't mean you're on his side. All it means is you're defending him, as is his right. And I don't buy for a minute this crap about Carl. That's a lawyer's cheap trick."

He looked around. "I hope everybody here understands that."

"Well, I don't."

Another voice heard from. The battle was truly joined. Brian Cooke, or Doctor Cooke, as he preferred to be called, even by his closest friends, though his doctorate was in science, would now be heard. "As far as I'm concerned," he said, his eyes riveted on Karen, "I think you should have let another lawyer handle this. I talked to Harold Clark today, and he says Caroline is devastated by this tragedy. You hurt her very much when you took this guy on as a client. It's a slap in the face to her. After all she's been through, it stinks. You should find another way to work out your differences with Caroline that doesn't involve wasting taxpayer money."

This could go no further. Karen held up her hands. "Look, all of you, let me say something here."

The music stopped.

Karen's gaze swept the room, took in the stares, absorbed the hostility expressed by many. It was, as Carl had said, a hard-nosed jury.

"Carl and I came here tonight," she said, "to help Fred and Mary celebrate their twentieth anniversary. I completely understand how troubling my presence here is to some of you. I debated coming, but I can't hide, and I did want to offer my best wishes to our hosts. Perhaps it *was* a mistake to come. The death of someone we all knew is a terrible shock. Even more shocking are the circumstances surrounding that death. I have no desire to spoil this lovely party, so I'll leave."

There were some shouts of protest.

"But before I leave," Karen added, "let me tell you a couple of things. As it happens, Jack Palmer was a client of mine before this terrible incident. In all truth, I wish that wasn't the case, but it is, and I'm forced to deal with that fact. Lawyers have certain obligations to clients. And I'm a lawyer.

"This case will be months getting to court. If any of you are offended by the fact that I'm representing the man accused of killing Dan DeFauldo, I understand. If you feel more comfortable avoiding me, I understand that, too. But I'm committed to defending the man, and so I shall."

She grabbed Carl's arm and looked into his eyes. He nodded. They turned to leave. There were more shouts that they should stay, but Karen ignored them. She and Carl said their good-byes to the Hamptons and stepped out into the cool night air.

Three blocks away, Ralph Vincenzo sat in his Lexus, the car having just been bailed out of the pound by one of his lawyer's lackies, smoking cigarette after cigarette, drinking Scotch from a silver flask, staring at the darkened DeFauldo house. It was near midnight. Still no sign of the bitch.

His hand tightened around the butt of the .38 stuck in the waistband of his trousers. Jesus. All he needed was five minutes, and he'd have the goddam truth. Fuck Victor and his crazy ideas. Walk into the feds and give up? Screw that! That made no damn sense at all. Jesus! Didn't Victor realize that investors were probably already running to the feds? They'd want to know what the hell was happening. Was their money safe? They'd want the feds to drag Ralph in and answer a whole lot of questions. They were all like old women worrying about their goddam money. They were on the damn phone before Dan's body was cold. Victor should have known that.

Hell, maybe he did. Maybe he was working *with* the goddam feds. Maybe he figured, with Ralph broke, he'd make himself look good by kissing some ass. Fucking lawyers were all the same. Parasites.

He was surprised the feds hadn't come after him while he was in the drunk tank. Reports of his arrest had been in all the papers. Maybe they were just slow. Maybe they were too busy. Assholes. Still, he had to be careful. His driver's license had been yanked. Damn! Where was Caroline?

If he parked here too long, somebody would get suspicious. He'd have to leave. Make a few calls, find out where the hell she was. It was only natural that he'd want to pay respects to the widow of his recently departed partner. Nothing to be concerned about there.

He turned the key and brought the engine to life.

By morning, Ralph's burgeoning paranoia had escalated to precarious heights. Rising after an almost sleepless night, he started working the phone. Within minutes, he'd learned that Caroline was staying with some people named Harold and Lila Clark. They lived in the same development.

It was bad news. It meant that the confrontation would have to wait. He wanted no witnesses in case something went wrong.

He packed his bags, not for another trip, but for a planned move to another location—an apartment somewhere, under another name. Any minute now, the feds would be banging on his door. Of that he was sure. He needed to be somewhere else. Maybe Vegas. No, not Vegas. He couldn't leave Palm Harbor until he'd talked to Caroline. No way.

Showered, dressed but unshaved, his suitcase packed, he drove to the Lexus dealer in Tampa and made a deal to get out of the lease for four thousand dollars in cash. Then he walked three blocks, suitcase in hand, and purchased a used Ford. He drove the Ford back to Palm Harbor and rented a small apartment near the corner of Alternate Nineteen and Alderman Road.

Taking a chance, he drove back to his condo, loaded up the Ford with some electronic gear, a TV, and the rest of his clothes, looking furtively over his shoulder the entire time. His answering machine was blinking, but he refused even to listen to the messages.

He drove back to the newly rented apartment. He arranged for some rented furniture, then hunkered down in his new digs, awaiting Caroline's expected return to her house.

In just a few days, Ralph had descended down a dark ladder into a bizarre new world of near-madness. He was drinking heavier now, eating less, and it showed. A small tremor had started in his right hand, and his eyes seemed to burn constantly. He looked like a man on the edge.

Twelve

Judge Joe Brown was, in the purest sense, a woman-hater. His enmity toward women oozed from every pore of his lumpy, ugly body. He felt justified in his hatred of women. He'd never met one yet who'd treated him right, not even his mother. Perhaps because of that, or his repulsive appearance, or his glaring insensitivity, the judge's relationships with women were abject failures. Three marriages had ended in divorce after embarrassingly short periods. He considered his posture toward women as a fair return.

And he *was* ugly. His pig-eyed round face was topped by a skull covered with large blotches that also marred his grotesquely huge cheeks and jowls, folds of hanging flesh the color of rotting whitefish. A heavy smoker, he coughed constantly, spitting up huge globs of phlegm that he hacked into a series of white handkerchiefs. There were times when his coughing spasms would bring a worried bailiff to his side, thinking the judge was about to suffer a seizure. The red-faced judge would angrily wave the bailiff away.

He was, in a word, disgusting.

His feelings toward Karen were a step beyond hate. She and the judge had tangled several times during his eleven-year tenure on the bench. Brown was hard put to disguise his loathing for her. For one thing, she reminded him of his second wife. For another, she was responsible for a high percentage of the judge's reversals, the worst in the entire Sixth Judicial District.

But the judge had friends. Discreet efforts to have the sixty-two-year-old jurist retire early fell on deaf ears. Anything of an official nature was certainly doomed to failure, for judges were rarely recalled unless they took bribes or committed other acts of outright malfeasance. Simple bad judgment was not, in and of itself, grounds for recall. Lawyers not in his good books, and that was most of them, were resigned to waiting him out. Five years ago, most had expected the wait to be a few years or less. He had fooled them all. Now, all bets were off.

On this bright sunny morning, the judge looked particularly insipid as he sat behind the bench in the crowded courtroom, his eyes bloodshot, the puffy bags beneath them a sour-looking purple color. He was angry. Karen was not going to be here to face the humiliation she deserved, in front of a room full of reporters. Instead, she was being represented by a puffed-up asshole Judge Brown hadn't seen in his courtroom in years.

He suffered a coughing spasm, spit into a handkerchief, drank some water, then glared at Brander Hewitt.

"You have a motion, Counselor?"

"I do, Your Honor."

"Let's hear it."

Brander walked to the lectern and stood behind it, looking dignified and outraged at the same time. "I ask Your Honor to dismiss Mr. Walsingham's motion on the grounds of relevancy. I have brought with me the incoming telephone records from the offices of Hewitt, Sinclair. These records prove that a telephone call initiated by Mr. Jack Palmer was received at our office, at which time Mr. Palmer asked Ms. Perry-Mondori to represent him. Since Mr. Palmer was in jail at the time the telephone call was made, it would have been impossible for Ms. Perry-Mondori to solicit him as a client. That being the case, the claim that Ms. Perry-Mondori sought out this case because of personal considerations is quite impossible."

Judge Brown looked at Jonathan. "Counselor?"

"Your Honor," Jonathan said in his booming, senatorial voice, "we have not claimed that Ms. Perry-Mondori solicited this case. We are claiming that had Caroline DeFauldo not been one of the victims who suffered at the hands of Jack Palmer, Ms. Perry-Mondori would not have *accepted* this case.

"Mr. Palmer has no money. He can't afford an attorney. But rather than allow Mr. Palmer to be defended by a public defender, Ms. Perry-Mondori took the case pro bono. Ms. Perry-Mondori has never before accepted a client charged with first-degree murder on a pro bono basis. Her pattern is firmly established. We submit that had there been no affair between Mrs. De-Fauldo and Dr. Mondori, Ms. Perry-Mondori would have refused to take *this* case as well. Her only motivation, therefore, is to use the criminal justice system as a venue for her threatened retaliation against Mrs. De-Fauldo."

Brander stood up. "Your Honor—"

Judge Brown waved a disdainful hand. "Sit down, Mr. Hewitt. I'm not going to waste time arguing the motion before we've heard the evidence. Mr. Hewitt, your motion is denied. Mr. Walsingham, call your first witness."

Jonathan smiled broadly, then said, "We call Mrs. Caroline DeFauldo."

Caroline stood up. She was blond, blue-eyed, and

beautiful, her soft hair bouncing off her shoulders, her high breasts stirring provocatively beneath a plain white blouse visible beneath the dark suit. Every eye in the room focused on her as she took the oath, then sat in the witness chair. Jonathan took his position at the lectern.

"Mrs. DeFauldo, would you tell the Court what happened on the evening of December fourteenth, two years ago?"

Caroline cleared her throat, then said, "Yes. I was visiting my husband at Morton Plant Hospital in Clearwater. He'd just undergone an operation for a herniated disc. He was lying in his hospital bed when a nurse came in and said she needed to do some tests. She said it would take about fifteen minutes. I stepped out into the hall to wait.

"While I was standing there, Dr. Mondori saw me. We'd been friends for some time, and it was because of that friendship that Dan ... my late husband ... wanted Dr. Mondori to perform the operation. Anyway, Dr. Mondori suggested I wait in his office, which was just down the hall. I agreed.

"Once we were in his office, he asked me if I wanted a drink. I said sure. So he fixed drinks and then sat down beside me on the sofa. He said Dan was recovering well and would be fine in a few weeks. Then he said Dan wouldn't be able to have sex for about a month, until the muscles in his back healed. He laughed and said I was going to really suffer.

"I asked him what he meant, and he said he could tell I was hot. He said he was, too, and that his wife was kind of a cold fish. And then he kissed me."

She brought a tissue to her face and wiped a tear from her eye. "It was a time when Dan and I were having marital troubles. I was very vulnerable, and when

Dr. Mondori kissed me, I . . . well, I just lost it. I kissed him back. The next thing I knew, he got up and locked the door, turned off the lights except for a small lamp on his desk, then started taking off his clothes. I did the same. We made love on the sofa. It was a spur-of-the-moment thing. I'm not proud of it. But it happened."

Jonathan looked properly sympathetic. "While you were in the doctor's office, did his telephone ring?"

"Yes it did."

"Did he answer it?"

"Yes."

"Then what happened?"

"He talked for a few moments, hung up the phone, and then we continued making love."

"How long did all this take?"

"About fifteen minutes."

"Then what happened?"

"Dr. Mondori got dressed. He said he had to run. He left the office. I dressed in a hurry and left a few minutes after he did."

"Did you and Dr. Mondori continue this affair?" Jonathan asked.

"No. Dr. Mondori called me a couple of times, asking me to meet him, but I refused."

"As a result of this incident, did you and your late husband sever your friendship with the Dr. and Ms. Perry-Mondori?"

"No. We couldn't. It would look bad. People would ask questions. So we just went along as if nothing had happened."

"Did you ever tell your husband?"

"No. I was ashamed. I didn't want to hurt him. I was afraid that telling him would create problems. As I said, we'd had problems from time to time, but we'd always managed to work them out. We really tried to make our marriage work. And we succeeded."

"So, it is your testimony that two years ago, you and Dr. Mondori made love in his office, and no one was ever the wiser. Is that correct?"

"Not exactly."

"Would you explain?"

"Yes. About a month ago, Dan and I and Carl and Karen were playing tennis in a round-robin tournament at the club. After the tournament, I went to the women's locker room for a shower. Karen was there. We were alone. She told me that Dr. Mondori had told her about the incident the night before the tournament. I guess he felt guilty or something."

Brander was on his feet. "Objection! Hearsay."

Judge Brown scowled. "I don't see Ms. Mondori's name on your witness list, Counselor. Does that mean she's not going to be here to testify?"

"Her name is Ms. *Perry*-Mondori, Your Honor. Since this entire matter is a figment of the witness's imagination, I have advised—"

The judge smiled. "In that case, your objection is overruled."

"Your Honor!"

"Sit down, Counselor. The witness may continue."

Jonathan smiled, then said, "Go on, Mrs. DeFauldo."

"Karen told me that she would get even somehow. She said she didn't care how long it took, but that she'd find a way. She really frightened me. I tried to tell her what had happened, but she walked out. We haven't talked to each other since."

Jonathan waved a hand at Brander and said, "I have nothing further."

Judge Brown nodded at Brander, who stood up. "Mrs. DeFauldo," Brander said, "were there any witnesses to either the alleged sexual intercourse with Dr. Mondori or the alleged confrontation with Ms. Perry-Mondori?"

Caroline bristled with anger. "It's not alleged. It's what happened."

"Please answer the question."

"There were no witnesses."

"None at all?"

"No."

"I see. Have you had other affairs, Mrs. DeFauldo?"

Jonathan was on his feet with an objection. "Irrelevant, Your Honor."

"Sustained."

Brander gave the judge a look, then said, "After you left Dr. Mondori's office two years ago, did you go back to your husband's room?"

"Yes."

"Was the nurse still there?"

"No."

"I see. And up until a month ago, you were unaware that Ms. Perry-Mondori knew of the encounter. Is that your testimony?"

"Yes."

"You said that Dr. Mondori took off his clothes after he locked the door. Is that correct?"

"Yes."

"He was completely naked?"

"Yes."

"And you also took off your clothes. Is that correct?"

"Yes."

"This took place at what time of day?"

"It was about eight in the evening."

"I see. And the lamp on his desk was turned on, is that correct?"

"Yes."

"Do you remember how you were dressed that night?"

"No."

"Do you remember if you were wearing panty hose?"

"I always wear panty hose."

"I see. So you removed them."

"Of course."

"You said that you were vulnerable at that particular time, that you and your husband were having marital problems. What exactly was the source of those problems?"

Again, Jonathan objected. "Relevance."

"Sustained."

Brander's cheeks flushed. "Your Honor, the witness testified on direct examination that—"

Judge Brown pointed a fat finger at Brander. "I said the objection was sustained, Counselor. Move along."

Brander shook his head. "I have no more questions at this time, Your Honor. I'd like to reserve the right to recall this witness at a later time."

Judge Brown looked at Caroline and smiled. "You may step down, but stay available."

Caroline returned to her seat beside Jonathan.

"Call your next witness."

Jonathan nodded. "We call Brenda Havlock."

A large woman in her forties took the oath and the stand. Jonathan asked, "Ms. Havlock, please tell the Court your occupation."

"I'm a registered nurse."

"Thank you. And were you on duty at Morton Plant Hospital on the night of December fourteenth, two years ago?"

"I was."

"At about eight in the evening on the night in question,

did you administer some tests to a patient named Daniel DeFauldo?"

"I did."

"Was Mrs. DeFauldo in the room when you arrived to do the tests?"

"Yes."

"Did you suggest that she wait outside the room?"

"Yes."

"How long did these tests take?"

"About ten minutes."

"And did anything unusual happen?"

"Yes. I noticed that the patient's temperature was elevated. I went to Dr. Mondori's office to tell him about it, but his door was locked."

"Does the doctor normally lock the door to his office?"

"Only when he's not in the hospital."

"And he was there that night?"

"Yes."

"How do you know?"

"Because I had him paged. He arrived at the patient's room about five minutes later."

"And did you see Mrs. DeFauldo again?"

"Yes. As I was walking down the hall to attend to my next patient, she was coming toward me. It looked to me as if she was coming from Dr. Mondori's office."

"Thank you. That's all I have, Your Honor."

Judge Brown raised an eyebrow, then turned to Brander. "You may inquire, Counselor."

Brander pulled a file folder from his attaché case, opened it, and left it on the table. He faced the witness and said, "You have a most remarkable memory, Ms. Havlock. Your recall of details that occurred two years ago is incredible."

"Just ask your questions," the judge bellowed.

Brander nodded. "Ms. Havlock, you testified that on the night of December fourteenth, you administered tests to Mr. DeFauldo. Is that correct?"

"Yes."

"And you remember the events quite clearly?"

"Yes."

"How many patients were in your care that night?"

"Perhaps twenty."

"Twenty. Can you tell me the name of the patient you attended immediately before seeing Mr. De-Fauldo?"

She blushed, then said, "No."

"You said that you saw Mrs. DeFauldo coming from the direction of Dr. Mondori's office after you'd finished your work with Mr. DeFauldo, correct?"

"Yes."

"You testified you were on your way to see another patient. Can you tell me the name of that patient?"

There was a pause, then, "No."

Brander looked angry. "Then how is it that you remember so clearly your attending to Mr. DeFauldo, but none of the others?"

"Because I was looking for the doctor and his office door was locked."

"And that stuck in your memory?"

"Yes."

"Have you discussed your testimony with Mr. Walsingham prior to this morning?"

The woman looked at Jonathan, then said, "Well, he did come and see me and asked questions. But he never told me what to say."

"Did he refresh your memory in any way?"

"No."

Brander turned to face the judge. "May I approach the witness, Your Honor?"

"You may."

Brander handed the witness a document. "Would you tell the Court what this document is?"

"Yes. It's a patient chart."

"And whose chart is this?"

"It's Mr. DeFauldo's chart."

"If it please the Court, Respondent's Exhibit Number One, Your Honor."

"So noted."

Brander had the exhibit marked, then gave it back to the witness. "On page five, there is a notation signed by you. Would you read that please?"

She went through the file, found the notation, and said, "It says I notified Dr. Mondori of the patient's elevated temperature."

"And there is a note of the time. Please read that."

"It says eight-twelve p.m."

"And immediately under that notation, there is another line. Please read that line."

"It's a notation by Dr. Mondori. He prescribed Tylenol, a thousand milligrams."

"And the time?"

"It says eight-sixteen P.M."

Brander smiled. "You said you had the doctor paged, and that he showed up in Mr. DeFauldo's room within five minutes. Are you sure about that?"

"Yes."

"So, when Dr. Mondori arrived, you were both in the room with Mr. DeFauldo. Did you make the notation on the chart while the doctor examined the patient?"

"Yes."

"And four minutes later, Dr. Mondori made his notation, after examining the patient, correct?"

"Yes."

"Read the line under Dr. Mondori's notation."

"It says I administered one thousand milligrams of Tylenol."

"And the time?"

"8:18 P.M."

"I see. So you gave Tylenol to Mr. DeFauldo, then left the room. Was that when you saw Mrs. De-Fauldo?"

"Yes."

"So that would be sometime after 8:18, correct?"

"Yes."

"Thank you, Ms. Havlock."

Judge Brown looked confused. He told the witness to step down, then said to Jonathan, "Call your next witness."

"That's all we have, Your Honor."

"Very well."

Brander was on his feet. "Your Honor, I renew my—"

"Denied. Call your first witness, Mr. Hewitt."

Brander took a deep breath, then said, "I call Dr. Carl Mondori."

The courtroom door opened and Carl walked in, tall and straight. Behind him came a young man pushing what looked like a shopping cart filled with document boxes. As Carl took the oath, the young man placed the document boxes on Brander's table, then left. As Carl took the witness stand, Bander opened the boxes and removed the contents. He began piling file folders in four stacks on the table, each stack over a foot high. Judge Brown's eyes seemed to be bugging out of his head.

Brander smiled, then faced Carl. "Dr. Mondori," he said, "have you, at any time in your life, had sexual intercourse with Caroline DeFauldo?"

"No."

He looked at the judge. "May I approach the witness?"

Judge Brown, still staring at the stacks of documents, rubbed his forehead, then said, "Go ahead."

Brander handed Carl some documents. "Would you real the passages I have highlighted in the document marked Respondent's Exhibit Number Two?"

Carl leafed through the document. "Yes. It's a notation signed by myself that says I prescribed two milligrams of Ativan to a patient named Rose McCalley on the night of December fourteenth, two years ago."

"And what time is noted?"

"The time noted is 8:03 P.M."

"And beneath that notation is another. Would you read that, please?"

"Yes. It's a notation by a nurse. She administered the drug at 8:06 P.M."

"And the nurse's name?"

"Betty Clover."

"Thank you. Now, in the—"

Judge Brown waved a hand in the air. "Hold it! The witness may step down temporarily. I'll see counsel in chambers."

The two lawyers took their seats in the judge's chambers. The court reporter extended the spindly legs of her shorthand machine and prepared to take down the official record. Judge Brown lit a forbidden cigarette and turned on a large fan to disperse the smoke.

"This has gone far enough," the judge grumbled. "There may or may not have been a sexual liaison between Dr. Mondori and Mrs. DeFauldo. I don't know. The evidence is pretty muddy. She says one thing, he says another. There are no witnesses to corroborate

Mrs. DeFauldo's claim of malice on the part of Ms. Mondori."

"*Perry*-Mondori," Brander corrected, his eyes sparkling with anger.

"Whatever. Women with three and four names are a pain in the ass." He looked at the stenographer, who nodded.

"And," the judge continued, "if I let Mr. Hewitt continue to display his talent for detailing the mundane, we'll be here forever.

"I'm the judge assigned to the Palmer case. I have complete confidence that I'll be able to discern whether or not Ms. Mondori is properly representing her client or engaging in some bullshit catfight. You'll have to leave that to me, Jonathan. That's all there is to it. We've wasted enough time. The motion to have Ms. Mondori removed from the case is denied. If you have a problem with that, Jonathan, take it wherever you like. In the meantime, both of you can get the hell out of my chambers. I've got a busy day ahead."

Thirteen

It was Karen's turn to give Brander a hug when he returned to the office in triumph.

"Thank you," she said softly.

Brander shook his head. "Don't thank me. I've succeeded in pouring salt into an open wound, that's all. Judge Brown will be really out to get you now. The man is demented."

"No harm done. He's been after me and every female attorney for years. Maybe this will finally drive him over the edge."

"One can hope. But let me warn you about Caroline, Karen. She's formidable, and very convincing on the stand. You said you didn't think she was clever enough to have engineered this attempt to get you off the case. I disagree. You'd be well advised to reassess your opinion of her."

Out of the corner of her eye, she saw a weary Colin enter the pit. She waved him to her office. "I've got to go," she said to Brander. "Thanks again, and I'll do as you suggest."

Colin was half asleep in the chair when Karen entered her office. Judging from his rumpled appearance and the weary look in his eyes, Karen figured he'd been working nonstop since Friday. Associates had a habit of doing that.

"So, how are you making out?" she asked.

"I hear we're still on the case," he said.

"We are, indeed."

"Well, I've managed to uncover a few nuggets you might find interesting," he said, smiling proudly. "I have to warn you, though. I haven't had time to write a report. All I have are my rough notes."

Karen held up the coffeepot. "Like some?"

He shook his head. "No more. I've been living on the stuff. I'm getting very jumpy."

She took her position behind her desk and looked at him sternly. "How much sleep have you had in the last forty-eight hours?"

"Not much, but it's okay."

"No, it isn't. I know I asked you to do this, and I appreciate the effort, but there's a limit. From here, you go home and get some sleep. You look exhausted. Don't think I'm being kind. I'm not. Tired people make mistakes, and we can't afford any."

His look was that of a man whose life sentence had just been commuted to probation.

"So . . . what have you got?" she asked.

He leafed quickly through his notes, three legal pads filled with them. "First, and probably most important," he said excitedly, "I talked to a security guy over at the Tarpon campus by the name of Wallace. He saw two people necking in a car on October 28, at 10:08 in the evening. He was going to tell them to leave and then thought better of it. I guess he's a romantic. He figured they were a couple from one of the adult classes."

His tired eyes managed a twinkle. "But he did write down the tag number, just in case it wasn't so innocent."

Karen could feel the adrenaline start to surge through her veins. "And?"

"The car is an Acura, registered to none other than Caroline DeFauldo."

Karen leaned forward. "Did he see any faces?"

"No. It was night, and the windows of the Acura were tinted. But it has to be them, doesn't it?"

Karen shrugged. "It doesn't *have* to be them, but it's reasonable to assume it *was* them." She rubbed her hands together. "You did well, Colin. What time did class break up?"

"Ten," he answered. The guard says that the car was gone on his second pass, which was about forty minutes later."

Karen beamed. "Very good. What else?"

"Well, I've talked to about twenty of the people who attended the classes. Most of them say they noticed that Caroline and Palmer were pretty friendly, but there was no touching or feeling going on. Just a lot of looks. Sure, there are some who claim the two were having an affair, but it's just gossip. There's not a shred of evidence to support their claims. I still have others to talk to. We'll see.

"And I talked to six families in the general area of the DeFauldo house. Three of them say they heard gunshots being fired, but only one called 911."

Again, he consulted his rough notes. "The DeFauldos live at 2773 Bridgemont Way. Mr. and Mrs. Paul Hendershot live in the house right next to them, 2765. Paul Hendershot says he heard three to five shots, all in quick succession. He called 911 almost immediately. The house on the other side, at 2785, is empty. The people who own it are in Europe on vacation. Name is Corwell. Older couple.

"Then, there were two neighbors across the street who also heard the shots. One says he thought he heard five or six shots, but wasn't sure. The other neighbor says there might have been eight shots. Both thought at first they were hearing firecrackers. They didn't call the police in case it was a false alarm. Apparently, there are some kids in that area who like to raise hell."

Karen knew that was certainly true. "Okay, what else?"

"I talked to two men who played poker with Dan De-Fauldo that night. They said he was losing and pretty upset about it. He left at ten-thirty, which was quite unusual. So was the fact that he was losing. He usually wins, but even when he loses, he almost never gets upset. And he never leaves that early."

"Never?"

"According to the two I talked to, Dan was almost always the last to leave, and that was usually between two and three in the morning."

Karen nodded. "That's great stuff, Colin. Anything else?"

"I have lots more, but it's just background stuff."

"What about the DeFauldos?"

"Well, the neighbors were quite willing to talk about the sounds of the gunshots, but they clammed up about anything else. All they'd say was that the DeFauldos were fine people, blah, blah, blah. They seem to be well liked. I guess I'm not as charming as you'd hoped. I'm sorry about that."

She smiled at him. "Keep trying. You're bound to find some gossipy people soon enough."

"I hope you're right. As far as the credit agencies are concerned, there's nothing much there. The usual stuff. I don't have the contacts to dig much deeper. Maybe you'd better hire a private investigator for the background stuff."

"Okay. It may come to that."

"As for Mr. DeFauldo's business dealings, that was

on my list for today. His office was closed Friday. The sign on the door says it will be open Tuesday. What with his partner being arrested for drunk driving, that will complicate matters, but I checked. Mr. Vincenzo is out on bail. As soon as I've grabbed some sleep, I'll go over to his house. I have the address. And I still have to check out the restaurant."

"There's plenty of time," Karen said.

Colin nodded. "Did you read the morning paper?"

"I did."

"I think it's a bit odd that she had him cremated. Odder still that there's no funeral."

Karen tapped a pencil on her desk. "I agree with you. It's odd, but it happens. The press is implying that Caroline is too distraught to function, but we know that isn't true. Brander says she was as sharp as a tack this morning. There's no memorial service scheduled, either. At least not for now. Caroline is still staying at the home of a friend."

"She's functioning pretty damn well," Colin said. "When I drove by the DeFauldo house this morning, there were three vans parked in the drive. I stopped and talked to the workers. They say Caroline made the arrangements to have the house fixed up herself."

Karen felt a sudden surge of adrenaline. "Really? That *is* interesting."

Colin beamed. "I thought you might think so."

"Well, with the body released and the house no longer off limits, the investigation must be complete. That means the autopsy report should be available."

"I hope you don't mind," Colin said tentatively, "but I inquired with the ASA's office as soon as I got in. I talked to Brad Keats and told him I was assisting you. He said most of the file was ready, so I sent a messenger down to pick it up.

Karen's eyebrows shot up. "I'm impressed. You learn fast," she said, pleased. "Putting you in the second chair was my best idea in weeks."

"Thanks, Karen."

"Okay. Go home. Get some sleep. I'll see you in the morning."

Colin, almost bursting with pride, left the office. Karen smiled. The compliment she'd given him was earned. He was doing a terrific job.

When the messenger delivered the file, Karen was surprised by its heft. Though it had been just days since the death of Dan DeFauldo, the file was already almost an inch thick. Even in this age of hi-tech electronics, the major bureaucracies still devoured paper at an extraordinary pace. Were it not for the fact that most used recycled paper, the various government agencies could justly be accused of being responsible for the deaths of thousands of American trees in any given week.

Karen started going through the file. It included the preliminary statements given by Jack Palmer and Caroline DeFauldo taken within minutes of the arrival of sheriff's deputies; a formal statement given later by Caroline DeFauldo; a report on her medical examination; a report by the Crime Scene Unit, including photographs taken at the scene; a report by Detective Simms complete with interview with Lucille and Paul Hendershot, the neighbors who had first called 911. There was also the autopsy report, complete with photos, on the examination of the body of Dan DeFauldo. Transcripts of both 911 telephone calls were included.

As usual, Assistant State Attorney Brad Keats was being graciously complaisant, at least in these initial stages. He'd attached a note saying that additional material would be sent to Karen as soon as it became available.

Karen read the autopsy report file. It was filled with stunning surprises.

Dan DeFauldo had died from injuries caused by a hollow-point slug that had ripped through his aorta. Death had been almost instantaneous. A total of four hollow-point .380 slugs were found in the body; one in the chest, one in the abdomen, and two in the head. Another wound was found in the upper right leg, but the bullet had exited the leg and was later found underneath the body.

The wound to the aorta had been the fatal shot. DeFauldo was already dead when the two slugs smashed into his head. No powder residue was found on the body. Not anywhere.

From an analysis of the blood spatters, the slug paths, and surrounding tissue, it was determined that the first shot to penetrate the body entered the leg. The second shot to penetrate entered the abdomen. The third was the aorta wound. Those three shots, plus the two that hit the wall, were fired from a position estimated to be three feet above the floor directly in front of the fireplace, about ten feet away from the victim.

The two shots to the head, one directly through the right eye, the other two centimeters below the eye and one centimeter to the right of the nose, were presumed to have been fired from a position above the victim. All heart activity had stopped, which meant the first of the head shots was fired at least thirty seconds after the shot that struck the aorta. The victim, already dead, had to be lying on the floor.

There was no powder residue on the head.

The neighbors had heard but one series of shots. How was that possible? And Jack Palmer had said nothing about shooting Dan in the head. What was going on here?

Her adrenaline pumping, Karen used a yellow marking pen to highlight the section, then read on.

One of the head shots had gone through Dan De-Fauldo's glasses. Two small fragments of plastic were found imbedded in the brain at the site of the slug coming to rest. They were assumed to have been captured by the slug as it passed through the glasses. Another smaller fragment of plastic was also found at the same site, and it was of a different composition. The M.E. had simply underlined the fact that it had been found. No effort had been made to positively identify any of the particles.

Karen highlighted that section as well.

All of the slugs were from bullets used in a Walther PPK, a nine-millimeter-caliber semiautomatic using the shorter, less powerful .380 bullets. Seven slugs and seven spent cartridges were accounted for, which meant the gun had been fully loaded with six in the clip and one in the barrel.

The gun found at the scene was a nickel-plated Walther PPK, serial #A074633, once a German-made weapon but now manufactured by Interarms in Alexandria, Virginia. It was identified as being the murder weapon. Latent prints found on the gun matched those of Jack Palmer. No other latents found on the gun. No latents were found on the shell casings.

Karen highlighted that section, too.

An ATF check—the Federal Bureau of Alcohol, Tobacco, and Firearms—had listed the gun as being sold a year before to an establishment called Rocky's Guns in Ocala. A request had gone to Ocala police to check with Rocky's in an attempt to determine the purchaser.

The State of Florida did not maintain records of gun sales to consumers. That was left to the dealers.

Karen leaned back in her chair as she digested this information. Bells seemed to be ringing in her ears. Warning bells.

She quickly scanned Caroline's official statement. It had been extensively expanded since the first statement was given. When Karen reached the part where Caroline explained the shooting, she read each word with care.

"He just started shooting for no reason. Dan fell to the floor. I was screaming. Jack stuck the gun in my mouth and said if I didn't shut up, he'd kill me, too. Then he looked at Dan's body. He was very agitated. He told me I was to call the police and tell them it was self-defense. I was to say that we were lovers, that Dan had found us, and that Jack had mistaken the keys in Dan's hand for a gun. He told me if I didn't go along, he'd either kill me himself or arrange for my death.

"I was terrified. I told him I would do whatever he asked. He had this evil smile on his face. Then, he went over to Dan's body and fired two shots into Dan's head. He pointed the gun at me again and told me to get dressed. He did the same. Then, he told me to call 911. I did. He kept looking out the window. As soon as he saw lights approaching, he told me to open the front door. He put the gun on the floor and stood near the fireplace beside me. The police came rushing in the front door."

Karen grabbed the crime scene photos, the ones depicting Dan DeFauldo lying on the floor, face up, in the DeFauldo living room. The full chain of keys near his hand was clearly visible. The man's white shirt and the carpet were both stained with blood. Dan's face was badly marred, but there was little blood. His glasses were askew, one lens smashed. His familiar toupee, often subject to snickering behind-the-back comments, was undisturbed.

Here was a very successful and supposedly intelligent man who wore a toupee that was so obvious as to be laughable. Karen had often wondered what the man actually saw when he looked in a mirror. Was he blind? The weatherman Willard Scott often joked about his own toupee, but when he wore it, it looked real. Dan's seemed more like roadkill.

His face was fatter than she remembered, the features more pronounced and somewhat distorted, as if the photo had been taken with a fish-eye lens. It hadn't, of course, but the camera angle made his nose larger, placed his eye sockets farther apart. She hadn't seen Dan for two months, and he'd been alive then. Now, in death, the extreme trauma of the head shots had deformed his face more than she would have expected.

She looked at another photo. The large diamond pinkie ring that everyone assumed was fake graced Dan's left hand.

There was a close-up shot of the Walther on the floor. The slide was open, meaning the gun was empty.

The Crime Scene Unit had checked for prints on the gun and the casings, and had given the house a thorough examination. Caroline had explained that a maid visited the house weekly, and had been there the day of the killing. Dan and Caroline's prints were found in only a few locations, as were Jack Palmer's. Palmer's prints were not found anywhere on the toilet he claimed he'd used. Some unidentified prints were found inside the medicine cabinet. Probably the maid's.

Karen reread that paragraph, then leaned back in her chair and thought about her conversation with Detective Simms. He'd told her the crime team had used the laser on the toilet. There was no mention of it in the report, but that was not significant. Often the reports mentioned results, not how the results were achieved.

She studied the 911 transcripts. The neighbor had been slightly tentative. Three to five shots had been fired, all in quick succession. The transcript of Caroline's call to 911 was more revealing. It read:

On Time: 2314:26   11/10

ED (Emergency Dispatcher): "This is 911. Who do you need, paramedics, police, or fire?"

CC (Calling Citizen): "I need the police."

ED: "Your location?"

CC: "2773 Bridgemont Way."

ED: "What city?"

CC: "Palm Harbor."

ED: "Hold on. I'll connect you."

Hand-off Time: 2314:54

On Time: 2314:57

PCSD (Pinellas County Sheriff's Dispatcher): "Pinellas Sheriff."

CC: "I need the police."

PCSD: "What's the problem?"

CC: "My husband has been shot."

PCSD: "What's your location?"

CC: "2773 Bridgemont Way. Palm Harbor."

PCSD: "Hold on."

Hold time: :09

PCSD: "All right. Units are already on the way. Are you all right?"

CC: "Yes."

PCSD: "Stay with me here, okay?"

CC: "Okay."

PCSD: "Is your husband breathing?"

CC: "No. He's dead."

PCSD: "Are you sure?"

CC: "I'm sure."

PCSD: "How did this happen?"

CC: "A man shot him."

PCSD: "Is the man there?"

CC: "Yes."

PCSD: "Are you in danger?"

CC: "I'm not sure."

PCSD: "Can the man hear what I'm saying?"

CC: "No."

PCSD: "Does he know you've called us?"

CC: "Yes. He said I was to call you."

PCSD: "Is he drunk or on drugs?"

CC: "I don't think so."

PCSD: "Are there any children in the house?"

CC: "No."

PCSD: "Just you and the man?"

CC: "Yes."

PCSD: "How far away is he from you?"

CC: "I don't know. About ten feet."

PCSD: "Does he have a gun?"

CC: "Yes."

PCSD: "What is the man doing?"

CC: "Just sitting on a chair. We're in the kitchen."

PCSD: "Listen carefully. If our officers come in there, are they going to be shot at?"

CC: "I don't know. I have to go now."

PCSD: "Wait! Stay with me here."

Contact Terminated: 23:17:25

They were both in the kitchen when the call was made. Jack was coolly watching Caroline call 911. Odd. Odder still, his prints had not been found in the kitchen.

Here was a man who had supposedly raped and murdered, then sat in a chair and watched as his victim called the police. And he was holding a gun that was empty. And all this immediately after putting two slugs into the head of a man already dead.

It didn't add up.

According to the hospital report, Caroline had engaged in sexual activity within a few hours prior to her being examined. There were no bruises on her body, no abrasions or lacerations in her vagina. A small amount of seminal fluid had been found, but there had been no ejaculation. The seminal fluid had been tested, and its blood type matched Jack Palmer's. Jack Palmer's skin had been found beneath Caroline's false fingernails.

There was one more thing. Two small dots of soft material found on one of the living-room tables had been determined to be candle wax.

Karen looked at her watch. Her mind was whirling, filled with a hundred unanswered questions, but they would have to wait. She was due in Family Court, having requested an emergency hearing on behalf of a man charged with murder who wanted to talk to his children on the telephone. She'd go there first; then she'd have a long talk with Jack Palmer.

If anything, Jack Palmer looked worse than he'd looked the first time Karen had seen him. There were deep pouches under his red-rimmed eyes. His sallow skin seemed lifeless as it hung on his bony face. The defeat that had marked him earlier now permeated his very being, his every move, his voice, even his breathing.

"Are you sleeping?" she asked, as they huddled together in one of the small lawyer-client conference rooms.

He shook his head.

"You should talk to the doctor. They can give you something to help you sleep."

"It won't help," he protested. "When I close my eyes, I can still see that guy standing there . . . looking at Caroline. I can still hear Caroline screaming at me. 'Shoot! Shoot! Shoot, you stupid bastard!' And I did. I can hear the gun making that awful sound. I can smell the stink of it. I can see him falling to the floor, all covered with blood. I know it was self-defense, but what the hell does it really matter? I killed a man. Jesus Christ! I'm afraid to sleep."

"You look like you're not eating, either."

"I'm not hungry."

"This is not good, Jack. You'll make yourself sick if you don't eat and sleep properly. I need your help on this case. Your kids need you, too. You can't help anyone if you become ill."

At mention of his children, his eyes showed a spark of life. "What about my kids? Ellen still won't let me talk to them."

Karen took a deep breath, then said, "I talked to your wife myself. She refuses to cooperate. So, this morning, I petitioned on your behalf in Family Court. The judge issued a show-cause order, and the summons will be delivered to your wife today. What all this really means is your wife will be required to appear in court within twenty days. I'll present your request to talk to your kids, and she'll either not show up, or show up and explain why she's doing what she's doing.

"Since I've already talked to her, I can assure you that she has no grounds to keep you from speaking to your children. Your request is sure to be granted. If she fails to comply with the court order, she'll be held in contempt and jailed until she does."

The life drained from his eyes. "If I understand you correctly, that means she can get away with this for twenty more days. Is that right?"

"I'm afraid so."

He shook his head. "I don't think I can last another twenty days. What if she still refuses even after the judge says she has to?"

"As I said, she'll be jailed, the kids will be given to HRS, and you'll talk to them immediately."

"Jesus," he said softly. "What a mess."

Karen opened her attaché case, removed the file, and placed it on top of the case. "Prosecutors are required to give defense lawyers all details pertaining to the case against a defendant. This is just some of what they've got on your case. Looking it over, I've got some questions I need to discuss with you. I need your full attention, Jack"

"Okay," he said. But his eyes seemed vacant.

"I've been going over Caroline's statement," she said. "You told me that after Dan was shot, you crawled over to his body."

He forced himself to look at her. "That's right. Did she say different?"

"I'll get to that later. You told me you were feeling nauseous. Is that right?"

"Yes. I thought I was gonna throw up all over the body. I ran to the bathroom."

"You were sick where?"

"In the toilet."

"You said you threw up several times."

"I did."

"Did any of it happen to miss the toilet?"

He thought for a moment, then said, "I don't think so. I lifted both lids and had my head halfway down the thing. I remember . . . God, it's so stupid . . . but I was worried about making a mess."

"Did you touch anything?"

He looked confused.

"I mean," she explained, "where were your hands when you were being sick?"

He sighed. "They were wrapped around the toilet. The room was spinning. I was holding on for dear life."

"Are you absolutely sure about that?"

He gave her a curious look. "Yes, I'm sure. What's the problem?"

"Nothing. What happened after you were sick?"

He thought for a moment, then said, "I flushed the toilet and washed my hands."

"And then?"

"I went back to the living room. Like I said, Caroline was dressed. She'd placed a blanket over her husband's body."

Karen took a deep breath. "When you last saw the body, it was where?"

"On the floor, like I said before. Face up. I don't understand. Why are you asking all these questions again?"

She threw him a weak smile. "Just doing my job, Jack. Details are so important. I want to make sure I have everything down. Was the body bloody?"

"Very. There was blood on his chest and his stomach. And some on his leg."

"What about his face?"

Jack seemed surprised. "His face? There was no blood on his face. In fact, he still had his glasses on. I remember I thought it weird that the glasses hadn't fallen off when he fell. His eyes were wide open. He was staring at the ceiling."

The warning bells were ringing louder now, clanging like those used on busy sea-lanes. This wreck of a man in front of her couldn't possibly be the accomplished liar he'd have to be if Caroline was telling the truth. There was nothing in Jack Palmer's past to suggest he was so violent a man. Not even his wife, as filled with bitterness as she was, has so much as hinted that Jack Palmer was a violent man. But if Jack *was* telling the truth, the cunning that had created this incredibly complex scenario for death was beyond anything Karen had ever experienced.

This was no spur-of-the-moment crime. This was a carefully planned, flawlessly executed assassination. And one impossible to pull off without help.

Karen resumed her questioning. "And the gun Dan was using? Where was it?"

"Like I told you before. It was lying beside the body. Maybe a foot away from his hand."

"Did you touch it?"

"No. I didn't touch it. I'm sure."

"Did you happen to see a set of keys?"

"Keys?"

"Yes, keys. Is it possible you could have mistaken a set of keys in Dan's hand for a gun?"

He made a face. "I know that's what Caroline said. I already told you she lied. How many times do I have to say it? It's not true. It was a gun. I swear to you. I wasn't feeling well, but I know what I saw."

Karen pressed him further. "And when you came out from the bathroom, the body was covered up. The gun as well?"

"Right."

"And then?"

"Caroline was standing there, real cool, telling me the police were coming. I got dressed, and they came in the door right then."

"She'd called the police while you were in the bathroom?"

"Yes."

"Was the front door open or closed?"

"It was . . . come to think of it, it was open."

She made a note, then said, "Let's get back to the time you spent in the bathroom. Can you remember how long you were in there?"

"Not really. I was so sick. I guess it was because I'd shot the man."

"But you said earlier you were feeling sick *before* Dan showed up."

He looked at her, then said, "That's right. I was."

"You're sure?"

He took a deep breath, exhaled, then said, "I'm sure. Look, I realize I'm not making much sense. It's hard to think. It really is."

"I'm sure," she said. "That's why you *must* get some sleep. Can you understand how important it is that your brain is running on all cylinders?"

"I guess you're right. I'll talk to the doctor. I promise."

"Good." She smiled at him. "Now, getting back to the bathroom, did you close the door when you were in there?"

"Yes. I mean . . . it was going to be gross, you know?"

"Okay. And can you tell me what you heard while you were in there?"

"You asked me that before. I couldn't hear anything. I was heaving so much."

"You're absolutely sure about this?"

"Absolutely. I heard nothing except my own sound."

"Okay. Can you tell me, and this is really important, how much time elapsed between the time you came out of the bathroom and the time the police arrived?"

He thought for a moment. "I would say about one minute. I remember I was still naked. I put on my briefs, then my socks. Then I put on my shirt and pants. Then my loafers. I was fully dressed when the police arrived. That would take about a minute."

"The bathroom has two doors, one leading to the living room, and one leading to the pool. Did you notice if the door leading to the pool was locked?"

"No. My mind was on other things."

"When you left the bathroom and returned to the living room, did you close the door behind you?"

"Oh, yeah. I always do. Turned the light off, too."

Karen nodded. "One more thing, and then we're done."

He sighed.

"You said that Caroline screamed when you were making love."

"Yes?"

"When was that again?"

He hesitated a moment, then said, "She screamed. I remember it scared the hell out of me. But before I could say anything, the light in the kitchen was on, and everything started happening."

"So she screamed immediately before the kitchen light was turned on?"

"Yes."

Karen patted his arm. "Okay. That's enough for now. Tomorrow, you'll take a polygraph test. Wednesday is your arraignment. I want you rested for both, so talk to the doctor. Promise?"

There was a touch of hostility in his voice as he said, "I said I'd talk to the doctor, and I will."

"Good," she said, rising to her feet. "I'll see you tomorrow."

She opened the door. A guard approached. And then she heard Jack's plaintive voice behind her. "Mrs. Perry-Mondori?"

She looked back into Jack's haunted eyes.

"Do you believe me?"

It was never a good idea for a defense attorney to tell a client she believed his story. In some people, it encouraged then to be creative, serving only to make the attorney's job that much more difficult. So Karen stalled. "I think it's time you called me Karen, Jack."

He would not be deterred. "Okay. Do you believe me, Karen?"

"It's not important whether I believe you or not," she said. "What's important is that this case is properly investigated. You've been given the quick shuffle. My job is to make sure you receive due process."

He shook his head. "I have to know. And I have to know now. Do you believe me?"

The hell with it. "I believe you, Jack. I believe every word. You were just as much a victim as Dan DeFauldo."

He sighed in relief.

"Hang in," she said. "Trial won't be for at least five months. That gives us plenty of time."

It was the wrong thing to say. At the sound of the words "five months," the light seemed to go out of his eyes.

"But I'm going to go for a preliminary hearing," she added quickly.

"A what?"

"A preliminary hearing. There are a lot of unanswered questions here. For example, no fingerprints were found on the shell casings. That's very unusual. And Caroline says you shot her husband in the head after he was already dead. Someone should have heard those shots. No one did. We have witnesses who will back up parts of your story. They heard only one series of noises."

"I still don't understand," Jack said. "What happens at a preliminary hearing?"

"We present the evidence we've gathered so far. Then we ask the court to order the police to reopen this investigation. And while that's being done, we'll ask that you be released. It's a long shot, but if it works, you could be out of here in a month or less."

A flicker of hope came back into his eyes. "Is there a chance?"

She hesitated for a moment, then said, "Yes."

Her eyes carefully scanned his face. "Jack, we talked about you seeing a doctor."

"I'll do it, I said I would."

"Yes, well, it's not that I don't trust you to keep your word, but I'm going to arrange for an immediate appointment with the jail psychiatrist. He's a friend of mine. It'll have more impact if the request comes from me, okay?"

He didn't look happy. "A shrink? What? you think I'm crazy?"

"Not at all. I'm no expert, but I think you're depressed. You have every right in the world to be depressed, but depression is something that needs to be treated. As I said, I need you at full strength, Jack."

He hung his head. "If you think so . . ."

"Good. I'll set it up. And Jack?"

"What?"

"When you talk to the doctor, let it all out. Hold nothing back. Okay?"

He simply nodded.

fourteen

"They tell me you haven't been eating," Dr. Philip Eisen said softly.

No answer.

Jack Palmer, embarrassed, gazed at the floor. Growing up, he'd been taught that discussing problems with a stranger was a sign of weakness in a man. And he believed it. He *was* weak. Useless, in fact. A man so stupid he'd allowed himself to be manipulated into committing murder. What did it matter that he'd been trying to protect his own life and that of the woman who'd tricked him? The police said it was murder, and that's all that counted. He was in jail, wasn't he? And even though his lawyer said she believed him, even though she'd agreed to take his case, he knew it was hopeless. Once the police said you were a murderer, that was it.

Besides, and this was the key thing, he had no money. He knew about lawyers. Lawyers needed money. He'd never thought about money when he'd called Mrs. Perry-Mondori. He'd been in such a panic, so scared. All he wanted was to get out of this terrible jail. Money hadn't even been a consideration. And while she'd agreed to take his case, he was sure she'd change her mind soon enough. Once she realized how hopeless his case was, she'd drop him like a hot rock.

Why should a woman like her waste time on a loser who couldn't pay her fee?

He'd eventually be given a public defender who didn't really give a damn. Why should he?

Damn it all. He was so stupid.

"They tell me you haven't been eating," the doctor repeated.

Jack looked at the man, his expression blank. The doctor seemed friendly enough. The room was small, not much bigger than Jack's cell. Except it had chairs and a desk and a phone. And a window.

Outside the window, Jack could hear and see cars driving by, people talking—free people, able to come and go as they pleased. Not Jack. He was locked in here like some animal in a cage. Couldn't even talk to his kids. Ellen had turned her back on him, refused to let him hear the voices of his children. And why not? He'd cheated on her, something he'd promised never to do, something he'd never *intended* to do.

But Caroline had been so sweet, so flattering, so understanding, so incredibly beautiful. And when she'd told him she wanted him to make love to her, he'd felt like a real man for the first time in his life.

It had all been a lie. He deserved his fate. Stupid people deserved what they got. That was the way the world worked.

"Jack?"

"Yes?"

For the third time, the doctor tried to penetrate the almost visible barrier between himself and his patient. His face showed no emotion as he addressed this obviously disturbed man. "They tell me you haven't been eating."

At last, Jack's attention focused on the doctor. "Oh. Yeah. Well, I'm not very hungry."

"You have to eat."

"I guess."

The doctor smiled. "Why don't you tell me how you feel?"

Jack looked at him as if he were the crazy one. "You want to know how I feel?"

"Yes."

"What difference does it make?"

"I'm interested in helping you, Jack."

"Why?"

"Because you're in here, because you're not eating, not sleeping, because you're frightened. I want to help you deal with it. If you tell me how you feel, I think I can help you."

Jack threw him a bitter smile. "No one can help me."

"Why do you say that?"

"Because it's the truth," Jack said apathetically. "I made a stupid, stupid mistake. My life is as good as over. My wife is going to divorce me. I guess she should. Not much point staying married to me. I'll probably never see my kids again. I have no money and no future. I'll probably spend the rest of my life in prison if they don't execute me. They may as well do it. It really doesn't matter anymore."

The doctor wrote something on a small notepad. "What was the mistake, Jack?"

Jack hesitated. "It was more than one, I guess."

"Can you tell me the worst one? The one that landed you in here?"

Jack sighed. "I was a fool. I let a woman trick me into killing her husband."

"How did that happen?"

Jack shrugged.

"Can you tell me about it?" the doctor asked.

"Why?"

"Because I'd like to know."

Jack grimaced. "Do I have to talk to you? I mean, is it a law or something?"

The doctor shook his head. "Are you uncomfortable talking with me?"

"Yes."

"Why?"

"Because I don't like talking about myself. Especially now. I never liked to talk about myself, and then, the one time I did, it got me in here."

The doctor nodded. "I see. Well, I'm supposed to make a report, Jack. I'm also trying to help you. If you don't talk to me, I'll not be able to do either of those things. The people I work for will be unhappy. Your lawyer will be unhappy. And when they get unhappy, they take it out on me. Maybe you could tell me a little of what happened so I can make my report. As a favor. Could you do that?"

Jack stared at him for a moment. "I met this woman . . ."

Doctor Eisen listened as Jack haltingly told his story. The evaluation was supposed to take fifty minutes, but once Jack got talking and the fifty minutes were up, the doctor forgot about time. They were well past an hour when the doctor asked the standard questions designed to help in a determination of Jack's mental condition. It was hardly necessary. The man was a textbook example of clinical depression, a man with admitted low self-esteem to begin with, his life shattered by what had happened. After the killing and Jack's arrest, there was little left but a hollow shell.

"So," Doctor Eisen said, "you haven't been able to talk to your children at all?"

Jack shook his head.

"But Ms. Perry-Mondori went to court and had a summons issued, did she not?"

"Yes, but Ellen can sit on it for twenty days. And she will. She hates me."

"Has she ever said so in those words?"

"She's said it many times."

"Before this incident?"

"Yes."

"Why did she say she hated you before this incident?"

"She thinks I'm a loser. I work very hard, I never get drunk, I'm home whenever I'm not working, but that's not good enough for her. She wants things we can't afford. I try my best, but I don't make enough money."

"How do you feel about her?"

"I don't really know."

Dr. Eisen put down his notebook. Leaning forward, his hands clasped together, he said, "Jack, everyone makes mistakes. It's part of life."

"Not like this one."

"You think not? Let me share this with you. I'm a very happy man, Jack. I have a lovely wife and three wonderful children. I love them all very much and would never knowingly do anything to hurt them. But I'll be candid with you. If I were given the same choice you were, if I were approached by a very sexy, beautiful woman who told me she wanted me to make love to her, I might well have acted just as you did."

Jack looked stunned. "You?"

"Yes. Any man would be tempted, and very few would be able to walk away from such a proposition. And further, I think that had I been in the situation you were in, being in that house, confronted by a man with a gun in his hand, I would have reacted just as you did.

The self-preservation instinct is very strong, Jack. It's a mark of your good sense that you reacted as you did."

Jack's eyes brightened. "Really?"

"I assure you. Karen tells me she's convinced you're innocent. It wasn't so much that you made a mistake. It's more that you encountered someone who recognized your basic personality, that of a gentle, kind, caring person. Someone took advantage of you, Jack. It happens often to caring people. And from what you've told me, I'd say your future is much brighter than you think."

"Come on."

"I'm serious. I've known Karen Perry-Mondori for many years. She's an excellent attorney, one of the best criminal lawyers in the state. She believes in you, Jack. I sense you're afraid that she'll stop believing in you at some point. I assure you, if you've told the truth, and I believe you have, Karen will not rest until you're free."

Jack shook his head. "She wants me to take a lie detector test."

"Does that bother you?"

"It's just that, well, it seems to me, if she believes me . . ."

"Never try to second-guess your lawyer, Jack. If Karen wants you to take a lie detector test, it's probably because she wants to use it to build some public support for your cause."

"I never thought of it that way."

In his five years of working for the county, Dr. Eisen had seen them all; the poseurs, the pathological liars, the mentally deficient, the sociopaths, psychotics, the confused first-timers. Rarely did he encounter a man like Jack Palmer, totally vulnerable, completely open, guileless, a time virgin in the criminal cosmos. It wasn't Eisen's job to make judgments as to guilt or innocence.

It was his job to make sure the patient was mentally able to assist in his own defense.

"Karen doesn't lie to her clients, Jack. She's not going to drop you. And money is not an issue. You need to trust her, and you need to remain healthy."

Jack nodded. "If you say so."

Dr. Eisen made some notes. "I'm going to place you on medication, Jack. We won't start the complete therapy until after the lie detector test, because some of the medications can affect the results. But I am going to place you on antidepressant medication immediately."

"Antidepressants?"

"Yes. You're clinically depressed, Jack. Because of what's happened to you, there's a chemical imbalance in your brain. That imbalance can be corrected by medication."

"I don't like taking pills."

"None of us do, Jack. But if you don't start eating and take your medication voluntarily, I'll have to place you in the hospital, where you'll be fed intravenously while strapped down on the bed. Is that what you want?"

Jack hung his head. "No."

"Okay. I'm not trying to be tough on you, but it's important that you be well. You should be aware that this medication takes some time to start working, usually a couple of weeks. We can't wait for two weeks for you to start eating, now can we?"

"I guess not."

"Remember what I said about the hospital. That's not something I want to do."

"I understand."

"I'm not trying to frighten you, Jack. You'll come to my office to take your medication. I'll also set up appointments for continuing sessions. As I said before, I want to help you. I fully understand why you feel the way you do. But it doesn't have to be that way. We need to work together, Jack. Will you work with me?"

"I'll try my best."

"Good."

Dr. Eisen picked up the phone and called the guard. He shook hands with Jack, then watched as the man shuffled out of the office, the guard beside him. Dr. Eisen then placed a call to the jail commander. He asked the commander to place Jack Palmer under a suicide watch, one that was as unobtrusive as possible.

The commander assured Dr. Eisen that it would be done.

Fifteen

By the time Karen got back to her office, the mid-afternoon sky had darkened considerably, matching Karen's mood perfectly. She was becoming more angry with each passing hour.

She was fast becoming convinced her client was an innocent man. The police—driven by the usual desire to wrap up cases as quickly as possible—had been much too quick to accept Caroline's carefully constructed charade. The investigation should have been much more extensive. Karen could understand, if not appreciate, their actions, but understanding failed to cool her anger. For if Jack Palmer was innocent, Caroline DeFauldo was a liar. And if Caroline DeFauldo lied about Jack Palmer, she probably lied about Carl.

Things were beginning to come into focus. To serve her own selfish needs, Caroline DeFauldo had tried to destroy Karen's marriage. That was every bit as unforgivable as her clever, conniving scheme to murder Dan. In most people's minds, murder was the ultimate crime. To Karen, what Caroline had tried to do to Carl and her was even worse. It was personal. It was evil. It was sick. It would be avenged.

Her thoughts returned to Jack. In theory, the accused was presumed innocent until proven guilty beyond a reasonable doubt. In actual practice, it was too often just the opposite: Napoleonic law—where the accused was presumed guilty until proven innocent. It wasn't the first time the police had acted presumptuously, nor would it be the last. While there were some niggling details that might have been disturbing to a semiperfectionist, the bulk of the evidence supported Caroline's story. The state had enough to convince a jury, or so they believed, and that was all that was needed. In these days of strained budgets, the pressure to close cases sometimes squelched the urge to investigate beyond the obvious. Spending money investigating relatively minor details that may or may not support a case was a waste of taxpayers' money. In the matter of one Jack Palmer, it was being left to Karen to prove the innocence of her client, and the cost of such an investigation would be borne entirely by her firm.

As thunder and lightning boomed and flashed outside the thick plate-glass windows of her office, Karen went about the business of setting up two large portable white-faced display boards. The display boards were the kind that allowed the use of thick-tipped, water-based, ink pens in many colors, their markings easily erasable with a dry cloth. Karen often used these display boards to map out strategies, especially in complex cases with many unanswered questions. When not in use, the boards were covered by white sheets and kept in a closet.

As she worked, she was haunted by the thought that she had acted exactly as had the police. She had judged Carl guilty based purely on a statement made by Caroline. And she'd been wrong. She knew that now.

She felt ashamed. She picked up the phone and called the hospital. She was told Carl was in the operating room. She left a message.

Returning her attention to the Palmer case, she drew

a layout of the DeFauldo house on the first board, the layout copied from a sales brochure procured from the house's builder. The floor plan was a popular one, and its design, in varying elevations, was still being used throughout the area by the same building contractor.

She drew the room outlines in black ink, the furniture positions in green. She added the positions of Caroline and Jack at the time the shots were fired, their positions based on statements given to the police. She marked the position of Dan's body in yellow, and the shell casings in blue. Finally, she marked the sight lines, the path of the bullets, in orange.

On the second board, she marked down the times of calls to 911, times of police unit arrivals, and other pertinent information. Then, after stepping back and admiring her handiwork, she reviewed the material sent her by Brad Keats—again.

Liz stuck her head in the door. "There's a guy on the phone for you. Won't give his name, but I think he's a cop."

"He won't give his name?"

"Nope. You want me to put it through?"

Karen shrugged, then said, "Okay."

She recognized the voice immediately. "This conversation never took place, understand?"

"Okay."

"Got a call from the feds. They've had some complaints from nervous investors about a company called Vinde Investments. Ring any bells?"

"It sure does."

"Well, we're talkin' real money here. Millions. The feds are trying to find Ralph Vincenzo. It seems some investors are worried about the money they placed with Dan DeFauldo before he was killed, so the feds went to see Ralph. Couldn't find him. When they talked to his secretary, she said he was off to France to close a really big deal when DeFauldo was killed. She says he's been back since, but she can't find him, either. She says the French deal might have been less than kosher because Ralph wouldn't let her type the papers like he usually does.

"So now the feds are really curious, but they can't find Ralph. He's closed the office, moved out of his condo, and turned his car back into the dealer. The feds can't figure out if the money is still here or not, but the guess is it's long gone with Vincenzo."

"Very interesting," Karen said.

"I thought you'd think so. The feds want our help in finding Vincenzo, but if he's flown the coop, I have no idea how we're supposed to find him. I dunno if it means anything, but I thought you should know."

"I really appreciate your letting me know," she said. "Does that mean—"

"It means," Charlie Simms said, "that I still think your guy did it. But maybe he was working for somebody, you know? Maybe he was working for Vincenzo. If that's the case, maybe he could talk to us, help us out a little, make himself a deal. That's all I was thinking. Unofficially, that is. Like I said, I never made this call."

Karen almost laughed out loud. "You think my client and Ralph are connected?"

"It's a possibility."

"And you think my client killed Dan DeFauldo for money? Is that what you're saying?"

"I'm saying you should talk to him, that's all."

"Listen to me," she said firmly. "I don't know Ralph Vincenzo from a hole in the ground, but I do know my client. Not as well as I should, perhaps, but I know him. There's no way on God's earth he would kill a man unless it was in self-defense. There's also no way he would even know Ralph Vincenzo. Ralph and Jack live in different solar systems.

"But," she said, her voice almost a whisper, "have you considered the possibility that Caroline DeFauldo and Ralph Vincenzo might be working together?"

There was silence for a moment, and then the line went dead.

Karen hung up the phone and sat at her desk thinking about what had just transpired. Had she heard right? Charlie was no fool He couldn't possibly think that Jack Palmer was Ralph Vincenzo's paid assassin. But he'd called. What was he really trying to tell her?

Her mind whirling, she asked Liz to come into her office. Liz had her steno pad ready.

"I want you to phone Tallahassee and request a copy of the incorporation papers for Vinde Investments."

"Okay."

"Then I want you to place some classified personal ads in both local papers. Make them blind ads, with a P.O. box. That should keep the kooks at bay. In the first one, I want anyone who has ever done business with Vinde to contact us. In the second, I want anyone who has sold a Walther PPK privately during the last six months to come forward. Offer a reward. Say a thousand dollars. Make it contingent. You know the drill."

Liz nodded. "Anything else?"

"No. That's it."

As soon as Liz went back to her desk, Karen picked up the phone and placed a call to a private investigator named Bill Castor. Castor was an ex-cop, a fine detective who'd worked on many of Karen's cases. Karen liked and trusted him.

"I was wondering when you'd call," he said when he

came on the line. "I've been following this Palmer thing on the tube. Looks like you could use some help."

"I can use all the help I can get," she said. "The problem is this one is pro bono. I have no budget. So I'll only be able to use you where it's absolutely essential."

"I understand," he said. "So what can I do for you?"

"I need deep background information on three people: Dan and Caroline DeFauldo, and Ralph Vincenzo. Everything you can get. I've got an associate collecting the public stuff, so don't waste your time on that. What I'm after is the buried treasure."

There was a pause. "You've got no budget."

"Exactly."

"Are you saying you want this off the clock?"

"No," Karen said. "I want it legit. Just try to keep it as low as you can."

He chuckled. "You always were a stickler. Okay. I'm on it."

When Colin arrived at the office, it was nearly four in the afternoon. He looked refreshed.

"Come in here," Karen commanded.

Colin did as he was told and stood staring at the display boards, then smiled at Karen. "We're going to solve the crime, right?"

Karen grinned. "We're going to get the known facts straight in our minds," she said. "Then, we're going to examine and explore the unknown."

"Sounds interesting."

"Let's hope. Ready?"

"Ready," he said, his voice filled with enthusiasm.

"First," she said, "let us assume that Jack Palmer is lying."

Colin gave her a worried look.

"For the purposes of this exercise," she added.

"Oh. I get it. Okay."

Karen stood by the first board and pointed to the front door. "All right. Jack Palmer appears at Caroline's door at approximately eleven o'clock on the evening of November tenth. He points a gun at Caroline and tells her to disarm the alarm system. He is obviously aware of how the system works because he tells her not to simply turn it off, but to enter the code that will disarm it. Caroline does as she is told."

Colin nodded.

Karen held up a finger. "First question: Is it possible Jack Palmer would know about security systems?"

Colin thought for a moment, then said, "Sure. There are so many of them around, most people would know how they operate. But he'd have no way of knowing if she had entered the right code. With a gun in her face, she probably would."

"Why?"

"Because that's the proper procedure," he said. "While the people who sell the systems don't always make it clear, the police advise homeowners that, in a situation such as this, the best thing you can do is follow instructions. Home invaders can go crazy if the cops show up. Your chances of staying alive are better if you cooperate, as horrible as that may be."

Karen was impressed. "So you think Caroline's statement relating to the security system is credible."

"To a jury? Yes."

"Okay," Karen said. "Next, Jack takes Caroline to the area in front of the roaring fireplace, tells her to take off her clothes, and proceeds to rape her. According to Caroline's statement, she might have mentioned during dinner that her husband was playing poker at Innisbrook with some friends. Possible?"

Again, Colin said, "Sure. I see what you're driving at. Assuming Jack knew she'd be alone in the house makes everything that follows more plausible."

"Exactly." Karen ran a hand through her hair. "What do you know about rapists?"

Colin shrugged. "Not very much."

"Tell me what you do know, no matter how insignificant."

"Well," he said, stroking his imposing chin, "as I understand it, rape is an act of violence. It's more a power thing than a sexual thing. In fact, it has little to do with sexual desire at all, contrary to popular opinion."

Karen's eyebrows shot up. "Well, well. That's very good, Colin. You'd be surprised how many law enforcement people, including judges, still don't accept that as fact. And if we assume that rape is not a sexual act, which it certainly is not, why would Jack Palmer want to rape Caroline in front of a roaring fireplace?"

"Well, on the surface, it makes no sense," Colin said. "But, when it comes to sexual assault, it's impossible to know what's running through a sick mind. Mr. Palmer might have had this crazy fantasy that needed to be played out."

Karen groaned. "Anyone ever tell you you're too damn logical?"

"Not really. Is that bad?"

She smiled. "No. But you're one hell of a devil's advocate."

"Sorry."

"Don't be. This is exactly the point of the exercise. Both Jack and Caroline agree that the sexual contact occurred there, right?"

"Right."

Karen nodded. "Most juries will have no trouble accepting Jack's choosing the fireplace setting as a rational act within the context of a rape. Agreed?"

"Agreed."

"Okay. Let's back up a little, to the time prior to the shooting. Dan DeFauldo is playing poker at Innisbrook with his regular Wednesday night group. According to the two men you talked to, Dan appeared nervous. He was losing heavily, and his friends figured his nervousness was due to his losing, even though he'd lost many times before. Then, at ten-thirty, Dan says he wants to leave and go home, which he does. What does that suggest to you?"

Colin thought it over for a moment, then said, "What are you suggesting, that he was on a schedule?"

Karen shook her finger at him. "I'm not suggesting anything. We're still assuming Jack is lying. Given that, why would Dan leave early?"

Colin thought for a minute, then said, "He could have been upset about something none of the other players knew about. Other than that, I haven't a clue."

A loud crash of thunder rattled the window. The storm was building in intensity. "All right," Karen said. "Let's move on. The first call to 911 was placed at eleven-thirteen by the next-door neighbor Hendershot. He claims he heard several shots fired in quick succession. At eleven-fourteen, Caroline calls 911. We can assume that the shooting took place prior to eleven-thirteen, right?"

"Right."

Karen smiled. "Okay." She stepped in front of the first board and used a pencil to follow the action. "Now, according to Caroline, Dan enters the house through the garage door entrance to the kitchen. He turns on the kitchen light. He walks into the living room, the house keys still in his hand, and sees Caroline and Jack together. Jack sees Dan, grabs his gun, and fires five times. Dan falls to the floor. Jack threatens Caroline for at least thirty seconds, then walks over to Dan's body and fires two more shots into Dan's head."

She leaned against the edge of her desk. "That's pretty brutal stuff. How do we counter?"

"You'd need a shrink to testify. Maybe two or three."

Karen shook her head. "Juries are notoriously suspicious of shrinks. Besides, the state can bring in someone who'll testify that anyone is capable of violence."

Colin sighed. "So how *do* we counter?"

"With facts."

"What facts?"

"I don't know yet. According to Caroline's statement, Jack had insisted that the lights be turned off in the living room. Once again, it would appear that Jack had insisted that this be a romantic rape. Possible?"

Colin shrugged. "Well, if we follow along on the fantasy thing, yes, it's possible."

Karen held up her finger again. "Caroline says Jack shot Dan in the head *after he was dead* as a warning to her. Possible?"

"I dunno," Colin said. "Maybe he was a little nuts. Maybe he was scared."

Karen shook her head. "Those aren't the actions of a frightened person; they are the actions of a very composed, possibly crazy person. And if Jack is crazy, why wouldn't he have exhibited these tendencies earlier? Why isn't there some record of previous violent acts?"

She tapped the board with her index finger. "Again, we have Caroline insisting there were two series of shots, the ones that initially hit Dan in the body together with the two that missed, then two more shots to the face later. The forensics material confirms Caroline's story to a point, which is to say that there was a gap of at least thirty seconds between the first shots and the second shots. Question: How come the neighbors didn't hear the second shots?"

"I have no idea," Colin said.

Karen stared at the board, thinking. Then, "Jack says he never heard them, either. Why would he lie about that? He didn't deny the first shots"

Colin pursed his lips for a moment, then said, "That one's easy. The first shots were supposedly fired in self-defense. The second two were not. He might admit to the first and not the second."

Karen frowned. "You're quite right, assuming he's lying. But again, why would the neighbors not hear the second shots?"

Colin shrugged. "Could be any number of reasons. Witnesses are notoriously unreliable, as you know. It depends on how much stock the jury gives any one of them."

Karen picked up a legal pad, looked at it for a moment, then said, "Okay. Another question: The gun had Jack's prints all over it, but the shell casings were free of prints altogether. That suggests that whoever loaded the gun used gloves, and then only after cleaning the shells. If Jack brought the gun with him, why would he be so careful when loading it, but so cavalier about the actual shooting?"

"That really makes no sense at all," Colin said. "Not if we're still assuming Jack is lying."

"We are," Karen said. "And here's something else to ponder. The medical examiner found traces of plastic in Dan's brain, some of which is assumed to have come from the glasses he was wearing. All of the bullets were hollow points. The slug that went through one of the lenses probably picked up small pieces of the lens. But there is a small piece of frosty-colored plastic that is completely unidentified. Any guesses as to what that might be?"

"Not a one."

"And this," she added. "There's no stippling on Dan's body. That means the shots all had to have come from at least six feet away. Can you explain to me how Jack stood over Dan's body and fired two shots into the man's head from six feet above him?"

Colin thought for a moment. "Did the slugs exit the head?"

"No."

Colin looked at the chair. "Mind if I sit?"

"Go ahead."

He got comfortable, studied the board for a moment, then said, "That one's not so hard. Dan's head could have been cocked to one side when he was lying on the floor. If Jack was standing off to the side, it would have been easy to be six feet away. The force of the shots could have moved the head to the full straight-ahead position in which it was found."

Karen's jaw dropped. The man was right. It had never occurred to her, just one of the reasons she liked to conduct this exercise. The problem was that, with each passing moment, Jack's prospects were becoming as dark as the sky outside. As if to emphasize the point, a flash of lightning zapped the ground very close by, followed immediately by a tremendous crack of thunder. The lights went out.

"Oh, great," Colin said.

It was so dim in the room they could hardly make out the board.

"Let's continue," Karen said.

"I'm glad this isn't on a computer," Colin said.

"Me, too. Okay. After shooting Dan, Jack tells Caroline she is to call the police. When the police arrive, she is to claim that Jack mistook the keys in Dan's hand for a gun. Question: Why not kill Caroline?"

"Because he thought she would back up his story," Colin said. "If he kills her, he has to make a run for it."

Karen nodded. "Yes, and his car was parked a block away, remember? In the dark, he could easily have made a run for it without having anyone catch the tag number or even the color of the car. Why take a chance on Caroline not sticking to the story? Especially when he'd displayed such cold, dispassionate cruelty. Put yourself in his shoes for a moment. Would you want to leave a witness, even encourage her to call the police?"

Colin shook his head. "I can't put myself in his shoes."

The lights came back on. Outside her office, Karen could hear the sound of scattered applause. She studied the board for a moment, then said, "Here we have a man so vicious he kills Dan on sight, then pumps two more bullets into Dan's brain. He spares Caroline, but tells her to call the police. Why on earth would he hang around? Why wouldn't he kill Caroline and run like hell?"

"I'm afraid I have a difficult time with this," Colin said.

"Why?"

"Because I don't for a second believe Jack did this."

Karen smiled at him. "You have to take a step back and look at this the way a jury will see it. Evidence, that's what they see. And the evidence supports Caroline's story. We have to be able to argue against that evidence, understand?"

"I understand. But it's still tough."

"You bet it is. The important thing to remember is that the bulk of Caroline's version of the events is plausible. The jury will tend to accept the credible aspects and dismiss the not so credible, unless the not so credible are so glaring as to be totally unacceptable."

She sat on the edge of her desk and sighed. "At the moment, I'd say Caroline's story will hold up. And that is a very big problem for us."

Colin looked suitably depressed.

"Let's switch over," Karen said. "We'll assume that everything Jack said is true. This time you take it, and take it from the top."

Colin looked at the two boards, then said, "Okay. Jack has been set up, right?"

"Right."

Colin stroked his chin as he talked. "All right. Jack comes to the house at a prearranged time. Caroline is waiting for him, all decked out, as is the living room. The fire is roaring, candles are blazing, and the stereo is playing. Drinks are waiting. Jack and Caroline start to make love. Then Dan enters the house."

"Stop right there," Karen said. "If we assume Jack is telling the truth, why would Dan enter the house at that exact time?"

Colin stiffened as a concept took hold. "Of course. He had to have been set up as well. Caroline had to have said something or done something to make him break away from the poker game and come home."

Karen stared at him intently. "So you're saying Dan had to know what was going on back home. That would be the reason he left the poker game early, so he could confront his wife with another man."

Colin was staring at the board. "Sounds crazy, I know. But there can be only one reason Dan entered the house when he did. He *had* to have been set up.

Perhaps Caroline enlisted the aid of a neighbor to call him, saying he or she saw Jack enter the house."

"There were no phone calls for Dan," Karen said. "You checked that out yourself."

He was crestfallen. "Right. Well, okay, maybe somebody drove up there . . ."

"Not enough time," Karen said, interrupting. "But you're right about one thing. Dan came home at that moment because he was programmed *ahead* of time. There's no other way any of this fits. Caroline had to know Dan would walk in the house at that exact moment."

Colin sighed. "That's going to be real tough to prove."

"Now you're beginning to understand," Karen said.

Colin shook his head. "What reason would Dan have for coming home? That's the question, right?"

"Right."

He pursed his lips as he talked it through. "He was playing poker. He was nervous. He received no calls. He knew he was to be home at a certain time. He had to. But I'm damned if I can think of why."

"Okay," Karen said. "Let's move forward. According to Jack, when Dan walked into the living room and saw them together, he had a gun in his hand. Where the hell did it come from?"

"More important," Colin said, "where the hell did it get to? That's the real question."

"Here's another," Karen said. "How could Caroline be sure Jack would fire the gun she handed him?"

"She *couldn't* be sure," Colin said.

"Okay, if that's the case, isn't that taking a pretty big risk? What if Jack can't fire the gun? What if Jack was frozen by shock and fear. Caroline could have been killed. How could she have prevented that?"

Colin stared at her. "The only way would be to ensure that Dan's gun couldn't fire."

Karen smiled at him. "Very good. Which means she had to have had access to the gun Dan used. But it's still taking a chance. If this went down the way Caroline says it did, Jack could have hesitated just long enough for Dan to take Jack's gun away from him, then use it on both of them.

"On the other hand, if it *was* a setup, there are only two possible explanations. Either Dan was a part of it, or he wasn't. Is it reasonable to assume that Dan would be a party to his own death?"

"No."

"In which case, he wasn't a part of it. In which case, this was a premeditated execution planned by Caroline."

"That's how it looks to me," Colin said.

"If that's true, explain to me how Caroline could get her husband to be so cooperative, to enter the house at the right time, to be so completely predictable."

Colin shook his head. "I can't."

"Nor can I," Karen said. "Nor can I explain why Jack's fingerprints are not on the toilet. Why would he lie about a thing like that?"

While Colin pondered that, she picked up a document. "Jack says he started feeling sick *before* the shooting. He thought it was because of the excitement, but what if it wasn't? What if his drink was laced with something that would make him sick?"

Colin looked confused. "I don't follow you."

Karen threw the document back on her desk. "If we assume that Caroline set this up, she needed Jack out of the room for a few minutes after Dan was shot."

"Why?"

"To get rid of the evidence: the candles, the gun in

Dan's hand, and anything else indicating that she and Jack had consensual sex. Jack says that when he entered the house, Caroline was waiting by the fireplace with a drink for him and one for herself. Baileys Irish Cream."

"And?"

"Every mother knows about a drug called ipecac, a brown syrup that induces vomiting. You never know when a kid may have taken something that requires an immediate stomach evacuation. The drug is also misused by bulimics. Let's say Caroline put ipecac in Jack's drink. Jack looks at the body, feels ill, and heads for the bathroom. Caroline swings into action. She douses the candles, throws on the lights, takes the gun and puts the car keys beside Dan's hand, grabs the glass Jack used, then throws everything into a sack that she hides somewhere. But first, she picks up the gun and puts two slugs in her husband's head."

Colin stared at her.

"If Jack is telling the truth," she said, "who else would do it? And why did Caroline do it?"

Colin thought for a moment, then said, "I'd guess that Jack only *thought* Dan was dead."

"Not so. Dan *was* dead. The autopsy proves that. He was dead as soon as he hit the floor."

"Then he might have twitched. That sometimes happens. Or maybe Caroline thought he twitched. Whatever."

"It could have happened that way," Karen said. "Okay. We'll assume that's what happened. Then Caroline gathers up the stuff, puts it in a sack, and gives it to a cohort."

"A cohort?"

Karen nodded. "If Jack Palmer is to be believed, Caroline had to have had help. It's the only way this scenario works. Because the police didn't find Jack's prints on the toilet, it means someone wiped them off *after* he left the bathroom. There is access to the bathroom from the outside."

Colin looked distressed. "This would have to have gone off like clockwork."

"I know that. This same person, the accomplice, earlier took the sack of evidence from Caroline, then went outside to the pool area. As soon as he knew Jack had left the bathroom, he entered it from the outside and wiped the toilet free of prints." She sighed. "In fact, it's the only way this could have happened the way Jack says it did."

Colin stared at her.

"Do you think a jury will buy his story?" Karen asked.

Colin slowly shook his head.

"Neither do I," she said.

"You mentioned an accomplice," Colin said.

"Yes. Dan DeFauldo was worth more alive than dead, Colin. He carried no life insurance whatsoever. If money wasn't the reason, what was Caroline's motive for killing him? Another man? It has to be. It's the only motive that makes sense to me."

"A secret lover?"

Karen nodded. "Either Caroline has a secret lover or . . ."

"Or?"

"Or Caroline's story is every bit as credible as Jack Palmer's. And if we go into court with two credible stories, Caroline's is the one they'll buy. We have to find her lover, Colin."

"Any ideas?"

"Only one that makes any sense at all."

"Who?"

She turned and looked at Colin with an intensity that frightened him. "Ralph Vincenzo."

"What!"

Karen told him about the tip, but not the tipster. "The police are hinting that Jack might have been working with Vincenzo, but that's poppycock. It's more likely Caroline and Vincenzo are working together. If true, we'd have a strong motive. If Ralph and Caroline were an item and thinking about stealing money from the company, getting rid of Dan would be a natural, wouldn't it?"

Colin, his eyes wide, nodded. "But . . . if Vincenzo has flown the coop, why is Caroline still here?"

"She's waiting for Jack's trial to be over and done with. With Jack convicted for the murder of her husband, Caroline's movements are not in question. If she had not waited, the murder investigation might still be underway. By staying, she deflects any attention that might come her way." She threw her pencil on the desk. "And I think that's exactly what's happened."

"It's perfect," Colin said, looking glum.

"Not at all," Karen insisted. "This is not a perfect crime. It's up to us to find the imperfections. I simply will not allow that woman to get away with this. I'd never be able to live with myself."

Colin looked at her approvingly. "If I was ever in trouble," he said softly, "you're just the kind of person I'd want defending me."

She smiled at him. "Thanks. But if we don't crack this case, I'm not much of a lawyer. If I let Caroline DeFauldo outsmart me, I belong in some other occupation."

Colin grinned. "I thought you said we weren't supposed to let these things get personal. We're supposed to be objective. Isn't that what you said?"

"I *am* being objective. And don't throw my words back at me. I really hate that, Colin."

There was no sting to her rebuke. Colin grinned, then hung his head in mock submissiveness. This was a serious case, he knew. A man's life hung in the balance. But Colin couldn't help being excited. He was learning more by working with Karen than he would have in six months of law school. He had complete faith in his mentor. She'd find a way to win this thing. In the meantime, he was having the time of his life.

When Karen arrived home, Carl was sitting at the bar, looking morose, a drink in his hand. She stood behind him, staring at the profile of his face, trying to think of the right words. "You never returned my call," she said.

"I was busy."

She took a deep breath. "Caroline was lying about you. I know that now. And I apologize. Can you forgive me?"

"Well, well," he said. "What changed your mind?"

"Please! I'm very, very sorry, Carl." She poured some white wine into a glass. "You have every right in the world to be angry." Tears formed at the corners of her eyes and started falling down her cheeks. "I'm asking you to forgive me. What else can I do?"

"Don't cry," he said. "You know I'm a sucker for tears."

"I can't help it. I feel like a fool."

"Good. You deserve it."

"I'm not perfect."

"Nor am I."

She wiped at her tears with a tissue. "It's not much fun being falsely accused, is it?"

"Not hardly."

"It happened to me, too."

"I wouldn't place your motives and my faithfulness in the same category."

"I'm sorry. Is it impossible for you to understand why I could make such a terrible mistake? If you put everything in context, I reacted as many women would. Blind faith is not necessarily the mark of intelligence, Carl. Haven't you ever wondered about my fidelity?"

"No."

"Oh, so you take me for granted?"

"No. I trust you."

"Blindly?"

"No. And stop cross-examining me. I can't turn my emotions on and off like a faucet."

"You're hurt, right?"

"Of course I'm hurt."

"And you need time to let the wounds heal?"

"Exactly."

"All right. Let me know when you feel better."

He slammed a hand on the bar counter. "Very clever. I'm the aggrieved party, but you're twisting it around so I'm the one feeling guilty."

Karen smiled. "I'm a woman. Women play by different rules. We have to in order to survive."

His face softened. "Yes."

"Yes, what?"

"You *are* a woman."

He leaned forward and kissed her. The weight of the world lifted from her shoulders.

And later that night, like giddy teenagers, they tiptoed down from the bedroom in their terry cloth robes, slipped out to the darkened pool area, and slid naked into the still-warm water. Above and behind them, a lone whippoorwill screeched news of their arrival.

Small, slowly drifting puffs of cloud occasionally obscured the half-moon floating serenely in the night.

Both storms had passed; a storm of nature, and a storm of doubt.

Carl took her into his arms and kissed her, then lifted her up and placed his arms under her buttocks, somehow managing to keep both their heads above water as he carried her to the end of the pool.

"I'm so sorry," she whispered. "Can you ever forgive me?"

"Forget it," he said. "I understand. There are times I take you for granted, too. I forget how lucky I am, how exciting you are, how wonderful it is to be in love with you."

She kissed him, then said, "You're still in love after all these years?"

"Yes."

"Even after what I put you through?"

"Very much so. Which makes me a masochist."

She kissed him deeply. "I'm still in love with you, too. The thought of you—"

"Stop it," he commanded.

They had reached the underwater ledge in the deep end. Carl released Karen, slid onto the ledge, then drew her up so that she straddled him. Her breasts bobbed gently on the surface of the water. Carl took one of them in his mouth.

"Someone might see us," she said, looking around. Lights still glowed from a few windows that faced their backyard.

"Nonsense," he said. "It's as dark as pitch out here."

"Carl, the moon is bright when the clouds pass."

He nuzzled her ear. "Where's your spirit of adventure?"

"Carl . . ."

He kissed her. And then she felt his urging. Suddenly, he was there. Almost involuntarily, her body started moving, sending a parade of small silver-topped ripples moving away from them.

His lips were at her ear. "Just one caution," he whispered.

"What?"

"When you reach that magic moment, don't scream as loudly as you usually do."

The darkness failed to dim the mirthful gleam in his passionate eyes.

Sixteen

Brad Keats was one of over a hundred assistant state attorneys prosecuting criminal cases in Florida's Sixth Judicial District. Like all the ASAs, he endured dreadful hours, a constricted budget, and unrelenting pressure. If all the cases in the Sixth Judicial District went to trial, the waiting list would be at least three years. By law, cases had to go to trial within six months, a physical impossibility if there were no plea bargaining. The only way the system functioned at all was to plead out the vast majority of cases, have the accused agree to accept a penalty for a lesser crime in exchange for a shorter than normal sentence.

The defense lawyers were well aware of the bazaar-like conditions that prevailed. They played the game to the hilt, often holding out until the day before trial before striking a reasonable bargain. The system creaked along like some ancient automobile, leaking oil, its transmission slipping, piston rings worn out, gears shot, bearings burned, tires flat, a dysfunctional bureaucracy barely able to drag itself through another day.

Soon, it would collapse entirely. Meanwhile, the pressure to keep the old machine moving was relentless.

Brad Keats, unlike many of his peers, seemed to

thrive in this strange, toxic atmosphere polluted by divergent views and twisted political agendas. Tall and handsome, married with four kids, the daily grind—this total immersion in the acidic brew of cynicism and hypocrisy—never seemed to eat away at his cheerful nature. Those who didn't know him well sometimes mistook his usual sunny disposition as a signal that Brad's approach to his job was indifferent, that he didn't care because the criminal justice system was so screwed up, it simply didn't matter anymore.

They were wrong.

Brad was a tiger in sheep's clothing. He hated criminals, especially the violent ones. The career criminals, the nonviolent scammers and thieves, even the hookers and dopers, those he could almost tolerate. Like Karen, he thought he understood. But he despised the killers, the rapists, the abusers, anyone who resorted to violence for whatever reason. They were beyond redemption or change. He was obsessed with putting them away for as long as possible.

Jack Palmer was a case in point.

Brad had always wanted to be a prosecutor. Nothing more, except perhaps to become a judge. He was good at his job, understood the complete workings of the system, a man who treated defense attorneys with the respect they deserved for simply doing their jobs. He believed in the system, felt that making it work was more important that fighting for changes that would never come. Not in a democracy, at least.

He waved Karen into his cramped, cluttered office, stood up, shook her hand, then said, "Coffee, Jack Daniel's, cocaine?" His gray eyes seemed even softer than usual.

"Thanks," Karen said laughing, "but I'll pass. How've you been?"

He waved a hand over a desk piled high with files. "Wonderful. You know how many homicides we had in Pinellas last night alone?"

"I have no idea."

"Three," he said ruefully. "Hillsborough had two. All in one night. I've got my secretary checking, like she's got nothing else to do, but I'm curious what the record is for a single week. This week has been a doozy. It's really getting out of hand, and those clowns in Tallahassee just keep smiling away like zoned-out druggies."

"Maybe you should run for public office," she said, taking a seat.

"Bite your tongue."

"Speaking of homicide," Karen said.

Brad sat down, flipped through some manila file folders and opened one. "Right. One Jack Palmer. You get your copies?"

"Yes, thanks."

"You want to plead this out right now?"

She laughed. "Wow, you *are* busy."

"I am, indeed." He leafed through the file. "Let's see. One Mr. DeFauldo was killed during the commission of a felony, to wit, something we laughingly call sexual battery. Why are we so loath to call it rape anymore?"

"Good question," Karen said.

"Well, call it what you will, the charge is Murder One. But I'm prepared to offer Murder Two right now. At least that keeps the guy out of the chair. Hell, the way things are right now, he'll be out in fifteen or less. Murder ain't what it used to be."

"Slow down," Karen said.

Brad leaned back in his chair and crossed his arms

over his chest. "Let me guess. You have a problem, right?"

"I have several," she said.

He grinned. "You realize, of course, that I am—unofficially speaking, of course—forbidden to make your life easy, that I am instructed to treat you like a cockroach, that I would be well advised to display extreme hostility toward you at such times as we are together in the public eye."

"I wouldn't have it any other way," she said.

"So?"

"Jack Palmer has no record. He's never been arrested or even accused of anything violent. He's the salt of the earth, reliable, trustworthy, a family man. He doesn't own a gun and never has. Now, all of a sudden, this mild-mannered guy goes crazy and rapes and kills? That makes no sense to me at all."

"It happens all the time, Karen. And you know it. Next?"

"The hospital report provides no evidence of rape. In fact, the report suggests that Caroline was sexually aroused. That could indicate consensual sex."

"It could, but I can have a doctor testify that some women secrete vaginal fluids while being raped. It's a medical fact. Strike that one. Your doctor and my doctor would cancel each other out. Anything else?"

"Uh-huh. How is it that the lab found Palmer's fingerprints on the murder weapon and no prints at all on the shell casings? Why would a man be that careful and that stupid at the same time?"

Brad shrugged. "I have no answer. Not that I need one."

Karen picked at some lint on her skirt. "Come on, Brad. There are patterns with most violent crimes. This one just doesn't fit any of the profiles. If Jack Palmer took the trouble to make sure there were no finger-prints on the shell casings, it would indicate premeditation. Since he's accused of raping Caroline, it would further indicate he planned to kill her, leave the casings behind, but take the gun with him. If that was his intent, why did he kill Dan DeFauldo and not Caroline? Why did he stay?"

Brad leaned forward, drummed his fingers on the file folder, and said, "Because he didn't expect Mr. De-Fauldo to show up. He was told earlier that DeFauldo was playing poker until two or so in the morning. When DeFauldo arrived home early, your boy pan-icked. Then, the whole plan went out the window. He decided to go to plan B. Bluff it out. But he didn't count on Mrs. DeFauldo displaying the courage she did. End of story."

Karen had to give him credit. He'd been doing his homework. "Then there's the little matter of the two gunshots to the head," she said. "Caroline DeFauldo says my client fired those head shots sometime after the first shots, and at close range. But the M.E. says the shots had to be fired from at least six feet away."

Brad tapped the file folder. "Mrs. DeFauldo says your client went over to the body and fired two shots into Mr. DeFauldo's head. She doesn't say how far away your client was when he fired the shots. It could have been ten feet, for all we know."

"Then explain to me why all the witnesses, with the singular exception of Caroline, say all the shots were fired at the same time. The neighbor who called 911 . . . what's his name . . . Hendershot . . . says that. I have two additional witnesses who say the same thing, not to mention my client. But the autopsy report proves that the head shots were fired at least thirty seconds af-ter the first shots."

Some of the softness left Brad's eyes. "You know as well as I do that witnesses are notorious for being wrong on facts. The one who called 911? Hendershot? He was probably on the phone when the head shots were fired. As for the others, maybe they were hiding in a closet. Who knows? You want to put them on the stand, be my guest, but I don't see a conflict here. The evidence clearly supports Mrs. DeFauldo's statement."

He leaned forward. "As for your client's story, he says Dan DeFauldo had a gun. Okay. Where is it? There was no time for Mrs. DeFauldo to dispose of it, and the police searched the area inside and outside the house. They found zip."

"I know, but—"

"Your client admits he fired the first shots. Okay. I'm willing to accept that, given his state of panic, he might have mistaken the keys in DeFauldo's hands for a gun. I'm being generous by knocking this down to Murder Two."

Karen rolled her eyes skyward. "Are you telling me that Jack Palmer, a man never before involved in anything violent, thinks he sees keys instead of a gun, then kills a man, then stands over him and pumps two more slugs into the man's head? Why would he do that?"

"I'm just giving you an out, that's all."

Karen shook her head. "I don't think Jack Palmer fired those head shots."

His eyebrows rose. "What are you suggesting? That she did it?"

Karen took a deep breath, then said, "That's exactly what I'm suggesting."

For a moment, Brad appeared stunned. "You're serious!" he said.

"Yes, I am."

He laughed at her. "Incredible. You should hear

yourself. If your client's story is to be believed, Caroline DeFauldo orchestrated this whole thing. She managed to have her husband walk in the house at eleven o'clock at night on his regular Wednesday poker night, when for years he's never made it home until two or three in the morning. She also managed to have her husband not fire the gun in his hand, the gun we can't find. God! The woman would have to be a genius. Does she strike you as a genius?"

He'd struck a nerve. Karen didn't answer.

"Your guy is lying through his teeth," Brad said firmly. "Plain and simple. I'm no shrink, but the way I hear it, things weren't so wonderful at the Palmer home. Maybe your guy was a little frustrated. He gets the hots for Caroline DeFauldo and gets a little carried away. Who the hell knows? But the *evidence,* that stuff we hold so dear, supports everything she says and nothing he says. We have to go with the evidence."

Karen sighed. She was getting nowhere. "The autopsy report mentions an unidentified piece of plastic found in the victim's brain. I'd like it identified."

Brad shook his head. "It's not important. We can't afford unnecessary lab work."

Karen tried another tack. "I've been given to understand that there may be some money missing from Dan DeFauldo's company. I'm also given to understand that Dan's partner is missing."

"Where'd you hear that?" he asked sharply.

"It's all over town," she said.

"That's not part of this case," he said.

"But it might be."

"Might be? I don't deal with what might be. I deal with evidence. And the evidence says your client is guilty as hell."

"Brad—"

He cut her off with, "Look, Karen, the evidence says your client raped Caroline DeFauldo and shot her husband to death. That's what the grand jury is going to say, and that's what a jury is going to believe."

"Brad—"

"Let me finish. Why not be smart? Do the right thing, and let's both of us get on with it."

"Indulge me just this once, will you?"

He leaned back in his chair and put his hands behind his head, a bored expression on his face. Karen stared into his eyes and tried hard to impart the sincerity that gripped her so strongly. "I'm having him go on the box this afternoon. If he passes, will you at least consider reopening the investigation?"

Brad shook his head. "No way. If he's a good enough liar to have you fooled, he'll beat the box with ease. As for Mrs. DeFauldo, she has no motive. Did you know her husband carried no life insurance?"

"Yes." It was pointless to pursue the issue. "I'd like to depose Caroline DeFauldo as soon as possible."

"I'm sure you would."

"Well?"

"As I understand it, she's very distraught at the moment."

"Come on, Brad. Do I have to get a court order?"

The smile was back on his face. "I'm sure you'll find Judge Brown very accommodating."

She felt her jaw tightening. "So, that's the way it is? I have to petition the court for everything?"

"Don't say I didn't warn you."

"This stinks."

He was running out of patience. "Karen, the guy is guilty. I have some important things to do, okay?"

Karen jumped to her feet, turned on her heel, and strode quickly out of his office.

* * *

Jack Palmer looked frightened as the various attachments were fastened to his body: the blood pressure cuff on his upper left arm, the two respiration indicators around his chest, the galvanic skin reflex readers on the tips of the index finger and ring finger of his right hand. The test was set to take place in one of the larger rooms used by lawyers and their clients within the jail. This one contained a small table and four chairs, just roomy enough to get the job done.

Jack sat at the end of the table facing away from the operator, Phil Gorman, one of the best polygraph operators in the country. Karen stood by the door, her arms crossed over her chest.

"Just relax," she said to Jack. "Phil is not going to try to trick you. He's going to ask you about thirty questions with yes or no answers. Just tell the truth, that's all."

Jack twisted his head around and looked at the strange machine with the long, thin pens, and the smaller machine beside it. "What's the little machine for?"

"It's a Psychological Stress Analyzer," Phil told him. "When we match the results of the polygraph with the PSA, we get a more complete evaluation."

Jack turned back to face Karen. "Why are you doing this, Karen? You said you believed me. You also said we can't use this in court."

"I do believe you, Jack. And we can't use it in court. But this case is about to take a new turn."

"What do you mean?"

"It's something I don't normally like to do, but I'm faced with a recalcitrant prosecutor and a Stone Age judge who doesn't like me very much. I'm taking this public. If I play my cards right, you're about to become a celebrity."

He looked concerned. "I'm not sure I want that."

"Don't worry. You'll be safely tucked away in here. I'll be the one taking the heat."

Phil checked a dial, then nodded. Karen patted Jack's hand and said, "Okay. Phil's ready. Relax as much as you can, give honest answers, and we'll see you in about fifteen minutes. Okay?"

"Okay," he said. But his voice wavered.

Karen waited outside while Gorman administered the test. If Jack passed, she would do as she said, go public. She'd announce the results of the test, have Phil there to back her up, then launch a media campaign designed to impress as many prospective jurors as possible. All it took was one, one who believed that Jack Palmer was simply a patsy. Preconditioning potential jurors was one possible way to achieve that goal.

It wasn't exactly ethical. Press conferences were fine, but presenting inadmissible evidence to the media was sleazy. The trick was in getting a reporter to ask the right question. A lawyer could hardly be censured for answering a question with an honest answer.

The test itself concerned her. Polygraph tests, even in the hands of an expert like Phil, were tricky. Subconscious guilt on the part of the subject could lead to negative results. And here was a man ridden with guilt over the fact that he'd killed a man, even though he believed it was self-defense. As well, Jack Palmer was a man with very little self-esteem. With an ego that diminished, anything was possible.

Inside the room, Phil had instructed Jack to look at the wall. Then, he asked Jack the control questions, the ones designed to set the machine's parameters, like, "Is your name Jack Palmer? Are you married?" Now, with both machines properly adjusted, he asked, "Do you know Caroline DeFauldo?"

"Yes."

Another adjustment to both machines. The name alone had caused a strong reaction.

"Do you live in Tampa?"

"No."

"Do you have children?"

"Yes."

"Did you have dinner with Caroline DeFauldo on the night of November tenth?"

"Yes."

Better this time. One final adjustment.

"Do you own a car?"

"Yes."

"Did you rape Caroline DeFauldo on the night of November tenth?"

"No."

"Do you live in Palm Harbor?"

"Yes."

"Did you shoot Dan DeFauldo on the night of November tenth?"

"Yes."

"Is your wife's name Ellen?"

"Yes."

"Are you thirty-six years old?"

"Yes."

"Was Dan DeFauldo pointing a gun at you when you shot him?"

"Yes."

"Did you believe your life was in danger on the night of November tenth?"

"Yes."

"Is your daughter's name Mary?"

"No."

"Did Caroline DeFauldo hand you a gun on the night of November tenth?"

"Yes."

"Had you ever seen that gun before?"

"No."

"Is your daughter's name Sally?"

"Yes."

"Did you believe Caroline DeFauldo's life was in danger on the night of November tenth?"

"Yes."

"Are you a salesman?"

"Yes."

"Do you know a man named Ralph Vincenzo?"

"No."

"Have you been married more than once?"

"No."

"Did you shoot Dan DeFauldo in the head when he was lying on the floor?"

"No."

"Did you see a gun on the floor near Dan DeFauldo after he fell to the floor?"

"Yes."

"Was it the same gun he had in his hand?"

"Yes."

"Have you answered every question I have asked you today in a truthful manner?"

"Yes."

Phil waited for a few moments, then reached forward and switched off both machines. As he unhooked the attachments, Jack looked up and asked, "How did I do?"

"It'll take five minutes to check the results. Why don't you go into the next room with your lawyer? I'll be there in a jiffy."

Jack did as instructed.

"Don't look so worried," Karen chided him. "I'm sure you did well."

Jack gave her a sorrowful look. "I don't know."

"Did you lie?"

"No, but I hear that those machines can make mistakes."

"That's true," she told him. "But that usually happens when the operator is inexperienced. Phil is a pro, believe me."

They waited. Then Phil stuck his head in the room, a wide smile on his face. "You passed both with flying colors."

Jack Palmer started to weep.

Seventeen

It was happening, just as he'd figured it would. It was all coming apart. The investors were screaming at anyone who'd listen. They were all over the newspapers and on TV. The feds were looking for him, looking hard. It was only a matter of time before the bastards found him. And then what? How was he supposed to explain what happened to the money? How was he supposed to convince them that Caroline had stolen the money and killed her husband to boot? They wouldn't buy that in a million years.

Ralph Vincenzo swallowed the last of his drink and fixed another. He looked terrible. He'd eaten very little the past few days. He hadn't bathed or shaved, brushed his teeth, or so much as changed clothes. He reeked of booze, tobacco, and stale sweat. His eyes were red-rimmed and clouded, his lips dry, his throat tickling from the onset of some viral infection. He looked at his watch, lit a cigarette, and switched on the television set. Then, he fell into a worn upholstered chair. The six o'clock news was filled with the usual reports: car crashes, murders—and a clip from a news conference.

"Attorney Karen Perry-Mondori asked for the public's help today," the breathless blond bubblehead announcer said, "in a news conference held at her office this afternoon. The attorney is representing Jack Pal-

mer, the man charged with the murder of local investment broker Daniel DeFauldo. Ms. Perry-Mondori
claims her client is innocent of the charges and wants
the public to help her prove it. Jim Gladden reports
from Clearwater."

Ralph leaned forward, trying hard to make his eyes
focus properly. He could just make out a young man
with a microphone in his hand standing in front of an
office building. "Karen Perry-Mondori," the man was
saying, "one of the area's top criminal lawyers, insists
her client is innocent of the charges now pending
against him. In a press conference held this afternoon,
the lawyer called on the public to help in finding the
evidence she says will prove her client's innocence."

The scene switched to a room crowded with media
people. An attractive woman stood at the back of the
room, her face almost hidden by a bank of microphones. "According to the authorities," the woman was
saying, "the gun used to kill Daniel DeFauldo has been
traced to an Ocala gun dealer who says he sold the gun
at an Orlando gun show because he was overstocked.
The name and address of the buyer is false. The gun is
a Walther PPK, and I'm asking anyone with information as to who might have bought this weapon at that
gun show to come forward.

"I'm also asking anyone who invested money with
Mr. DeFauldo's company to get in touch with me. As
you know, the FBI is investigating Vinde Investments
for possible fraud. I have information that suggests the
murder of Dan DeFauldo is connected to the recent
collapse of that company."

Reporters were screaming questions. Ralph couldn't
make out the questions, but he heard the lawyer's answer.

"I'm saying that Jack Palmer told the truth when he

said that he shot Dan DeFauldo in self-defense," she was saying. "You can draw your own conclusions as to the inferences. The gun that killed Dan DeFauldo was never owned by Jack Palmer. I'm asking that the person who sold that gun come forward and identify the person to whom the gun was sold. Justice demands it. It's the key to this case."

Another babble of questions. Again, Ralph heard only the answer.

"Yes. Jack Palmer was given a lie detector test and a voice stress test this afternoon." The lawyer turned to her right and smiled at a man. "The test was administered by Mr. Phil Gorman, a man with fifteen years' experience in tests such as these. Mr. Gorman will soon tell you that Jack Palmer passed both tests unequivocally. Jack Palmer did not rape Caroline DeFauldo, nor did he shoot Dan Fauldo in cold blood. Jack Palmer shot Dan DeFauldo in self-defense."

"Then, what happened to the other gun?" someone asked. Ralph could make out that question.

"I can't answer that question," the lawyer said. "All I can tell you is that it was there. The police didn't find it, but I think they would if they'd just keep looking. The fact that the police don't seem very interested in pursuing this investigation is not unusual. When police departments have a suspect in custody, they stop looking. It's standard procedure. And since the police don't have much interest in reopening this case, I'm asking for the public's help in preventing a terrible injustice."

Another reporter asked, "Are you saying Caroline DeFauldo is lying?"

The lawyer smiled. "I'm saying that Jack Palmer told the truth when he was asked if Dan DeFauldo pointed a gun at him. I'm saying he told the truth when he said he didn't rape Mrs. DeFauldo. I'm saying he told the truth when he said he was enticed to have an affair with Mrs. DeFauldo."

A woman yelled a question. "If Mrs. DeFauldo is the seductress you claim she is, isn't it possible she also seduced your husband? And isn't that the real reason you took this case?"

"I didn't say Mrs. DeFauldo is a seductress. I said my client claims he was seduced. I believe my client is telling the truth. As for my reasons for taking this case, I've made several statements relative to that question. Nothing has changed. With regard to Mrs. DeFauldo's claim that she had an affair with my husband, had Brander Hewitt been allowed to continue with his presentation at the recent hearing, you all would have learned that Mrs. DeFauldo was lying. The evidence proves that my husband could not possibly have been in two places at once.

"It seems to me that Mrs. DeFauldo had other reasons for wanting me off this case. I won't presume to know what they are, but I'm looking forward to the opportunity of proving that Jack Palmer is telling the truth. It shouldn't have to be that way, but it sometimes is in criminal cases."

The announcer was back. "And the FBI confirms that they have been unable to find Ralph Vincenzo, the late Dan DeFauldo's partner in the investment company. Obviously, this case is getting more complicated by the moment, Jill."

The bubblehead was now talking to the reporter. "Has Caroline DeFauldo any comment on this?"

"Not a word," the reporter said solemnly. "Mrs. DeFauldo moved back into her Palm Harbor home this morning. We tried to get a comment from her, but she refused to answer the door or the telephone. We also tried to talk with attorney Jonathan Walsingham, but he had no comment. He was, however, clearly upset by the implications made today by Jack Palmer's lawyer. I'm sure we'll be hearing something from him soon."

Ralph stood bolt upright, his mind whirling. He almost fell, then caught the arm of the chair and steadied himself. She was back home, the bitch. At last! Time to have a talk. Time to find out what the hell was going on.

He ran the back of his hand over his lips. By rights, he should wait until dark. That would be the smart move. But he'd waited too damn long already. He was going crazy cooped up in this shitcan apartment, hiding out like some goddam criminal. He hadn't done anything wrong. It was her! And when he was through with her, she'd set the feds straight. She'd tell them the truth or face the goddam consequences. He had to make her believe that.

He picked up the gun from the coffee table and tucked it into his pants behind his belt. Then he threw on his jacket and walked unsteadily toward the door.

He climbed into his car and aimed it toward Alternate Nineteen. At this hour, traffic was heavy. He waited impatiently, drumming his fingers on the steering wheel, talking to himself, practicing the speech he'd use on Caroline.

The traffic started to move. Ralph turned right at Alderman, drove a half mile, then turned left at the entrance to Autumn Woods. Four blocks to Bridgemont Way. He pushed hard on the accelerator.

He parked right in front of the house, climbed out of the car, and tottered toward Caroline's front door. Already, his hand was on the butt of the gun.

"Hey!"

He heard a voice behind him. He turned and saw a

man in a suit and tie standing beside a car parked across the street.

"Where are you going?" the man shouted.

"None of your fucking business," Ralph yelled, then turned away.

"Stop!" the voice yelled.

Ralph took the gun out of his pants and pointed it in the general direction of the man. "Keep your nose out of this, asshole. Just back off, understand?"

"Put the gun down!"

Another voice, this one from a man standing behind a car parked thirty feet away. Another man in a suit and tie. Pointing something. A gun? He couldn't really tell. "Security officer!" the man screamed. "Put the gun down. Now!"

"Not until I talk to Caroline," Ralph yelled. "Just get the fuck out of here before you get hurt."

"Put the gun down!" the voice insisted.

Ralph wasn't a stupid man. A stupid man wasn't capable of putting deals together the way Ralph had done. While not exactly brilliant, he wasn't close to being stupid. But he *was* drunk. And frustrated. And worn out. He'd worked hard all his life and now everything was gone. Caroline had stolen six million dollars and arranged to have her husband killed, and nobody gave a damn. They were letting her off while they hounded the hell out of Ralph. It wasn't fair.

For days he'd brooded about it. For days, he hadn't slept right, hadn't thought about anything except sticking a gun in Caroline's face and forcing the bitch to tell the truth. For days, he'd been slipping faster and faster down the road to madness. His head hurt, his stomach hurt, and his throat was killing him. He was out of his mind with rage, disillusionment, self-pity, and remorse for trusting Dan in the first place. A potent brew of emotions skewed by alcohol. And it made Ralph do something very stupid.

Instead of putting the gun down, he took aim at one of the men who would bar him from talking to Caroline.

It was a fatal error.

First the noise, then the pain in his chest, unlike anything in his experience. Ralph stared uncomprehendingly at the man who had shot him. Jesus! Who was this guy? He pointed his own gun, tried to pull the trigger. Another excruciating pain took his breath away. He tried to keep his arm straight, but couldn't. He saw it drop, saw the gun slip from his fingers, saw the asphalt driveway rise up and slap him in the face.

He felt dizzy. Hot and cold at the same time. There was a strange buzzing in his ears. He couldn't move.

He felt someone touch him, roll him over, and then he was staring at the sky, drifting, consumed with pain.

He saw a face. A man's face. A stranger.

"I have to talk to Caroline," Ralph mumbled through cracked lips.

"Take it easy, fella."

The sky was getting darker. What was blue was now black. There were no stars, no sound, no man. Nothing. The pain was gone.

He thought he heard the sound of his own voice, but it couldn't be. He wasn't talking. He was too tired to talk. Too tired to explain. He'd just lie here and sleep awhile. He'd feel better soon. He was sure of it.

Karen lay in bed, Carl beside her, both of them intently watching the eleven o'clock news. The death of Ralph Vincenzo was the lead item. Caroline DeFauldo's driveway was lit up like a baseball stadium, as TV cameras focused on the bloodstains and news reporters interviewed the police spokesman on the scene.

The reports were incomplete. No one knew what Ralph Vincenzo was doing at Caroline's home, nor did anyone know why he had a gun in his hand. The police had taken statements from the security people guarding Caroline and declared they did not expect to press charges. There were two witnesses to the shooting, both of whom claimed that the security guards were acting in self-defense.

Caroline was not available for comment.

The second story covered Karen's news conference. The station's investigative reporter was wondering aloud if the death of Ralph Vincenzo was connected to the death of former partner Dan DeFauldo, and if so, where did Jack Palmer fit in? It was all very confusing, he said.

When they broke for a commercial, there was the bizarre sight of Caroline DeFauldo, wearing a tight, low-cut sweater, standing in the middle of an acre of new automobiles, waxing enthusiastic about the dealer.

"Tired of being treated like a nobody?" she asked. "Come see us at Don's Ford. We'll treat you right. You'll be driving a brand-new Ford before you know it, with terms to suit any budget. So, come on down. I'll be looking for *you*!" She pointed at the camera and proffered a sexy smile.

Karen threw her pillow at the TV set, then switched it off.

"Great timing," Carl groused. "Bet they paid extra to get that time slot."

"She's becoming ubiquitous," Karen snarled. "I have the feeling she's laughing out loud."

"She who laughs last . . ."

"I have a question," Karen said.

"Shoot."

"Bad choice of words, love."

"Sorry. What's the question?"

"Why were there two armed security guards at Caroline's place?"

Carl stared at her. "Why, indeed. You think she was expecting Ralph?"

"Uh-huh. But why would he want to kill her? And how come she was expecting him? If that's what this all means."

"What else could it be?"

She sighed. "That's what I have to find out."

Eighteen

"You're late, Counselor," Judge Brown shouted.

"My apologies, Your Honor. I'm late because—"

"Save it," the judge bellowed. "Does the defendant waive reading of the specifications?"

"He does, Your Honor. If I might—"

Brown growled something indistinguishable, then looked at Jack Palmer. "Mr. Palmer, you are charged with murder in the first degree. How do you plead?"

"Your Honor," Karen said, "the defense wishes to—"

"That will be *enough*," Brown bellowed. "I want to hear your client's plea."

Jack, unaware of the reason behind Karen's agitation, mumbled a weak, "Not guilty."

Brown nodded. "The defendant pleads not guilty. All right. Now, as to bail . . . "

"The state requests bail be denied," Brad Keats said. "This is a capital case, Your Honor. The defendant is a serious flight risk."

Judge Brown looked at Karen.

"The defendant is not a flight risk in the least, Your Honor. He has a wife and two children, and strong roots in the community. But Your Honor, before we discuss—"

Brown's face was becoming purple with rage. "We're not going to try the case today, little lady, so let's get on with it. Bail is set at one million dollars. As to a trial date—"

"Your Honor," Karen exclaimed, "the defense requests an emergency preliminary hearing!"

Brown looked ready to explode. Gavel in hand, he pointed it at Karen like a weapon. "Don't interrupt me again, Counselor. I'm warning you."

Behind her, a squadron of attorneys shifted uncomfortably in their chairs, like hapless Christians awaiting their exposure to the lion. They were next. If Karen Perry-Mondori was getting this hard a time, what horrors could they expect?

Karen, her own cheeks flaming, persisted. "Your Honor, I've tried to talk with the prosecutor before this arraignment. If Your Honor would bear with me for just a moment."

The judge ignored her. "Trial date is set for April fifth. Is that acceptable?"

"Acceptable to the state," Brad said.

"Not acceptable to the defense," Karen said firmly.

Judge Brown grunted. "What *is* your problem? A little PMS this morning?"

The room was shocked into silence. Karen knew she could walk out if she wanted. Walk out and file a complaint. Everyone had heard him say it. But not everyone would *admit* to having heard him say it. Power did that to the less powerful. But even if there were ten people who would admit to having heard Brown say it, he'd receive nothing but a slap on the wrist, and, in the end, Karen would be chasing her own tail. For no good reason.

She gritted her teeth, fixed him with the laser glare, and said, "I have several problems, Your Honor. Aside from your disgraceful comment, I have the problem of requesting an emergency preliminary hearing."

He looked at her for a moment, realized he'd stepped over the line, and did a most unusual about-face. "I withdraw the PMS comment. Uncalled for. An emergency preliminary hearing? On what grounds?"

Those behind Karen started breathing again.

"On the grounds that I believe the death of Ralph Vincenzo is directly related to this case."

The judge looked at the complaint. "Who the hell is Ralph Vincenzo? He's not listed in this complaint."

Karen tried to make him understand. "Your Honor, Ralph Vincenzo is, or was, the partner of—"

"I don't want to hear it," he bellowed. "His name is not on this complaint. Motion denied. You are entitled to a preliminary hearing. However, my docket is pretty full at the moment. Let's say January fifteen. How's that suit you?"

"Not at all," Karen said. "May we approach?"

Judge Brown slapped his hand on the bench. "No, you may not. I won't have you standing in front of my bench and giving me arguments, Counselor. If you have something to say, put it in writing and move it through channels. This is my court. Here, we do things my way. Understand?"

"Yes, Your Honor," Karen hissed.

"You have anything else?"

"I do. But in view of the comments just made by Your Honor, I'll present my motions in writing."

"You do that."

She turned to Colin. "Give the motions to the clerk now."

Colin reached into his bag, pulled out the motions he'd worked on most of the night, and walked to the clerk's desk. As he did so, Brown stared at Karen and said, "I have something to say to you. I don't want you shooting your mouth off to the press again, understand?"

"Are you imposing a gag order, Your Honor?"

"Not yet," he said. His rheumy eyes were filled with undisguised loathing. "I don't like imposing gag orders, but if you force me to do it, I will."

Karen's own glare had become a living thing. Swallowing hard, she said, "I understand, Your Honor."

Brown slammed his gavel. "Next case."

The bailiff called the next case. Karen turned to Brad. "We have to talk," she said, sotto voce. Before Brad could answer, Brown leaned forward and boomed. "We're done with you, Ms. Mondori. Get out of my courtroom."

He was forever getting her name wrong. Was it deliberate? Probably. Could she do anything about it? Not likely. Karen grabbed a confused Jack Palmer's hand and whispered, "Don't let all this bother you, Jack. Things are progressing nicely. Hang in."

Jack, wide-eyed, looking a little better this morning, said, "I don't understand."

"I can't talk now. I'll come and see you tonight. I'll explain everything."

Jack nodded as the judge screamed, "Ms. Mondori?"

"I'm leaving, Your Honor."

It was an hour before Brad walked out of the courtroom. Karen was waiting for him in the hallway. She'd worked up a good head of steam. "Did you have anything to do with Judge Brown's behavior?"

Brad grinned. "If I did, do you think I'd tell you?" He started walking toward the elevator. "I can't talk to you now. I have to get ready for another trial. Strange as it may seem, Jack Palmer is not the only person in Pinellas County charged with a serious felony."

Karen ignored the rebuff and struggled to keep up

with Brad's long strides. "Ralph Vincenzo," she said, "was about to storm into Caroline DeFauldo's house when he was killed by security people she'd hired. Why would she hire security people? Because she was expecting Ralph to show up, that's why. And why was Ralph there with a gun in his hand? Because he wanted to know, as do a few other people, what happened to all that money."

They had reached the elevator. The door opened. Karen and Brad jammed themselves inside. Down at ground level, Karen followed Brad into his rabbit-warren office, pecking away at him like a chicken after seed. "Can't you see it?" she said. "This whole thing is one giant setup. Jack Palmer was in Caroline De-Fauldo's house at the exact moment Dan DeFauldo walked in because Caroline choreographed it that way. She wanted her husband dead."

Brad took of his jacket, threw it over the coat rack, then slumped in his chair. "I thought I told you I have to get ready for court. What is it with you? I've never seen you so irritatingly obsessive."

She wanted to spit in his eye. "Damn it, Brad, this case should be reopened."

He steepled his hands and glared at her. "I'm not going to argue with you any longer. If you want to go over my head, feel free. But I suspect those motions Colin dropped on the clerk's desk contain that very request."

Karen opened her briefcase the threw copies of the motions on his desk. "I want a court order to depose Caroline, preferably before she disappears. The way things are going, that isn't out of the question. I also want the Florida Department of Law Enforcement to take a look at the materials found in Dan DeFauldo's brain during the autopsy. I feel they may provide important clues. And then, as I said in court, I'm asking for an emergency preliminary hearing. An innocent man is wasting away in jail. Did you know he's being treated by a psychiatrist for depression?"

"No."

"It's true. He's suicidal, Brad. I'm going to lose this guy unless we get this straightened out real fast. I'll send you a copy of the doctor's report."

"Along with another motion?"

"You have it in your hands."

He looked at it quickly, then threw it on his desk with the others. "I saw the ads you ran in the paper. Any of the investors come forward yet?"

"No. I have an appointment in Tampa this afternoon to discuss that very issue."

Brad laughed. "With whom? The feds?"

"Yes."

"Geez. You're really pulling out all the stops."

"I have to. You won't lift a finger."

He glared at her. "Frankly, I think everything you're doing is just for publicity."

"You can't possibly think that," she said.

"I'm afraid so, and it troubles me. When you decided to take this case pro bono, I was somewhat astonished, but I figured you were using the case to bolster your campaign to make all lawyers rich." He leaned back in the chair. "Now, I see something else. I see a woman racking up a few hundred thousand dollars' worth of free publicity. I thought you were more ethical than that, Karen."

It was probably the cruelest thing he'd ever said to her in all the time they'd known each other. It cut her deeply. She picked up her attaché case, slung her handbag over her shoulder, and prepared to leave.

"Karen," he said softly.

"What?"

"I'll set up the depo with Mrs. DeFauldo. It's to be conducted in my interview room, and I'll set it up as soon as possible. The rest is up to the judge."

"Thanks," she said coldly.

It was raining hard when Karen reached the federal building on Zack Street in Tampa. She parked the Beemer in a public lot a half block away, got out, opened her umbrella, and hurried to the rear entrance of the building. She went through security, then onto the elevator and up to the sixth floor.

The FBI agent assigned to the Vinde Investments case was a muscular, crew-cut, square-jawed man named Tom Foote. He showed her to a seat in his small, austere office, then sat behind a beat-up walnut desk. The rain pounded noisily against the window.

"So," he said, "you're Karen Perry-Mondori. I've heard a lot about you."

"Good or bad?"

He smiled. "Depends on how you define the terms. A couple of the guys say you worked them over pretty good on the Baxter case."

She remembered. "It didn't do much good. I still lost."

"Not from lack of trying. How can I help you?"

She took a deep breath, then said, "Are you aware I'm defending the man accused of killing Dan DeFauldo?"

"I am. Kinda hard to miss unless you've been off the planet for a few days."

She let that slide. "You folks are investigating Vinde Investments. I think there's a connection between what happened at Vinde and the deaths of Dan DeFauldo and Ralph Vincenzo."

He seemed amused. "How so?"

"You first. What can you tell me about Vinde?"

Foote folded his hands in front of him. "Not much, I'm afraid. I can confirm that we are investigating the company, but that's about it. We have a policy of not discussing ongoing investigations. It's out of my hands. But I'd be interested in your thoughts on the connection you mentioned."

Karen shook her head. "Mr. Foote, I believe in two-way streets. I'll be happy to share with you what I know, but I'm not simply going to be a conduit for information. I have a client rotting away in jail, an innocent man who has been sucked into some grandiose scheme resulting in somebody getting very rich. I need help, and I'm prepared to give you quid pro quo. But there's no free ride."

Foote smiled, showing perfect teeth. "I'd like to help you, really. But I'm pretty new at the bureau. I can't afford to get in trouble."

"Trouble? What trouble?"

He shrugged.

"So I came all the way over here for nothing? Thanks a lot."

He shrugged again. "Maybe . . . maybe if you *did* tell me what was on your mind, I could take it upstairs. If the resident-agent-in-charge saw that you were trying to help us, he might be inclined . . . "

Karen stood up. "I've been at this awhile, Agent Foote. So have you, obviously."

He leaned forward, sighed, then said, "Sit down, please."

Karen sat.

"This is off the record, okay?"

"Agreed. That goes for me as well."

"Fine. This is a little complicated, but bear with me."

"I will."

"Okay. Vinde Investments was running two operations: one legitimate and one that was essentially an offshore tax evasion scheme. Whoever took the money took it all. We've been interviewing investors, but most of them were involved in the legitimate investments. For obvious reasons, the ones involved in the tax-dodge deal aren't at all eager to talk to us. We've asked the people we've talked to not to discuss this case with you or anyone else, and that's why none of them have contacted you to this point."

"Why?"

"Because we like to conduct our investigations without a lot of conflict with other investigations. Your client is of no interest to us."

"Go on."

"I'm not prepared to tell you how the offshore operation was conducted, but I can tell you that millions of dollars are missing and only two people had access to that money. As you might imagine, those two people were Dan DeFauldo and Ralph Vincenzo. Now, with both of them dead, things are going to get sticky."

"Do you know where the money went?"

"Yes. It was transferred from a New York bank to a Swiss bank, and from there to a bank in the city of Kralendijk, on the island of Bonaire in the Netherlands Antilles. The trail ends there. We're working through diplomatic channels to try and trace it further."

"Do you know who took it?"

"We're not sure. And that's all I'm able to tell you."

Karen thought for a moment, then said, "Are you aware of the details surrounding my case?"

"Only what I see on television and read in the newspapers. I assume they've made the usual errors."

"These transfers . . . were they done electronically?"

"For the most part, yes."

"Using codes?"

"Yes."

Karen nodded. "Consider this, Agent Foote. Let us assume that Caroline DeFauldo somehow knew those codes. Would it be possible for her to make the transfers?"

"I guess it would."

"Just for the sake of discussion, let's assume that she did. When were the transfers made?"

"I'm not at liberty to say."

"Before Mr. DeFauldo's death?"

"Yes."

"Isn't it curious that Dan DeFauldo was killed after the transfers were made? Isn't it even more curious that Ralph Vincenzo gets killed a few days later while attempting to force his way into Caroline DeFauldo's house?"

"Yes, that is, as you say, curious. However, the explanations we've examined to this point seem to fit."

"Really? Isn't it possible that Caroline DeFauldo took the money and arranged for the deaths of her husband and Ralph Vincenzo?"

"I see where you're headed. It's a nice theory, but it won't fly."

"Why not?"

"Because the last transfer, the one that took place in the Netherlands Antilles, was done in person, by a man we assume was Ralph Vincenzo. In addition, we gave Mrs. DeFauldo a polygraph test, at which time we asked her about her involvement in the money transfer. She claims she knows nothing—and she passed the polygraph test."

Karen felt her stomach flip. She couldn't very well challenge the results of Caroline's polygraph test without compromising the results of the test given Jack. "Did you happen to ask her about the murder of her husband?"

He smiled. "No, we didn't. That has nothing to do with our case."

"It may have everything to do with your case."

"Well, we'll handle our end without your help. No offense."

"None taken. So you think Ralph Vincenzo orchestrated this deal, right?"

"We think so."

"And Ralph traveled to the Netherlands Antilles, went into a bank, and walked away with six million bucks. Is that what you're telling me?"

"That's how it looks, yes."

"Then, explain something to me. Why the hell would he come back?"

"I'm sorry I had to rush off like that," Karen said.

"It's okay. I know how busy you are."

"Dr. Eisen says you've been eating. Good for you. How do you like Eisen?"

"He's okay. Sure asks a lot of questions."

"That's his job, trying to find out what makes you tick. Once he's got you figured out, he'll set you straight. You'll feel a lot better, believe me."

Jack Palmer shrugged. "I hope you're right."

Karen and her client were jammed into one of the small lawyer-client interview rooms. All around her, similar discussions were being conducted, for evening provided the best time for lawyers to see their clients. Offices were usually closed, phones silenced, computers turned off. In the evening, a lawyer could concentrate on the business at hand.

"I want you to know that we're making great progress," Karen said.

"Really?"

"Yes. Ralph Vincenzo's death has cast a new light on this case. Doubt, wherever it comes from, increases our chances for success, even if the preliminary hearing fails. Your chances are improving with each passing moment. I want you to believe that."

"I'll try."

"I've talked to one of our divorce specialists. He tells me that if you're acquitted, you and your wife will probably be granted joint custody of the children should there be a divorce. That means she can't take the children to some other state without your permission."

"You're sure?"

"I'm positive. And no matter what happens, you'll be able to talk to your kids in a matter of days. Your wife cannot stop you from seeing them, either. You just have to hang in there."

"I will," he said earnestly. "God, I miss them. I never realized how much they meant to me until now."

"I'm sure they feel the same way about you, Jack."

"I hope so."

"Listen to me. You're a decent person. What happened to you can't change that. And I'm going to fight for your freedom with every ounce of energy I have. This has become a mission for me."

Jack smiled. "Because of what Caroline said about your husband?"

It was a question that gave her hope. For the first time since he'd been arrested, Jack Palmer was aware of events outside his own world of pain and anguish. Dr. Eisen was working his magic.

"Partly," Karen said. "But mostly, I resent what she

did to you. It was cruel and evil, and I won't rest until she pays for it."

The smile left Jack's face. "How will I ever be able to repay you for what you're doing?"

"Don't even think about that. Think about your future. You've got one, Jack. You'll get another job, and you'll see your kids, and eventually, you'll meet a woman who loves you for what you are. You keep thinking positive thoughts, and I'll do what I do best. Okay?"

"Okay," he said.

He sounded as if he meant it.

Nineteen

The deposition of Caroline DeFauldo did not take place at Brad's office as planned. Instead, it took place at Jonathan Walsingham's plush offices, at Jonathan's insistence. Since Caroline was not a suspect, simply a witness, Brad was hard put to argue.

Jonathan sat with his client, looking confident and relaxed, apparently unruffled by his failure to have Karen thrown off the case. There was a smug smile on his lips, his Armani suit gleamed, and his dyed black hair was perfectly in place, like everything in this magnificently appointed conference room.

The room fairly screamed of success, furnished in rich mahogany with fine fabric upholstery, original oils on the expensively papered walls, the large mahogany conference table shining like a mirror, the Wedgwood-filled china closet in one corner gleaming with its gold-trimmed booty. Even the view was magnificent, overlooking one of the thousands of sprawling marinas that helped make Florida such a mecca for those in love with the sea.

Caroline was dressed in a severe dark blue suit that deemphasized her magnificent body. Her lovely face was skillfully made up, her eyes misty, her entire visage the personification of the still-grieving widow being put upon by a sleazy lawyer trying to make a name for herself. Her husband had been shot to death in cold blood by this lawyer's raping, murdering client, and here she was being forced to submit, for the second time, to another rape of sorts—an attack on her honor.

At one end of the long table, a court stenographer sat with fingers resting on the keys of a shorthand machine. At the other end of the table, Brad Keats looked bored. And across the table from Jonathan and Caroline, a very nervous Colin sat next to Karen, his eyes wide with excitement, his mouth slightly open in anticipation, this being his first deposition in a major criminal case.

Karen made short work of the preliminaries, then got right down to business. Since Caroline was the only witness, other than Jack, to the death of her husband, the object of this exercise was to get a statement, made under oath, that might conflict with statements made later during the preliminary hearing. If the statements *did* conflict, the doors were thus opened for a more expansive cross-examination than would normally be the case.

To Caroline, she said, "Would you explain when and how you first met Jack Palmer?"

Caroline looked at Jonathan. He nodded.

"I met him at an adult education center in Tarpon Springs. We were both taking a course in word processing."

"Do you recall the date?"

"Yes. It was Thursday, October seventh."

Karen made a note, then asked, "Can you tell us what happened that night?"

"What do you mean?"

"Did Jack Palmer say or do something that you might have considered as being forward?"

"No, he didn't," she said.

"Okay, how about the next time you met him?"

"I never met him, as you're saying. I attended classes. He also attended the same classes. I don't appreciate your inferences."

Jonathan smiled. Brad stared at the ceiling and shook his head. "I'm not inferring anything," Karen said, discomforted by her own defensiveness. "You attended a total of five classes with Mr. Palmer, is that right?"

"I wasn't *with* Jack," she said. "I was there, and so was he, but we weren't together."

The woman had been carefully coached. Jonathan looked more superior than usual.

"But you talked to each other during those classes, is that correct?"

"Of course we talked. I talked to most of the people there."

"Did you ever talk with Mr. Palmer after class?"

Caroline took a deep breath, then said, "Perhaps I did, if only for a few moments, like on our way to our cars or something."

"Did you and Mr. Palmer ever sit together inside a car and talk?"

"No."

"You never sat inside a car together, either his or yours?"

"No."

"Did Mr. Palmer ever come on to you?"

"Not until that awful dinner," she said.

"So, up to that point, you felt safe with him, is that correct?"

"Up until that terrible night, yes."

"For the record, when you say 'that terrible night' are you referring to the night of November ten?"

"Yes."

"During the five sessions you attended, did you ever come on to Mr. Palmer?"

"No!"

"Objection," Jonathan thundered, in his most outraged voice. "Mrs. DeFauldo is a *victim*. She doesn't have to sit here and be subjected to this kind of scandalous innuendo."

Karen smiled. "There's no jury here to impress, Jonathan. I asked her a direct question, and she answered it. There's no innuendo. Can we move on?"

Jonathan waved a finger in the air. "Watch yourself, Karen."

Karen ignored the comment. "When you talked to Mr. Palmer on the way to your cars, what did you and Mr. Palmer talk about?"

"He did most of the talking," she answered. "He said he wanted to be a writer. So did I, so we talked about that a lot. We also talked about books we'd read, movies we'd seen, sort of comparing notes."

"You say you talked a lot. Is that correct?"

"Well, not really."

"But you just said you and Mr. Palmer talked about being writers a lot. How long did these conversations last?"

"They weren't conversations. He said he wanted to write, and I said I did, too. That was all."

"You said you also talked about movies and books. That would take more than a few seconds, wouldn't it?"

"Yes. I guess it would. Maybe a minute or two."

Finally, a small chink in the armor. "You both wanted to be writers, is that correct?"

"I just said that, yes."

Karen made a note. "What kind of stories do you write?"

"All kinds."

"Can you give me an example?"

"Not offhand."

"I see. Have you ever written a romantic story?"

"I may have."

Karen leaned back in her chair and tapped her pencil on the table. "Jonathan, would you tell your client that being evasive is just going to drag this out?"

Jonathan gave Caroline a nod. "Go ahead. You have nothing to be ashamed of. She's just trying to rattle you."

Karen looked at the court stenographer. "Please note that I am objecting to the characterization of me made by Mr. Walsingham." Then, to Caroline, she said, "Isn't it true that you told my client you were interested in writing romance novels?"

Caroline hesitated, then said, "Yes, that much is true."

"I ask you again, have you ever written a romantic story?"

She hesitated, then said, "Yes."

"About how many?"

"I don't know."

"Just a rough estimate."

Her eyes blazing with hostility, Caroline said, "Twenty, okay?"

Karen pressed her. "Did any of these stories involve a rich woman and a gardener?"

"No."

Karen's eyebrows shot up. "Really. What kind of stories were they?"

Caroline waved a hand in the air. "Just fluffy little things, all right?"

"Could you give me an example?"

Caroline sighed deeply, then said, "One was about a

woman who had lost her husband in the Vietnamese War. She finds a new love. Nothing earthshaking."

"That's one. What else?"

Jonathan held a finger in the air. "You're badgering her, Karen. Cut it out."

Karen let it go. "Do any of your stories involve rich women?"

"No."

"Do any of your stories involve handsome gardeners?"

"No."

"Did you ever show Mr. Palmer anything you'd written?"

"No. Why would I?"

"Isn't it true that you showed Mr. Palmer a short story involving a rich woman and a gardener?"

"Objection," Jonathan said. "She's already answered that question. She said she didn't show Mr. Palmer any of her stories. She also said she never wrote a story involving a rich woman or a gardener. Move on, Karen."

"Very well," Karen said. "Her answer is no, is that correct?"

"Correct," Jonathan said. "How many ways does she have to say it?"

"Thank you," Karen said. "Mrs. DeFauldo, did you ever tell Mr. Palmer you were unhappy in your marriage?"

"Of course not."

"Did you ever tell Mr. Palmer your husband was not paying much attention to you?"

Her eyes narrowed as she said, "No!"

"Did you ever tell Mr. Palmer you were dissatisfied with your sex life?"

"I'm going to object to this whole line of questioning,"

Jonathan said. "There's no need for these kinds of questions, Karen."

Karen looked at him sternly. "I think there is. Mrs. DeFauldo claims she was raped by my client. My client claims he was seduced by Mrs. DeFauldo. I'm trying to determine if there was any reason for my client to think he was being seduced. Mrs. DeFauldo's discussions with him are relevant."

Jonathan shook his head. "You're trying to embarrass Mrs. DeFauldo, that's all."

Karen smiled. "Are you instructing your client not to answer the question?"

It was an old trick. If Jonathan answered yes, this deposition would be over. Karen would appear before a judge and ask for a ruling on the question. If the judge ruled against her, another deposition would be scheduled at her expense. If, however, the judge ruled in Karen's favor, the cost of the second deposition, one much costlier, would be borne by Jonathan. In this case, the judge being Joseph Brown, the odds were against Karen. But unless Jonathan was very sure of himself, he was better off having his client answer.

Jonathan frowned, then looked at Caroline. "Let's humor them for a bit. Go ahead."

Caroline, blushing now, said, "I never discuss my sex life with anyone."

"No one?"

"No one. It's personal."

Karen suppressed a smile. "Let's get back to the writing for a moment. Did Mr. Palmer ever show you anything he'd written?"

"Yes. He gave me some chapters of a book he was working on."

"Did you read what he gave you?"

"Yes."

"And did you give it back to him?"

"I did."

"What did you say about his work, if anything?"

"I told him I thought he was going to be a good writer someday."

Karen's eyebrows rose. "Really. And what did he say?"

"He said he hoped I was right."

"So you encouraged him."

"Only in his writing. I genuinely thought it was pretty good."

"And you never asked him to read any of your work?"

Jonathan started to object, but Karen said, "Withdrawn. Strike the question." She took a moment, then looked at Caroline and said, "At some point, you decided to have dinner with Mr. Palmer, is that right?"

Jonathan smiled broadly, then said, "Objection. Karen, let's not twist things around."

Karen returned his smile, then looked at Caroline. "Let me rephrase. At some point, there was an agreement to meet for dinner. Would you tell us how that came about?"

Caroline cleared her throat, then said, "Well, Mr. Palmer had been talking to me all along, like I said, about writing, but it was as two friends would talk. There was never anything sexual about it. If I'd thought there was a risk, I never would have agreed to meet him for dinner, but he seemed so troubled, so I did."

"Why was he troubled?"

Caroline hesitated, then said, "He told me he was having trouble at home. He also said he was worried about his job. He said he couldn't talk to his wife about these things. So he asked if I would have dinner with him."

Karen looked at her notes. "Earlier, you said that all you and Mr. Palmer talked about was the fact that both of you wanted to be writers. That, and how you felt about certain movies and books. Now you're saying that you talked about his personal life, including his fears about his job and the fact that he couldn't talk to his wife. So, do you wish to correct your earlier statement?"

"No. It was at the last class that we attended that he brought it up. I didn't discuss it with him. He just blurted out things about his problems and asked me to have dinner with him."

Karen looked incredulous. "And you agreed?"

"Yes."

"Why?"

"Because I felt sorry for him."

"I see. You felt sorry for him, and you wanted to have dinner with him because it would make him feel better."

"Objection," Jonathan said softly. "Let's not put words in her mouth, okay?"

Karen shrugged. "She said she felt sorry for him."

"Why don't you move on?" Jonathan said.

Karen threw her pencil on the table. "I'm trying to understand why she had dinner with him. She said she felt sorry for him. Feeling sorry for someone and having dinner are two different things. I'm trying to determine if they are linked in this case."

"Of course they are," he said.

"Then let your client answer the question," Karen said sharply.

Jonathan glared at her for a moment, then told Caroline to answer. "I had dinner with him because I felt sorry for him," Caroline said.

"Had you not felt sorry for Mr. Palmer, would you have had dinner with him?"

"No."

"So, in fact, it is your testimony that you agreed to have dinner with him only because you felt sorry for him and were willing to listen to him discuss his personal problems."

"I guess that's right. I know it was a mistake. I was just being kind."

"Who set the place and time?"

"Mr. Palmer did. He said he was usually on the road three nights a week, but he was coming home early the next week. He wanted to meet in Tampa on Wednesday night."

"What was the date agreed upon?"

She brushed a tear from her eye. "The night Dan was killed."

"At what time were you to meet?"

"Eight-thirty."

"Where?"

"At a place called Cafe Creole in Ybor City."

Karen glanced at her list of questions, made a note, then said, "You and Mr. Palmer both live in Palm Harbor. Do you have any idea why Mr. Palmer wanted to eat in Tampa?"

"Yes. He told me. He said he didn't want anyone to get the wrong idea if they saw us. He thought it was better to eat in Tampa."

"Did you tell your husband you were having dinner with Mr. Palmer?"

"I did."

"And what was his reaction?"

"He said it was fine. I'm an actress. There are times when I have dinner with people in the theater or businesspeople who want to discuss a possible commercial deal. Dan understood this. He wasn't jealous at all."

"But this wasn't business, was it?"

"No. I told Dan that Mr. Palmer was depressed. I was trying to cheer him up. My husband thought that was a very honorable thing to do."

"Was that the word he used, *honorable*?"

"Yes."

"What did you and Mr. Palmer talk about during dinner?"

Caroline squirmed in her chair. "Well, at first, he talked about the same things he always talked about, his job, his family, the fact that he wasn't getting anywhere in his life. He said he really wanted to be a writer. Then, after dessert, he started coming on to me. I told him to stop."

"But before he started coming on to you, he told you a lot about himself. Did you offer suggestions, engage in conversation, or otherwise contribute to this discussion?"

"No. He talked, and I listened."

"You said nothing?"

"Not very much at all."

Karen looked deep into the woman's eyes. "What exactly did he say when he came on to you?"

"He said he thought I was beautiful, that his wife didn't like sex, and that he wanted to have sex with me."

"Just like that?"

Caroline looked at Jonathan. The lawyer patted her hand. "Just tell her what you can recall to the best of your ability."

"That's the gist of it," Caroline said. "He was quite bold. I told him I was disappointed in him, and left immediately."

"Did he follow you?"

"Not then. I left the restaurant and got into my car. It took about an hour to get home."

Karen nodded. "And you arrived home at what time?"

"I guess it was about ten-thirty."

"Was your husband home?"

"No."

"Did you know where he was?"

"Yes. He was playing poker with some friends. He always played poker on Wednesday night."

"Did you husband's poker games usually end at around eleven o'clock?"

"No."

"What time, then?"

"I wouldn't know. I was always asleep when he got home."

"He never woke you?"

"No. My husband was very considerate."

"Have you any knowledge as to why your husband left this particular game early?"

"No. We never had the opportunity to discuss it."

"Other than poker nights, what time did you and Mr. DeFauldo usually retire?"

"About eleven."

"And you go to sleep at eleven?"

"No. We would go to *bed* at eleven. Dan and I would usually watch the news, maybe one of the talk shows until twelve-thirty or so, then go to sleep."

"But on the night of November ten, you didn't go to bed at eleven, did you?"

"No. I was very upset by what had happened at the restaurant. I felt like a fool for having tried to help Mr. Palmer. I had thought Mr. Palmer was a friend. When he came on to me at dinner, I was shocked. So, when I came home, I started a fire, showered, and changed. I was trying to calm down."

Karen looked at her notes. "You're an attractive actress and a model. You said earlier that you often dine with associates or businesspeople. Isn't it true that men come on to you all the time?"

"Yes, it is," Caroline said without hesitation. "But it always upsets me, if that's what you're driving at. I know it shouldn't, but it does. I'll never get used to that kind of crassness if I live to be a hundred."

Karen took a deep breath. Caroline was formidable, a brilliant and resourceful adversary. She'd dazzle a jury with her verbal footwork and her calculated composure. Karen had greatly underestimated her considerable intelligence. At least Karen had had the foresight to fight for this deposition. It gave her insight that would help at the hearing.

"Did you have a drink when you got home?"

"Yes."

"Do you remember what you drank?"

"Yes. It was a Baileys Irish Cream."

Karen nodded. "So you started a fire, showered, and changed. What did you wear after you changed clothes?"

"I wore relaxing clothes."

"Could you be a little more specific?"

"It was a white blouse and black skirt. Long."

"The same clothes you wore to the hospital later that night?"

"Yes."

Karen pulled a photograph from her pile of documents. "This is defense Exhibit One for the purposes of this deposition, and will form part of the record. It is a color photograph taken by the police, identified as A663, of the clothes Mrs. DeFauldo was wearing when she arrived at the hospital." She showed the photo to Caroline. "Are these the clothes you were wearing?"

"Yes."

"You call those relaxing clothes?"

"Yes, I do."

"Did you wear a brassiere?"

"Of course."

"Did you wear panties?"

"Yes."

"You were upset. You came home close to the time you would normally retire, knowing your husband was probably going to be late. You started a fire in the fireplace, showered, then got dressed. You put on underwear and a brassiere, then a blouse and a long skirt. What do you normally wear to bed?"

"Nothing. I sleep in the nude."

"Always?"

"Always."

"Then why would you put on a brassiere and panties when you knew you were going to be alone?"

Caroline's face was becoming flushed. "Because I felt like it."

"Not because you were expecting anyone?"

"Objection!" Jonathan yelled.

"Withdrawn. Okay, you had a drink in your hand, you were relaxing by the fire . . . was the stereo on?"

"Yes."

"How long did all this take, the showering, changing, starting a fire, fixing a drink?"

"I don't know. Maybe a half hour."

"What happened then?"

"The doorbell rang."

"What time was that?"

"I guess it would be about eleven."

"Are you sure?"

"No."

"Are you saying you have no idea of the time frame?"

"That's what I'm saying."

Karen pulled out a document. "This is a copy of part of the preliminary police report, number 333499, prepared by a Deputy Cox, in which you gave a statement. For our purposes, we'll call it defense Exhibit Two, and it will form part of this record. Do you recall making a statement to Deputy Cox?"

"I do."

"Do you recall that you stated that Mr. Palmer showed up at your door approximately five minutes after you arrived?"

"I may have said that."

"Well, you did say that. You now state that you're not sure of the time frame. Is your earlier statement incorrect?"

Caroline sneered. "Not at all. I gave that report at a time when I could see my husband lying dead on the floor. I could barely function. I was in shock. I'd been brutally raped and my husband murdered. It was all I could do to remember my own name."

Jonathan smiled. He had good reason to. Other than some minor inconsistencies, his client was continuing to perform brilliantly.

Karen forged on. "What did you do when the doorbell rang?"

"I went to the door and looked through the peephole. I saw it was Mr. Palmer. I thought he was coming by to apologize. I opened the door, and Mr. Palmer stuck a gun in my face. He told me to disarm the alarm system. He said he knew all about the codes and if anyone showed up, he'd kill me on the spot." She put a fluttering hand to her forehead. "I was so shocked!"

Karen shook her head. "You thought he was coming by to apologize?"

"I did. The only reason I agreed to have dinner with him was because I felt sorry for him. I thought he was a decent person. I guess I still wanted to believe that."

Karen suppressed a groan. "What kind of gun was he holding?"

"I don't know."

"Can you say what the gun looked like?"

"It was small. Chrome."

"What happened then?"

Tears started to form in the corners of her eyes. She dabbed at them with a white handkerchief, then said, "He raped me."

Karen hesitated for a moment, then said, "Could you go into a little more detail, please? He was at the front door. What happened after you opened the door and he put the gun to your head and told you to disarm the alarm system?"

"I did as I was told with the alarm. He told me to go to the fireplace." Caroline looked at Jonathan. He patted her hand and nodded. She dropped her head and let the tears stream down her face as she related the events. "He was acting very strange. He told me to take off my clothes. I begged him not to do this, but he insisted. So, I took off my clothes. He did the same. Then he told me to lie on my back on the floor in front of the fireplace. I did so. Then . . . he lay on top of me. I tried to fight him off. I scratched him on the face. But he still raped me."

Karen made a note, then said, "Where was the gun?"

"He'd put it on the floor out of my reach."

"And what did he do when you scratched him?"

"He laughed."

"He laughed?"

"Yes."

"And then?"

"And then he raped me."

Karen dropped her voice about ten decibels as she asked, "Did he penetrate?"

"Yes."

"Did it hurt?"

Jonathan was about to object, then dropped his hand.

"Of course it hurt," Caroline said.

Karen picked up a copy of the hospital report. "According to the doctors who examined you, there were no bruises on your body, no tears or abrasions on your vaginal walls, no sign at all of—"

"Your client had scratches all over his face and chest," Jonathan bellowed.

Karen glared at him. "To continue, the medical report states that you showed signs of being aroused."

Caroline looked Karen straight in the eye. "I can't help that. I am almost constantly moist in that area. It's hormonal, something my gynecologist will testify to. I've been treated for it several times, but the side effects of the treatment are unpleasant. There's a medical name for the condition that escapes me at the moment."

"It's called leukorrhea," Jonathan said.

"Yes, that's it," Caroline said.

"And the name of your gynecologist?"

"Dr. Philip Summers."

Karen could feel her body beginning to tense. The woman had an answer for everything. "Did Mr. Palmer ejaculate?" she asked.

"He didn't have time. Dan came in from the garage and yelled something. Then, Mr. Palmer started shooting him. Dan fell to the floor."

"Dan came in from the garage, you say. Through the kitchen?"

"Yes."

"Did he turn on the kitchen light?"

"Yes."

"Did you notice the light go on?"

"No. I didn't notice anything until I heard Dan's voice."

"What did he say?"

"He called my name. He was shocked, I could tell."

"Then what happened?"

"Jack picked up the gun and started firing. Dan fell to the floor."

"What did you do then?"

"I don't recall."

Karen's eyebrows shot up again. "You don't recall? You were in your living room, naked, your husband lying on the floor shot and bleeding, and the man who shot him standing there beside you. Can't you recall if you said or did anything?"

Caroline dabbed at her eyes, then said, "I was in shock. I may have screamed, I don't know. I know I eventually went over to Dan. He was lying on his back, all bloody. I tried to get him to speak, but he didn't. I knew then he was dead."

"You were still nude?"

"Yes."

"Where was Mr. Palmer?"

"He was putting on his clothes."

"Did Mr. Palmer ever leave the living room?"

"Yes. When he told me to call the police. He stood by the entrance to the kitchen while I made the call. He'd finished dressing, then came up to me and said that I was to tell the police that we were making love, that we had both thought Dan had a gun in his hand and was going to kill us. He pulled a handkerchief out of his pocket, reached into Dan's pocket, and pulled out his keys. He placed them beside Dan's hand. He told me to say that we both mistook the keys in Dan's hand for a gun. He said if I didn't go along with him, he'd either kill me himself or have someone else do it. Then . . ."

She started crying.

"May I suggest a short recess?" Jonathan said.

"No!" Caroline exclaimed. "I want to get this over with."

Karen pressed on. "What happened after Mr. Palmer threatened you?"

"He . . . stood over my husband . . . and fired . . . two shots . . . into his face."

"Just like that?"

"Yes."

"Did he wrap the gun in anything?"

"No."

"How far away was he standing from your husband?"

"About six or seven feet. Off to the side a bit. After he shot Dan again, he told me that's what I could expect if I didn't lie to the police. Then, he said I could get dressed and call the police."

Karen leaned back in her chair. "He made no move to leave?"

"No."

"Why do you think that was?"

"Objection," Jonathan snapped.

"Withdrawn. So Mr. Palmer told you that you were to back up his story, which was that your husband entered the room with what you both thought was a gun in his hand. Correct?"

"Correct."

"But there was only one gun, is that what you're saying?"

"Yes."

"Have you ever been at your husband's office?"

"Of course."

"Are you familiar with the operation of the computer?"

"No."

"But you have a computer at home, do you not?"

"Yes."

"So you are familiar with the operation of a computer."

"Yes, but Dan's was different. I have no idea how it works."

"Did your husband ever discuss with you the handling of the company's cash accounts?"

"No. My husband never discussed business with me at all."

"Did Ralph Vincenzo ever discuss company business with you?"

"No."

"Have you ever met with Ralph Vincenzo socially?"

"Not alone, no. I've attended functions with Ralph and my husband, but I've never been alone with Ralph in my life."

"On the day Ralph Vincenzo was killed, he was coming to see you. Do you know why?"

"I have no idea."

"But you were expecting someone. You had hired security guards to protect you. Why did you do that?"

There was a wisp of a smile on Caroline's lips as she said, "Because Mr. Palmer had threatened to have me killed. I knew he was in jail and that I'd disobeyed his instructions. I was afraid he would hire somebody, as he said he would, to come and kill me."

It was a great answer, one Karen had expected. It all

fit so nicely, this incredible story concocted by a woman with a heart of absolute stone.

"I see. And somebody did try to kill you, didn't they?"

"Objection!" Jonathan cried. "No one knows what was in Ralph's mind. He was drunk."

Karen sighed. "I'll withdraw the remark. Mrs. De-Fauldo, your husband carried no life insurance, is that correct?"

"That's true."

"Did you and your husband ever discuss having life insurance?"

"Yes."

"But he never took out a policy. Why was that?"

"My husband had a heart condition. He was uninsurable."

"What kind of heart condition?"

"One of his heart valves was bad. He could have had it fixed, but Dan was afraid of having open heart surgery. His father died on the operating table during an operation for the very same thing. But Dan was stubborn. I tried for years to change his mind, but I never could."

"As I understand it," Karen said, "the money in the company has disappeared. How are you going to live?"

Caroline sighed. "I have no idea. We had a few thousand dollars in our joint account, but that's all. I'll have to place the house on the market. Other than that, I don't know what I'll do. I earn money from my modeling, but it isn't nearly enough. I guess I'll have to get a regular job."

It was almost too much. Much more of this, and Karen would vomit. She shuffled some papers, then said, "I have just two more questions, and then we're through here. Prior to the night of November ten, did you ever kiss Jack Palmer?"

"No, I did not!"

"I see. Have you been unfaithful to your husband at any time in the last year?"

Jonathan slammed his hand on the table. "That's it. That question is irrelevant and unconscionable. You're a disgrace, Karen."

Karen smiled sweetly. "Thanks for your cooperation, Mrs. DeFauldo."

The deposition was over.

Outside, a smiling Brad Keats passed Karen and Colin on his way to his car. "She makes quite a witness, don't you think?"

Karen smiled. "She does, indeed. She's good, Brad. Real good. But as good as she is, she lied three times. See you at the prelim."

She left him standing there, wondering if she was just bluffing.

An hour after Caroline's deposition, Brad Keats joined Jonathan Walsingham for a hastily called joint press conference held in the very same room used for the taking of the deposition. Amid all the luxury, a very wealthy lawyer and a hardworking prosecutor lowered the boom on Karen. Brad was the first to speak.

"It's become clear to me," he said, "that the defense attorney representing Mr. Jack Palmer is seeking to try this case in the media rather than the proper forum, which is a court of law. In doing so, she demeans the very system she is sworn to support.

"Just so everyone here understands the facts of this case, the police investigation into the death of Mr. Daniel DeFauldo was extensive and complete. The gun used was recovered, analyzed, and found to be the murder weapon. Fingerprints matching those of the suspect now in custody, Mr. Jack Palmer, were found on the weapon. In fact, Mr. Palmer has confessed that he shot Daniel DeFauldo and has signed a statement to that effect.

"The attorney for the defense has made much of the fact that her client passed a lie detector test. In point of fact, lie detector tests are not admissible in court, and for good reason. They are notoriously unreliable. The fact that someone passes a lie detector test means nothing. As prosecutors, we rely on evidence to determine whether or not there is reason to bring charges against a certain suspect.

"The evidence in this case is irrefutable. In addition to the murder weapon, there is strong evidence that the suspect raped Mrs. DeFauldo, that he viciously fired bullets into the already dead body of her husband, and that he threatened Mrs. DeFauldo with death if she refused to corroborate the cock-and-bull story he fabricated for the police.

"I call on the defense attorney to stop using the media to confuse potential jurors and obfuscate due process. I call on her to stop her obvious efforts to subvert the system of justice we all hold so dear."

Brad stepped away from the forest of microphones and stood back as Jonathan took his place.

"I have very few remarks," Jonathan said, his voice booming. "More of a warning."

He stared directly into the cameras, using no notes, wearing his most outraged expression, and said, "Earlier today, Mrs. Caroline DeFauldo took her own polygraph test, a test given at her insistence. Naturally, she passed the examination, as we all knew she would.

"The conduct of the attorney representing Mr. Jack Palmer, the man who viciously raped Caroline De-

Fauldo and murdered her husband, is unconscionable. She is trying to create an atmosphere of confusion by casting doubt on the veracity of Caroline DeFauldo's statements, her morality, and her very being. I can assure you Mrs. DeFauldo will not stand still for any more of this, nor will I. If the attorney for the defense utters another comment of a derogatory nature relative to Caroline DeFauldo, we will launch the biggest slander suit this county has ever seen.

"As a longtime member of the bar, I'm going to be seeking sanctions against Ms. Perry-Mondori. She is, in my opinion, a disgrace to the profession. She is unfit to practice law in this county or any other county. And that's all I have to say. This circus has to stop. And it will stop. I assure you."

He stepped back from the microphones.

Neither Brad nor Jonathan answered questions.

Twenty

With the less-than-wonderful deposition of Caroline DeFauldo complete, it was back to the display boards for Karen and Colin. Caroline, much to Karen's dismay, was a strong witness with near-heroic persuasive powers, a woman capable of bewitching many a juror. If it came down to a case of Caroline's word against that of a namby-pamby Jack Palmer, there would be no contest. The head-to-head battle of key witnesses would be lost. Now it was a case of harvesting every ounce of supportive evidence, and that evidence had to be hard evidence. Yesterday's press conference had turned the tide. The press hostility index had risen ten notches.

Karen and Colin repeated the exercise they had used several times in the past few days, tracing the steps of those involved, matching the physical evidence against the conflicting statements of Jack Palmer and Caroline DeFauldo. But this time, they unceremoniously dumped one of the possible scenarios.

The autopsy performed on the body of Ralph Vincenzo had shown he had an alcohol content of .23. He was drunker than even that figure would indicate, for the analysis of his digestive tract had shown he'd eaten very little in the past few days. He had two viral infections and one bacterial infection, which the M.E. attributed to a weakened immune system brought about by a combination of extreme stress and vitamin deficiency. In short, the man had gone over the edge, driven there by despair and anguish.

The idea of Ralph's being Caroline's secret lover now made no sense at all. But questions still remained. What was he doing at her house, half out of his mind and with a gun in his hand? If Ralph was the one who'd transferred the money, why had he returned? What was his beef with Caroline? Was it possible Ralph wasn't the man with the money? And, if not, did he think Caroline had stolen the money? Had she reneged on some deal they'd made? None of it made sense.

At the deposition, Caroline had hinted that Ralph might have been coming after her at the request of Jack Palmer, but that was patently ridiculous. No one could find a connection between Jack Palmer and Ralph Vincenzo. No one would. There was no connection.

But what *was* Ralph doing there?

A police search of Ralph's rented apartment had revealed little. It was assumed Ralph was hiding out from the feds. That sounded right. But the question kept haunting Karen, refusing to be set aside. If Ralph had stolen the money as the FBI surmised, and had appeared in person at a bank in the Netherlands Antilles, what was he doing back in town? Why take the chance of being caught?

Karen had posed that very question to FBI Agent Foote. He'd simply shrugged. If the FBI had actual knowledge of the reason for Ralph's movements, they weren't talking. All Foote would say was that they were looking into it. Big help.

Around and around they went until Colin finally complained of a headache.

"I'm getting one as well," Karen said. "Let's knock it off for now.

"I'll help clean up," he said, looking at the piles of documents cluttering Karen's desk.

"No," she said. "Leave it. I'll just have to dig them out again tomorrow. I won't be able to work on anything else until I have this one clear in my mind. If you get any bright ideas during the night, call me."

"I will," he said.

"Try to get some sleep. We have those pretrial hearings tomorrow. Did I tell you Judge Brown wants to conduct them in chambers?"

"No. How come?"

"He probably doesn't want the press to hear what we have to say. I'd be willing to bet money that he'll impose a gag order. After all the press conferences, things are getting a little out of hand."

"I'll be ready," Colin said.

Despite her admonition to Colin, Karen kept at it for another hour. With the headache threatening to develop into something worse, she finally gave it up for the day. The phone rang as she was about to leave the office. It was Bill Castor, the private investigator she'd hired.

"How's it going?" he asked.

"Terrible."

"I called you at home, but your husband said you were still at the office."

"I'm above to leave. What have you got for me?"

"Not much, I'm afraid. You want me to fax this stuff to you? It's all written up."

"Sure, Bill. Anything interesting?"

"Not really."

"Well, thanks for the effort."

"Anytime."

Karen hung up the phone and walked to the communications center. The fax was coming off the machine. The cover sheet indicated three pages. She looked around the office. At this hour, near seven, half of the associates were still at work. The nineties' work ethic; sixty to eighty hours a week if you wanted to keep your job. Bill 200 hours a month or take a hike. And it wasn't just at Hewitt, Sinclair. It was the same everywhere. Walter Sinclair wasn't prepared to accept anything less than a five percent increase, so the whip was out.

She pulled the fax from the tray and took it back to her office. At first blush, Bill had been right. There wasn't much. Ralph Vincenzo was an only child. His parents were dead. His ex-wife lived in California.

Dan DeFauldo was born and raised in Chicago, the oldest of three children. He was the only one in the family to get through high school. Upon graduation, he went to the University of Illinois on an academic scholarship, then to work for a Chicago investment firm. Five years later, he moved to New York, where he met both Caroline and Ralph. He'd been married once, and that was to Caroline. Both he and Ralph had moved to Florida to start their own firm four years ago. Until now, there'd been no complaints from clients. On the contrary, most of their clients thought the company was one of the best in the business.

Dan's father was deceased, but his mother, once a warehouse worker with Sears, was still alive, living in a rest home in a Chicago suburb. She was suffering from Alzheimer's disease. The second son, Michael, had been born severely retarded. He was now forty, two years younger than Dan, and institutionalized in a Chicago facility. The third child was the youngest of the trio, a daughter named Rose, who worked as a waitress. At thirty-six, she'd been married twice, had no kids, no money, and not much future.

There was a note that said Rose regularly removed Michael from the institution for about a month a year. She would bring him to her apartment and take care of him, giving him some brief respite from his bleak sanitarium life. In fact, she'd just taken him out again two weeks ago. According to Bill Castor, if there was any affection in the family at all, it existed only between Rose and Michael.

As for Caroline, she was the illegitimate daughter of a New York stripper named Heaven Sent (her legal name). Caroline had left home at the age of eighteen, worked as a waitress and occasional model, and attended night school where she graduated as an accountant, then joined a New York investment firm where she eventually met Dan. Karen grudgingly gave her full marks for that achievement, but it raised another interesting point. If Caroline was trained as an accountant, the possibility that she could make the money transactions took a quantum leap.

But the FBI said it was Ralph.

Karen finally shook off thoughts of Ralph and moved to something else. With two fragmented and dysfunctional families like this, a jury could understand why Caroline had not bothered with a standard funeral or memorial service. Not good.

There was much to do before the preliminary hearing. And unless Karen found the needed evidence, Jack would spend months in jail awaiting trial. Could he survive? That was not at all a certainty. While his spirits were slightly lifted because of his treatment and a glimmer of hope provided by Karen's enthusiasm for his chances, Karen knew that Jack Palmer's spirits would be crushed if the preliminary hearing failed to set him free. She'd made a serious mistake in the handling of this case; she'd allowed the reality of Jack Palmer's fragile emotional state to penetrate the wall that all lawyers were supposed to keep between themselves and their clients. Now, she was paying for it, feeling a deep sense of misplaced responsibility.

Damn!

Judge Brown seemed to sag in his high-backed leather chair. Probably suffering from another hangover, Karen thought, as she and Brad took seats directly in front of the judge's desk. Colin sat to the right and slightly behind Karen. A court reporter sat with her little portable shorthand machine near the door.

Like all of the court reporters who worked with Brown, she would enter the sum and substance of the judge's remarks, not the words verbatim. Those who recorded the judge's remarks word for word did so only once. Transcripts of his remarks went through a sanitary cleansing process. "Little lady" became "counsel for the defense," while "the stupid bastard" might be transcribed as "the defendant."

Judge Brown hacked, spit into his handkerchief, then said, "I thought we'd discuss this quietly and calmly in chambers this morning. Thanks to both of you, the press boys are buzzing around this case like flies on horse shit."

He held up a document. "This is called a gag order. Do you both understand what a gag order is?"

"Yes, Your Honor."

A chorus of two voices.

"Well, I'm not so sure. You've both got mouths on you the size of refrigerators. So let me spell it out in words you two dummies will understand. There is to be no mention of this case to anyone outside the direction

of this court. Not a goddam word. No more press conferences, no more letters to editors, no more billboards,
no ads on TV, no lectures, no seminars, no nothing.
You got it?"

"Yes, Your Honor."

"Good. Now as far as these proceedings are concerned, I don't need any histrionic bullshit from anyone, so let's get this over with as quickly as possible. I
have things to do."

"Yes, Your Honor."

"First," the judge said, "as to the defense request to
depose Mrs. DeFauldo, I understand this request has
been withdrawn as the deposition has already been
conducted. Correct?"

Karen said, "Correct, Your Honor."

Judge Brown gave Karen a rare smile. "Maybe
you'll do us all a favor and withdraw the whole mess."

"I can't," she said.

His jaw stiffened. "Of course you can't. You're a
lawyer, right? Lawyers like to keep the meter running
all the damn day, every damn day. Wouldn't be doing
your job otherwise." He gave the court reporter a look.
She nodded her complete understanding.

"All right," the judge said, "what's all this about
brain tissue?"

Karen cleared her throat, then said, "The autopsy report on the victim indicates that three small pieces of
plastic material were found in the brain of the victim at
the sites where the slugs came to rest. The state has refused to request a lab analysis of that material. The defense requests that the analysis be done."

"Why?"

"As we have stated in our motion, the material may
be evidence. We're entitled to have access to *all* the
evidence, no matter how insignificant it may appear."

The judge looked at Brad. "So, what's the story?"

Brad shrugged. "It means nothing, Your Honor. It's not an issue. The defendant has confessed to pulling the trigger. The autopsy report, combined with the forensics report, proves that the slugs from the gun the defendant used caused the death of the victim. There's no challenge being made to that. The material found in the brain of the victim is irrelevant."

"I agree," the judge said.

"Then," Karen said, "would you allow the defense to have the FDLE lab analyze the material, provided we keep the chain of evidence intact? Whatever information we learn will be offered to the prosecution."

The judge looked at Brad, who shrugged again. "We have no objection. I'm just trying not to waste the taxpayers' money. If Ms. Perry-Mondori wants to spend money like a drunken sailor, that's fine with me."

The judge scribbled on the document. "So ordered." He glared at Karen. "Now, as to your request that the investigation be given back to the police, I've read your motion and see nothing at all that warrants the case being reopened. Motion denied."

"Your Honor—"

He raised a hand. "There you go interrupting again. I thought I told you not to do that."

"Sorry, Your Honor."

He picked up anther document. "Regarding the doctor, the shrink who talked to the defendant, if you want to call him as a witness, that is your right. There's no doctor-patient privilege in this state. You have any objection, Brad?"

"No, Your Honor. However, if Ms. Perry-Mondori is going to call the doctor as a witness, we'd request that the court appoint an independent psychiatrist as a witness for the state. One who has examined the defendant."

Judge Brown looked at him and shook his head. "This doctor *already* works for the state. He's sure as hell not biased in favor of the defendant. I thought you were interested in saving taxpayers' money."

Brad blushed. "Well, yes, of course. But . . . "

"Request denied. I'm sure the good doctor will tell it like it is." He smiled. "Good. Another one out of the way." The judge had worked his way through the pile in jig time. Obviously, he had other things on his mind. Probably a drink.

He fixed his rheumy eyes on Karen. "As for the little lady's request for an emergency preliminary hearing, I see no emergency." He threw her another smile.

Karen's stomach turned.

"However," he continued, "I see my docket has a couple of holes due to some late-in-the-game plea bargains. So . . . " He leaned back in his chair and grinned. "You want a preliminary hearing, little lady, you got it. Starts Monday morning, nine o'clock sharp. How's that grab you?"

Karen was stunned. It would mean she'd be cramming for the next three days with little to work with. But she could hardly refuse. In the first place, she'd asked for the emergency hearing. To refuse to accept an early prelim date would make her look stupid. It would also mean more months of incarceration for her client.

She nodded. "That's fine, Your Honor. I appreciate the consideration. We'll be ready."

Brad was red-faced. "Your Honor, this is a little too soon for us. The arraignment was only a couple of days ago."

Judge Brown turned his head and faced Brad. "You're

the guy who said there's no need for further investigation. You've got everything you need, you said. You said the defendant admitted shooting the victim and the evidence was solid. So what are you worried about?"

Brad's face reddened even further. "Nothing. It's just, well, we like to fully prepare for—"

"It's not a trial, mister, it's a prelim. I don't want the little lady firing incendiary letters off to Tallahassee saying I'm being the big bad wolf again, that I treat women badly, that I don't have the greatest respect for all the women of the bar, even the short ones. I want to put a stop to that crap right now. She wants a quick prelim, she's got it."

The room fell silent. The judge seemed immensely pleased with himself. "Anything else?"

Brad shook his head.

"Not me," Karen said.

"Well, if there's nothing else, you can both get the hell out. I've got things to do."

"Let's go over this again," Karen said, sitting on the edge of her desk. "You've talked to the waiter, and he says there was nothing unusual going on."

"Exactly," Colin said. "They seemed like two businesspeople during dinner. No holding hands, none of that. Caroline left first. Jack stayed around, finished his coffee, paid the bill, then left. The waiter says he figured they'd had a spat of some sort."

Karen picked up a legal pad and drew a line through the waiter's name. "He's out for sure. And the neighbors?"

"I can't find a one who will say that Caroline ever screwed around. The ads we put in the papers have brought forth zip, even the ads in the Orlando papers.

If she did have a boyfriend, they were certainly discreet. I can't find anyone who saw her with another man."

Karen nodded. "If she's as clever as she appears to be, being discreet would be the way she'd handle it. And Dan's poker pals are sticking to their story. They all say the same thing. He seemed to be upset about losing, got up, and left the game. The fact that he's never acted that way before won't help us at all."

She sighed. "Well, the FDLE lab will have the report for us Friday afternoon. Let's hope it opens up something, but it's probably nothing."

There was a knock at the door, and Carl walked in, a smile on his face.

"Hi!" Karen exclaimed, happy to see him. "What are you doing here?"

Carl, dressed in a suit and tie, said, "I came to whisk you away to dinner. You've been working much too hard. It's almost ten."

Karen looked at her watch. "Is it ten already?"

"I'm afraid so. Michelle and a friend went to Tampa to see the opera. The baby-sitter has arrived, and I'm starving. Aren't you?"

Karen suddenly felt cold. Her hand went to her mouth. "The opera?"

Carl gave her a rueful smile. "It's okay."

It wasn't okay at all. She felt awful. "Oh, my. You bought those tickets three months ago. I completely forgot. I'm so sorry, Carl."

He shrugged. "You've been a little preoccupied," he said. "There'll be other operas."

"And other cases," Karen said, her body sagging. "This is not the way I want to live. I've let everything slide. I've been behaving like an idiot."

Carl gripped her arms and looked down into guilt-filled eyes. "Stop beating yourself up. You have to eat. Doctor's orders." He tilted his head toward Colin. "You're welcome to join us, Colin."

Colin shook his head. "I'm too tired to eat. But thanks for asking."

"I'll just freshen up," Karen said, walking out of the office. She would rather have crawled into a hole. Carl was an opera freak, and opera came to the Tampa Bay area infrequently. She'd let him down. Coming so close after her acceptance of Caroline's affair story, it was more than humiliating. She felt as if she were on autopilot, destroying her marriage through sheer stupidity.

Colin reached for his jacket. Carl looked at Karen's cluttered desk. "Is she always this messy at work?"

Colin laughed. "Not at all. We've been working on the Palmer case as you might expect. Autopsy reports, depositions, police reports, lab reports, the usual."

"How's it going?" Carl asked as he idly picked up some photos.

"I'll leave that for Karen to explain," Colin said. "I'm not sure I really know at this point. Good night, Dr. Mondori."

"Good night."

As Colin was heading out the door, Carl shouted. "Colin, what's this?"

Colin looked at the photo in Carl's hand. "That's one of the photos from the medical examiner's file. It's a shot of the late Mr. DeFauldo."

"You're sure it's him? I can't see his face."

"Oh, sure. You can see the identification number on the back of the photo. Case and file number. There's also a tag on his wrist. Same number as on the other shots."

Carl looked at some of the other photos, then returned

his attention to the one he'd first picked up. He kept staring at it intently.

"Something wrong?" Colin asked.

"Probably not," he said. "Good night, Colin."

"Thanks again for the invitation to dinner."

"You're quite welcome."

When Karen returned, she saw her husband sitting at
her desk, using a magnifying glass to examine one of
the photos. "I'm really sorry, Carl. I *have* been preoccupied. I should never have taken this damn case. You
were right."

He raised a hand to stop her. "It's really no big deal.
I don't feel much like opera anyway. Not tonight."

"Why? What happened?"

He put down the photo and magnifying glass and
stared at the ceiling. "My third operation of the day
was supposed to be routine, a patient with a small fragment of the L4-L5 disc pressing against a nerve. Duck
soup, right? Except the patient had a goddam heart attack about an hour in."

"Oh, no."

"We've got him all strapped up in the brace, right?
No time to bring him down. The code team comes in
and tries to work. Impossible. I'm slapping staples in
while they're trying to move the brace. Chaos! The guy
is in full cardiac arrest. I finally get him stapled up and
step back. They're trying everything, but it's not working."

"Did he make it?"

Carl shook his head. "He was dead from the time the
alarm went off. Apparently, he had an aortic aneurysm
that got past everyone. It burst while we were working
on him. No previous record of heart trouble, but you
can be sure I'll get sued."

"Why?"

"He was twenty-eight, Karen. Twenty-eight-year-old men aren't supposed to die while being operated on for a herniated disc. When they do, it's always because some doctor screwed up. Has to be. Nothing ever happens unless *somebody* screws up, right?"

She touched his hand. "I'm sorry, Carl. I really am. But you've been through this before. You'll be fine."

He sighed. "We'll see. At least I know where to find a good attorney."

"Absolutely. Do you really feel like eating out? It's late. I can fix something at home."

"I was hoping you'd suggest that." He handed her the photo he'd been examining, a puzzled look on his face. "Who's this?"

Karen looked at the photo and said, "It's Dan De-Fauldo. It's a shot taken at the morgue with Dan lying facedown. They always take lots of photos. Why do you ask?"

"Are you sure it's Dan?"

She looked more closely at the photo. "Yes, I'm sure. There's the ID number and—"

"Karen, something is very wrong."

As Karen looked at him, she felt a sudden chill. "Wrong? What do you mean?"

He took the photo from her hands, looked at it again, then said, "Remember the hearing? The one where Caroline claimed she and I made love in my office?"

"I could hardly forget," Karen said.

"Exactly. And it was all about Caroline visiting her husband after I'd operated on his back, right?"

Karen seemed puzzled. "What are you driving at?"

Carl handed her the photo. "The photo you have in your hand is of a man with the same basic height and build as Dan, but it's not Dan DeFauldo."

Karen felt her heart begin to pound. "What?"

Carl gave her a look. Admittedly, she was exhausted, but Carl was somewhat surprised Karen hadn't picked up on this before. It wasn't like her. "Take another look," he said. "There's no scar from my operation. I'm good, Karen, but I'm not that good. If this is a photo of Dan DeFauldo, there should be a two-inch scar right along the spine at the L4-5 location. This body has no scar at all."

Karen, her fingers trembling, stared at the picture, then at her husband. Her eyes were wide, the adrenaline coursing through her veins.

"This isn't Dan DeFauldo," he repeated. "Not unless this photo got mixed up with another one. Is that possible?"

"It's possible," Karen said breathlessly, "but highly unlikely."

She slumped to a chair, threw her head back, and stared at the ceiling. "My God!"

Now Carl looked confused. "I don't get it. If this isn't Dan, who the hell is it?"

Karen didn't answer. Suddenly infused with new energy, she leaped up and rummaged through the other photos on her desk. She grabbed one and handed it to Carl. "Tell me what you see."

He studied it for a moment, then said, "I see a man with two gunshot wounds to the face. It looks like Dan, all right. Hard to tell with all the damage. But . . . the distance between the eyes, even with the trauma, doesn't seem quite right. And the nose seems a little large."

"Would you have thought this was Dan DeFauldo?"

He looked at the photo again. "I guess I would."

"You sure would if Caroline said it was Dan."

"No question. But if this isn't Dan . . . "

Karen grabbed the phone.

"Who are you calling at this hour?" he asked.

"A private investigator named Bill Castor. He works twenty-four hours a day."

"Nobody works—"

Her raised hand cut him off. "Bill? Karen Perry-Mondori. Yes. Listen, can you get your hands on a photo of Michael DeFauldo? Yes. Prints, too, if possible. I need the whole package yesterday. You will? Great. Cost is no object. No, you heard right. Thanks."

Karen hung up the phone, walked slowly toward her husband, leaned over, and kissed him on the lips. "Thank you," she said, huskily.

"You're welcome."

"Have you got X-ray plates, MRI plates, surgery notes, anything in writing?"

"Sure. I've got the entire file."

Karen kissed him again. "Thank you, my love. You've just broken this case wide open. And with it, you've saved another life."

He was staring at the picture. "I heard you on the phone. Are you saying this is Michael DeFauldo?"

"I'm not sure, but I'm guessing it is."

"Who's Michael?"

Karen sighed. "Michael DeFauldo is Dan's retarded brother. He's two years younger than Dan."

Carl stared at her. The implications were beginning to sink in.

"Exactly."

He was astounded. "So, you were right all along. About Caroline and Dan and the whole thing. This *was* a setup."

"Yes, it was." As she said it, she could literally feel the heavy blanket of discouragement being lifted from her narrow shoulders.

"What are you going to do?" Carl asked.

"I'm not sure. As you pointed out, it's possible this

photo got mixed up with another one, but I doubt it. In any event, I need more direct evidence. Once I have it all put together, I'll go to the prosecutor." She fought the impulse to rub her tired eyes. "Then again, maybe I won't."

Carl look mystified. "Would you care to explain that to me?"

She smiled at him. "Sure. Over dinner."

Twenty-one

The jigsaw puzzle was almost complete.

Karen and Colin reinterviewed witness after witness. Karen talked to agent Foote at the FBI, told him what she suspected, and asked for a special favor. Foote, playing it close to the vest as usual, said he'd think about it.

Karen sent Colin to Chicago to interview Rose Halliday, née DeFauldo. Colin's instructions were to tell her that he was there to discuss the death of Dan DeFauldo. He was *really* there to determine Michael's whereabouts. In the event Michael could not be found, Colin was to return without revealing his mission to Rose. That would have been cruel.

Bill Castor came through with faxed photos and prints of Michael DeFauldo on Friday morning. That same afternoon, the FDLE report on the analysis of the small plastic pieces found in Dan's brain arrived. Karen studied it for a minute, then let out a sigh. Then, Colin called. He was on his way home.

"Did you find Michael?"

"Did you think I would?"

"No."

"You were right," he said, his voice filled with sadness. "I have the whole setup, Karen. We've got her."

Karen sighed. "Well done, Colin."

"I should be thrilled, but I feel terrible," he said. "Don't you think she should be told?"

"I wish we could, but there's still a slim chance we're wrong. Once we prove it in court . . . "

"I understand."

"Not much fun, is it?"

"No."

"Try to keep things in perspective, Colin. We're fighting to get an innocent man released. While the road may be filled with emotional potholes, the final destination will give you a tremendous sense of satisfaction."

"I'm sure that's true. But . . . "

"What?"

"She's a very caring person. So innocent. I feel like a shit."

Karen gave him some more words of encouragement, then hung up the phone. She leaned back in her chair, feeling the familiar rush of adrenaline coursing through her body. Vindication was not far away. More important, freedom for her client was close.

At six, the normal business day at an end, Karen called Brad Keats at his home. She told him only some of what she knew, hoping he would end the conversation before she had to reveal everything.

"I'm sorry to trouble you at home," she said amiably, "but I've uncovered some new evidence. We should discuss it before Monday."

She heard a sigh at the other end of the line. "What new evidence?"

She chose her words carefully. "Well, for example, one of those little pieces of plastic they found in Dan's brain turned out to be from a milk jug. It's very important."

"A milk jug?"

"Yes."

"I don't see the significance."

"You don't? Well, if we could meet, I'd be happy to explain the significance to you."

There was a hesitation, then, "I don't think so, Karen. This is the third or fourth time you've bugged me on this case. I meant what I said at that press conference. You keep coming up with these crazy theories that turn out to be nothing but time-wasters. You've become a glory-seeker. You just like pulling my chain."

"How can you say that?" she protested, her voice as sweet as fresh honey. "I'm the one who's been pressing for an emergency prelim. I've agreed to the Monday hearing, haven't I? I'm just trying to save you some embarrassment, Brad. Jack Palmer is innocent. I'm going to prove it on Monday. I'm asking you for the last time to drop the charges while you take a look at the evidence I've gathered. If I'm pulling your chain, you can always refile the charges."

"Forget it." he said harshly. "You can present your evidence in court. and don't call me at home again."

Karen held her breath for a moment, then said, "Whatever you say, Brad. Just write down in your journal that we had this conversation, okay? I wouldn't want anyone to think I was being unprofessional."

She was smiling as she hung up the phone.

By Sunday, Carl had resigned himself to the fact Karen would be out of touch for the entire weekend. He'd gone golfing with some doctor buddies. Michelle had taken Andrea for a boat ride on the Gulf of Mexico. The child seemed to have weathered the storm created by her teasing classmates. But Carl and Karen had pledged to take her out of school for a week as soon as the Palmer case was over. They would spend the week together, as a family, building up Andrea's confidence.

Karen was closeted in her office with Colin, reading documents, working her chart boards, trying to put together the final touches on a presentation that would have her client out of jail by Monday night. With the preliminary hearing just hours away, her concentration was at a high pitch. Perhaps it was this focus, this extreme intensity, that triggered the creative impulse. Whatever the reason, the idea hit her with the force of a bolt of lightning, literally taking her breath away.

She was standing in the file room with a key in her hand, a key that would open a cabinet holding some documents she thought might prove useful. But it wasn't the documents that stirred her imagination; it was the key in her hand. She turned it over and over as a small scene kept replaying in her mind—an uncomplicated scene: Rosemary Perkins at the door making sure Karen still had keys to Rosemary's house in case of emergency. Neighbors were like that, trusting, sometimes dependent, for there were always little things that needed to be attended to when a house was left empty for any length of time.

Again, she turned the key in her hand. Then she dashed back to her office and called Charlie Simms. He was at home, she was told. She called him there.

"It's my day off," he complained.

"I'm sorry, Charlie, but I need a cop in on this, one who can testify in court if need be. I can't take the chance that Judge Brown will rule this evidence, if it exists at all, is inadmissable. With you there, my chances improve."

She heard a groan. "You're something. You realize I'm watching some of my old pals on the tube? There's a doubleheader today."

"So, we can do it tonight after the games. After dinner, if you like. That would even be better. It'll be dark then."

"Do what?"

She told him.

When she hung up the telephone, Colin was staring at her, his face a portrait of confusion. "What was *that* all about?"

"I'm not sure," she said.

At nine-thirty that evening, Karen, Colin, and Detective Charlie Simms stood by the front door of a house owned by Mr. and Mrs. Paul Hendershot. The house was another example of modern Florida architecture, a Spanish design featuring stressed brick, curved window openings, and a red tile roof. It stood next to the DeFauldo house, itself glowing from within with warm yellow light. Karen shivered involuntarily.

She took a deep breath and rang the doorbell. The light over the door blinked on and the door opened.

Paul Hendershot, an attractive man of about fifty, tall and lean, looked perplexed as he peered at the badge being held by Charlie Simms. He looked at Karen and scowled, then at Colin, then back at Charlie. "I recognize the lawyers," he said derisively, "but who are you?"

"Detective Simms," Charlie said. "Pinellas County Sheriff's Office. I'm here unofficially, sir. We're sorry to bother you. There's nothing to be concerned about. We'd just like to ask your cooperation on something. May we come in?"

"Unofficially?"

"That's right, sir. You can close the door in my face if you like. But we'd all sure appreciate the chance to talk to you."

Like most law-abiding citizens, Hendershot had a certain respect for law enforcement officers—and a certain curiosity as to why a cop was standing at his front door on a Sunday evening. Reluctantly, he waved the visiting trio into the living room. "My wife has gone to bed, so let's not be noisy. What's this all about?"

Charlie looked at Karen. "This is your show," he said laconically.

"Mr. Hendershot," Karen began, "you may or may not know that there is a preliminary hearing tomorrow morning concerning the death of Dan DeFauldo."

"So I understand," he said harshly. "And you are the woman who is defending the man who killed him. You have a lot of gall coming around here. Dan and Caroline are . . . were . . . dear friends. I thought you were also their friend. Maybe the only friend you lawyers have is a dollar bill."

Karen let the harsh words roll off her shoulders. "I realize this is an imposition, and I understand your position. But I must tell you that there are some issues in this case still unresolved. If you've been following the case, you know that I feel my client is innocent."

Hendershot frowned. "I wouldn't have expected you to say anything else. But there was no need to drag Caroline through the mud. I hope her lawyer nails you good. I think what you've done is disgraceful all the way through."

Karen's cheeks reddened, but she held her tongue.

"We're just trying to get at the truth," Karen said. "And you strike me as the kind of man who would want the truth to come out."

Hendershot glared at her. "What truth? Your truth?" He pointed a thumb at Colin. "Look, your flunkie has been out here twice already. I've told him everything I know." He was getting agitated. "What is all this, anyway? Why did you bring a policeman with you?"

Karen decided to get to it. "Would you happen to have keys to any of your neighbors' homes?"

He seemed offended. "What are you suggesting?"

"I'm not suggesting anything. I hold keys that allow me access to the homes of three of my neighbors. When they go away on vacation, I check and see that everything is okay. I just wondered if you and your wife had the same kind of arrangement with your neighbors."

"Sure," he said. "We do things for each other, yes."

"Then you have keys to some of your neighbors' houses?"

"Yes."

"Which neighbors?"

"Well, we have keys to the DeFauldo home and the one next to it, the Corwell house."

"And the Corwells are away."

"Yes. They're in Europe. So what?"

Karen took a deep breath, then said, "There is a possibility that evidence relating to this case is stashed somewhere in the Corwell house. I'm asking you to voluntarily let us into the house for a look around. Detective Simms is here to take possession of the evidence, should any turn up."

Now Hendershot was really confused. "I don't know what you're talking about. The Corwells have been away in Europe for over a month."

"That's just it," Karen said. "And you have a key to their house. Do you happen to know if the DeFauldos also have a key to the Corwell house?"

"I believe they do, yes." Hendershot's eyes narrowed. "Are you trying to tell me that Caroline hid something in the Corwell house?"

Karen didn't know exactly how to answer that question. Charlie sensed her discomfort and stepped in. "Not exactly," he said. "She thinks someone else hid it. And I'm not trying to be coy, sir. If the stuff is there, that's one thing. If it's not, it will go a long way to clearing up a matter that needs clearing up. You said you were upset about the treatment of your friend. You'll be doing her a favor if you let us in."

Hendershot gave that some thought.

Charlie pressed. "This will only take a few minutes. And we'll be grateful. How about it?"

Hendershot looked at them both for a moment longer, then turned and walked into the kitchen. He opened a drawer, pulled out a set of keys, then said, "Let's go."

They walked quietly past the DeFauldo house to the front door of the Corwell place. Hendershot opened the door, read the tag on the key, then entered the code that would disarm the alarm system.

Charlie closed the door behind him and said, "Let's all stay together. If we find something, we can all testify under oath as to what we saw."

They went from room to room, starting with the living room. Nothing. Then they went to the kitchen. They found evidence that someone had been using the place recently; a plastic garbage bag filled with used TV dinners and beer cans. There were some snacks in the refrigerator that were still reasonably fresh.

Charlie started giving Karen looks. "You want any of this stuff?"

"Yes," she said, her heart pounding. "I want it all. It proves someone was living here while the Corwells were away."

"But not who."

"Depends on what the lab has to say."

Hendershot looked stunned. "I never saw anyone enter or leave this house," he said.

"When's the last time you were in here?" Charlie asked.

"I haven't been in here recently. We all take turns. Sometimes Lucille and I look after the place, and sometimes the DeFauldos do it. And vice versa. This time, it was left to Dan and Caroline."

They finished searching the main floor, then went to the second floor. One of the beds in the guest bedroom was unmade, and the guest bathroom was a mess.

"Do the Corwells have a maid?" Karen asked.

"No. We do, and so does Caroline. Same woman. But the Corwells do all their own housekeeping."

Finally, they reached the garage, with space for three cars, a Cadillac and a Taurus taking up most of the space. After a short search, they found nothing of interest. Karen leaned against one of the cars, her disappointment obvious.

"It was worth a shot," Charlie said. "Maybe this garbage will yield some prints."

"Can I leave now?" Mr. Hendershot asked.

"Sure," Charlie said. "We appreciate your cooperation. We'll let you lock up."

"Okay."

"Wait!"

Karen was staring at the ceiling. "Mr. Hendershot, do you have keys to the cars?"

"The cars? Yes. Why do you ask?"

She pointed to a rope hanging from the ceiling. "If we're to get that stairway down and take a peek in the attic, we'll have to move one of the cars."

Hendershot nodded, pressed a button on the wall that opened the garage door, then climbed into the Taurus. He fired it up and backed it into the driveway.

Karen pulled down the stairway. Charlie flicked on his flashlight and preceded her up the stairs. When he reached the attic over the garage, he switched on the attic light and put his flashlight away.

"Well, I'll be goddamned."

"What is it?" Karen asked.

"You stay there."

Charlie took a few steps into the attic. In seconds, he was coming back down the stairs, holding another green plastic garbage bag in his hand. Karen could hardly contain herself.

When Charlie reached the garage floor, he opened the bag and shone his flashlight inside. He let out a big sigh. "I'll be goddamned again," he said. "You just hit the jackpot, Karen."

Karen looked inside the bag. There was a nickel-plated semiautomatic handgun that she guessed to be a nine millimeter, a small liqueur glass, some used candles still in their holders, a towel, some rubber gloves, a small brown bottle, and an empty milk jug.

Charlie pulled a pair of rubber gloves from his jacket pocket, put them on, then carefully examined the treasure. The small bottle was labeled ipecac. The milk jug had two holes in the bottom—each about nine millimeters in diameter.

It was all there.

Success made Karen feel weak. She leaned against the Cadillac, her eyes closed, her breath coming in short bursts.

"I don't get it," Mr. Hendershot said, rubbing his head.

"You will," Karen said. "Tomorrow. I need you to testify as to what you saw tonight."

Charlie shook his head. "You can't go to court with this. You gotta give this stuff to the ASA."

"At this hour?"

Charlie was insistent. "Then I'll give it to him in the morning."

"You could do that," she said, "but Brad's so stubborn he'll probably insist that my client put that stuff in the attic. Besides, I've given Brad several opportunities to reopen this case. He pushed me away every time. If I do this by the numbers, he'll take three weeks to cut through the red tape. On the other hand, if I drop this bomb on him in court tomorrow, my client will be free before the day is out."

Charlie, gripping the plastic bag firmly in his massive hand, said, "Maybe you just want to humiliate him. That's not too smart, Karen."

"Maybe not," she said. "And maybe he has it coming. But, in all seriousness, it's not enough to get the charges against my client quietly withdrawn. Unless all this comes out, people will assume that some smart-ass lawyer got Jack Palmer off on a technicality."

She took a deep breath. "I want you to take it to the FDLE lab. Will you?"

Charlie made a face. "If I do that, my black ass will be in a sling. I don't work for you, Karen. I'm a cop. I work for the county."

"I know," she said softly. "If you handle that evidence the usual way, it won't get the whole job done. A man will be released from jail, the charges dropped, but people will always wonder. And you put him there, Charlie. You bought Caroline's story, and you put my client away. You don't owe me anything, but you owe *him* something."

Charlie thought for a moment, then shook his head. "You know, you can really hit below the belt. Are you always this tough?"

She grinned. "Only with ex-football players. Will you take it to the lab?"

He hesitated. "I don't know. I have to tell the sheriff about this, Karen."

"He's probably asleep by now. Tell him after you take the stuff to the lab, okay?"

"Once I do tell him, he's gonna tell Keats."

"Maybe," she said. "Then again, maybe not. The sheriff couldn't reopen the case unless Keats asked him to. Maybe the sheriff will be just as happy to see this proceed. Politics is a funny business."

Charlie threw his hands in the air in a gesture of surrender. "Your husband must have the patience of Job. God, you're a pisser. Okay. When do you need me in court?"

Karen wanted to kiss him. "You'll be witness number two," she said. "I need you there by nine-thirty at the latest. But you're not done here just yet. We need to go shopping."

He gave her a querulous look. "We need to do what?"

"You heard me. Get the stuff from the kitchen, and I'll fill you in."

Charlie headed for the kitchen. Hendershot stood there scratching his head. "Would you mind telling me what all this means? After all, I let you in here."

Colin remained quiet, but it was clear he was just as confused as Hendershot.

Karen patted Hendershot on the shoulder. "Yes, you did. Thank God for people like you, Mr. Hendershot. You'd better bring that car back in here."

Hendershot, still scratching his head, went to the car. Karen's eyes followed him. Beyond, standing in the street, wearing a white dressing gown, her arms wrapped around herself, Caroline DeFauldo stood gaping at them, the expression on her face one of intense shock. It was all Karen could do not to wave to her.

"Well, well. What do we do now?" Charlie said, returning with the kitchen goodies, his gaze also fixed on Caroline.

"That's up to you," Karen said. "You're the police officer. I'm just defending a client."

"She might take off."

"She might at that," Karen said. "You do what you think is right."

Hendershot parked the car and stepped out.

"I never got an answer from you, Mr. Hendershot," Karen said.

"About what?"

"Will you testify as to what happened tonight?"

"Do I have to?"

"I could get a subpoena, but I'd rather not."

He looked at her for a moment, then said, "I'll be there."

Karen thanked him, then said, "I hope you're not too tired right now."

"Why?"

"We're just getting started. I have to be in court tomorrow at nine. I'll need your help for a couple more hours."

"For what?"

She explained what she wanted to Charlie, Colin, and Hendershot. And as she did so, she watched Caroline slink back home.

Twenty-two

The small courtroom was packed and buzzing with whispered conversation. The media coverage of this case, keen ever since the contentious battle of the press conferences, had continued to build. Now, even some stringers for a few of the many New York-based tabloid TV shows were covering the hearing. Karen's eyes were still swimming with bright spots created by flashing camera lights as she entered the courthouse, refusing to answer questions, her head high, a look of determination on her face.

There were others there besides media, even a few ASAs, obviously drawn like bees to honey by fast-spreading divergent rumors. Rumor one was that Judge Brown had pressed Karen into a quick preliminary hearing, where, supposedly unprepared, she was expected to fall on her face. Rumor two was that she had something hot and was about to make Brad Keats and the sheriff's office look very bad. It wasn't just the retirees who had a good grapevine.

Like all courtrooms in this austere building, this one was pretty ordinary, with painted walls and wooden benches, a drab room lit by harsh fluorescent bulbs in the ceiling. The carpet on the floor and the thick walls gave the courtroom a hushed quality, and the low ceilings prevented voices from echoing. No marble columns, no statuary, just two limp flags flanking the unimposing bench soon to be occupied by His Honor Judge Joe Brown.

Jack Palmer was brought in dressed in his best suit, looking much less depressed. Karen squeezed his arm.

Suddenly, Brad Keats burst through the courtroom door, trailing an assistant pushing what looked like a small grocery cart filled with documents. Brad rushed up to Karen, his face red with anger. "I hear you've been playing detective," he declared. "Why didn't you call me?"

She gave him the laser look usually reserved for judges. "This all happened very late last night. There was no time. Besides, the last time I called you at home, you told me never to do it again. I take you at your word."

"When it suits you." He looked around. "Where's Simms?"

"He'll be here," she said confidently. "So will a lot of other people."

There was genuine concern in his eyes. "Like who?"

Karen handed him a large manila envelope. "This is a list of exhibits and witnesses. It's all I have. Most of the evidence will be in the form of testimony."

Brad opened the envelope and leafed through the pages. "You're still trying to turn this into a circus, aren't you? You could have brought the evidence to me before coming here."

"There wasn't time, Brad."

He glared at her. "You're gloating. If this stuff is as exculpatory as you seem to think it is, I'll consider dropping the charges, but I need time to look it over."

"I'd rather present it in court," Karen said coldly.

"Why?"

"Because I want it all on the record. I want Jack

Palmer cleared completely. That can happen only if the evidence, every last ounce of it, gets presented here and now."

He was furious. "Well, if you think you can walk all over me, you have another think coming. I'm going to ask for a continuance until I've had the chance to examine this so-called evidence."

Karen smiled. "Go ahead. Judge Brown hates my guts. He might just give it to you. But I'll demand that he remove the gag order and let me hold a press conference."

"He won't remove the gag order."

There was an edge to her voice as she said, "Then I'll be in contempt. Once the press hears all of this, the contempt might swing over to someone else. I told you this case was a six-hour wonder. You should have listened."

Brad glared at her. "You do what you have to do, and I'll do what I have to do."

"All rise!"

Judge Brown entered the courtroom looking particularly poorly. He shuffled rather than walked to the bench, his shoulders hunched, his facial and body language screaming news of a hangover of monumental proportions. He found his seat, slammed his gavel, and closed his eyes as the clerk finished the standard intonation.

His voice raspy, the judge said, "Just for everyone's edification, the gag order imposed earlier is still in effect in this case." He peered out into the gallery. "I see we are privileged to have some members of the press here today. Well, I can't keep the press out of here. Heavens, no. Can't have that. Whole country would go down the tubes. But there are witnesses outside this room who are to stay outside until they are called. And while they're out there, I don't want anyone telling them what's going on, is that clear? No contact with the witnesses whatsoever. They all have tags on their chests saying 'witness' in big block letters, so don't try to pretend you don't know who they are. This is a preliminary hearing, not a trial, but anyone who tries to talk to a witness, lawyers excepted, will be held in contempt of court."

He looked at Karen, coughed a few times, then said, "Ms. Mondori, you may call your first witness."

That wasn't her name, but, as usual, she let it go. He never got it right. Never would.

Suddenly, Brad Keats was on his feet. "Your Honor, the state wishes to ask for a continuance."

Judge Brown glared at him as if he were some disgusting insect. "A continuance?"

"Yes, Your Honor."

"On what grounds?"

"New evidence has been discovered, Your Honor. Evidence having a direct bearing on this case."

"Are you telling me you want to withdraw the charges?"

"Not yet, Your Honor. We just want time to examine this new evidence. I would also ask that you direct counsel for the defense to hand over any other evidence she may have and stop this grandstanding."

The judge waved a hand at Karen. He had a cruel smile on his face. "What say you, little lady?"

"We'd like to proceed directly, Your Honor. The only other evidence I have is already in the hands of the proper authorities, to wit, a detective with the Pinellas County Sheriff's Office. All of the evidence will be presented at this hearing. We would ask that Your Honor allow counsel to litigate its relevance to this case."

Brown coughed again, spit into his handkerchief, then said, "I guess that's the way it's supposed to work. The request for a continuance is denied. Call your first witness, Ms. Mondori."

Brad seemed ready to explode. Karen repressed a smile and looked around. A beaming Colin was sitting next to Jack Palmer. Palmer, still unaware of everything that had happened over the weekend, looked hopeful nonetheless.

Karen faced Judge Brown, and in a clear voice, said, "The defense calls Dr. Henry Proctor."

Instead of Henry, the door at the back of the room opened, and Jonathan Walsingham stormed in, his hand in the air. "Your Honor!"

Brown slammed his gavel. "What the hell is going on here? Has everybody gone nuts?"

Jonathan stood by the bar that separated the working pit—Karen liked to call it the stage—from the spectator section. Jonathan stood tall and straight, a uncommon look of panic on his noble face. "Your Honor, I'm Jonathan Walsingham. As an Officer of the Court, I request an opportunity to speak to the Court regarding this matter."

Judge Brown's face was turning purple again. "Whom do you represent?"

"Caroline DeFauldo."

The judge glanced at the papers in front of him. "To the best of my knowledge, Caroline DeFauldo is listed as a witness for the prosecution. Now I see she's being called by the defense as well."

"That is correct, Your Honor. I must speak with her before she testifies, but I can't find her."

The judge glared at Brad and Karen. "Well, since she's on both your lists, does either of you know where she is?"

"I do," Karen said. "She's in police custody awaiting a first appearance. She's being held as a material witness."

"What's she doing in jail?" the judge thundered.

"The police have evidence that the witness may flee to avoid giving testimony to this Court, Your Honor."

Brown looked mystified. He turned to Walsingham and said, "Well, now you know. Have at it, Counselor."

Jonathan whirled and almost ran from the courtroom. Karen leaned toward a stunned Brad Keats, smiled sweetly, and said, "I think Jonathan wants to cut a deal for his client. Surprised?"

Brad sank into his chair, smoldering.

Pinellas County Medical Examiner Henry Proctor finally entered the room, took the oath, and sat in the witness chair. Henry, an old hand at trials, was a joy in that he always testified in layman's terms. Juries could understand him without the examiners having to ask the same question thirteen different ways.

Karen stood up but stayed at her table. "Dr. Proctor, would you please state your occupation."

Proctor stated his qualifications.

"Did you examine the body of a man identified as Dan DeFauldo?"

"I did."

"Do you have knowledge as to how the identification was made?"

"I do. The man was carrying identification papers: Social Security card, credit cards, driver's license. As well, he was wearing certain items of jewelry known to belong to Dan DeFauldo. His wife claimed he was Dan DeFauldo. But the official identification was made by two close friends, Harold and Lila Clark."

"Is that it?"

"Not at all. As a matter of course, we take fingerprint impressions, dental impressions, samples of blood and tissue samples, all of which are kept for future use should there ever be a question at a later time."

"Thank you," Karen said. "Is there a possibility that a mistake could have been made in the identification?"

Henry squirmed in his seat. "That possibility always exists. In this case, the face of the victim was distorted by the trauma caused by two gunshot wounds. However, because of the certainty of the identification made by personal friends and the presence of personal items on the victim's remains, we thought the identification was properly made."

"Nevertheless, if someone were to present evidence that cast suspicion on this identification, you'd eventually be able to correct any mistakes because of the fingerprint impressions, dental impressions, and samples of blood and tissue samples that were kept. Is that correct?"

"Yes."

"Has it ever happened?"

"Has what ever happened?"

"Has a body ever been wrongly identified?"

"Of course. It happens everywhere. It's rare, but it happens."

"Thank you, Doctor. Did you perform an autopsy on the person you identified as Mr. Dan DeFauldo?"

"Yes."

"What were your findings?"

"I discovered that Mr. DeFauldo died of a gunshot wound that tore a hole in his aorta. He also had two gunshot wounds to the head, and two other wounds to his body, one in the abdomen and one in his right leg."

"Can you determine, with reasonable certainty, when the shots were fired?"

"Yes. Death occurred at approximately 11 P.M on the evening of November ten. The heart wound was immediately fatal. The shots to the head came at least thirty seconds after the death of the victim."

"Did you find two slugs in the victim's brain?"

"Yes. They were nine-millimeter hollow-point slugs that were later identified as having been fired by a Walther PPK .380 handgun."

As was also his habit, the verbose doctor was testifying to more than was asked. In this case, Karen had no objection. "Did you find anything else in the victim's brain?"

"Yes. We found three small pieces of plastic that have not been identified."

"Why not?"

"Because neither the sheriff's office nor the state attorney's office asked us to."

"At the request of this Court, did you subsequently forward these small pieces of plastic to the Florida Department of Law Enforcement's Tampa lab?"

"Yes, I did."

Karen picked up two photographs and turned to the judge. "For the purpose of identification, we ask that these photographs be entered as defense Exhibits One and Two respectively."

A tired judge waved her toward the clerk's table. Karen had the exhibits marked, then said, "Permission to approach the witness, Your Honor?"

Brown waved her forward. Karen showed Proctor the first photo, a shot of the victim lying on the morgue table on his back. "Is this a photograph of the person you have identified as Dan DeFauldo?"

"Yes."

She showed him Exhibit Two, a photo of the victim lying facedown. "And this one?"

"Yes."

"Dr. Proctor, Exhibit Number Two is a photograph of a man lying facedown on a table at the morgue. Is that correct?"

"Yes."

"And that man was identified as Dan DeFauldo, correct?"

"Correct."

"Take another look at the photo, Doctor. Do you see a scar anywhere in this photo?"

The doctor took a moment, then said, "No, I do not."

"To the best of your recollection, did the body you identified as Dan DeFauldo have any scars?"

"No, it did not."

"Is it safe to say then, that this photograph is an accurate photograph of the man you identified as Dan DeFauldo?"

"Yes."

"Thank you, Doctor. I now direct your attention to an autopsy report that was done on a man identified as Ralph Vincenzo."

Brad was on his feet. "Objection. Ralph Vincenzo has nothing to do with this case."

"In fact, he does," Karen said. "I'm just trying to save some time rather than recalling the witness later."

"I'm all in favor of anything that saves us time," the judge said, "but I fail to see the significance. The objection is sustained."

Karen nodded. "I have no further questions at this time, but I would like to ask that Dr. Proctor stay close. I may have some more later."

Judge Brown leaned forward. "How long is this going to take, little lady?"

"We should be through by the end of the day, Your Honor."

"Very well. See that you are. You have some cross, Mr. Keats."

Brad simply shook his head.

"The witness is temporarily dismissed," Judge Brown growled. "Call your next witness, Ms. Mondori."

Again, she resisted the impulse to correct him. "The defense calls Detective Charles Simms."

Charlie lumbered into the courtroom, his football knees creaking noisily as he made his way to the pit, took the oath, and climbed into the witness chair. He looked tired and very unhappy, having some idea as to what lay ahead. His dismay at being perceived as having screwed up during the initial investigation was somewhat tempered by the knowledge that he was about to help set things straight. Still, he was the point man for what was bound to be a torrent of criticism once all of this was over. Karen admired him for his obvious willingness to take the heat.

"Detective Simms," Karen began, her voice sounding warm and friendly, "you were in charge of the investigation into the death of a man later identified as Daniel DeFauldo, correct?"

"Yes."

She folded her hands across her chest and said, "Can you describe how you conducted the initial stages of the investigation?"

Charlie made a face, shifted his big frame in the witness chair, pulled out a small notebook, then read from it. "After receiving a radio call from dispatch, I arrived at 2773 Bridgemont Way in Palm Harbor at approximately 11:40 P.M. on the evening of November ten. There were several uniformed officers on the scene, some paramedics, and a body on the floor, and two witnesses I subsequently identified as Caroline DeFauldo and Jack Palmer.

"Evidence consisted of the body, of course, also a semiautomatic handgun, specifically a Walther PPK, and some spent shell casings. I called the Crime Scene Unit. They were pretty busy, so I called for more uniformed officers to keep the crime scene from being contaminated."

"What do you mean by contaminated?"

"Well, in any murder scene, evidence is everywhere, even things you can't see with the naked eye. It's important that nothing be disturbed until the Crime Scene Unit arrives. They are the experts, and they make sure that all the evidence is properly handled. So I had the officers seal off the house. Then I talked to the two witnesses."

"And you took their statements?"

"Yes, I did."

"And after taking their statements, did you then arrest Jack Palmer?"

"Yes."

"Why?"

"Because of a combination of evidence, the statements made, and the actions of the defendant."

"Please explain."

"Well, the defendant took a punch at me. I figured he had a violent streak. Based on that and the evidence, it wasn't hard to accept Caroline DeFauldo's account of what had happened."

"Did you read Jack Palmer his rights before you questioned him?"

"Not at first, but as soon as he became a suspect, I read him his rights and had him sign a waiver."

"Then what happened?"

"I took him to the jail and booked him in."

"Did you subsequently return to the DeFauldo house?"

"Yes. I waited for the Crime Scene Unit to arrive."

"And when did they arrive?"

"At approximately 5 A.M. on the morning of November 11."

"And how long were they there gathering evidence?"

"About six hours."

Karen looked at her notes, then asked, "According to all of the evidence gathered—specifically the initial statements made by both Caroline DeFauldo and Jack Palmer, the calls made to 911 by both Paul Hendershot and Caroline DeFauldo, the subsequent interviews with witnesses who claimed to have heard the sound of gunfire, and the Crime Scene Unit—are you able to determine a time when the shots that killed Daniel DeFauldo were fired?"

"Yes. The shots were fired at approximately 11:12 P.M. on the evening of November 10."

"How approximate?"

Charlie started to smile. He knew where Karen was headed with this. And well he should have. "I'd estimate plus or minus one minute at the outside."

"And when did the first police unit arrive at the house?"

"At 11:20 P.M."

Karen nodded. "I now direct your attention to the statements made to you by Caroline DeFauldo and Jack Palmer. They were not in agreement as to the series of events, were they?"

"No."

"Can you tell me, in brief, Caroline DeFauldo's version of the events of the evening of November tenth?"

Charlie read Caroline's initial statement. Karen then asked him to read Jack Palmer's statement. When he'd finished, Karen said, "Both statements are in agreement that the shots were fired sometime after eleven o'clock, correct?"

"Yes."

"So it would be reasonable to assume that the gunshots heard by the neighbors are the shots that were fired inside the DeFauldo house, correct?"

"Correct."

"And since we know that the police arrived at 11:20, and given your assurance that the time of the shots being fired could have been 11:11 P.M., we can be sure that a maximum of nine minutes elapsed between the time the shots were fired and the arrival of the police. Is that correct?"

"Correct."

"Can there be any mistake about that?"

"No."

Karen smiled, then said, "All right. According to Jack Palmer's statement, when he entered the house after being invited, he discovered two logs burning in the fireplace. Did you see evidence of logs in the fireplace?"

"Yes. They were still burning when I arrived."

Karen looked at her notes. Here, there was no jury to impress, no need for posturing. For one thing, Judge Brown was unimpressed; for another, the facts would speak for themselves. Accuracy was more important than perception. "Mr. Palmer also said that there were several candles burning. His statement says that there were at least a half dozen. Did you find any burning candles?"

"No."

"Mr. Palmer also said that there was a glass of liqueur waiting for him when he arrived, and that he drank it. He described it as Baileys Irish Cream. Did you find any evidence at the scene to support that statement?"

"No."

"Mr. Palmer also states that when Daniel DeFauldo entered the house, he was holding a gun in his hand. Mr. Palmer described the gun as a large handgun, possibly nickel-plated, pointed at him and Caroline DeFauldo. Did you find such a gun during your initial investigation?"

"No."

"So, because you were unable to verity the statements made to you by Mr. Palmer and the evidence available to you at that time supported the statement given you by Caroline DeFauldo, you were convinced that Mr. Palmer was lying, is that correct?"

"Yes."

"And you arrested him."

"Yes."

Karen took a few steps away from the lectern. "Mr. Palmer also said that he became ill immediately after shooting Daniel DeFauldo, and that he went to the bathroom to be sick. That bathroom has two entrances: one leading to and from the living room, the other to and from the outside pool area. Is that correct?"

"Yes."

"To your knowledge, did the Crime Scene Unit find any of Mr. Palmer's fingerprints in that bathroom?"

"No, they did not."

She returned to the lectern. Judge Brown looked at her, the expression on his face one of extreme interest. Either that, or he was in some kind of trance. "Now," she said, "and this is a hypothetical question, if everything Mr. Palmer said was true, such items as the gun supposedly in Daniel DeFauldo's hand, the glass of Baileys Irish Cream he drank, and the candles . . . all of that would have to be gathered up and taken away by someone before the police arrived, would it not?"

"Hypothetically speaking, yes. It wasn't there, so if it existed, someone had to take it away."

Karen made a note. "Again, hypothetically speaking, had you found this evidence during your initial investigation, would you still have arrested Mr. Palmer?"

"Not then. We would have had the evidence analyzed. Depending on the results of that analysis, we would determine who was telling the truth."

Karen pressed her point home. "So, for Mr. Palmer to be considered a liar, it was important that the additional evidence be moved to a location where you wouldn't be likely to find it, hypothetically speaking, of course."

"That would be true."

"Objection!" Brad cried. "All this conjecture has nothing to do with the facts of this case."

Karen looked at the judge and said, "It has everything to do with the case, Your Honor. And I'll tie it all together before this day is done."

"Overruled. Get on with it."

Karen threw Brad a cruel smile, then turned her attention back to Charlie. "Now, getting away from the hypothetical, in the statement given you by Caroline DeFauldo, she claimed that Jack Palmer stood over her dead husband and fired two shots into his head, is that correct?"

"Yes."

"And according to the M.E.'s report, these shots were fired at least thirty seconds after the first shots were fired, correct?"

"Yes."

"But Jack Palmer's statement includes the comment

that he fired only one series of shots. He also claims he heard no other shots, correct?"

"Correct."

"And the witnesses you interviewed, with the singular exception of Caroline DeFauldo, all claimed they heard but one series of shots, is that not so?"

"That is true."

"Once you completed your report, you turned it over to the State Attorney's office, is that correct?"

"Yes."

"And the case was assigned to Assistant State Attorney Brad Keats. Did Mr. Keats ask you to continue your investigation?"

"No. He was satisfied with my report."

"In other words, case closed."

"Yes."

"All right. Did you receive a telephone call from me yesterday at approximately one o'clock in the afternoon?"

"Yes."

"And what was the reason for my call?"

"You said that you had reason to believe that there was some evidence relating to the case hidden in a house located next door to the DeFauldo house. You asked me to accompany you on a legal search of the house."

"And did you agree to accompany me?"

"Yes."

"How did we achieve this legal search?"

"Well, you didn't have a search warrant, so we asked a neighbor named Paul Hendershot to voluntarily let us into the house."

"That's legal?"

"Yes. Since Mr. Hendershot had a key given him by

the owners of the house, he was the legal guardian of the house."

"He had a key?"

"Yes. The owners of the house, people named Corwell, are away in Europe. They left a key to the house with the Hendershots. According to Mr. Hendershot, the Corwells also left a key with the DeFauldos."

Brad immediately jumped to his feet, yelling, "Objection! Hearsay."

"Sustained," Judge Brown bellowed.

"Your Honor, Mr. Hendershot will verify what he said when he testifies later."

"No matter. The objection is sustained."

Karen walked to the clerk's table. "Your Honor, I have a poster here I'd like to have marked as defense Exhibit Three. The poster depicts the location of the three houses we are about to discuss."

"Very well."

Karen had the poster marked, then placed it on an easel. She returned to the lectern. "Detective Simms, please explain what is depicted on the poster."

"Yes. The house on the left belongs to Mr. and Mrs. Hendershot. The house in the middle belongs to Mrs. DeFauldo, and the house on the right is owned by Mr. and Mrs. Corwell."

"How far is it from the side door of the DeFauldo house to the side door of the Corwell house?"

"About forty feet."

"Thank you. Now, when Mr. Hendershot agreed to let you and me into the Corwell house, what did we do?"

"We entered the house with Mr. Hendershot and proceeded to make a search."

"Did we find anything?"

"Yes."

"Explain to the Court what we found."

"We found a plastic garbage bag in the kitchen containing used TV-dinner containers, along with some food and plastic utensils. We also found some food in the refrigerator. Then, in the attic above the garage, we found another plastic garbage bag containing a nickel-plated nine-millimeter semiautomatic, six used candles still in their holders, a towel, a liqueur glass, a small bottle of ipecac, an empty gallon milk jug, and a pair of rubber gloves."

The spectator section started buzzing. Judge Brown slammed his gavel and screamed, "Quiet!"

Brad was on his feet. "Your Honor, I ask that this testimony be stricken from the record and the evidence be ruled as inadmissible."

A tired Judge Brown looked down through clouded eyes. "And why would you want to do that, Mr. Keats?"

"Because there is no evidence as to who placed that material in the Corwell house, nor is there probable cause for the search to have been made in the first place."

The judge looked at Karen.

"Your Honor," she said, "there will be evidence presented at this hearing that will clearly establish who put the evidence in that attic. As for probable cause, the search was voluntary. Mr. Hendershot is ready to testify that he, as legal guardian of the house, gave his permission for us to conduct the search. No probable cause is required."

Judge Brown turned to Detective Simms. "Is it your testimony that this was a voluntary search?"

"Yes, Your Honor."

"You were a witness to Mr. Hendershot giving permission to enter the building?"

"Yes, Your Honor."

"Then I don't see a problem. Objection overruled."

The spectators buzzed anew. Brown slammed his gavel. "If you don't keep quiet, I'll clear the court."

Karen asked Charlie, "What did you do with the items we found?"

"I took them to the Florida Department of Law Enforcement Regional Crime Lab in Tampa. There, I handed them over to Crime Lab Analyst Rick Joel and asked him for an immediate analysis."

"Thank you. Now, before we were through that night, what did you and I do, with Mr. Hendershot and Colin McBride as witnesses?"

Charlie took a deep breath, then said, "We went shopping at the Kash-N-Karry store at the corner of Alderman and U.S. Highway 19."

"And what did we buy?"

"We bought a towel, a half-dozen candles, a water pistol, a liqueur glass, some plastic garbage bags, and a jug of milk."

"What did we do then?"

"We went back to the Hendershot house, dumped the milk, then placed the empty jug and the other items we'd bought on the lawn of the Corwell house, at a spot approximately fifty feet from the side door. Then, while you and your associate timed me and Mr. Hendershot watched, I gathered the items up, put them in a plastic bag, and using the keys given me by Mr. Hendershot, entered the Corwell house, hiding the bag in the same spot we'd found the original bag. Then I returned to the front lawn."

"How long did all this take, Detective?"

"It took thirteen minutes."

"Why did it take so long?"

"Because the stairway to the attic above the garage

was blocked by a car. Before I could get to the attic, I had to open the garage door, move the car, lower the stairs, hide the bag, put the car back in the garage, close the garage door, and leave."

"You testified earlier that a maximum of nine minutes elapsed between the time the shots were fired in the DeFauldo house and the arrival of the first police unit. Correct?"

"Correct."

"But in our re-creation of what might have happened, it took thirteen minutes, correct?"

"Correct."

"As a police officer with many years of experience, can you say with certainty that it would have been impossible for either Caroline Defauldo or Jack Palmer to have gathered up these items and hidden them in the Corwell house in nine minutes?"

"It would have been impossible, yes."

"And when the initial police units arrived, a standard search was made of the area, correct?"

"That is correct."

"And they found the Corwell garage door to be closed and locked, correct?"

"Correct."

"And when you talked to witnesses who had heard the shots being fired, they stated that they had looked out their front windows after hearing the shots. They all said the Corwell garage door was closed, did they not?"

"Objection," Brad screamed. "Hearsay."

"Sustained."

Karen smiled. "So, hypothetically speaking, if Mr. Palmer's statement to you was true and the evidence he claims he saw in the DeFauldo house was there, and if that evidence was removed while Mr. Palmer was being sick in the bathroom, it would have been impossible for Caroline DeFauldo to have gathered up that evidence, taken it to the Corwell house, hide it, then return to the house within nine minutes, is that not so?"

"That's true."

"In their statements, neither Caroline DeFauldo nor Jack Palmer mentioned leaving the house for any reason, correct?"

"Correct."

"But if someone did leave the house to hide the material, it would have to be either Caroline DeFauldo, Jack Palmer, or someone else, is that not true?"

"Objection!" Brad yelled. "She's asking for a conclusion."

Judge Brown leaned forward. "Not really. This is an exercise in logic, Mr. Keats. And I want to hear the answer."

Charlie licked his lips, then said, "You said hypothetical. Yes. Someone else would have had to have hidden the stuff."

"And since the time frame disallows either Jack Palmer or Caroline DeFauldo from leaving the premises and hiding the bag, it would seem logical that someone else hid that bag, would it not?"

"Objection!"

"I withdraw the question, Your Honor. I have nothing further."

Judge Brown nodded to Brad. "Your witness."

Brad leaped to his feet. "All this talk about some so-called evidence. Do you have any direct knowledge that Caroline DeFauldo put that plastic bag in the Corwell house?"

"No."

"So in fact, anyone could have put it there, isn't that true?"

"I just said that, yes."

"And for all you know it could have been put there two days after Daniel DeFauldo was shot. Isn't that true?"

"Yes."

"In fact, someone could have gathered up this stuff and hidden it in the Corwell house in an effort to draw suspicion away from Jack Palmer, isn't that so?"

"Objection," Karen said softly. "Calls for a conclusion."

"Overruled. I'll allow it," the judge said.

Charlie took a deep breath, then said, "It's possible, yes."

Brad threw a pencil on his table in disgust and sat down. "That's all."

Karen rose to her feet. "Redirect, Your Honor?"

"Go ahead."

She smiled at Charlie. "The material we gathered is in the hands of the FDLE, correct?"

"Yes."

"You made sure that the chain of evidence was not broken, isn't that true?"

"That's true."

"Thank you. That's all I have. The defense calls Mr. Paul Hendershot."

Judge Brown held up a hand. "In the interests of brevity, Ms. Mondori, I'll take your word and the word of the police officer as it relates to the finding of the evidence. If this witness is being called simply for the purposes of corroboration, I see no need."

Karen almost fell over. "Thank you, Your Honor."

"Before you call your next witness, we'll take a fifteen-minute recess."

"All rise!"

Brad was at her side before the judge had managed to leave the room. "We have to talk," he said.

"Your place or mine?"

"Let's try one of the witness rooms."

"Give me a minute to talk to my client," Karen said.

Brad turned away and Karen sat beside Jack. "Do you have any idea what's going on here?" Karen asked.

"Not really. But I *think* you're winning. Are you?"

Karen couldn't help it. She laughed. "Yes, Jack. We're winning."

She leaned closer. Colin, sitting on the other side of their client, also moved closer. "Here's what's about to happen," Karen told Jack. "The prosecutor wants to talk to me because he knows his case is about to be blown to smithereens. You didn't murder Dan; you were set up, and the prosecutor is beginning to understand what really happened. He's going to ask me to agree to a deal. He drops the charges against you and you walk out of this court a free man."

Jack looked incredulous. "Really?"

"Really."

"Oh, my God! It's over?"

"That's what I want to talk to you about."

"I don't understand," Jack said.

"I'll explain. If we agree to this, you're free, but the case will remain open. It will take some time for the police and the prosecutor to file charges against Caroline. In the meantime, the press will report only that the charges against you were dropped. People won't know what to think. In some minds, you'll always be guilty.

"What I want to do, but only with your permission, is to present everything we've got—if we can pull it off. The evidence proves that Caroline set you up. We want to present that evidence today. If we do, the press will know you were duped and will report the whole story, not just the part about the charges against you being dropped. It will allow you to walk out of here knowing that *everyone* knows you were innocent. But it means you'll be here for a few more hours.

"I know how badly you want to see your kids. I won't blame you a bit if you tell me you want this ended right now. But if you can endure a few more hours, you'll be further ahead."

Jack looked at her with tears in his eyes. "Ms. Perry-Mondori, if you asked me to walk on cut glass with my bare feet, I'd do it."

"You're sure?"

"I'm positive. God bless you, Ms. Perry-Mondori."

Karen rubbed his shoulder. "Why don't you call me Karen, okay?"

Twenty-three

"Okay," Brad said, looking properly humble, "I was out of line the other night. I apologize. I'll have the evidence checked out, and if it's everything you think it is, I'll make sure the investigation is reopened and release your client."

They were alone in one of the small rooms just off the hall used by lawyers and witnesses, sitting across from each other at a small oak table.

"Brad," Karen said, "if you drop the charges, my man walks, and that's the object of the exercise. That's great as far as it goes. But I'm asking you not to do that just yet."

He looked astonished. "Why not? It's what you've been pressing for from the beginning."

"I know. But I've spent a fortune getting lab work done, hiring private investigators, the whole nine yards. In all humility, I'm ready to hand you this case on a silver platter. Since the work is already done, you'll have little trouble making your next case, the case where you nail Caroline DeFauldo for conspiracy to commit murder."

He glared at her. "I'm supposed to be grateful, is that it?"

"No. If I'm allowed to continue, everyone will know that Jack Palmer did not commit this crime. They'll know it without question. But if you drop the charges, it'll be months before you get around to trying Caroline. By then, people will have forgotten what happened here today. Jack will always have a cloud over his head. That's just not fair."

"I don't have to be fair."

"I know that."

"I don't need to be humiliated, either. Why should I sit there and let you make me look like a jerk?"

"It's the police who will be humiliated," she said. "And so they should be. They closed this case far too soon. Jack Palmer deserves to be completely cleared. If you want to drop the charges, I can't stop you. Judge Brown will be only too happy to get this over with. But by letting me continue, you'll be doing all of us a great service, not just Jack Palmer. And in the end, you'll serve yourself as well."

Brad grinned at her. "Incredible. You once suggested I run for office. Now it's you who sounds like the politician, and I don't mean that as a compliment."

"I'm sorry you feel that way."

He threw a hand in the air. "You know, I used to think you were a pretty fine attorney. But you've been acting very strangely ever since you took this case on."

"That's because I was scared," she said. "Haven't you ever been scared?"

"Of what?"

"Of screwing up."

He sighed. "Spare me the phony humanity."

Karen's jaw tightened. "Okay. Let's put all the cards on the table. My client was railroaded, and you now know it. I'm not blaming you for that, because you had to go with what you had. But you know I'm telling the truth when I say that we too often sacrifice people for the sake of protecting our precious egos. I'm asking you to make an exception in this case. Charlie Simms, the lead investigator, was man enough to come in here and eat crow, damn it! Take a good look at Jack Palmer. A few days ago, he was close to suicide. His life is a disaster. The least we can do is to let him walk out of here with as much dignity as he can muster. You have that power. Use it!"

Brad shook his head. "Judge Brown will never allow it. Once he realizes what's going on, he'll call a halt to your munificence."

"Don't be too sure about that. Judge Brown and the sheriff are longtime adversaries. It goes back to a time when Brown was a prosecutor and the sheriff was a defense attorney. The sheriff beat Brown so many times, Brown hated him with a passion. Still does. Knowing the sheriff will be pilloried by the media will give the decrepit old bastard some real satisfaction."

Brad smiled. "You've got all the bases covered, haven't you?"

"I try, Brad."

"If this costs me my job, what then?"

"It won't. But if it does, come see me."

"No thanks. I wouldn't be caught dead working with you."

Karen looked hurt. "Do you really mean that?"

"Of course not, you idiot."

"The defense calls Dr. Carl Mondori."

Carl strode into the room, took the oath, then the witness box. He smiled at his wife, obviously proud of her, and related the story about the operation. Karen entered some X-ray plates and MRI scan plates into evidence, then asked some questions. Summing up, she said, "Is it your testimony, Dr. Mondori, that the man identified as Daniel DeFauldo is, in fact, someone else?"

"Yes."

"Thank you. No further questions."

"Cross, Mr. Keats?" Judge Brown asked.

Brad shook his head. Judge Brown's eyebrows shot up. He looked at Karen quizzically. "I'm waiting for a motion, Counselor."

Well, he wasn't asleep. Since Brad had chosen not to cross-examine Carl, he was giving tacit approval to Karen's contention that the body found in the De-Fauldo residence was someone other than Dan. That meant the charges were in error. As such, Karen could have them dismissed forthwith. The judge was wondering why she hadn't.

"Your Honor," she said, "we'd like to present all of our witnesses first, if Your Honor will allow it."

Judge Brown stared at Brad. "You're going along with this?"

Brad stared at his hands. "Yes, Your Honor."

"I'll see counsel in chambers," he thundered. "Now!"

Judge Brown doffed his black robe, hung it up on a coatrack, shuffled behind his desk, then flopped into his chair like a beached whale. "Does someone want to explain to me what the hell is going on here?"

The court reporter's fingers flew over the keys. Karen looked at Brad. Brad shrugged. Karen faced the judge. "Your Honor, we've been gathering evidence ever since my client was arrested. We're still gathering it. We'd like the opportunity to present it to the Court."

Judge Brown's lips turned into a sneer. "Who the hell do you think you are, Ms. Mondori? This is real life, little lady, and from what I've seen, the prosecutor has ample reason to take another look at this case. If the body is not that of Daniel DeFauldo, the case against your client is moot. New charges will have to be filed. In the meantime, he walks. That's the goddam law. Are we practicing law or playing games? What I'm seeing here is a grandstand play by a woman who wants to put on a one-man show. Excuse me. One-*woman* show."

"Your Honor, I don't—"

"Don't interrupt! You have this terrible habit of interrupting. Have you no manners?"

Karen remained silent.

"The way I have this figured," the judge continued, "the two of you are trying to make somebody look bad. Who is it, me?"

"Not at all, Your Honor," Karen said. "All I'm trying to do is to present all the evidence I've managed to pull together. When Jack Palmer walks out of this courtroom, I want him to be able to look everyone in the eye and know that *they* know he's completely innocent. At the same time, by presenting the evidence, it guarantees that the police will have ample probable cause to arrest the people who *are* responsible."

Judge Brown shook his head. "God save us all from do-gooders. You're making it impossible for whoever is responsible for this mess—and it doesn't take a rocket scientist to determine that you think that Daniel and Caroline DeFauldo are the bad guys—to get a fair trial. Every piece of evidence you bring into this court will be talked about in the newspapers and seen on TV before these people have been arrested. That's not justice. That's overkill. As I said before, it's not your job to make cases, it's your job to defend your client."

"As an officer of the Court," Karen said, "I have a greater responsibility, and that's to see that justice is served."

The judge coughed, then said, "Justice will be served best if the charges against your client are withdrawn and a reinvestigation of this case begun. And that's what I'm going to order."

Brad cleared his throat.

"What!" the judge barked. "Speak up!"

"Can we go off the record?" Brad asked.

"Jesus Christ!" Brown nodded to the stenographer. "What is it now?"

"Karen has a point, Your Honor. It doesn't happen often, but there are times when we get the wrong person. Maybe we do have an obligation to do more. Maybe admitting we screwed up isn't enough. Maybe the evidence should come out now. As for another trial, evidence is evidence. Let the chips fall where they may. Caroline DeFauldo has been making fools of us all. I'm not all that concerned about her goddam rights.

"And another thing. The only person who will look bad after all of this hits the fan is the sheriff. Karen asked the police several times to reopen the case, and they refused. After this fiasco, the sheriff will be made to look like a complete asshole. I can guarantee you, *I'm* not going to take the heat for this screwup, and that leaves the sheriff. Between the media, Karen, and the State Attorney's office, we should be able to settle the man's hash pretty good, don't you think?"

Judge Brown stared at the man for a full twenty seconds. "This is a complete farce," he complained. "You're both abusing this Court."

Brad and Karen looked properly contrite.

"But," the judge added, "who am I to interfere in these marvelous machinations. I have nothing else to do but lie in the sun. Let it never be said that I spoiled anyone's fun. Carry on, Counselors."

Karen almost fell off her chair. She looked at Brad. His mouth was hanging open.

"Let's get *on* with it," the judge thundered.

"Yes, Your Honor."

Back in the courtroom, Karen let out a deep breath, then said, "The defense calls Robert Paul."

An intense-looking man of about thirty-five, dressed in civilian clothes, took the oath, then the stand.

"Would you tell the Court your occupation?" Karen asked.

"I am a forensics technician employed by the Pinellas County Sheriff's Department."

"With respect to the death of Daniel DeFauldo on the night of November 10, were you in charge of the analysis of evidence gathered by the Crime Scene Unit at the scene?"

"Yes, I was."

Karen held up a document. "Defense Exhibit Four, Your Honor. May we have it marked?"

"Go ahead."

Karen had the exhibit marked, then handed it to Mr. Paul. "We've already heard testimony from the medical examiner. You've read his report. Would you tell us your findings not covered in the M.E.'s report?"

"Yes." Paul quickly leafed through the document in his hands. "We found seven slugs: two in the wall, four in the victim, and one underneath the victim. We were able to determine that two of the slugs were fired from a Walther PPK. The other slugs were too distorted for proper identification to be made."

Karen held up a gun. "For the purposes of this hearing, we ask that this gun be marked as defense Exhibit Five, Your Honor."

Judge Brown nodded.

After having the weapon marked, Karen handed it to the witness. "Is this the weapon from which the slugs you found were fired?"

Paul examined it, then said, "Yes. It has my mark."

"Did you check this weapon for fingerprints?"

"Yes. We found two latents that matched those of the defendant."

"No others?"

"No."

"Did you attempt to ascertain ownership of this weapon?"

"Yes. We were successful to a point. We contacted the Alcohol, Tobacco and Firearms Bureau, and asked for a trace."

"Do you have their report?"

Paul pulled a document from his pocket, "Yes, I do."

Karen turned to the judge. "I would like to have the ATF report entered into evidence, Your Honor. Defense Exhibit Six."

Judge Brown looked at Brad. "No objection," the prosecutor said.

The judge shook his head. "I am at your service. Think of me as a rubber stamp."

Karen, barely able to contain her continuing astonishment at the judge's behavior, had the report marked. She gave it back to Mr. Paul. "Would you tell us what is in the report?"

"Surely. The ATF reported that the gun was sold by the manufacturer to a gun shop in Ocala. The gun shop sold it to a man who then took it to a gun show in Orlando approximately three months ago. The man sold it at that show. He did not keep a record of the sale, nor did he remember to whom he had sold the gun. He does remember, however, that he sold two guns to the purchaser, who he says is a man."

"He sold two guns. What was the other one?"

"It was a nickel-plated Colt nine-millimeter semiautomatic."

"Did he say why he sold the guns?"

"Yes. He said he bought them for protection after there were some burglaries in his neighborhood. But his wife became nervous with guns in the house, so he decided to get rid of them."

"Should he have kept records of the sales?"

"No. He was a private citizen. He is not required to do so under Florida law."

"I see. So there is no direct evidence to connect this gun with the defendant, is that correct?"

"That is correct."

"Did you find empty shell casings near the victim?"

"Yes. We found seven. We determined that the shell casings matched the slugs from the Walther."

"Did you find any fingerprints on the shell casings?"

"No."

"Is that normal?"

"Not in my experience."

"Please explain what other fingerprints you found and where."

"We found fingerprints belonging to Jack Palmer, Caroline DeFauldo, Daniel DeFauldo, Martina Contrare, and one other person as yet unidentified, in various places in the DeFauldo home."

"Any others?"

"No."

"Who is Martina Contrare?"

"She's a maid. She cleans the DeFauldo house once a week."

"And how did you determine Daniel DeFauldo's prints?"

"By matching them against the fingerprints on the body."

"Did you send the Daniel DeFauldo prints to the FBI for further checking?"

"Not then."

"What do you mean by that?"

"Well, up until last night, I was satisfied that they were the prints of Daniel DeFauldo. Then I received a telephone call from Mr. Keats asking me to send the prints to Washington for checking. They were sent late last night."

"When do you expect to have the results?"

"In about three weeks."

Karen smiled. "I see. Now, did you find any latents in the bathroom closest to the living room?"

"Yes. We found latent prints on the inside of the medicine chest that matched those of Caroline De-Fauldo and the unidentified person previously referred to."

"But not those of Dan DeFauldo?"

"That is correct."

"Did you find any latents on the toilet or tub?"

"None at all."

"Mr. Paul, if I were to show you two fingerprint cards here in this courtroom, how long would it take you to determine if there was a match?"

"About thirty seconds."

Karen turned to the judge. "I have no more questions at this time, but I request that Mr. Paul remain available."

Judge Brown sighed. "And why not? So ordered. Do you have a cross, Mr. Keats?"

"No, Your Honor."

"Of course not. Why would you? Call your next witness, Ms. Mondori."

"The defense calls Rick Joel."

Judge Brown coughed, spit into his third handkerchief of the morning, then said, "You told me this would be over today, little lady."

"It will, Your Honor."

"It better be. Call the witness."

A tall, black-haired man entered the courtroom, placed a cardboard box on Karen's table, was sworn, and took the stand. He looked exhausted.

"Would you tell the Court your occupation?" Karen said.

"Yes. I'm a crime laboratory analyst with the Florida Department of Law Enforcement."

Karen faced the judge. "Your Honor, Mr. Joel has been with the FDLE for fifteen years. He's previously been declared an expert witness by this Court."

Brown waved a hand. "Yes, yes. Let's get on with it."

Karen turned her attention back to the witness. "Mr. Joel, as the result of an order issued by this court, did you examine some small pieces of plastic taken during an autopsy from the brain of a man identified as Daniel DeFauldo?"

"Yes."

Karen held up two small glassine bags. "For the purposes of this hearing, defense Exhibits Seven and Eight, Your Honor."

"Go ahead."

Karen had them marked, then gave them to Joel. "The bag marked Exhibit Number Seven, can you identify the contents?"

"Yes. These are small shards of plastic that match the plastic used in the lens of the glasses worn by the deceased."

"How did they get into his brain?"

"The bullets used were hollow points. By their nature, hollow-point slugs have a small opening at their tip. This allows for expansion of the slug on contact. As the slug passed through the glasses, two small plastic fragments were captured and driven into the brain along with the slug."

"And have you identified Exhibit Number Eight?"

"Yes. That is a small piece of plastic from a milk jug."

"Can you hypothesize as to how that piece of plastic was found imbedded in the brain of the deceased?"

"Yes. In the same way the pieces from the glasses were imbedded. The slug passed through a milk jug before it entered the brain of the deceased."

"A milk jug?"

"Yes."

"Did you have contact with Detective Charles Simms of the Pinellas County Sheriff's Department during the past twenty-four hours?"

"Yes."

"Would you explain the circumstances?"

"Yes. I received a telephone call from Detective Simms while I was at home. The time was eleven-thirty in the evening. Detective Simms requested that I officially receive some evidence and conduct certain tests. He explained that he wanted it to be done immediately. I told him to meet me at the lab."

Karen looked incredulous. "A detective calls you up at home, asks you to work through the night, and you say okay? How come?"

"Because I owe him."

"Would you explain?"

"Yes. Two years ago, we had a homicide in Pinellas County. The sheriff's office had a suspect in mind, but there wasn't enough evidence to make an arrest.

Detective Simms worked for weeks on his own time to finally crack the case."

"Why was the cracking of that case important to you?"

"Because the victim was a friend of mine. In my opinion, Detective Simms made a special effort without which I doubt a arrest and conviction would have been made. I told him at that time if he ever needed a favor, I was available."

"And so he called in his marker last night?"

"Yes."

"What did he bring you?"

"He brought me two plastic garbage bags filled with various items. He also brought me copies of a case file."

"And did you conduct tests on the items he brought you?"

"I did."

"Would you tell the Court the results of those tests?"

He removed a folded document from his inside jacket pocket, then said, "Where would you like me to start?"

"Let's start with having your report marked as defense Exhibit Nine."

After marking, Karen said, "Please tell us about the milk jug."

Karen noticed that Brad Keats's eyes were beginning to glaze over. The judge, surprisingly, seemed quite chipper, if a little confused.

"The milk jug had two bullet holes in its base. I measured the diameter and found the holes to be approximately nine millimeters wide. I also found powder burns on the inside of the jug consistent with the type of bullets found at the scene of the DeFauldo killing.

When I compared the milk jug to the plastic sample I'd received earlier, I found them to be identical."

"Which means?"

"Which means that the two slugs fired into the head of Daniel DeFauldo on the night of November tenth were fired through a milk jug."

Karen opened the cardboard box and extracted the milk jug. "Defense Exhibit Ten, Your Honor."

Judge Brown nodded and waited patiently as it was marked. Karen handed it to Joel. "Is this the milk jug?"

After looking at it, he said, "Yes."

Karen looked perplexed. "As an expert, can you tell me why someone would fire a gun through a milk jug?"

"There's only one possible reason," Joel answered. "A milk jug can often act as a silencer."

Again, there was a buzz from the spectator section. Judge Brown slammed his gavel. Karen waited, then asked, "Did you find any fingerprints on this particular milk jug?"

"Yes."

"Were you able to match them to any fingerprints in the case file given you by Detective Simms?"

"Yes. The fingerprints on the milk jug matched those of Caroline DeFauldo."

The room erupted. Judge Brown banged his gavel, to no avail. Reporters started streaming for the door. By the time order was restored, Judge Brown had had enough for now. "Court will stand in recess for one hour," he bellowed.

Twenty-four

"Mr. Joel," Judge Brown cautioned as court resumed after lunch, "I remind you that you're still under oath."

"Yes, sir."

"You may proceed, Ms. Mondori."

"Thank you, Your Honor."

Behind Karen, the room was jammed. There were people and reporters standing outside in the hall, being moved about by burly bailiffs trying to keep the hallways clear. With a short report on one of the national news telecasts and local radio and television stations giving hourly reports, the hearing had become the hot ticket for crime buffs and professionals alike.

Karen was in her element, on stage, doing what she liked best—winning her case. Today, there was the added bonus of knowing she'd helped drag a man up from the engulfing depths of despair. But the best bonus of all was yet to come.

Jack Palmer's eyes were shining, his entire body galvanized with energy. The dark mood had lifted, replaced by hope. That hope would not be dashed.

"Mr. Joel," Karen began, "you have already explained the use of the milk jug and its exculpatory pertinence in this hearing. As an expert, can you state that the use of the milk jug would explain why no witnesses other than Caroline DeFauldo claimed to have heard the second shots, the ones fired into the head of the person identified as Daniel DeFauldo?"

It was a blatantly leading question, one that would be thrown out in a normal hearing. But this hearing was far from normal.

"In my expert opinion, yes, it would."

"And in your expert opinion, those shots, the ones to the head, were fired by Caroline DeFauldo, correct?"

"That would be my reading of the evidence, yes."

"Can you give us a reason as to why?"

"Based on the evidence already presented, it is clear to me that the person lying on the ground at the De-Fauldo home when the shots were fired was not Daniel DeFauldo. Rather, it was someone who looked some-what like him, possibly a relative. The shots were prob-ably fired to alter the facial features of the body to aid in misidentification."

Karen reached once again into the cardboard box and removed a nickel-plated Colt semiautomatic. "I'd like this marked as Defense Exhibit Eleven."

"Go ahead," the judge said. His entire demeanor had changed. He was alert, intense, and very much inter-ested, almost licking his lips at the thought of the pounding his longtime enemy the sheriff was going to take.

Karen had the Colt marked, then handed it to Mr. Joel. "Did you examine this weapon?"

"I did."

"And what did you find?"

"First, I found fingerprints matching those of the person identified as Daniel DeFauldo, the decedent. I also found fingerprints matching those of Caroline De-Fauldo. Finally, I found that the firing pin had been filed down."

"Which means?"

"The gun was inoperable."

"It couldn't be fired?"

"No."

"If this is the gun alluded to in Mr. Palmer's statement to the police, is there any way Mr. Palmer could have known the gun could not be fired?"

"I can't answer that."

"But Mr. Palmer was justified in thinking his life was in danger if, in fact, a man was pointing this gun at him."

"That's correct."

Karen removed the liqueur glass from the box, had it marked as Defense Exhibit Twelve, then handed it to the witness. "What did you find when you examined this glass?"

"I found fingerprints matching those of Jack Palmer and Caroline DeFauldo. I also found traces of Baileys Irish Cream and a syrup called ipecac."

"What is ipecac?"

"It's a chemical used to induce vomiting."

"How quickly does ipecac act?"

"Usually within ten minutes."

Karen picked up a document. "According to Jack Palmer's statement, he claims he felt ill before the person identified as Dan DeFauldo entered the house. He further claims that he was violently ill immediately after shooting the man. Based on the evidence you found in and on that glass, is that statement credible?"

"Yes. If Jack Palmer swallowed ipecac in the period immediately prior to the shooting, he would be unable to prevent the vomiting."

"And is it hypothetically possible that he was given ipecac to ensure he would be in the bathroom for a few minutes immediately following the shooting?"

"Yes."

"Thank you." Karen held up the small bottle of ipecac. "Defense asks that this be admitted into evidence, Your Honor. Exhibit Thirteen."

"Go ahead."

After having the bottle marked, Karen showed it to the witness. "Did you check the contents of this bottle found with the other items delivered to you by Detective Simms?"

"I did."

"And what did you find?"

"It's exactly as the label says. Ipecac."

"Did you find any fingerprints on the bottle?"

"Yes."

"And were you able to identify those prints?"

"Yes. They belong to Caroline DeFauldo."

Karen held up the rubber gloves. "I'd like these gloves marked as defense Exhibit Fourteen, Your Honor."

Judge Brown simply waved a hand. Karen had the gloves marked, then handed them to Joel. "Mr. Joel, did you examine these gloves?"

"Yes."

"And what did you find?"

"We found fingerprints on the inside of the gloves matching those of Caroline DeFauldo."

"Did you find anything on the outside of the gloves?"

"Yes. We found more prints matching those of Caroline DeFauldo. We also found powder burns that are consistent with the kind of bullets used in the murder weapon."

"And based on that evidence, can you hypothesize as to what might have happened?"

"Yes. I would hypothesize that Caroline DeFauldo

put on the rubber gloves, then fired the Walther at some time."

"You testified that fingerprints were found on the weapon itself. Can you hypothesize as to why Caroline DeFauldo wore rubber gloves at all?"

"Yes. The rubber gloves prevented powder burns from getting on her skin."

"Is it likely that this occurred on the evening of November tenth?"

"It's possible. That's all I can say."

"But you can state that Caroline DeFauldo handled all of the items you brought with you today at some time, is that not true?"

"Yes, that's true."

"And it's possible that all of this took place on the evening of November tenth, correct?"

"It's possible, yes."

Karen removed the candles and their holders from the cardboard box and placed them on the clerk's desk. "Defense Exhibits Fifteen through Twenty, Your Honor."

The items were marked.

"Did you find fingerprints on these candles?"

"Yes."

"And whose were they?"

"They matched those belonging to Caroline De-Fauldo."

"Did you find anything else that we haven't discussed?"

"Yes. I checked both plastic bags. On one, I found fingerprints matching those of a man as yet unidentified. On the other, I found those same prints, and prints matching those of Caroline DeFauldo."

"Are those unidentified prints the same as those found on the inside of the medicine chest?"

"Yes."

Karen pulled a small striped towel from the cardboard box, had it marked, and handed it to the witness. "What did you find on this towel?"

"We found gun oil which is identical to that found on the Walther PPK. We also found traces of gun powder residue that matches the residue found on the rubber gloves and the milk jug."

"Can you explain what all this means?"

"Based on my examination of the evidence, I would deduce that at some point in time, Caroline DeFauldo put on a pair of rubber gloves, then picked up the murder weapon. She pushed the barrel of the murder weapon into a milk jug, then wrapped the towel around the opening to make for a tighter fit. She then fired the murder weapon twice."

Karen smiled at the witness, then said, "That's all I have."

Judge Brown sighed, looked at Brad, who was shaking his head, then said, "I see there is to be no cross. You may call your next witness, Ms. Mondori."

"Thank you, Your Honor. The defense calls Caroline DeFauldo."

It took twenty minutes for Caroline to be brought from the jail to court. Jonathan Walsingham, looking grave, was with her. Being held as a material witness, Caroline was not dressed in prison clothes. She wore a red suit over a white silk blouse. The beautiful woman who had so captivated Jack Palmer looked frightened as she took the oath, and then sat in the witness chair. As for Palmer, he stared at Caroline, his eyes filled with pure hatred.

Karen faced her witness, smiled, and said, "Good afternoon, Mrs. DeFauldo."

Caroline said nothing.

"Mrs. DeFauldo," Karen began, "approximately an

hour after the unfortunate death of your husband, you gave a statement to the police, is that correct?"

"Yes."

"And in a later meeting with me, attended by your attorney, you gave another statement, is that correct?"

"Yes."

"In both statements, you claim that the defendant murdered your husband, correct?"

"Yes."

"Were either of those statements true?"

Caroline shot a look at a crestfallen Jonathan Walsingham, then said, "I refuse to answer the question, exercising my rights under the Fifth Amendment."

"I see. You're afraid you might incriminate yourself?"

"I refuse to answer that question, exercising my rights under the Fifth Amendment."

"Very well. Do you know if your late husband has any siblings?"

"Yes."

"Can you give us their names?"

"He has a brother named Michael, and a sister named Rose."

"Have you ever met Michael?"

"Yes."

"Would you describe the circumstances?"

"Dan and I went to Chicago and visited with him."

"Where?"

"At the Northbrook Institute for the Mentally Challenged."

"Is that where Michael resides?"

"Yes."

"Why is that?"

"He's retarded."

"I see. And when is the last time you saw Michael?"

"About a year ago."

"In Chicago?"

"Yes."

"Has Michael ever come to your home to visit?"

Caroline stiffened. "No. Never."

Karen looked at the judge. "That's all I have at this time, Your Honor. But I would ask that the witness remain in court until after I've recalled an earlier witness."

"The witness is so instructed."

Caroline walked slowly from the stand and took a seat next to Jonathan. She looked very pale.

"The defense recalls Robert Paul to the stand."

Robert Paul entered the courtroom and took the stand. The judge reminded him he was still under oath.

Karen pulled a faxed document from one of her files, and then a fingerprint card. "We'd like these two exhibits marked as next in order, Your Honor."

"Go ahead."

Karen had the exhibits marked, then handed them to the witness. "Mr. Paul, earlier today, you testified that if given two fingerprint impressions, you would be able to determine if they matched within thirty seconds, correct?"

"Yes."

"I ask you now to look at the two exhibits I've handed you, and tell the Court if they are a match."

Paul looked at the exhibits, put on glasses, and looked at them again, then nodded. "They are the same."

"You're sure?"

"Yes."

"Would you read what it says on the fax sheet?"

"Yes. It comes from the Chicago Police Department. It's a certified true copy of a fingerprint set belonging to one Michael DeFauldo, a resident in the Northbrook Institute for the Mentally Challenged."

"Thank you. And would you now read what it says on the second exhibit."

"Yes. It is a certified copy of a fingerprint set taken by the Pinellas County Medical Examiner's Office from one Dan DeFauldo, deceased."

"The two sets of fingerprint impressions are of the same person?"

"Yes."

"Thank you, Mr. Paul."

Paul left the stand, and Karen stood at the lectern. "Your Honor, the evidence presented here today gives us a clear indication of the events that resulted in the death of Michael DeFauldo. The defense moves for a dismissal of all charges against the defendant."

Judge Brown glanced at Brad.

"No objection, Your Honor. The state wishes to publicly apologize to the defendant. It is clear he is innocent of these charges. We also ask that a bench warrant be issued for the immediate arrest of Caroline and Daniel DeFauldo."

Judge Brown made a note, then turned to the bailiff. "The bailiff will take Mrs. DeFauldo into custody. A warrant will be issued for the arrest of Daniel De-Fauldo."

The bailiff moved quickly. Caroline's wrists were handcuffed behind. She was led out of the room, a thoroughly chagrined Jonathan Walsingham walking dutifully by her side.

The judge turned to Jack. "Stand up, young man."

Jack Palmer stood.

"You won't get an apology from me, Mr. Palmer," the judge thundered. "The police arrested you because of the evidence that was available to them, evidence

that any normal-thinking policeman would find suffi-
cient to hold you for trial. They were simply doing
their jobs. If there is blame to be assessed, it lies firmly
on the shoulder of the sheriff of this county, who, when
asked to reopen the case by the Assistant State Attorney, refused to do so. This entire fiasco could have
been prevented if the sheriff had carried out his respon-
sibilities with even a modicum of diligence.

"You should be thankful that there are lawyers like
Ms. Perry-Mondori who care enough to seek the truth.
You're a lucky man, Mr. Palmer. And you're free to
go." He slammed his gavel. "This Court is adjourned."
It was the first time Judge Brown had addressed Karen
by her correct name.

The room exploded. Karen and Colin hugged Jack,
whose face was flooded with tears. Brad Keats stood
nearby, waiting for a chance to shake Karen's hand.
When he finally made it, Karen whispered, "What was
that all about?"

"My letter to the sheriff?"

"Exactly."

"Oh, they'll find one in his in-basket soon enough.
Properly backdated, of course. I have some friends on
the force."

"That's cruel," Karen said.

"So's life. We all have to protect ourselves, Karen.
You do good work. If I do get fired, I may give you a
call."

"Anytime, Brad. And thanks."

"Sure."

Twenty-five

There were four of them crammed in the small room at the Pinellas County Jail: Brad Keats, Charlie Simms, Jonathan Walsingham, and an unusually calm Caroline DeFauldo.

Caroline wore no makeup and was dressed in the plain blue coveralls issued every prisoner in the maximum-security section. The effect was startling. The glamour was gone. And with it, much of her intrinsic arrogance. Instead of the frightened expression most first-time prisoners wore, Caroline seemed almost acquiescent.

But she wasn't talking.

For the last ten minutes, in a voice strangely devoid of passion, Caroline insisted that the police were wrong, that they had misinterpreted the evidence, that a terrible mistake had been made. It seemed to Charlie that she was doggedly playing out the last act of a Broadway play while knowing the play was closing at the end of this performance.

It was time to bring down the curtain. Charlie took three photos from his jacket pocket and placed them on the table in front of Caroline. "The first one," he said, "was taken on a beach near Buenos Aires. According to the FBI, the woman has been identified as a prostitute by the name of Alicia Gamez. Looks a little like you, Mrs. DeFauldo."

Caroline picked up the photo, looked at it, then placed it back on the table without comment.

"The second one was taken in the city," Charlie continued. "The Rolls is a couple of years old, but we understand the dealer has ordered a new one for your big-spending husband."

He tapped the third photo. "And this photo shows him just outside a villa near the coast. He's making arrangements to buy the place. The woman with him is another prostitute. Your husband seems to have a thing for expensive hookers, Mrs. DeFauldo."

Caroline looked at both photos, then put them back on the table.

"Here's the thing," Charlie said. "The way I see it, you were set up just like you set up Jack Palmer. Your husband, with your help, has pulled off the perfect crime. He's down there in Argentina having a good time, and you're up here in jail. Doesn't seem fair, somehow."

"The United States has no extradition treaty with Argentina," Brad noted. "We can't touch him. But you knew about that didn't you?"

Caroline said nothing. Brad looked at Jonathan. "Why don't you fill her in, Jonathan?"

Jonathan picked at his tie for a moment, then said, "What's being suggested here is that you tell them what you know. As your lawyer, I can tell you that the evidence against you is more than strong. It's utterly damning. I can also tell you that if you cooperate, the chances are good that you'll spend many less years in prison than you would otherwise. That's really what we're talking about, Caroline."

"And I'll add one extra bonus," Brad said.

"What's that?" Caroline asked.

"Well, as we said, there is no extradition treaty with

Argentina. However, the Argentinean government has the right to deport noncitizens for any reason they choose to cook up. They don't have to, mind you, but they might be persuaded to do so. I can't guarantee it, but I can tell you that the State Department might be more inclined to give it a shot if you were to decide to help us. Don't you think it would be interesting to see your husband in an American court where you can testify and watch the expression on his face?"

She smiled for the first time. "I think I'd like that. Yes. But I'd need some guarantees."

"There are no guarantees," Brad said coldly. "The way things stand now, we're going to put you away for life and then some. I really don't need your statement. We know what happened. But if you feel like talking to us, it saves the cost of a trial. It also sets the record straight, makes people feel better, you know? It's up to you. Frankly, I don't really give a shit. What you and your husband cooked up is unspeakable."

Caroline looked at Jonathan. "If I talk, how long would I be in prison?"

Jonathan's gaze fell to the table. "Fifteen years minimum," he said. "But that's contingent on getting Dan back. If they fail to get Dan back, you'll be in for at least twenty-five. That's the deal they're offering."

"I'll be an old woman when I get out."

"Even older if this goes to trial and you're convicted," Brad said. "You could be in there forever. At least this way you get to smell the flowers again. Assuming we can get our hands on your husband, fifteen years can go pretty quickly if you put the time to good use. You could write those books you talked about. They say solitude is good for a writer."

She took a deep breath, exhaled, then said, "What are the chances you *can* get him back?"

Brad shrugged. "Let me put it to you this way. If Dan continues to spend money at the rate he's spending it now, he'll be broke in a few years. Once that happens, the Argentinean government will probably lose all interest in him. Matters of principle usually involve bigger fish. On the other hand, if he watches his pennies and greases the right palms, he could stay there for the rest of his life. Of course, since he's got a bad ticker, he might drop dead from all the sex he's having. In which case we couldn't care less what you have to say."

He leaned back in his chair and added, "If it was me, I'd be inclined to get things on the record while the offer is on the table. You never know what tomorrow can bring."

The room felt silent. Finally, after a minute or so, Caroline said, "What do you want to know?"

They brought a stenographer into the crowded room. She had to stand. Caroline told them that Dan had first broached the idea after he'd sold the first six of the Ducerne deal investments. There was then over a million dollars in the escrow account, and the way things were going, it would surely hit the full 4.8 million. With that and the other accounts, they could go to Paraguay with over six million in their jeans. They'd visited Asunción a year ago and loved it. And six million dollars would last a lifetime in Paraguay. They'd never have to work again. Dan had said that having Michael killed would be doing the poor bastard a favor. He had no life. He was just taking up space. All they needed was a mark.

At first, Caroline had been against it. Not because it was inherently evil, but because she was afraid they'd be caught. But Dan had been so sure they could pull it off. Timing was the key. They had to plan and plan and wait for the right moment. And when Caroline met Jack, she knew she'd met the mark. She smiled when she got to that point.

"He was such a nerd. God! I'd say something nice to him, and he'd light up like a Christmas tree. I kissed him once. His heart was pounding so hard even I could hear it."

"How did you know Jack would actually fire the gun?" Charlie asked.

"That was a risk, sure. But I had him figured out pretty good. If he was alone, he might not have. But he thought he was saving my life, the stupid jerk. That's what made him shoot."

"What about Ralph?" Charlie asked. "As soon as he got back from France, he'd know the money was gone."

"Dan was supposed to kill Ralph the next night," Caroline said matter-of-factly. "He was supposed to kill him right outside his condo and make it look like a robbery. There was no way Dan could be a suspect because Dan was supposed to be dead. What with all the killings that we have around here, it would look just like another one. As for me, I had the perfect alibi. I was living with friends at the time. I was never out of their sight for a second.

"Dan already had a ticket for the flight to Paraguay. He was to leave on Friday, the twelfth. When I realized Ralph was still alive, I knew something had gone wrong. Dan had been hiding in the house next door. We weren't supposed to take a chance and meet. But I told my friends I needed to take a walk alone and went over to the Corwell house to see if Dan was still there. He wasn't."

"Why did you leave the garbage bag in the kitchen?"

"I thought about that, but I figured I could take care

of that later. I was so upset that Dan had left without taking care of Ralph. Jesus. I used a pay phone to call the hotel in Paraguay where Dan was supposed to be staying under another name. He wasn't there. That's when I realized what he'd done to me." She looked into Jonathan's eyes. "But what could I do?"

It was incredible. She was actually seeking sympathy. Charlie wanted to puke.

"How'd you beat the lie detector test?" Charlie asked.

Caroline smiled. "Easy. I took some Inderal before both tests, the one with the FBI and the one Jonathan gave me. Everybody knows that old trick."

Charlie shook his head. Not everybody, he thought.

"Who wiped Jack's prints off the toilet?"

"Dan. After I gathered up the stuff and handed it to Dan out the side door, he went around the back and used the towel in the bag to wipe the toilet." She smiled. "About five seconds after Jack came out. The timing was pretty slick, don't you think?"

Charlie didn't answer. "Who bought the guns?"

"Dan. When I saw that bitch's press conference, I was worried the guy who sold Dan the guns might remember him. But he didn't, thank God."

It occurred to Charlie that Caroline DeFauldo had gone past the point of confessing. The acquiescence expressed earlier was gone, replaced by a sick bravado. Now she was bragging, as if what she and her husband had done was an accomplishment. There was not a scintilla of remorse, no hint of even the slightest humanity.

"We did our research," Caroline continued. "We knew Jack was broke, that he could never afford a good attorney. We figured the public defender's office would assign some jerk who'd walk it through. Then, once Jack was convicted, I could flee the country, and nobody would ever know where I went, or care for that matter. Dan would be waiting for me."

She laughed bitterly. "I guess I was just as big a fool as poor old Jack."

They stared at her, saying nothing, all of them feeling cold inside.

"Let's move on," Charlie said. "How'd you get Michael to cooperate?"

"That was easy," Caroline said. "Michael was like a big puppy dog, anxious to please. Dan stashed him in the Corwell house before he went off to play poker. Dan handcuffed him to a drain pipe in the kitchen so he couldn't wander off." She laughed. "He told him it was a game we were playing and that when Dan got back, we'd really have some fun."

She took a deep breath, then said, "So, when Dan got back from poker, he put his toupee on Michael's head, dressed him in Dan's clothes, right down to the ring and glasses ... even the underwear. He told Michael we were all rehearsing for a movie, that he was to pretend to walk into the living room and shoot two people on the floor. They waited in the garage until I gave them the signal."

"What signal?"

"I let out one hell of a scream. Michael came in right on cue. Poor bastard. He had no clue. Dan was hoping that Jack would shoot him in the head. When he didn't, I had to do it. We had the milk jug ready. I felt bad about that."

"I'm sure you did," Brad said. "Where'd you get the milk jug idea?"

"I read it somewhere. Like I said, we did our research."

"We never found the handcuffs. Where are they?"

She shrugged. "Dan must have taken them with

him." And then she smiled. "Funny. If Dan hadn't screwed it all up and buried the garbage bag someplace in Tampa like he was supposed to, this would never have happened. None of you would be any the wiser."

Again, the room grew quiet. All eyes were on Caroline.

Finally Brad said, "You still don't get it, do you?"

"Get what?"

"Why do you think Dan left the bags in the house?"

She stared at him for a moment, then sighed. "So you'd find them, right?"

"You got it."

She sighed. "Karen screwed it up. She's never liked me. I could see it in her eyes the first time we met. I never dreamed she'd take this case. I had no idea she even knew Jack Palmer."

"So," Brad said, "you tried to get her off the case with the story about you and her husband, right?"

Caroline shook her head. "No. That wasn't a story. It was true. I have no reason to lie now, do I?"

The room was silent for a moment. Then Brad turned to the stenographer. "Strike the question and the answer."

The stenographer nodded. Caroline smiled. "What are you doing? Trying to protect her? It's a waste of time. She'll learn the truth eventually."

"We'll have this typed up and you can sign it," Brad said.

"Fine. Mind if I ask you something?"

"What's that?"

"There's no law in Florida that says I can't profit from the sale of a book, is there?"

Brad shook his head. "I'm not aware of one."

Caroline smiled. "Good. Well, that's it, then."

* * *

Brad stayed behind when Caroline was taken back to her cell and the others dispersed. He stepped into the room next to the one used for the interview. The room was occupied by a man wearing earphones and operating a small machine. When Brad entered the room, the man removed the earphones and leaned back in his chair.

"Well?" Brad asked.

"She's telling the truth. All except one part."

"Which part?"

"There was a part where she said, 'So, you tried to get her off the case with the story about you and her husband, right?' And she said, 'No. That wasn't a story. It was true. I have no reason to lie now, do I?' She was lying through her teeth at that point. What a bitch!"

Brad grinned. "Tell me about it."

Twenty-six

They had to go all the way to Canada, but it was worth it. Watching Andrea play in the snow was something to see, her cheeks red from the cold, her teeth sparkling in the sunlight, her eyes gleaming like diamonds. She was enthralled by the snow, by the mountains, by the strange vista so new to her. Even the heavy ski suit and boots and mitts and fur hat brought her joy. For it was different from anything in her brief experience.

Karen and Carl sat on a wooden bench and drank it all in. They'd been here for two days, and already, they were a family again. Andrea's hated teacher had prepared studies to keep her abreast of the work she'd miss, and the evenings were spent with that. But the days were given over to having fun.

Andrea stopped rolling around in the snow and looked up at a mountain. She'd never seen mountains before. Even after two days, they fascinated her.

"If you think that's big," Carl called out, "wait until tomorrow. Tomorrow, we take the train through the mountains all the way to the Pacific Ocean. Along the way, you'll see some really big mountains."

"How big?" Andrea asked.

"Wait and see."

Andrea ran and dived into a pile of snow, screaming in glee.

"This was a great idea," Karen said.

"Absolutely. We should do it more often."

"Let's."

"We both work too damn hard."

"I agree."

"So what do we do?"

"Work less. Play more."

"Think we can do it?'

"We can do anything if we put our minds to it."

He took her in his arms and kissed her. Andrea watched them from the pile of snow.

She was smiling.